ROME

In a thousand years she grew from a village of shepherds to a world-girdling power which traded with China, and whose borders were the borders of Western Civilization.

CITY AND WORLD

Wracked by war, rotted by internal decay, she survived for centuries more: the greatest empire men had ever known; the greatest empire men would ever know.

ETERNAL

The empire and the men who built it died, but the dreams they wake in the minds of later generations will never die.

THE ETERNAL CITY

C·I·T·Y

DAVID DRAKE

BAEN
BOOKS

THE ETERNAL CITY

Copyright © 1990 by David Drake,
Martin Harry Greenberg, and Charles G. Waugh

A Baen Books Original

Baen Publishing Enterprises
260 Fifth Avenue
New York, N.Y. 10001

ISBN: 0-671-69857-5

Cover art by John Rheaume

First printing, January 1990

Distributed by
SIMON & SCHUSTER
1230 Avenue of the Americas
New York, N.Y. 10020

Printed in the United States of America

CONTENTS

ACKNOWLEDGMENTS

"Delenda Est" by Poul Anderson—copyright © 1955 by Mercury Press. From *The Magazine of Fantasy and Science Fiction*. Renewed © 1983 by Poul Anderson. Reprinted by permission of the Scott Meredith Literary Agency, Inc., 845 Third Avenue, New York, NY 10022.

"Nightfall on the Dead Sea" by R. Faraday Nelson—copyright © 1977 by Ray Nelson. Reprinted by permission of the author.

"The Prince" by C.J. Cherryh—copyright © 1985 by C.J. Cherryh. Reprinted by permission of the author.

"An Elixir for the Emperor" by John Brunner—copyright © 1988 by Brunner Fact and Fiction, Ltd. From *The Best of John Brunner*. Reprinted by permission of Ballantine Books, a division of Random House, Inc.

"Some Very Odd Happenings at Kibblesham Manor House" by Michael Harrison—copyright © 1969 by Michael Harrison. Reprinted by permission of the author.

"Time Grabber" by Gordon R. Dickson—copyright © 1952 by Greenleaf Publishing Company; copyright © 1980 by Gordon R. Dickson. Reprinted by permission of the author.

"Survey of the Third Planet" by Keith Roberts—copyright © 1966 by Mercury Press, Inc. From *The Magazine of Fantasy and Science Fiction*. Reprinted by permission of the author and his agent.

"Don't Be a Goose" by Robert Arthur—copyright © 1941 by Popular Publications, Inc. Reprinted by permission of the agents for the author's Estate, Scott Meredith Literary Agency, Inc., 845 Third Avenue, New York, NY 10022.

"Survival Technique" by Poul Anderson & Kenneth Gray—copyright © 1957; renewed © 1985 by Poul Anderson. Reprinted by permission of the Scott Meredith Literary Agnecy, Inc., 845 Third Avenue, New York, NY 10022.

"Ranks of Bronze" by David Drake—copyright © 1975 by UPH Publishing Coroporation. Reprinted by permission of the author.

"Kings of the Night" by Robert E. Howard—copyright © 1930 by The Popular Fiction Publishing Company. From *Weird Tales*. Reprinted by permission of Glenn Lord, agent of Alla Ray Kuykendall and Alla Ray Morris.

Introduction

The Creation of Rome

I've had occasion to study a number of foreign languages over the years—besides the Latin I took in high school because it was that or Spanish, and I was even less interested in Spanish.

There was German during the brief period as an undergraduate when I thought I was going to be a chemistry major and step up to big pay as a patent attorney. (Not a bad plan—but not a plan for me, I soon realized.)

Classical Greek later, because I'd gotten back into Latin and figured I wouldn't have much problem with Greek. (I had a lot more problem than I was willing to expend the effort to solve.)

Vietnamese, courtesy of a Defense Language Institute accelerated course that left me with a high level of reading and verbal comprehension . . . for about three minutes, before my mind made a determined effort to eradicate all the memories of my time in uniform that *could* be eradicated.

And most recently, the French that I taught myself to read in a firebase with a friend's correspondence-course materials. The main result of that was a lot of puzzled looks from other soldiers when they found the yellow-covered paperback in my pocket was *Theatre de Moliere*— and not one of the BeeLine Books making the rounds of the camp (*Juicy Lucy* was particularly popular, as I recall).

Other languages are incidents of the past, like wide ties

(or ties at all, now that I've got only occasional reason to costume myself in a suit). I still do much of my pleasure reading in Latin, and even more of my reading involves studies in Roman history and society.

Rome owns a major part of my soul; and, as this tiny sampling makes clear, Rome has been a part of the background of science fiction and fantasy as long as the genres have existed.

I think the reason for the field's fascination with Rome is that no other culture has been as effective at creating myths and clothing those myths in the appearance of reality. Almost every Western adult knows myriad things about Rome—and virtually everything he or she knows is a myth.

Some of the myths are obvious. Most of the familiar tales of gods are Greek in origin anyway, whether or not they're retailed (as Edith Hamilton does) under the names of their Roman more-or-less cognates.

Of course Rome wasn't founded by refugees from Troy. Of course the babes Romulus and Remus (in the unlikely event they existed at all) weren't suckled by a she-wolf. Livy, a historian of the first century B.C. explains in the manner of a modern debunking historian that the folk of that time referred to prostitutes as "she-wolves," and that's no doubt how the legend arose.

The explanation is a good example of what I mean about myth. Livy didn't have a clue as to how the people of the eighth century B.C. referred to *anything*. He had virtually no access to records going back before the third century. He—or a near contemporary with no more evidence than Livy had—made up the bit about she-wolf meaning prostitute seven hundred years in his past.

That myth fitted the milieu of Livy's day better than the earlier version, crafted for a less rationalistic age. But both versions were lies.

When a Roman historian needed more material, he made it up. When a genealogist working for a powerful Roman family needed noble deeds and ancestors, he made them up. When a Roman general needed an incident to justify his conquest of this tribe or that, he . . . well, you get the picture.

Almost everything literary sources tell us about Rome before the third century B.C. is a myth, and quite of lot of what we're told of later periods (when accuracy was possible) is mythical also. (Jim Baen, having recently reread *The Gallic Wars*, commented that Julius Caesar would've made a hell of an SF writer. Jim was right.)

The myths keep accumulating, even in learned circles. Some of them are silly, like the pompous pronouncements about Vergil and Horace being poor men (they were both from wealthy landowning families), or—a pet peeve of mine—that Juvenal was a misogynist. It's beyond me how anybody could take at face value the statements of a man who says, "And what I *really* hate about women is sitting next to one at dinner and learning she's a lot smarter and better read than I am!"

And some of the new myths are nasty ones, like Gibbon's dictum that Rome was felled by the rise of Christian superstition. That was an attempt, for Gibbon's own purposes, to supplant the myth that the corrupt morals of the early emperors brought the empire down four centuries later.

I said that much of what we "know" about Rome is myth. I didn't mean that the myths were false.

In one sense, the truth or falsehood can't be judged. Livy wasn't there to see Horatius stand at the bridge, facing down the whole Etruscan army . . . but I wasn't there either. Maybe Tarquin raped the chaste wife of one of his commanders; maybe Cincinatus put down his plow handles to assume supreme power in a crisis; maybe Brennus tossed his sword onto the already false scales and snarled, "Woe to the vanquished!"

But that's not the point. The myths were absolutely true as archetypes of what Romans—and other cultures for millennia after Rome was ruin and memory—believed should have happened.

There *is* no truth in the absolute sense regarding human interactions. For an example of the problem: was Mao Tze-dung a great man? A myth that touches the souls through the ages has more reality than the events that someone present may have remembered during his or her brief lifetime.

Welcome, then, to some of the resonances that Roman archetypes have struck across the whole fabric of fantasy and science fiction.

Dave Drake
Chapel Hill, NC

DELENDA EST

Poul Anderson

The hunting is good in Europe 40,000 years ago, and the winter sports are unexcelled anywhen. So the Time Patrol, always solicitous for its highly trained personnel, maintains a lodge in the Pleistocene Pyrenees.

Agent Unattached Manse Everard (American, mid-twentieth A.D.) stood on the glassed-in veranda and looked across ice-blue distances, toward the northern slopes where the mountains fell off into woodland, marsh and tundra. He was a big man, fairly young, with heavy homely features that had once encountered a German rifle butt and never quite straightened out again, gray eyes, and a brown crew cut. He wore loose green trousers and tunic of twenty-third-century insulsynth, boots handmade by a nineteenth-century French-Canadian, and smoked a foul old briar of indeterminate origin. There was a vague restlessness about him, and he ignored the noise from within, where half a dozen agents were drinking and talking and playing the piano.

A Cro-Magnon guide went by across the snow-covered yard, a tall handsome fellow dressed rather like an Eskimo (why had romance never credited paleolithic man with enough sense to wear jacket, pants, and footgear in a glacial period?), his face painted, one of the steel knives which had hired him at his belt. The Patrol could act quite freely, this far back in time; there was no danger of upsetting the past, for the metal would rust away and the strangers be forgotten in a few centuries. The main nuisance was that female agents from the more libertine periods were always having affairs with the native hunters.

Piet van Sarawk (Dutch-Indonesian-Venusian, early twenty-fourth A.D.), a slim dark young man with good looks and a smooth technique that gave the guides some stiff competition, joined Everard, and they stood for a moment in companionable silence. He was also Unattached, on call to help out in any milieu, and had worked with the American before. They had taken their vacation together.

He spoke first, in Temporal, the synthetic language of the Patrol. "I hear they've spotted a few mammoth near Toulouse." The city would not be built for a long time, but habit was powerful.

"I've got one," said Everard impatiently. "I've also been skiing and mountain climbing and watched the native dances."

Van Sarawak nodded, took out a cigaret, and puffed it into lighting. The bones stood out in his lean brown face as he sucked in the smoke. "A pleasant interlude," he agreed, "but after a time the outdoor life begins to pall."

There were still two weeks of their furlough left. In theory, since he could return almost to the moment of departure, an agent could take indefinite vacations; but actually he was supposed to devote a certain percentage of his probable lifetime to the job. (They never told you when you were scheduled to die—it wouldn't have been certain anyhow, time being mutable. One perquisite of an agent's office was the longevity treatment of the Daneelians, ca. one million A.D., the supermen who were the shadowy chiefs of the Patrol.)

"What I would enjoy," continued van Sarawak, "is some bright lights, music, girls who've never heard of time travel—"

"Done!" said Everard.

"Augustan Rome?" asked the other eagerly. "I've never been there. I could get a hypno on language and customs here."

Everard shook his head. "It's overrated. Unless we want to go 'way upstairs, the most glorious decadence available is right in my own milieu, say New York. If you know the right phone numbers, and I do."

Van Sarawak chuckled. "I know a few places in my own sector," he replied, "but by and large, a pioneer society has little use for the finer arts of amusement. Very good, let's be off to New York, in—when?"

"1955. My public *persona* is established there already."

They grinned at each other and went off to pack. Everard had foresightedly brought along some mid-twentieth garments in his friend's size.

Throwing clothes and razor into a small handbag, the American wondered if he could keep up with van Sarawak. He had never been a high-powered roisterer, and would hardly have known how to buckle a swash anywhere in space-time. A good book, a bull session, a case of beer, that was about his speed. But even the soberest of men must kick over the traces occasionally.

Briefly, he reflected on all he had seen and done. Sometimes it left him with a dreamlike feeling—that it should have happened to *him*, plain Manse Everard, engineer and ex-soldier; that his ostensible few months' work for the Engineering Studies Company should only have been a blind for a total of years wandering through time.

Travel into the past involves an infinite discontinuity; it was the discovery of such a principle which made the travel possible in 19,352 A.D. But that same discontinuity in the conservation-of-energy law permitted altering history. Not very easily; there were too many factors, the plenum tended to "return" to its "original" shape. But it could be done, and the man who changed the past which had produced him, though unaffected himself, wiped out the entire future. It had never even *been;* something else existed, another train of events. To protect themselves, the Daneelians had recruited the Patrol from all ages, a giant secret organization to police the time lanes. It gave assistance to legitimate traders, scientists, and tourists— that was its main function in practice; but always there was the watching for signs which meant that some mad or ambitious or careless traveler was tampering with a key event in space-time.

If it ever happened, if anyone ever got away with it . . . The room was comfortably heated, but Everard shivered. He and all his world would vanish, would not have existed at all. Language and logic broke down in the face of the paradox.

He dismissed the thought and went to join Piet van Sarawak.

Their little two-place scooter was waiting in the garage. It looked vaguely like a motorcycle mounted on skids, and an antigravity unit made it capable of flight. But the controls could be set for any place on Earth and any moment of time.

> *"Auprès de ma blonde*
> *Qu'il fait bon, fait bon, fait bon,*
> *Auprès de ma blonde*
> *Qu'il fait bon dormir!"*

Van Sarawak sang it aloud, his breath steaming from him in the frosty air, as he hopped onto the rear saddle. Everard laughed. "Down, boy!"

"Oh, come now," warbled the younger man. "It is a beautiful continuum, a gay and gorgeous cosmos. Hurry up this machine."

Everard was not so sure; he had seen enough human misery in all the ages. You got case-hardened after a while, but down underneath, when a peasant stared at you with sick brutalized eyes, or a soldier screamed with a pike through him, or a city went up in radioactive flame, something wept. He could understand the fanatics who had tried to write a new history. It was only that their work was so unlikely to make anything better. . . .

He set the controls for the Engineering Studies warehouse, a good confidential place to emerge. Thereafter they'd go to his apartment, and then the fun could start.

"I trust you've said good-by to all your lady friends here," he murmured.

"Oh, most gallantly, I assure you," answered van Sarawak. "Come along there. You're as slow as molasses on Pluto. For your information, this vehicle does not have to be rowed home."

Everard shrugged and threw the main switch. The garage

blinked out of sight. But the warehouse did not appear around them.

For a moment, pure shock held them unstirring.

The scene registered in bits and pieces. They had materialized a few inches above ground level—only later did Everard think what would have happened if they'd come out in a solid object—and hit the pavement with a teeth-rattling bump. They were in some kind of square, a fountain jetting nearby. Around it, streets led off between buildings six to ten stories high, concrete, wildly painted and ornamented. There were automobiles, big clumsy-looking things of no recognizable type, and a crowd of people.

"Ye *gods!*" Everard glared at the meters. The scooter had landed them in lower Manhattan, 23 October 1955, at 11:30 A.M. There was a blustery wind carrying dust and grime, the smell of chimneys, and—"

Van Sarawak's sonic stunner jumped into his fist. The crowd was milling away from them, shouting in some babble they couldn't understand. It was a mixed lot: tall fair roundheads, with a great deal of red hair; a number of Amerinds; half-breeds in all combinations. The men wore loose colorful blouses, tartan kilts, a sort of Scotch bonnet, shoes and high stockings. Their hair was long and many favored drooping mustaches. The women had full ankle-length skirts and hair coiled under hooded cloaks. Both sexes went in for jewelry, massive bracelets and necklaces.

"What happened?" whispered the Venusian. "Where are we?"

Everard sat rigid. His mind clicked over, whirling through all the eras he had known or read about. Industrial culture—those looked like steam cars, but why the sharp prows and figureheads?—coal-burning—post-nuclear Reconstruction? No, they hadn't worn kilts then, and they still spoke English—

It didn't fit. There was no such milieu recorded!

"We're getting out of here!"

His hands were on the controls when the big man jumped him. They went over on the pavement in a rage of fists and feet. Van Sarawak fired and sent someone else down unconscious; then he was seized from behind. The mob piled on top of them both, and things became hazy.

Everard had a confused impression of men in shining coppery breastplates and helmets, who shoved a billy-swinging way through the riot. He was fished out and supported while handcuffs were snapped on his wrists. Then he and van Sarawak were searched and hustled off to a big vehicle. The Black Maria is much the same in all times.

He didn't come out of it till they were in a damp and chilly cell with an iron-barred door.

"Name of a flame!" The Venusian slumped on a wooden cot and put his face in his hands.

Everard stood at the door, looking out. All he could see was a narrow concrete hall and the cell across it. The map of Ireland stared cheerfully through those bars and called something unintelligible.

"What's happened?" Van Sarawak's slim body shuddered.

"I don't know," said Everard very slowly. "I just don't know. That machine was supposed to be foolproof, but maybe we're bigger fools than they allowed for."

"There's no such place as this," said van Sarawak desperately. "A dream?" He pinched himself and lifted a rueful smile. His lip was cut and swelling, and he had the start of a gorgeous shiner. "Logically, my friend, a pinch is no test of reality, but it has a certain reassuring effect."

"I wish it didn't," said Everard.

He grabbed the rails, and the chain between his wrists rattled thinly. "Could the controls have been off, in spite of everything? Is there any city, anywhen on Earth—because I'm damned sure this is Earth, at least—any city, however obscure, which was ever like this?"

"Not to my knowledge," whispered van Sarawak.

Everard hung onto his sanity and rallied all the mental training the Patrol had ever given him. That included total recall . . . and he had studied history, even the history of ages he had never seen, with a thoroughness that should have earned him several Ph.D.'s.

"No," he said at last. "Kilted brachycephalic whites,

mixed up with Indians and using steam-driven automboiles, haven't happened."

"Coordinator Stantel V," said van Sarawak faintly. "Thirty-eighth century. The Great Experimenter—colonies reproducing past societies—"

"Not any like this," said Everard.

The truth was growing in him like a cancer, and he would have traded his soul to know otherwise. It took all the will and strength he had to keep from screaming and bashing his brains out against the wall.

"We'll have to see," he said in a flat tone.

A policeman—Everard supposed they were in the hands of the law—brought them a meal and tried to talk to them. Van Sarawak said the language sounded Celtic, but he couldn't make out more than a few words. The meal wasn't bad.

Toward evening, they were led off to a washroom and got cleaned up under official guns. Everard studied the weapons: eight-shot revolvers and long-barreled rifles. The facilities and the firearms, as well as the smell, suggested a technology roughly equivalent to the 19th century. There were gas lights, and Everard noticed that the brackets were cast in an elaborate intertwined pattern of vines and snakes.

On the way back, he spied a couple of signs on the walls. The script was obviously Semitic, but though van Sarawak had some knowledge of Hebrew through dealing with the Jewish colonies on Venus, he couldn't read it.

Locked in again, they saw the other prisoners led off to do their own washing—a surprisingly merry crowd of bums, toughs, and drunks. "Seems we get special treatment," remarked van Sarawak.

"Hardly astonishing," said Everard. "What would you do with total strangers who appeared out of nowhere and used unheard-of weapons?"

Van Sarawak's face turned to him with an unaccustomed grimness. "Are you thinking what I am thinking?" he asked.

"Probably."

The Venusian's mouth twisted, and horror rode his voice:

"Another time line. Somebody *has* managed to change history."

Everard nodded. There was nothing else to do.

They spent an unhappy night. It would have been a boon to sleep, but the other cells were too noisy. Discipline seemed to be lax here. Also, there were bedbugs.

After a bleary breakfast, Everard and van Sarawak were allowed to wash again and shave. Then a ten-man guard marched them into an office and planted itself around the walls.

They sat down before a desk and waited. It was some time till the big wheels showed up. There were two: a white-haired, ruddy-cheeked man in cuirass and green tunic, presumably the chief of police; and a lean, hard-faced half-breed, gray-haired but black-mustached, wearing a blue tunic, a tam-o'-shanter, and insignia of rank—a golden bull's head. He would have had a certain hawklike dignity had it not been for the skinny hairy legs beneath his kilt. He was followed by younger men, armed and uniformed, who took up their places behind him as he sat down.

Everard leaned over and whispered: "The military, I'll bet. We seem to be of interest."

Van Sarawak nodded sickly.

The police chief cleared his throat with conscious importance and said something to the—general? The latter turned impatiently and addressed himself to the prisoners. He barked his words out with a clarity that helped Everard get the phonemes, but with a manner that was not exactly reassuring.

Somewhere along the line, communication would have to be established. Everard pointed to himself. "*Manse Everard*," he said. Van Sarawak followed the lead and introduced himself similarly.

The general started and went into a huddle with the chief. Turning back, he snapped: "*Yrn Cimberland?*"

"*No spikka da Inglees*," said Everard.

"*Gothland? Svea? Nairoin Teutonach?*"

"Those names—if they are names—they sound a little Germanic, don't they?" muttered van Sarawak.

"So do our names, come to think of it," answered Everard

tautly. "Maybe they think we're Germans." To the general: "*Sprechen Sie Deutsch?*" Blankness rewarded him. "*Taler ni svensk? Niederlands? Dönsk tunga? Parlez-vous français?* Goddammit, *¿habla usted español?*"

The police chief cleared his throat again and pointed to himself. "*Cadwallader Mac Barca,*" he said. "*The general hight Cynyth ap Ceorn.*"

"Celtic, all right," said Everard. Sweat prickled under his arms. "But just to make sure—" He pointed inquiringly at a few other men, being rewarded with monickers like Hamilcar ap Angus, Asshur yr Cathlaan, and Finn O'Carthia. "No . . . there's a distinct Semitic element here too. That fits in with their alphabet—"

Van Sarawak's mouth was dry. "Try Classical languages," he urged harshly. "Maybe we can find out where this time went awry."

"*Loquerisne latine?*" That drew a blank. "Ελλευίξεις?"

General ap Ceorn started, blew out his mustache, and narrowed his eyes. "*Hellenach?*" he snapped. "*Yrn Parthia?*"

Everard shook his head. "They've at least heard of Greek," he said slowly. He tried a few more words, but no one knew the tongue.

Ap Ceorn growled something and spoke to one of his men, who bowed and went out. There was a long silence.

Everard found himself losing personal fear. He was in a bad spot, yes, and might not live very long; but anything that happened to him was ridiculously insignificant compared to what had been done to the entire world.

God in Heaven! To the universe!

He couldn't grasp it. Sharp in his mind rose the land he knew, broad plains and tall mountains and prideful cities. There was the grave image of his father, and yet he remembered being a small child and lifted up skyward while his father laughed beneath him. And his mother— they had a good life together, those two.

There had been a girl he knew in college, the sweetest little wench a man could ever have been privileged to walk in the rain with; and there was Bernie Aaronson, the long nights of beer and smoke and talk; Phil Brackney, who had picked him out of the mud in France when machine guns were raking a ruined field; Charlie and

Mary Whitcomb, high tea and a low little fire in Victoria's London; a dog he had once had; the austere cantos of Dante and the ringing thunder of Shakespeare; the glory which was York Minster and the Golden Gate Bridge—Christ, a man's life, and the lives of who knew how many billions of human creatures, toiling and suffering and laughing and going down into dust to leave their sons behind them—*It had never been!*

He shook his head, dazed with grief, and sat devoid of real understanding.

The soldier came back with a map and spread it out on the desk. Ap Ceorn gestured curtly, and Everard and van Sarawak bent over it.

Yes . . . Earth, a Mercator projection, though eidetic memory showed that the mapping was rather crude. The continents and islands were there in bright colors, but the nations were something else.

"Can you read those names, Van?"

"I can make a guess, on the basis of the Hebraic alphabet," said the Venusian. He read out the alien words, filling in the gaps of his knowledge with what sounded logical.

North America down to about Colombia was Ynys yr Afallon, seemingly one country divided into states. South America was a big realm, Huy Braseal, with some smaller countries whose names looked Indian. Australasia, Indonesia, Borneo, Burma, eastern India, and a good deal of the Pacific belonged to Hinduraj. Afghanistan and the rest of India were Punjab. Han included China, Korea, Japan, and eastern Siberia. Littorn owned the rest of Russia and reached well into Europe. The British Isles were Brittys, France and the Low Countries Gallis, the Iberian peninsula Celtan. Central Europe and the Balkans were divided into many small states, some of which had Hunnish-looking names. Switzerland and Austria made up Helveti; Italy was Cimberland; the Scandinavian peninsula was split down the middle, Svea in the north and Gothland in the south. North Africa looked like a confederacy, reaching from Senegal to Suez and nearly to the equator under the name of Carthagalann; the southern continent was partitioned among small countries, many of which had purely African titles. The Near East held Parthia and Arabia.

Van Sarawak looked up. There were tears in his eyes.

Ap Ceorn snarled a question and waved his finger about. He wanted to know where they were from.

Everard shrugged and pointed skyward. The one thing he could not admit was the truth. He and van Sarawak had agreed to claim they were from some other planet, since this world hardly had space travel.

Ap Ceorn spoke to the chief, who nodded and replied. The prisoners were returned to their cell.

"And now what?" Van Sarawak slumped on his cot and stared at the floor.

"We play along," said Everard grayly. "We do anything to get at our scooter and escape. Once we're free, we can take stock."

"But what happened?"

"I don't know, I tell you! Offhand it looks as if something upset the Roman Empire and the Celts took over, but I couldn't say what it was." Everard prowled the room. There was a bitter determination growing in him.

"Remember your basic theory," he said. "Events are the result of a complex. That's why it's so hard to change history. If I went back to, say, the Middle Ages, and shot one of FDR's Dutch forebears, he'd still be born in the twentieth century—because he and his genes resulted from the entire world of his ancestors, and there'd have been compensation. The first case I ever worked on was an attempt to alter things in the fifth century; we spotted evidence of it in the twentieth, and went back and stopped the scheme.

"But every so often, there must be a really key event. Only with hindsight can we tell what it was, but some one happening was a nexus of so many world lines that its outcome was decisive for the whole future.

"Somehow, for some reason, somebody has ripped up one of those events back in the past."

"No more Hesperus City," whispered van Sarawak. "No more sitting by the canals in the blue twilight, no more Aphrodite vintages, no more—did you know I had a sister on Venus?"

"Shut up!" Everard almost shouted it. "I know. What counts is what to do.

"Look," he went on after a moment, "the Patrol and the Daneelians are wiped out. But such of the Patrol offices and resorts as antedate the switchpoint haven't been affected. There must be a few hundred agents we can rally."

"*If* we can get out of here."

"We can find that key event and stop whatever interference there was with it. We've got to!"

"A pleasant thought," mumbled van Sarawak, "but—"

Feet tramped outside, and a key clicked in the lock. The prisoners backed away. Then, all at once, van Sarawak was bowing and beaming and spilling gallantries. Even Everard had to gape.

The girl who entered in front of three soldiers was a knockout. She was tall, with a sweep of rusty-red hair past her shoulders to the slim waist; her eyes were green and alight, her face came from all the Irish colleens who had ever lived, the long white dress was snug around a figure meant to stand on the walls of Troy. Everard noticed vaguely that this time-line used cosmetics, but she had small need of them. He paid no attention to the gold and amber of her jewelry, or to the guns behind her.

She smiled, a little timidly, and spoke: "Can you understand me? It was thought you might know Greek—"

The language was classical rather than modern. Everard, who had once had a job in Alexandrine times, could follow it through her accent if he paid close heed—which was inevitable anyway.

"Indeed I do," he replied, his words stumbling over each other.

"What are you snakkering?" demanded van Sarawak.

"Ancient Greek," said Everard.

"It would be," mourned van Sarawak. His despair seemed to have vanished, and his eyes bugged.

Everard introduced himself and his companion. The girl said her name was Deirdre Mac Morn. "Oh, no," groaned van Sarawak. "This is too much. Manse, you've got to teach me Greek, and fast."

"Shut up," said Everard. "This is serious business."

"Well, but why should you have all the pleasure—"

Everard ignored him and invited the girl to sit down. He joined her on a cot, while the other Patrolman hovered unhappily close. The guards kept their weapons ready.

"Is Greek still a living language?" asked Everard.

"Only in Parthia, and there it is most corrupt," said Deirdre. "I am a Classical scholar, among other things. *Saorann* ap Ceorn is my uncle, so he asked me to see if I could talk with you. There are not many in Afallon who know the Attic tongue."

"Well . . ." Everard suppressed a silly grin. "I am most grateful to your uncle."

Her eyes rested gravely on him. "Where are you from? And how does it happen that you speak only Greek, of all known languages?"

"I speak Latin too."

"Latin?" She frowned briefly. "Oh, yes. The Roman speech, was it not? I'm afraid you'll find no one who knows much about it."

"Greek will do," said Everard.

"But you have not told me whence you came," she insisted.

Everard shrugged. "We've not been treated very courteously," he hinted.

"Oh . . . I'm sorry." It seemed genuine. "But our people are so excitable—especially now, with the international situation what it is. And when you two appeared out of thin air—"

Everard nodded grimly. The international situation? That had a familiar ring. "What do you mean?" he inquired.

"Oh, surely . . . of course you know. With Huy Braseal and Hinduraj about to go to war, and all of us wondering what will happen— It is not easy to be a small power."

"A small power? But I saw a map, and Afallon looked big enough to me."

"We wore ourselves out two hundred years ago, in the great war with Littorn. Now none of our confederated states can agree on a single policy." Deirdre looked directly into his eyes. "What is this ignorance of yours?"

Everard swallowed and said: "We're from another world."

"What?"

"Yes. A . . . planet of Sirius."

"But Sirius is a star!"

"Of course."

"How can a star have planets?"

"How— But it does! A star is a sun like—"

Deirdre shrank back and made a sign with her finger. "The Great Baal aid us," she whispered. "Either you are mad, or— The stars are mounted in a crystal sphere."

Oh, no! Everard asked slowly: "What of the planets you can see—Mars and Venus and—"

"I know not those names. If you mean Moloch, Ashtoreth, and the rest, of course they are worlds like ours. One holds the spirits of the dead, one is the home of witches, one—"

All this and steam cars too. Everard smiled shakily. "If you'll not believe me, then what do you think?"

Deirdre regarded him with large eyes. "I think you must be sorcerers," she said.

There was no answer to that. Everard asked a few weak questions, but learned little more than that this city was Catuvellaunan, a trading and manufacturing center; Deirdre estimated its population at two million, and that of all Afallon at fifty millions, but it was only a guess—they didn't take censuses in this world.

The prisoners' fate was also indeterminate. Their machine and other possessions had been sequestrated by the military, but nobody dared to monkey with them, and treatment of the owners was being hotly debated. Everard got the impression that all government, including the leadership of the armed forces, was a sloppy process of individualistic wrangling. Afallon itself was the loosest of confederacies, built out of former nations—Brittic colonies and Indians who had adopted white culture—all jealous of their rights. The old Mayan Empire, destroyed in a war with Texas (Tehannach) and annexed, had not forgotten its time of glory, and sent the most rambunctious delegates of all to the Council of Suffetes.

The Mayans wanted an alliance with Huy Braseal, perhaps out of friendship for fellow Indians. The West Coast states, fearful of Hinduraj, were toadies of the Southeast Asian empire. The Middle West—of course—was isolationist, and the Eastern states were torn every which way but inclined to follow the lead of Brittys.

When he gathered that slavery existed here, though not on racial lines, Everard wondered briefly if the guilty time travelers might not have been Dixiecrats.

Enough! He had his own and Van's necks to think about. "We are from Sirius," he declared loftily. "Your ideas about the stars are mistaken. We came as peaceful explorers, and if we are molested there will be others of our kind to take vengeance."

Deirdre looked so unhappy that he felt conscience-stricken. "Will you spare the children?" she whispered. "They had nothing to do with it." Everard could imagine the frightful vision in her head, helpless captives led off in chains to the slave markets of a world of witches.

"There need be no trouble at all if we are released and our property returned," he said.

"I shall speak to my uncle," she promised, "but even if I can sway him, he is only one of the Council. The thought of what your weapons could mean if we had them has driven men mad."

She rose. Everard clasped her hands, they lay warm and soft in his, and smiled crookedly at her. "Buck up, kid," he said in English. She shivered and made the hex sign again.

"Well," said van Sarawak when they were alone, "what did you find out?" After being told, he stroked his chin and murmured thoughtfully: "That was one sweet little collection of sinusoids. There could be worse worlds than this."

"Or better," said Everard bleakly. "They don't have atomic bombs, but neither do they have penicillin. It's not our job to play God."

"No . . . no, I suppose not." The Venusian sighed.

They spent a restless day. Night had fallen when lanterns glimmered in the corridor and a military guard unlocked the cell. The prisoners' handcuffs were removed, and they were led silently to a rear exit. A car waited, with another for escort, and the whole troop drove wordlessly off.

Catuvellaunan did not have outdoor lighting, and there

wasn't much night traffic. Somehow, that made the sprawling city unreal in the dark. Everard leaned back and concentrated on the mechanics of his vehicle. Steam-powered, as he had guessed, burning powdered coal; rubber-tired wheels; a sleek body with a sharp nose and a serpent figurehead; the whole simple to operate but not too well designed. Apparently this world had gradually developed a rule-of-thumb mechanics, but no systematic science worth mentioning.

They crossed a clumsy iron bridge to Long Island, here as at home a residential section for the well-to-do. Their speed was high despite the dimness of their oil-lamp headlights, and twice they came near having an accident—no traffic signals, and seemingly no drivers who did not hold caution in contempt.

Government and traffic . . . hm. It all looked French, somehow, and even in Everard's own Twentieth Century France was largely Celtic. He was no respecter of windy theories about inborn racial traits, but there was something to be said for traditional attitudes so ancient that they were unconsciously accepted. A Western world in which the Celts had become dominant, the Germanic peoples reduced to two small outposts . . . Yes, look at the Ireland of home; or recall how tribal politics had queered Vercingetorix's revolt. . . . But what about Littorn? Wait a minute! In *his* early Middle Ages, Lithuania had been a powerful state; it had held off Germans, Poles, and Russians alike for a long time, and hadn't even taken Christianity till the Fifteenth Century. Without German competition, Lithuania might very well have advanced eastward—

In spite of the Celtic political instability, this was a world of large states, fewer separate nations than Everard's. That argued an older society. If his own Western civilization had developed out of the decaying Roman Empire about, say, 600 A.D., the Celts in this world must have taken over earlier than that.

Everard was beginning to realize what had happened to Rome. . . .

The cars drew up before an ornamental gate set in a long stone wall. There was an interchange with two armed guards wearing the livery of a private estate and the thin steel collars of slaves. The gate was opened, and the cars went along a graveled driveway between trees and lawns and hedgerows. At the far end, almost on the beach, stood a house. Everard and van Sarawak were gestured out and led toward it.

It was a rambling wooden structure. Gas lamps on the porch showed it painted in gaudy stripes; the gables and beam-ends were carved into dragon heads. Behind it murmured the sea, and there was enough starlight for Everard to make out a ship standing in close—presumably a freighter, with a tall smokestack and a figurehead.

Light glowed through the windows. A slave butler admitted the party. The interior was paneled in dark wood, also carved, the floors thickly carpeted. At the end of the hall there was a living room with overstuffed furniture, several paintings in a stiff conventionalized style, and a merry blaze in a great stone fireplace.

Saorann Cynyth ap Ceorn sat in one chair, Deirdre in another. She laid aside a book as they entered and rose, smiling. The officer puffed a cigar and glowered. There were some words swapped, and the guards disappeared. The butler fetched in wine on a tray, and Deirdre invited the Patrolmen to sit down.

Everard sipped from his glass—the wine was an excellent burgundy type—and asked bluntly: "Why are we here?"

Deirdre smiled, dazzlingly this time, and chuckled. "Surely you find it more pleasant than the jail."

"Oh, yes. But I still want to know. Are we being released?"

"You are . . ." She hunted for a diplomatic answer, but there seemed to be too much frankness in her. "You are welcome here, but may not leave the estate. We had hopes you could be persuaded to help us. There would be rich reward."

"Help? How?"

"By showing our artisans and wizards the spells to make more machines and weapons like your own."

Everard sighed. It was no use trying to explain. They didn't have the tools to make the tools to make what was needed, but how could he get that across to a folk who believed in witchcraft?

"Is this your uncle's home?" he asked.

"No," said Deirdre. "It is my own. I am the only child of my parents, who were wealthy nobles and died last year."

Ap Ceorn snapped something, and Deirdre translated with a worried frown: "The tale of your magical advent is known to all Catuvellaunan by now; and that includes the foreign spies. We hope you can remain hidden from them here."

Everard, remembering the pranks Axis and Allies had played in little neutral nations like Portugal, shivered. Men made desperate by approaching war would not likely be as courteous as the Afallonians.

"What is this conflict going to be about?" he inquired.

"The control of the Icenian Ocean, of course. Particularly, certain rich islands we call Yyns yr Lyonnach—" Deirdre got up in a single flowing movement and pointed out Hawaii on a globe. "You see," she went on earnestly, "as I told you, the western countries like Brittys, Gallis, and ourselves, fighting Littorn, have worn each other out. Our domains have shrunken, and the newer states like Huy Braseal and Hinduraj are now expanding and quarreling. They will draw in the lesser nations, for it is not only a clash of ambitions but of systems—the monarchy of Hinduraj and the sun-worshipping theocracy of Huy Braseal."

"What is your religion?" asked Everard.

Deirdre blinked. The question seemed almost meaningless to her. "The more educated people think that there is a Great Baal who made all the lesser gods," she answered at last, slowly. "But naturally, we pay our respects to the foreign gods too, Littorn's Perkunas and Czernebog, the Sun of the southerners, Wotan Ammon of Cimberland, and so on. They are very powerful."

"I see. . . ."

Ap Ceorn offered cigars and matches. Van Sarawak inhaled and said querulously: "Damn it, this would have to be a time line where they don't speak any language I know." He brightened. "But I'm pretty quick to learn, even without hypnos. I'll get Deirdre to teach me."

"You and me both," said Everard hastily. "But listen, Van—" He reported what had been said.

"Hm." The younger man rubbed his chin. "Not so good, eh? Of course, if they'd just let us at our scooter, we could take off at once. Why not play along with them?"

"They're not such fools," answered Everard. "They may believe in magic, but not in undiluted altruism."

"Funny . . . that they should be so backward intellectually, and still have combustion engines."

"No. It's quite understandable. That's why I asked about their religion. It's always been purely pagan; even Judaism seems to have disappeared. As Whitehead pointed out, the medieval idea of one almighty God was important to science, by inculcating the notion of lawfulness in nature. And Mumford added that the early monasteries were probably responsible for the mechanical clock—a very basic invention—because of having regular hours for prayer. Clocks seem to have come late in this world." Everard smiled wryly, but there was a twisting sadness in him. "Odd to talk that way. Whitehead and Mumford never lived. If Jesus did, his message has been lost."

"Still—"

"Just a minute." Everard turned to Deirdre. "When was Afallon discovered?"

"By white men? In the year 4827."

"Um . . . when does your reckoning start from?"

Deirdre seemed immune to further startlement. "The creation of the world—at least, the date some philosophers have given. That is 5959 years ago."

4004 B.C. . . . Yes, definitely a Semitic element in this culture. The Jews had presumably gotten their traditional date from Babylon; but Everard doubted that the Jews were the Semites in question here.

"And when was steam (*pneuma*) first used to drive engines?"

"About a thousand years ago. The great Druid Boroihme O'Fiona—"

"Never mind." Everard smoked his cigar and mulled his thoughts for a while. Then he turned back to van Sarawak.

"I'm beginning to get the picture," he said. "The Gauls were anything but the barbarians most people think. They'd learned a lot from Phoenician traders and Greek colonists, as well as from the Etruscans in Cisalpine Gaul. A very energetic and enterprising race. The Romans, on the other hand, were a stolid lot, with few intellectual interests. There was very little technological progress in our world till the Dark Ages, when the Empire had been swept out of the way.

"In *this* history, the Romans vanished early and the Gauls got the power. They started exploring, building better ships, discovering America in the ninth century. But they weren't so far ahead of the Indians that they couldn't catch up . . . even be stimulated to build empires of their own, like Huy Braseal today. In the eleventh century, the Celts began tinkering with steam engines. They seem to have got gunpowder too, maybe from China, and to have made several other inventions; but it's all been cut-and-dry, with no basis of real science."

Van Sarawak nodded. "I suppose you're right. But what did happen to Rome?"

"I'm not sure . . . yet . . . but our key point is back there somewhere."

Everard returned to Deirdre. "This may surprise you," he said smoothly. "Our people visited this world about 2500 years ago. That's why I speak Greek but don't know what has occurred since. I would like to find out from you—I take it you're quite a scholar."

She flushed and lowered long dark lashes. "I will be glad to help as much as I can." With a sudden appeal that cut at his heart: "But will you help us in return?"

"I don't know," said Everard heavily. "I'd like to, but I don't know if we can."

Because after all, my job is to condemn you and your entire world to death.

When Everard was shown to his room, he discovered that local hospitality was more than generous. He was too tired and depressed to take advantage of it . . . but at least, he thought on the edge of sleep, Van's slave girl wouldn't be disappointed.

They got up early here. From his upstairs window, Everard saw guards pacing the beach, but they didn't detract from the morning's freshness. He came down with van Sarawak to breakfast, where bacon and eggs, toast and coffee added the last incongruous note of dream. Ap Ceorn was gone back to town to confer, said Deirdre; she herself had put wistfulness aside and chattered gaily of trivia. Everard learned that she belonged to a dramatic group which sometimes gave plays in the original Greek—hence her fluency; she liked to ride, hunt, sail, swim—"And shall we?" she asked.

"Huh?"

"Swim, of course!" Deirdre sprang from her chair on the lawn, where they had been sitting under flame-colored leaves in the wan autumn sunlight, and whirled innocently out of her clothes. Everard thought he heard a dull clunk as van Sarawak's jaw hit the ground.

"Come!" she laughed. "Last one in is a Sassenach!"

She was already tumbling in the cold gray waves when Everard and van Sarawak shuddered their way down to the beach. The Venusian groaned. "I come from a warm planet," he objected. "My ancestors were Indonesians—tropical birds."

"There were some Dutchmen too, weren't there?" grinned Everard.

"They had the sense to go to Indonesia."

"All right, stay ashore."

"Hell!" If she can do it, I can!" Van Sarawak put a toe in the water and groaned again.

Everard summoned up all the psychosomatic control he had ever learned and ran in. Deirdre threw water at him. He plunged, got hold of a slender leg, and pulled her under. They tumbled about for several minutes before running back to the house. Van Sarawak followed.

"Speak about Tantalus," he mumbled. "The most beautiful girl in the whole continuum, and I can't talk to her and she's half polar bear."

Everard stood quiet before the living-room fire, while slaves toweled him dry and dressed him in the local garb. "What pattern is this?" he asked, pointing to the tartan of his kilt.

Deirdre lifted her ruddy head. "My own clan's," she answered. "A house guest is always taken as a clan member during his stay, even if there is a blood feud going on." She smiled shyly. "And there is none between us, Manslach."

It cast him back into bleakness. He remembered what his purpose was.

"I'd like to ask you about history," he said. "It is a special interest of mine."

She nodded, adjusted a gold fillet on her hair, and got a book from a crowded shelf. "This is the best world history, I think. I can look up details you might wish to know."

And tell me what I must do to destroy you. Seldom had Everard felt himself so much a skunk.

He sat down with her on a couch. The butler wheeled in lunch, and he ate moodily.

To follow up his notion—"Did Rome and Carthage ever fight a war?"

"Yes. Two, in fact. They were allied at first, against Epirus. Then they fell out. Rome won the first war and tried to restrict Carthaginian enterprise." Her clean profile bent over the pages, like a studious child. "The second war broke out twenty-three years later, and lasted . . . hm . . . eleven years all told, though the last three were only mopping up after Hannibal had taken and burned Rome."

Ah-hah! Somehow, Everard did not feel happy about it.

The Second Punic War, or rather some key incident thereof, was the turning point. But—partly out of curiosity, partly because he feared to tip his hand—Everard did not ask for particulars. He'd first have to get straight in his mind what had actually happened, anyway. (No . . . what had not happened. The reality was here, warm and breathing beside him, and he was the ghost.)

"So what came next?" he inquired tonelessly.

"There was a Carthaginian Empire, including Spain, southern Gaul, and the toe of Italy," she said. "The rest of Italy was impotent and chaotic, after the Roman confederacy had been broken up. But the Carthaginian government was too venal to endure; Hannibal himself was assassinated by men who thought him too honest. Meanwhile, Syria and Parthia fought for the eastern Mediterranean, with Parthia winning.

"About a hundred years after the Punic Wars, some Germanic tribes invaded and conquered Italy." (Yes . . . that would be the Cimbri, with their allies the Teutones and Ambrones, whom Marius had stopped in Everard's world.) "Their destructive path through Gaul set the Celts moving too, into Spain and North Africa as Carthage declined; and from Carthage the Gauls learned much.

"There followed a long period of wars, during which Parthia waned and the Celtic states grew. The Huns broke the Germans in middle Europe, but were in turn scattered by Parthia, so the Gauls moved in and the only Germans left were in Italy and Hyperborea." (That must be the Scandinavian peninsula.) "As ships improved, there was trade around Africa with India and China. The Celtanians discovered Afallon, which they thought was an island— hence the 'Ynys'—but were thrown out by the Mayans. The Brittic colonies further north had better luck, and eventually won their independence.

"Meanwhile Littorn was growing vastly. It swallowed up central Europe and Hyperborea for a while, and those countries only regained their freedom as part of the peace settlement after the Hundred Years' War you know of. The Asian countries have shaken off their European masters and modernized themselves, while the Western nations have declined in their turn." Deirdre looked up. "But this is only the barest outline. Shall I go on?"

Everard shook his head. "No, thanks." After a moment: "You are very honest about the situation of your own country."

Deirdre shrugged. "Most of us won't admit it, but I think it best to look truth in the eyes."

With a surge of eagerness: "But tell me of your own world. This is a marvel past belief."

Everard sighed, turned off his conscience, and began lying.

The raid took place that afternoon.

Van Sarawak had recovered himself and was busily learning the Afallonian language from Deirdre. They walked through the garden hand in hand, stopping to name objects and act out verbs. Everard followed, wondering vaguely if he was a third wheel or not, most of him bent to the problem of how to get at the scooter.

Bright sunlight spilled from a pale cloudless sky. A maple stood like a shout of scarlet, and a drift of yellow leaves scudded across sere grass. An elderly slave was raking the yard in a leisurely fashion, a young-looking guard of Indian race lounged with his rifle slung on one shoulder, a pair of wolfhounds dozed with dignity under a hedge. It was a peaceful scene—hard to believe that men schemed murder beyond these walls.

But man was man, in any history. This culture might not have the ruthless will and sophisticated cruelty of Western civilization; in some ways it looked strangely innocent. Still, that wasn't for lack of trying; and in this world, a genuine science might never emerge, man might endlessly repeat the weary cycle of war, empire, collapse, and war. In Everard's future, the race had finally broken out of it.

For what? He could not honestly say that this new continuum was worse or better than his own. It was different, that was all; and didn't these people have as much right to their existence as—as his own, who were damned to nullity if he failed to act?

He shook his head and felt fists knot at his side. It was too big. No man should have to decide something like this.

In the showdown, he knew, it would be no abstract sense of duty which compelled him, but the little things and the little folk he remembered.

They rounded the house and Deirdre pointed to the sea. "*Awarlann*," she said. Her loose hair was flame in the wind.

"Now does that mean 'ocean' or 'Atlantic' or 'water'?" asked van Sarawak, laughing. "Let's go see." He led her toward the beach.

Everard trailed. A kind of steam launch, long and fast, was skipping over the waves, a mile or so offshore. Gulls flew up in a shrieking snowstorm of wings. He thought that if he'd been in charge, there would have been a Navy ship on picket out there.

Did he even have to decide anything? There were other Patrolmen in the pre-Roman past. They'd return to their respective eras and—

Everard stiffened. A chill ran down his back and into his belly.

They'd return, and see what had happened, and try to

correct the trouble. If any of them succeeded, this world would blink out of spacetime, and he would go with it.

Deirdre paused. Everard, standing in a cold sweat, hardly noticed what she was staring at, till she cried out and pointed. Then he joined her and squinted across the sea.

The launch was coming in close, its high stack fuming smoke and sparks, the gilt snake figurehead agleam. He could see the dwarfed forms of men aboard, and something white, with wings. It rose from the poopdeck and trailed at the end of a rope, mounting. A glider! Celtic aeronautics had gotten that far, at least—

"Pretty thing," said van Sarawak. "I suppose they have balloons too."

The glider cast its tow and swooped inward. One of the guards on the beach shouted. The rest came running from behind the house, sunlight flashed off their guns. The launch sped for the shore and the glider landed, plowing a furrow in the beach.

An officer yelled, waving the Patrolmen back. Everard had a glimpse of Deirdre's face, white and uncomprehending. Then a turret on the glider swiveled—a detached part of his mind assumed it was manually operated—and a cannon spoke.

Everard hit the dirt. Van Sarawak followed, dragging the girl with him. Grapeshot plowed hideously through the Afallonian soldiers.

There came a spiteful crack of guns. Men were emerging from the aircraft, dark-faced men in turbans and sarongs. *Hinduraj!* thought Everard. They traded shots with the surviving guards, who rallied about their captain.

That man roared and led a charge. Everard looked up to see him almost at the glider and its crew. Van Sarawak leaped up and ran to join the fight. Everard rolled over, caught his leg, and pulled him down.

"Let me *go!*" The Venusian writhed. There was a sobbing in his throat. The racket of battle seemed to fill the sky.

"No, you bloody fool! It's us they're after, and that wild Irishman did the worst thing he could have—" Everard slapped his friend's face and looked up.

The launch, shallow-draught and screw-propelled, had

run up to the beach and was retching armed men. The Afallonians realized too late that they had discharged their weapons and were being attacked from the rear.

"Come on!" Everard yanked Deirdre and van Sarawak to their feet. "We've got to get out of here—get to the neighbors—"

A detachment of the boat crew saw him and veered. He felt rather than heard the flat smack of a bullet into turf. Slaves were screaming around the house. The two wolfhounds charged and were gunned down.

Everard whirled to flee. Crouched, zigzag, that was the way, over the wall and out onto the road! He might have made it, but Deirdre stumbled and fell. Van Sarawak halted and stood over her with a snarl. Everard plunged to a stop, and by that time it was too late. They were covered.

The leader of the dark men snapped something at the girl. She sat up, giving him a defiant answer. He laughed shortly and jerked his thumb at the launch.

"What do they want?" asked Everard in Greek.

"You." She looked at him with horror. "You two—" The officer spoke. "And me to translate—No!"

She twisted in the arms that held her and clawed at a man's face. Everard's fist traveled in a short arc that ended in a lovely squashing of nose. It was too good to last: a clubbed rifle descended on his head, and he was only dimly aware of being carried off to the launch.

The crew left the glider behind, shoved their boat into deeper water, and revved it up. They left all the guardsmen slain, but took their own casualties along.

Everard sat on a bench on the plunging deck and stared with slowly clearing eyes as the shoreline dwindled. Deirdre wept on van Sarawak's shoulder, and the Vensusian tried to console her. A chill noisy wind blew across indifferent waves, spindrift stung their faces.

It was when the two white men emerged from a cabin that Everard's mind was jarred back into motion. Not Asians after all—these were Europeans. And the rest of the crew had Caucasian features . . . grease paint!

He regarded his new owners warily. One was a portly, middle-aged man of average height, in a red silk blouse and baggy white trousers and a sort of astrakhan hat; he was clean-shaven and his dark hair was twisted into a queue. The other was somewhat younger, a shaggy blond giant in a tunic sewn with copper links, leggined breeches, a leather cloak, and a horned helmet. Both wore revolvers at their belts and were treated deferentially.

"What the devil—" Everard looked around. They were already out of sight of land and bending north. The engine made the hull quiver, spray sheeted when the bows bit into a wave.

The older man spoke first in Afallonian. Everard shrugged. Then the bearded Nordic tried, first in a completely unrecognizable dialect but afterward: *"Taelan thu Cimbric?"*

Everard, who knew German, Swedish, and Anglo-Saxon, took a chance, while van Sarawak pricked up his Dutch ears. Deirdre huddled back wide-eyed, too bewildered to move.

"Ja," said Everard, *"ein wenig."* When Goldilocks looked uncertain, he amended it: "A little."

"Ah, aen litt. Gode!" The big man rubbed hairy hands. *"Ik hait Boierik Wulfilasson ok main gefreond heer erran Boleslav Arkonsky."*

It was not any language Everard had ever heard of—it couldn't even be the original Cimbrian, after all these centuries—but the Patrolman could follow it tolerably well. The trouble would be in speaking; he couldn't predict how it had evolved.

"What the hell erran thu maching, anyway?" he blustered. "Ik bin aen man auf Sirius—the stern Sirius, mit planeten ok all. Set uns gebach or willen be der Teufel to pay!"

Boierik Wulfilasson looked pained and suggested that the discussion be continued inside, with the young lady for interpreter. He led the way back into the cabin, which turned out to be small but comfortably furnished. The door remained open, with an armed guard looking in and more on call.

Boleslav Arkonsky said something in Afallonian to Deirdre. She nodded, and he gave her a glass of wine. It seemed to steady her, but she spoke to Everard in a thin voice.

"We've been taken, Manslach. Their spies found out

where you were kept. Another group is supposed to capture your machine—they know where that is, too."

"So I imagined," replied Everard. "But who in Baal's name are they?"

Boierik guffawed at the question and expounded lengthily on his own cleverness. The idea was to make the Suffetes of Afallon think that Hinduraj was responsible. Actually, the secret alliance of Littorn and Cimberland had built up quite an effective spy service of its own. They were now bound for the Littornian Embassy's summer retreat on Ynys Llangollen (Nantucket), where the wizards would be induced to explain their spells and the great powers get a surprise.

"And if we don't . . . ?"

Deirdre translated Arkonsky's answer word for word: "I regret the consequences to you. We are civilized men, and will pay well in gold and honor for your free cooperation; but the existence of our countries is at stake."

Everard looked at them. Boierik seemed embarrassed and unhappy, the boastful glee evaporated from him. Boleslav Arkonsky drummed on the table, his lips compressed but a certain mute appeal in his eyes. *Don't make us do this. We have to live with ourselves.*

They were probably husbands and fathers, they must enjoy a mug of beer and a friendly game of dice as well as the next man, maybe Boierik bred horses in Italy and Arkonsky was a rose fancier on the Baltic shores. But none of it would do their captives a bit of good, not when the almighty Nation locked horns with its kin.

Everard paused briefly to admire the sheer artistry of this operation and began wondering what to do. The launch was fast, but would need something like twenty hours to reach Nantucket if he remembered the trip. There was that much time at least.

"We are weary," he said in English. "May we not rest a while?"

"*Ja deedly*," said Boierik with a clumsy graciousness. "*Ok wir skallen gode gefreonds bin, ni?*"

Sunset smoldered redly to the west. Deirdre and van Sarawak stood at the rail, looking across a gray waste of waters. Three crewmen, their brown paint and Asian garments removed, poised alert and weaponed on the poop; a man steered by compass; Boierik and Everard paced the quarterdeck, talking. All wore heavy cloaks against a stiff, stinging wind.

Everard was getting some proficiency in the Cimbrian language; his tongue still limped, but he could make himself understood. Mostly, though, he let Boierik do the talking.

"So you are from the stars? These matters I do not understand. I am a simple man. Had I my way, I would manage my Tuscan estate in peace and let the world rave as it will. But we of the Folk have our obligations." The Teutons seemed to have replaced the Latins altogether in Italy, as the Saxons had done the Britons in Everard's world.

"I know how you feel," said the Patrolman. "It is a strange thing, that so many should fight when so few want to."

"Oh, but it is necessary." Almost a whine there. "You don't understand. Carthagalann stole Egypt, our rightful possession."

"*Italia irredenta*," murmured Everard.

"Huh?"

"Never mind. So you Cimbri are allied with Littorn, and hope to grab off Europe and Africa while the big powers are fighting in the East."

"Not at all!" replied Boierik indignantly. "We are merely asserting our rightful and historic territorial claims. Why, the king himself said—" And so on and so on.

Everard braced himself against the roll of the deck. "It seems to me that you treat us wizards rather hardily," he declared. "Beware lest we get really angered at you."

"All of us are protected against curses and shapings."

"Well—"

"I wish you would help us freely," said Boierik. "I will be happy to demonstrate to you the justice of our cause, if you have a few hours to spare."

Everard shook his head and stopped by Deirdre. Her face was a blur in the thickening dusk, but he caught a forlorn defiance in her voice: "I hope you are telling him what to do with his plans, Manslach."

"No," said Everard heavily. "We are going to help them."

She stood as if struck.

"What are you saying, Manse?" asked van Sarawak.

Everard told him.

"No!" said the Venusian.

"Yes," said Everard.

"By God, no! I'll—"

Everard grabbed his arm and said coldly: "Be still. I know what I'm doing. We can't take sides in this world, we're against everybody and you'd better realize it. The only thing to do is play along with these fellows for a while. And don't tell that to Deirdre."

Van Sarawak bent his head and stood for a moment, thinking. "All right," he said dully.

The Littornian resort was on the southern shore of Nantucket, near a fishing village but walled off from it. The embassy had built in the style of its homeland, long timber houses with roofs arched like a cat's back, a main hall and its outbuildings enclosing a flagged courtyard. Everard finished a night's sleep and a breakfast made miserable by Deirdre's eyes by standing on deck as they came to the private pier. Another, bigger launch was already there, and the grounds swarmed with hard-looking men. Arkonsky's eyes kindled, and he said in Afallonian: "I see the magic engine has been brought. We can go right to work."

When Boierik interpreted, Everard felt his heart slam.

The guests, as the Cimbrian insisted on calling them, were led into a great room where Arkonsky bent the knee to an idol with four faces, that Svantevit which the Danes had chopped up for firewood in the other history. There was a blaze on the hearth against the autumn chill, and guards posted around the walls. Everard had eyes only for the scooter, where it stood gleaming on the floor.

"I hear it was a hard fight in Catuvellaunan," remarked Boierik to him. "Many were killed, but our folk got away without being followed." He touched a handlebar gingerly. "And this wain can truly appear anywhere it wishes, out of thin air?"

"Yes," said Everard.

Deirdre gave him a look of scorn such as he had never known. She stood haughtily away from him and van Sarawak.

Arkonsky spoke to her, something he wanted translated. She spat at his feet. Boierik sighed and gave the word to Everard:

"We wish the engine demonstrated. You and I will go for a ride on it. I warn you, I will have a revolver at your back: you will tell me in advance everything you mean to do, and if aught untoward happens I will shoot. Your friends will remain here as hostages, also to be shot on the first suspicion. But I'm sure we will all be good friends."

Everard nodded. There was a tautness thrumming in him, and his palms felt cold and wet. "First I must say a spell," he answered.

His eyes flicked. One glance memorized the spatial reading of the position meters and the time reading of the clock on the scooter. Another look showed van Sarawak seated on a bench, under Arkonsky's drawn pistol and the rifles of the guards; Deirdre sat down too, stiffly, as far from him as she could get. Everard made a close estimate of the bench's position relative to the scooter's, lifted his arms, and chanted in Temporal:

"Van, I'm going to try to pull you out of here. Stay exactly where you are now; repeat, exactly. I'll pick you up on the fly. If all goes well, that'll happen about one minute after I blink out of here with our shaggy comrade."

The Venusian sat wooden-faced. There was a thin beading of sweat on his forehead.

"Very good," said Everard in his pidgin Cimbrian. "Mount on the rear saddle, Boierik, and we'll put this magic horse through her paces."

The big man nodded and obeyed. As Everard took the front seat, he felt a gun muzzle held shakily against his back. "Tell Arkonsky we'll be back in half an hour," he added; they had approximately the same time units here as in his world, both descended from the Babylonian. When that had been taken care of, Everard said: "The first thing we will do is appear in midair over the ocean and hover."

"F-f-fine," said Boierik. He didn't sound very convinced.

Everard set the space controls for ten miles east and a thousand feet up and threw the main switch.

They sat like witches astride a broom, looking down on a greenish-gray sweep of waters and the distant blur which was land. The wind was high, it caught at them and Everard gripped tight with his knees. He heard Boierik's oath and smiled wanly.

"Well," he asked, "how do you like this?"

"It . . . it is wonderful." As he grew accustomed to the idea, the Cimbrian gathered enthusiasm. "Why, with machines like this, we can soar above enemy cities and pelt them with fire."

Somehow, that made Everard feel better about what he was going to do.

"Now we will fly ahead," he announced, and sent the scooter gliding through the air. Boierik whooped exuberantly. "And now we will make the instantaneous jump to your homeland."

Everard threw the maneuver switch. The scooter looped the loop and dropped at a three-gee acceleration.

Forewarned, the Patrolman could still barely hang on. He never knew whether the curve or the dive had thrown Boierik; he only had a moment's hideous glimpse of the man plunging down through windy spaces to the sea.

For a little while, then, Everard hung above the waves. His first reaction was a cold shudder . . . suppose Boierik had had time to shoot? His second was a gray guilt. Both he dismissed, and concentrated on the problem of rescuing van Sarawak.

He set the space verniers for one foot in front of the prisoners' bench, the time unit for one minute after he had departed. His right hand he kept by the controls— he'd have to work fast—and his left free.

Hang on to your seats, fellahs. Here we go again.

The machine flashed into existence almost in front of van Sarawak. Everard clutched the Venusian's tunic and hauled him close, inside the spationtemporal field, even as his right hand spun the time dial back and snapped over the main switch.

A bullet caromed off metal. Everard had a moment's glimpse of Arkonsky shouting. And then it was all gone and they were on a grassy hill sloping down to the beach. It was 2,000 years ago.

He collapsed shivering over the handlebars.

A cry brought him back to awareness. He twisted around, looking at van Sarawak where the Venusian sprawled on the hillside. One arm was still around Deirdre's waist.

The wind lulled, and the sea rolled into a broad white strand, and clouds walked high in heaven.

"I can't say I blame you, Van." Everard paced before the scooter and looked at the ground. "But it does complicate matters greatly."

"What was I supposed to do?" There was a raw note in the other's voice. "Leave her there for those bastards to kill—or to be snuffed out with her entire universe?"

"In case you've forgotten, we're conditioned against revealing the Patrol's existence to unauthorized people," said Everard. "We couldn't tell her the truth even if we wanted to . . . and I, for one, don't want to."

He looked at the girl. She stood breathing heavily, with a dawn in her eyes. The wind caressed her hair and the long thin dress.

She shook her head, as if clearing a mist of nightmare, and ran over to clasp their hands. "Forgive me, Manslach," she whispered. "I should have known you'd not betray us."

She kissed him and van Sarawak. The Venusian responded eagerly, but Everard couldn't bring himself to. He would have remembered Judas.

"Where are we?" she chattered. "It looks almost like Llangollen, but no men— Have you taken us to the Happy Isles?" She spun on one foot and danced among summer flowers. "Can we rest here a while before returning home?"

Everard drew a long breath. "I've bad news for you Deirdre," he said.

She grew silent, and he saw her gather herself.

"We can't go back."

She waited mutely.

"The—the spells I had to use, to save our lives . . . I had no choice, but those spells debar us from returning home."

"There is no hope?" He could barely hear her.

Everard's eyes stung. "No," he said.

She turned and walked away. Van Sarawak moved to follow her, but thought better of it and sat down beside Everard. "What'd you tell her?" he asked.

Everard repeated his words. "It seemed the best compromise," he finished. "I can't send her back to—what's waiting for this world."

"No." Van Sarawak sat quiet for a while, staring across the sea. Then: "What year is this? About the time of Christ? Then we're still upstairs of the turning point."

"Yeh. And we still have to find out what it was."

"Let's go back to the farther past. Lots of Patrol offices. We can recruit help there."

"Maybe." Everard lay back in the grass and regarded the sky. Reaction overwhelmed him. "I think I can locate the key event right here, though, with Deirdre's help. Wake me up when she comes back."

She returned dry-eyed, a desolate calm over her. When Everard asked if she would assist in his own mission, she nodded. "Of course. My life is yours who saved it."

After getting you into that mess in the first place. Everard said carefully: "All I want from you is some information. Do you know about . . . about putting people to sleep, a sleep in which they may believe anything they're told?"

"Y-yes," she said doubtfully. "I've seen medical Druids do that."

"It won't harm you. I only wish to make you sleep so you can remember everything you know, things you believe forgotten. It won't take long."

Her trustfulness was hard to endure. Using Patrol techniques, Everard put her in a hypnotic state of total recall and dredged out all she had ever read or heard about the Second Punic War. That added up to enough for his purposes.

Roman interference with Carthaginian enterprise south of the Ebro, in direct violation of treaty, had been the last roweling. In 219 B.C., Hannibal Barca, governor of Carthaginian Spain, laid siege to Saguntum. After eight months he took it, and thus provoked his long-planned war with Rome. At the beginning of May, 218, he crossed the Pyrenees with 90,000 infantry, 12,000 cavalry, and 37 elephants, marched through Gaul, and went over the Alps. His losses en route were gruesome: only 20,000 foot and 6,000 horse reached Italy late in the year. Nevertheless, near the Ticinus River he met and broke a superior Roman force. In the course of the following year, he fought several bloodily victorious battles and advanced into Apulia and Campania.

The Apulians, Lucaninas, Bruttians, and Samnites went over to his side. Quintus Fabius Maximus fought a grim guerrilla war, which laid Italy waste and decided nothing. But meanwhile Hasdrubal Barca was organizing Spain, and in 211 he arrived with reinforcements. In 210 Hannibal took and burned Rome, and in 207 the last cities of the confederacy surrendered to him.

"That's it," said Everard. He stroked the coppery hair of the girl lying beside him. "Go to sleep now. Sleep well and wake up glad of heart."

"What'd she tell you?" asked van Sarawak.

"A lot of detail," said Everard—the whole story had required more than an hour. "The important thing is this: her knowledge of history is good, but never mentions the Scipios."

"The who's?"

"Publius Cornelius Scipio commanded the Roman army at Ticinus, and was beaten there. But later he had the intelligence to turn westward and gnaw away the Carthaginian base in Spain. It ended with Hannibal being effectively cut off in Italy, and the Iberian help which could be sent was annihilated. Scipio's son of the same name also held a high command, and was the man who finally whipped Hannibal at Zama; that's Scipio Africanus the Elder.

"Father and son were by far the best leaders Rome had—but Deirdre never heard of them."

"So—" Van Sarawak stared eastward across the sea, where Gauls and Cimbri and Parthians were ramping through the shattered Classical world. "What happened to them in this time line?"

"My own total recall tells me that both the Scipios were at Ticinus, and very nearly killed; the son saved his father's life during the retreat, which I imagine was more like a stampede. One gets you ten that in *this* history the Scipios died there."

"Somebody must have knocked them off," said van Sarawak on a rising note. "Some time traveler . . . it could only have been that."

"Well, it seems probable, anyhow. We'll see." Everard looked away from Deirdre's slumbrous face. "We'll see."

At the Pleistocene resort—half an hour after having left it—the Patrolmen put the girl in the charge of a sympathetic Greek-speaking matron and summoned their colleagues. Then the message capsules began jumping through space-time.

All offices prior to 218 B.C.—the closest was Alexandria, 250–230—were "still" there, two hundred or so agents altogether. Written contact with the future was confirmed to be impossible, and a few short jaunts upstairs clinched the proof. A worried conference met at the Academy, back in the Oligocene Period. Unattached agents ranked those with steady assignments but not each other; on the basis of his own experience, Everard found himself the chairman of a committee of top-bracket officers.

It was a frustrating job. These men and women had leaped centuries and wielded the weapons of gods; but they were still human, with all the ingrained orneriness of their race.

Everyone agreed that the damage would have to be repaired. But there was fear for those agents who had gone ahead into time before being warned; if they weren't back when history was re-altered, they would never be seen again. Everard deputized parties to attempt rescue, but doubted there'd be much success; he warned them sternly to return in a day or face the consequences.

A man from the Scientific Renaissance had another point to make. Granted, it was the survivors' plain duty to restore the original time track. But they had a duty to knowledge as well. Here was a unique chance to study a whole new phase of humankind; there should be several years' anthropological work done before—Everard slapped him down with difficulty. There weren't so many Patrolmen left that they could take the risk.

Study groups had to determine the exact moment and circumstances of the change. The wrangling over methods went on interminably. Everard glared out the window, into the prehuman night, and wondered if the saber-tooths weren't doing a better job after all than their simian successors.

When he had finally gotten his bands dispatched, he broke out a bottle and got drunk with van Sarawak.

Reconvening the next day, the steering committee heard from its deputies, who had run up a total of years in the future. A dozen Patrolmen had been rescued from more or less ignominious situations; another score would simply have to be written off. The spy group's report was more interesting. It seemed that there had been two Helvetian mercenaries who joined Hannibal in the Alps and won his confidence. After the war, they had risen to high positions in Carthage; under the names of Phrontes and Himilco, they had practically run the government, engineered Hannibal's murder, and set new records for luxurious living. One of the Patrolmen had seen their homes and the men themselves. "A lot of improvements that hadn't been thought of in Classical times. The fellows looked to me like Neldorians, 205th millennium."

Everard nodded. That was an age of bandits who had "already" given the Patrol a lot of work. "I think we've settled the matter," he said. "It makes no difference whether they were with Hannibal before Ticinus or not. We'd have hell's own time arresting them in the Alps without tipping our hand and changing the future ourselves. What counts is that they seem to have rubbed out the Scipios, and that's the point we'll have to strike at."

A nineteenth-century Britisher, competent but with elements of Colonel Blimp, unrolled a map and discoursed on his aerial observations of the battle. He'd used an infrared telescope to look through low clouds. "And here the Romans stood—"

"I know," said Everard. "A thin red line. The moment when they took flight is the crucial one, but the confusion then also gives us our chance. Okay, we'll want to surround the battlefield unobtrusively, but I don't think we can get away with more than two agents actually on the scene. The Alexandria office can supply Van and me with costumes."

"I say," exclaimed the Englishman. "I thought I'd have the privilege."

"No. Sorry." Everard smiled with one corner of his mouth. "It's no privilege anyway. Risk your neck, all to wipe out a world of people like yourself."

"But dash it all—"

Everard rose. "I've got to go," he said flatly. "I don't know why, but I've got to."

Van Sarawak nodded.

They left their scooter in a clump of trees and started across the field.

Around the horizon and up in the sky waited a hundred armed Patrolmen, but that was small consolation here among spears and arrows. Lowering clouds hurried before a cold whistling wind, there was a spatter of rain, sunny Italy was enjoying its late fall.

The cuirass was heavy on Everard's shoulders as he trotted across blood-slippery mud. He had helmet, greaves, a Roman shield on his left arm and a sword at his waist; but his right hand gripped a stunner. Van Sarawak loped behind, similarly equipped, eyes shifting under the wind-ruffled officer's plume.

Trumpets howled and drums stuttered. It was all but lost among the yells of men and tramp of feet, screaming horses and whining arrows. The legion of Carthage was pressing in, hammering edged metal against the buckling Roman lines. Here and there the fight was already breaking up into small knots, where men cursed and cut at strangers.

The combat had passed over this area and swayed beyond. Death lay around him. Everard hurried behind the Roman force, toward the distant gleam of the eagles. Across helmets and corpses, he made out a banner that fluttered triumphant, vivid red and purple against the unrestful sky. And there, looming gray and monstrous, lifting their trunks and bellowing, came a squad of elephants.

He had seen war before. It was always the same—not a

neat affair of lines across maps, nor a hallooing gallantry, but men who gasped and sweated and bled in bewilderment.

A slight, dark-faced youth squirmed nearby, trying feebly to pull out the javelin which had pierced his stomach. He was a cavalryman from Carthage, but the burly Italian peasant who sat next to him, staring without belief at the stump of an arm, paid no attention.

A flight of crows hovered overhead, riding the wind and waiting.

"This way," muttered Everard. "Hurry up, for God's sake! That line's going to break any minute."

The breath was raw in his throat as he panted toward the standards of the Republic. It came to him that he'd always rather wished Hannibal had won. There was something repellent about the cold, unimaginative greed of Rome. And here he was, trying to save the city. Well-a-day, life was often an odd business.

It was some consolation that Scipio Africanus was one of the few decent men left after the war.

Screaming and clangor lifted, and the Italians reeled back. Everard saw something like a wave smashed against a rock. But it was the rock which advanced, crying out and stabbing, stabbing.

He began to run. A legionary went past, howling his panic. A grizzled Roman veteran spat on the ground, braced his feet, and stood where he was till they cut him down. Hannibal's elephants squealed and lifted curving tusks. The ranks of Carthage held firm, advancing to the inhuman pulse of their drums. Cavalry skirmished on the wings in a toothpick flash of lances.

Up ahead, now! Everard saw men on horseback, Roman officers. They held the eagles aloft and shouted, but nobody could hear them above the din.

A small group of legionaries came past and halted. Their leader hailed the Patrolmen: "Over here! We'll give them a fight, by the belly of Venus!"

Everard shook his head and tried to go past. The Roman snarled and sprang at him. "Come here, you cowardly—" A stun beam cut off his words and he crashed into the muck. His men shuddered, someone screamed, and the party broke into flight.

The Carthaginians were very near, shield to shield and swords running red. Everard could see a scar livid on the cheek of one man, and the great hook nose of another. A hurled spear clanged off his helmet; he lowered his head and ran.

A combat loomed before him. He tried to go around, and tripped on a gashed corpse. A Roman stumbled over him in turn. Van Sarawak cursed and dragged him away. A sword furrowed the Venusian's arm.

Beyond, Scipio's men were surrounded and battling without hope. Everard halted, sucking air into starved lungs, and looked into the thin rain. Armor gleamed wetly, Roman horsemen galloping in with mud up to their mounts' noses—that must be the son, Scipio Africanus to be, hastening to his father. The hoofbeats were like thunder in the earth.

"Over there!"

Van Sarawak cried it out and pointed. Everard crouched where he was, rain dripping off his helmet and down his face. A small troop of Carthaginians was riding toward the battle around the eagles, and at their head were two men with the height and craggy features of Neldor. They were clad in the usual G.I. armor, but each of them held a slim-barreled gun.

"This way!" Everard spun on his heel and dashed toward them. The leather in his cuirass creaked as he ran.

They were close to the newcomers before they were seen. A Carthaginian face swung to them and called the warning. Everard saw how he grinned in his beard. One of the Neldorians scowled and aimed his blast-rifle.

Everard went on his stomach, and the vicious blue-white beam sizzled where he had been. He snapped a shot and one of the African horses went over in a roar of metal. Van Sarawak stood his ground and fired steadily. Two, three, four—and there went a Neldorian, down in the mud!

Men hewed at each other around the Scipios. The Neldorians' escort yelled with terror. They must have had the blasters demonstrated, but these invisible blows were something else. They bolted. The second of the bandits got his horse under control and turned to follow.

"Take care of the one you potted," gasped Everard. "Haul him off the battlefield—we'll want to question—" He himself scrambled to his feet and made for a riderless horse. He was in the saddle and after the remaining Neldorian before he was fully aware of it.

They fled through chaos. Everard urged speed from his mount, but was content to pursue. Once they'd got out of sight, a scooter could swoop down and make short work of his quarry.

The same thought must have occurred to the time rover. He reined in and took aim. Everard saw the blinding flash and felt his cheek sting with a near miss. He set his pistol to wide beam and rode in shooting.

Another fire-bolt took his horse full in the breast. The animal toppled and Everard went out of the saddle. Trained reflexes softened the fall; he bounced dizzily to his feet and staggered toward his enemy. His stunner was gone, no time to look for it. Never mind, it could be salvaged later, if he lived. The widened beam had found its mark; it wasn't strong enough to knock a man out, but the Neldorian had dropped his rifle and the horse stood awaying with closed eyes.

Rain beat in Everard's face. He slogged up to the mount. The Neldorian jumped to earth and drew a sword. Everard's own blade rasped forth.

"As you will," he said in Latin. "One of us will not leave this field."

The moon rose over mountains and turned the snow to a sudden wan glitter. Far in the north, a glacier threw back the light in broken shards, and a wolf howled. The Cro-Magnons chanted in their cave, it drifted faintly through to the veranda.

Deirdre stood in darkness, looking out. Moonlight dappled her face and caught a gleam of tears. She started as Everard and van Sarawak came up behind her.

"Are you back so soon?" she asked. "You only came here and left me this morning."

"It didn't take long," said van Sarawak. He had gotten a hypno in Attic Greek.

"I hope . . ." She tried to smile. "I hope you have finished your task and can rest from your labors."

"Yes," said Everard. "Yes, we finished it."

They stood side by side for a while, looking out on a world of winter.

"Is it true what you said, that I can never go home?" asked Deirdre.

"I'm afraid so. The spells—" Everard shrugged and swapped a glance with van Sarawak.

They had official permission to tell the girl as much as they wished and take her wherever they thought she could live best. Van Sarawak maintained that that would be Venus in his century, and Everard was too tired to argue.

Deirdre drew a long breath. "So be it," she said. "I'll not waste a life weeping for it . . . but the Baal grant that they have it well, my people at home."

"I'm sure they will," said Everard.

Suddenly he could do no more. He only wanted to sleep. Let van Sarawak say what had to be said, and reap whatever rewards there might be.

He nodded at his companion. "I'm turning in," he declared. "Carry on, Van."

The Venusian took the girl's arm. Everard went slowly back to his room.

NIGHTFALL ON THE DEAD SEA

R. Faraday Nelson

Vespasian's good son reigned little more than two years before he died, some say of poison, and Vespasian's evil son became Emperor of all the Roman Empire.

Even the gods protested, and Jupiter opened the heavens and poured out rain and lightning on the city of Rome for weeks without a break. During this storm an elderly retired centurion named Gaius Hesperian, partly to escape the weather and partly to escape the murderous whims of the new ruler, found shelter in a modest villa near the Tiber River, along the highway between Rome and the Port of Ostia.

In the evenings, fat Marius, whose business affairs had obliged him to spend his entire life within a day's drive of this villa, insisted on having couches set out on a sheltered porch overlooking his courtyard, and there he would eagerly question his guest about battles and barbarians and kings and princesses, and about the strange cults and superstitions prevailing in the distant lands at the rim of Rome's dominions.

Every night the same ritual would be repeated. Marius, in toga and tunic, would waddle excitedly about, urging the slaves to hasten and clear away the remains of supper and set out the couches on the porch.

A slave would ask, "What wine, master?"

And Marius would say, "Only the finest and oldest Falernian for my honored guest!"

And when the couches and a low table, on which was placed two goblets and a slender amphora of red wine, were set out, Marius would lead the old soldier to the porch and say, "Here! A little wine? A bit of good conversation before bed?"

Then Gaius Hesperian would sigh and nod and remove his helmet (for he still wore helmet, cape and armor, more from habit than necessity) and bow slightly, so that Marius could see the lamplight flicker on his bald head, and recline on the couch across from his host, resting his weight on his elbow, his still-muscular arm bulging.

The two men would watch the rain in the courtyard garden for a while, drinking their wine slowly, unmixed with water, for they both agreed that Falernian was too fine a wine to be watered, and for a long time neither man would speak.

It was always Marius who broke the silence. "Did you ever see the beautiful Princess Berenice of Judea?" or, "Do the Britons really paint themselves blue?" or, "The Black Nations to the south—are they any match for our legions in battle?"

And Hesperian would clear his throat and answer yes or no or perhaps and begin another story, for the old soldier had seen many things and spoke well, in a deep, rough, but resonant voice.

Then one night, after the silence had run longer than ever before and Marius was shifting uncomfortably, Hesperian said softly, "It's colder than usual tonight. Perhaps it would be better if we did not talk."

It was actually quite warm in spite of the rain, but Marius did not wish to be impolite. "Slaves!" he called. "Bring us a brazier of hot coals!" They hastened to do his bidding.

Hesperian smiled. "Can't do without your bedtime story, eh, Marius?"

Marius nodded sheepishly. "How else can I learn about that great wide world?" he demanded with an expansive gesture. "That world I can never see for myself?"

"But I'm afraid you've pumped me dry. There's no more to tell. You've heard it all."

Marius' dismay was only temporary. "Not so, Gaius!

What about that incident at the Dead Sea? You've often mentioned it—even been on the brink of telling me about it—but then you always changed the subject."

The centurion frowned. "Allow me to let that one story remain untold."

"No, no! I can tell by the way you speak of it that it must be something strange, something more fascinating than any tale of mere warfare and political intrigue. You must tell me that story, even if you never tell me another!"

"Marius, you don't understand. You live so near Rome, where one city leaves off around here, another begins. In all your life, I doubt if you've ever been for one minute in a place where, if you called for help, someone would not answer. It's a safe world, a world where you can feel secure. You'll be happier, better off, if you go on thinking all the world is like that."

"No, Gaius! I'm not happy, only bored! Tell me! Tell me about the Dead Sea!"

Hesperian raised his goblet and drank deep, then set it down and wiped his thin lips with his wrist. "Very well, Marius. I see you will not let me rest until you've heard it. I told you, did I not, that I once served in the Eastern Legions, near the Jewish temple city of Jerusalem?"

"Yes! Yes! Go on!"

I was young then and not yet a centurion. I commanded a troop of eight regular legionaries stationed in Bethany, just east of Jerusalem. There were those eight men, myself, and my clerk, Charon . . . ten Romans in all, left there to maintain order in a population of several hundred Jews and Greeks. The Jews and Greeks hated each other almost more than they hated us Romans. So I was regularly forced to investigate cases of violence and murder. It was cold comfort when my commanding officer, in one of his infrequent visits, told me I should be glad the Greeks and Jews were at each other's throats, because if they ever joined forces they would certainly have no trouble slaughtering our tiny band.

When I remember Bethany I get an overpowering impression of white. The buildings were all white, white and square and crude, without ornamentation. The land was white, bleached white and without a trace of grass, though there were a few palm trees inside the town. Even the sky was white, or so it sometimes seemed because of the blinding brightness of the sun. It was a special kind of white, I think—the white of dry bones, of a skull from which all trace of flesh has long since decayed away.

My troops, my clerk and myself, together with two horses and one donkey, lived in a single small barracks on the edge of town, and it was there, at a makeshift table in a dusty courtyard, that I dispensed Roman justice every day of the week except the Jewish Sabbath.

As I say, the majority of the cases were of violence between the Jews and Greeks, usually violence against property but occasionally violence against persons—murder, fistfights, minor riots. Somehow, in spite of the heat and the hatred that made our lives like a never-ending fever dream, we dealt with it all, at least until that evening—I think it was in autumn, though all the seasons seemed alike to me there—when, all the pending cases disposed of one way or another, I adjourned the court and, together with Charon, was gathering up my scrolls. Suddenly I heard the hysterical scream of a little girl and looked up to see a Jewish child in a torn and dirty tunic running toward me across the courtyard, bare feet flying and long black hair streaming behind her.

"Officer! Officer! Come quick!"

Charon caught her before she reached me and tried to hold her struggling little body. "Tomorrow, child. Tomorrow," he told her sternly.

"No! No! You must come now! It's my grandmother!" She burst into tears. "Now! Now!"

I could have sent a soldier with her to investigate, but court was over for the day, and I felt the need for a little exercise. "Let her go, Charon," I said, and the child, the moment she was free, dashed up to me and began tugging at my hand in a frenzy.

I let her lead me out of the front gate of the courtyard, while Charon, tall, gaunt and disapproving, followed after us.

"Calm down, child," I said as we hurried through the streets, our long shadows moving ahead of us. "Calm down and tell me what's wrong."

At first I couldn't understand a word of her broken babbling, but finally I made out "The blue man. The blue man."

"What blue man?"

"Grandma and I were walking—at the other end of the village. We'd been shopping. We had bread and cheese and wine. I noticed a shadow. Someone was following us." She stopped, her almost-black eyes round with remembered terror. "I warned Grandma."

"Go on," I prompted.

"We walked faster. He walked faster. We began to run. He came after us. He was too fast for Grandma. He caught up to her, tore the food out of her hands!"

"What did he look like?"

"I told you! He was blue. His skin was all over blue!" She looked as if she was on the verge of vomiting.

"Might be someone with leprosy," commented Charon.

"No!" she cried angrily. "A leper is white. This man was *blue*."

"Easy, child," I said softly. "What happened next?"

"He ran away. And Grandma . . . Grandma. . . ."

We turned a corner.

"There she is! You see?" she cried, pointing.

The old woman lay in a crumpled heap in the dust.

It was obvious she was dead, but I tried her pulse anyway, then examined her quickly in the failing evening light, trying to determine the cause of death. Neither then nor later could we find a mark on her.

"I don't understand," I said, standing up.

"Look at her face," said Charon.

The old woman's face was horribly contorted. It seemed impossible that a mere human face could show such terror. Wasn't that a mask? A mask carved by some master sculptor for some Greek horror play? No, it was real. The bulging eyes, the lips drawn back from the toothless mouth, the maze of tortured, twisted brown flesh; it was all real.

"Her heart, perhaps," I said.

He nodded. "Perhaps."

"Sometimes, when an old person sees something frightening. . . ."

"I've seen fear before, sir, but not like that. What did she see? What *could* she have seen?"

"I don't know. I just don't know."

I was curious.

I asked questions, alerted the troops before their tours of guard duty to be on the watch for a "blue man," even though I could tell it was only the strictness of Roman discipline that prevented them from laughing in my face.

"You're spending too much time on the blue-man thing," said Charon finally. "Old women die all the time. There are other, more important matters needing your attention."

"Perhaps you're right," I sighed.

But one week later I visited the little girl at her home, hoping to get from her a more complete description or some explanation of what she meant by a "blue man."

Her mother met me at the door of their poor dwelling. "I want to talk to your daughter," I said.

"I hope you can," she answered listlessly.

She led me into the dark interior, and when I saw the little girl sitting at the table, motionless, her eyes blank and unfocused, I understood what her mother meant.

"Do you remember me, child?" I asked.

She did not answer.

"She never speaks now," said the mother. "Not a sound. At night though—sometimes—she screams in her sleep."

I tried again to speak to the little girl, but it was useless. Those round dark eyes were looking at something else, something quite invisible to me . . . perhaps a man with blue skin.

For a while we got other reports of a strange man, always alone, who stole chickens, raided kitchens, even rooted around in garbage, but nobody else got a good look at him. He now appeared only at night, one shadow among many, for Bethany was very poorly lit. Charon pointed out that it was not certain that this was the same man who was supposed to have the blue skin and perhaps there was more than one man.

The only clue of any kind that came in during this period was a bit of cloth a merchant claimed to have torn from the cloak of the thief.

It was ordinary wool, dyed blue, but the merchant, who dealt in spices and perfume, claimed that it proved our thief was, in addition to his other crimes, also a grave robber.

"He steals from the dead as well as the living," insisted the bearded little Arab.

"How do you know?" I asked him . . . it was during one of those sessions at the table in the courtyard.

"Smell it!" he said triumphantly.

I sniffed the bit of cloth. It did have an odd aroma.

"You see, sir?" he said. "There are certain oils and spices that are used only to anoint a dead body. It's my business to know them, sir, by the smell. I tell you, sir, there's no doubt in my mind. That bit of wool came from the clothing of a corpse!"

Then, abruptly, the crimes ceased.

When I kept up my questioning and my admonitions to the men on watch, Charon chided me. "You seem unhappy that our thief has given up his life of crime."

"How can we be sure he's given it up?" I asked, annoyed. "He may be waiting, waiting for a chance to do something worse."

"Or," Charon pointed out with a grin, "he may have gone somewhere else"—he chuckled—"out of your jurisdiction."

Other cases came up, claiming my attention.

There was a band of Jewish highway robbers who called themselves an army of liberation.

There were some religious fanatics who went out into the desert to meet an angel and starved to death.

There was a gang of child cutpurses traveling with a Greek musician and his dancers.

And a woman turned up whom I'd known before, a woman who'd done some spying for us when she was younger but who, now that she'd lost her looks, had become very religious. She still painted her lips, and I couldn't blame her. They'd made her a small fortune. We'd paid her for the words those lips spoke; her victims had paid for her kisses.

Miriam Redhead, we'd called her, and we still called her Redhead now that her hair had all turned gray.

She'd come before me during the regular court session, and I didn't recognize her, what with the weight she'd put on and the way her hair had turned gray, but she recognized me.

"Gaius!" she cried.

"Do you know me, woman?"

"Of course. There's many a secret I whispered into those handsome Roman ears of yours, back when I was called Redhead!"

Even then I didn't recognize her.

It was only after the day's session was over that it all came back to me. She'd had a child. She'd said it was mine—and perhaps it was. I'd arranged for the child to be granted Roman citizenship and be adopted by a Roman family, though the parentage could never be established for certain.

The following morning she met me at the gates of our courtyard, where, as the guard later informed me, she'd been waiting for me for hours.

"There's no court today," I told her. "It's the Sabbath."

"I observe the Sabbath better than most these days," she said, fingering the white linen shawl she had over her head. "But this is a family matter."

"Does that make a difference? I know nothing of Jewish law."

"Some men spend a lifetime studying it and still do not know it all. So there's no shame if you are ignorant. But you remember me now, don't you?"

"Yes, Redhead. I was only a common soldier then, and you were . . ."

"I know what I was. And what have you been doing since then?"

"I've been posted to Spain, to Britain, and now back here. And you?"

She shrugged, standing barefoot in the dust with the white sun beating down on her, raising beads of sweat on her forehead. "I've found a great peace and—a great trouble." She glanced at me sharply and I saw that her glittering green eyes, at least, had not grown old. "You remember my brother?"

"I remember you had a sister."

"I had a brother too, older than me. Don't you remember him either?"

"Wait. Yes. I remember him now."

"He's lost, wandered away. I'm searching for him. Have you noticed any strangers? Someone who looked—a little familiar to you?"

I searched my memory, then shook my head.

"Please," she begged. "Try to remember. He's not like he was. You might not recognize him. He's—*changed*."

"Changed? In what way?"

There was a long silence, then she whispered, "I can't tell you that." She gave me a look of hopelessness, then turned to shuffle away.

"Are you sure he's still alive?" I called after her.

She glanced back at me, and there was a faint, strange, ironic smile on her lips. "Oh, yes, Gaius. That's the one thing I am absolutely sure of."

Every day for six days she came to question me about her missing brother, waiting her turn patiently with the other Jews and Greeks and Arabs who came to place their fates in my hands, but each time I could tell her nothing.

The Sabbath came again, and again she met me at the gate, and we talked, there in the blazing sun. I'd begun to feel easier with her, when an odd thought entered my head and I asked her, "Did you say your brother has changed?"

"Yes."

"Does he have—blue skin?"

There was a long silence, then she said, "So he *is* here. And you kept it from me!"

"No, no, don't misunderstand. It's only this minute that your brother and this man with the blue skin came together in my mind. We've had a mystery around here, and now, thanks to you, we may be able to solve it. Someone with a blue skin has been seen in the area, stealing things, hiding in the shadows. . . ."

"Where is he now?" she broke in. Her green eyes had suddenly come alive with a disquieting glitter, so that she looked almost insane.

"I don't know. I've had no new reports about him for months."

She turned away, her painted lips a grim line. "So he's gone, moved on."

She walked briskly away, her fat bare feet kicking up little puffs of white dust.

"Wait!" I called after her. "I have some questions to ask you!"

When she paid no attention, I let her go, thinking I could have one of my men drop around to the town's one inn and arrest her before the day was out. It was there I made a mistake. When my soldier arrived at her lodgings, he found she'd left, in spite of the Jewish prohibition against traveling on a Sabbath. The innkeeper claimed she'd joined an Arab camel caravan headed east, to the Essence monastery at Qumran, on the shore of the Dead Sea.

When I heard this, I turned to Charon and said, "Let's saddle up and go after her!"

Charon, however, pointed out that she was now outside my jurisdiction and that anyway a lost brother was not an important enough matter for me to postpone my regular sessions of court. I had to admit, very reluctantly, that he was right.

A week and a half later a mounted courier arrived from Qumran with the news that, I felt, gave me the excuse I needed for action.

The blue man had been seen along the shores of the Dead Sea in broad daylight. A monk had pursued him, while three other monks looked on, and had evidently trapped the stranger in one of the dead-end canyons or gullies that clefted the mountainous cliffs behind the monastery.

The three onlookers had watched the pursuit until it was out of sight and only became alarmed when, after a half an hour, their brother monk did not return.

They went looking for him.

And they found him.

His head had been torn from his body . . . not cut, as by sword or ax, but torn, twisted off as if by some being of far more than human strength.

This time, when I commanded Charon to have our

horses saddled, he had no arguments to offer, and within the hour we two were galloping east into the shimmering white wilderness of tortured boulders and huge grotesque hills sculpted by the wind into a thousand nightmare shapes, a wilderness where you could ride for hours without seeing a single spot of green.

We camped by the road that night; it would be all too easy to wander off the road and never find our way to anything but death, the following day, by sunstroke.

I looked out over the Dead Sea.

It was as flat as a marble floor; not a ripple disturbed its pale gray surface, and from that motionless water arose a frightful, somehow terrifying stench, unlike anything I'd ever smelled before . . . except, yes, there had been a time in Rome . . . I'd tried to forget it . . . when I'd seen a man covered with tar and burned alive. That was it! That was where I'd smelled that hideous smell before.

The monks had seen us coming from afar, and four of them ran out to greet us as we approached their low, plain buildings.

They took the bridles of our horses and led us to their stables. As I dismounted, one of them said in a low voice, "The woman is here. I think she wishes to speak with you."

"The woman?"

I followed him into the dim interior of one of the buildings, into a hall where, from the look of the tables, the monks ate their communal meals. There stood Redhead, pale, staring, with a monk's robe draped around her pudgy body.

"Your brother . . . he's killed a man," I began, setting down my shield.

"They shouldn't have chased him," she whispered.

"Be that as it may, things are serious now. You must tell me all about it, explain what's going on here."

"I'll tell you nothing until I have your word as a Roman officer that you won't go after him."

"I can't do that. You know I can't. He's a murderer. He must be brought to trial. Then, if there are extenuating circumstances . . ."

"Gaius, forget for a moment that you're a Roman soldier.

Let me talk to you as a man. I can tell you a secret, the greatest secret of all."

"I am a Roman soldier and I can never forget it."

"Not even for the secret of immortality?"

There was a long pause before I said softly, "There is no secret of immortality."

"Oh, no? When that poor dead monk was found, he was clutching something in his hand. I saw it when the body was brought in, and when nobody was looking, I took it."

She produced, from inside her voluminous robes, a small object wrapped in a white scarf. Carefully she unwrapped it and held it up for me to see.

It was a finger, a human finger.

"This is my brother's finger," she whispered. "That monk must have broken it off in the fight."

"By the gods!" I reached out to cover it up with the scarf again.

"No, Gaius. Wait. Look."

The finger moved, just a little, very slowly.

"It's alive," I said softly.

"Yes, Gaius, it is. Now do you believe me?"

She wrapped it carefully in the scarf and once again hid it in her robes. "No one need know, Gaius, but you and I."

I was speechless.

"Let him go, Gaius," she persisted. "Let him go, and you can watch the years pass like minutes, the centuries like days."

Suddenly, without warning, the door burst open and there was a pale, panting, wild-eyed monk. "The blue man!" he shouted. "They've seen him."

I turned, picked up my tall rectangular shield.

"No, wait!" she called, trying to clutch my arm.

I shook her off and followed the monk out the door, running, trying not to think.

"One of our brotherhood," panted the monk. "He found the blue man in the shed—where we store our food. This way."

We rounded the corner of a house.

"The blue man—he . . ." The monk broke off and glanced at me with fear-glazed eyes. "He killed him with a single blow of his fist."

We came in sight of a little cluster of monks.

I pushed my way through them.

There was a man lying there in the dirt, the side of his head smashed to a pulp.

Charon appeared at my elbow, sword in hand. "There are tracks, sir. Footprints, heading toward the cliffs."

"Let's get the horses."

"Too steep and rough, sir. We'll have to go on foot."

I paused and shaded my eyes with my hand. The cliffs were indeed too rugged for horses, perhaps even too rugged for men on foot.

"You monks," I said crisply. "Follow us."

Nobody moved.

One of the monks said softly, "We're men of peace, sir."

"What about you, Charon?" I turned to him. "Are you a man of peace, too?"

"No, sir." He carefully tested the blade of his shortsword with a gingerly fingertip.

"Then come on!"

When next I looked back, the monks were far behind and below us. Redhead was there, too, standing a little apart from the crowd. Then the footprints led us around a bend in the rocks, and we could see them no more.

"Where to now, sir?" demanded Charon.

The footprints had reached an area of bare rock, broad, gray and clean, and there they ended. I turned slowly around, studying the cyclopean boulders that surrounded us on all sides. The sky was a slender crack of light far above us.

"Let's scout around and see if we can pick up the track on the other side of this stone area."

"Yes, sir."

We searched for at least an hour, but there were no more tracks to be found.

"Might as well turn back," said Charon, wistfully returning his sword to its sheath.

I sighed and nodded.

We started back the way we had come.

Or so we thought.

It had been fairly cool, there in the shelter of the

boulders and cliffs, but now it was getting cooler yet. I looked up. The narrow area of sky that was still visible to us had turned a sullen, glowering red. It was dark down on the floor of the canyon where we stood, and it was getting darker.

"Sundown," said Charon with a faint smile.

"Are we lost, Charon?"

"Yes, sir. I believe so, sir."

I sat down on a pile of sand, Charon seated himself near me, near enough so he could reach out and touch me. The light continued to fade until I could no longer make out the outlines of Charon's head. I held up my hand before my eyes, but that, too, was invisible. Above, I could make out a few hard, unwinking stars, but otherwise there was blackness, blackness all around.

It would be suicide to try to move around in this darkness," I said. "We could fall over a cliff, bring down a rockslide on ourselves."

"Yes, sir."

"In the morning, when it's light, we'll find our way out."

"Of course, sir. And if we can't move, neither can our friend, the blue man."

I considered that a moment. "I wouldn't be too sure about that, Charon. He's had a chance to explore this area. He may be able to find his way around by feel by this time."

There was a long silence, then: "I see, sir."

I heard the sound of Charon drawing his sword and laying it gently on the sand beside him.

I was on the verge of dozing when I felt Charon touch my arm. He said nothing, so I sat listening, trying to decide why he'd touched me.

I could hear his breathing and mine. It was so still that even my pulse beat was clearly audible. I waited.

Finally I whispered, "What. . . ?"

His clumsy fingers fumbled across my face, found my lips, and firmly squeezed them closed.

Again I waited.

Then I heard it, quite plainly.

A distant sigh.

A faint rustle of cloth.

The sound came from the direction where, as I remembered it, the canyon extended backward and upward to what we had supposed was a dead end.

There was a long pause.

Then again the sound of breath, closer now.

The meaning of these sounds was unmistakable. Someone was, with infinite stealth, creeping slowly toward us down the narrow cleft, and I did not see how, in such a narrow passage, he could miss us.

Silently I drew my sword.

Charon moved. I could hear him carefully get to his feet. I, too, stood up and faced in the direction of expected attack. I heard Charon take a step, pause, then take another.

There was a sudden rush, followed by what must have been the thud of a fist against armor. Charon cursed. His sword whistled in the air, but failed to strike flesh. I held my sword at the ready, but dared not strike for fear of hitting my friend.

There was a pause, another rush, the sounds of a violent struggle. Charon cried out in pain. His sword clanged against rock, fell clattering underfoot, and I heard the stranger grunt with effort.

"Gaius!" called Charon desperately, and his voice was coming from somewhere higher than my head. The attacker must have lifted Charon high in the air. In spite of the risk, I stepped forward, thrusting my shortsword blindly into the void.

Charon cried out again, and by his cry I could follow the arc of his body as it sailed through the air to strike a distant cliff with a crash and scrape of metal against stone.

When the echo of this crash died away, there was silence again, absolute silence.

How could this demon be so quiet, I thought. Doesn't he have to move at all? Doesn't he have to breathe?

Then, very faintly at first, then stronger, the odor came to my nostrils, the odor the little bearded Arab perfume merchant had told me could only come from the oils and spices used to anoint a corpse. And there was another odor, too, the odor the perfume was intended to mask, the odor I'd smelled many times before on the battlefield, the sweet sick odor of decaying flesh.

I thrust my sword again into the blackness. There seemed to be nothing there. I took a cautious step backward, hoping to connect with the sheer rock face behind me and thus protect myself against attack from the rear, but somehow I had gotten turned around, and the rock was not there.

Ahead of me I heard a soft footfall, then another.

The odor grew stronger.

I went down on one knee, in defensive position, holding my great rectangular shield in front of me. Perhaps, I thought, he'll expect to find me in a standing position. Perhaps, by crouching, I'll surprise him and gain a few seconds' advantage.

He exhaled again, and I knew he was directly in front of me. I gripped my sword and waited.

Suddenly his fingers closed on my shield with an uncanny rasping noise, not like the sound of flesh against metal, but something drier, more rough and brittle. I thrust my sword forward and up and felt it connect with something, penetrate something, something more like ancient rotting wood than any human body. I drew it out, thrust again, but this time it was knocked from my hand by a blow so violent it sent the sword flying to clatter down some distant cliff into some unseen crevice.

I drew my dagger.

The dry fingers closed again on the rim of my shield and I slashed at them with my knife. A finger, perhaps two, severed from his hand, fell against my face and rebounded to land in the dust.

Why didn't he cry out? Could he lose fingers without feeling it?

Then came a terrible blow, a blow so powerful no mere man could have delivered it, a blow that cracked my shield in half. I slipped out of the shield, scrambled backwards. A hand closed on my cape. I unsnapped the clasp and let him tear the cape off me.

He touched me on the arm, and his touch was like ancient dry crumbling papyrus. I slashed at his hand and kept scrambling backward. Suddenly I found myself on a steep shelf of rock, sliding, falling, rolling over and over, and he—he was still with me! I clutched an outcropping, managed to check my fall.

He clutched my ankle and hung there, a terrible weight dragging me down. The small stones and pebbles we had dislodged kept on going—they fell a long, long way.

I realized I must be on the edge of some terrible drop.

He was pulling now, pulling himself up by my ankle.

I reached down with my knife and hacked, sawed and hacked again at his wrist, and that wrist . . . it was wood! I tell you it was wood!

But it broke.

Yes, it finally severed, under my frantic, feverish slashing, and he slid away and fell and hit something and fell again and finally, in a shower of loose rocks, thudded to a halt far below.

But that hand of his still clutched my ankle. I felt its fingers move—the hand was still alive!

I had to cut away the fingers, one by one, before I could finally be free.

I crept up the steep rock shelf and finally reached a level place where I felt in no more danger of falling, and there I lay back and closed my eyes, panting, gasping for breath.

After a while I felt better.

Then I heard it, far away and below me.

Someone was moving, slowly and painfully. Someone was moaning softly. He was still alive.

In a frenzy I began pulling loose every rock I could get my hands on and throwing them, throwing them into the darkness. Some of the stones were hitting him! I could hear him grunt with their impact!

And then he spoke, one whispered word, the only word he uttered during the entire struggle.

"Please. . . ."

I stopped throwing stones instantly, but it was too late. The stones I'd thrown already had started a minor avalanche, and it was several minutes before the last echo of the rock slide died away.

I listened carefully for an hour then, but there was no longer anything to hear.

Shortly after dawn the monks found us and took us back to the monastery. Charon was not dead, but it took many months for his ribs to heal, and he always after that walked with a slight limp.

Miriam Redhead made them go with her that afternoon to try and dig out her brother, but it was no use. There were tons of rocks on his body, and they were so placed that whenever the monks tried to remove one boulder, two others would fall in its place.

She was weeping when she returned and I tried to comfort her. "He's dead now. He can't suffer any more," I said.

She turned to me, her insane green eyes blazing with anger. "You fool, Gaius! If only that were true!"

Marius leaned forward, lowering his goblet, now empty, to the table. "Is that all?" he demanded.

The old centurion shrugged. "I warned you you'd find this story unsatisfactory, but you insisted on hearing it."

"But this man . . . the woman's brother. How do you explain. . . ?"

Gaius Hesperian swung his feet to the floor, then stood up and stretched. "Explain? There is no explanation. Out there on the rim of the Empire, these things happen, that's all." He yawned and began walking toward the door.

Marius called after him, "Wait! At least tell me one thing."

Hesperian paused. "What thing?"

"The brother's name."

"His name? What does that matter?"

"I don't know. Just tell me."

"Let's see. Oh, yes, now I remember."

"Yes? Yes?"

"Lazarus," he said.

Marius sat for a long time alone on the porch, watching the rain, before he finally went to bed.

THE PRINCE

C.J. Cherryh

The foundations shook. The lights went out. The computer went down.

"*Dannazione—!*"

Lights went up again. The monitor came up on a blank screen and the disk drive hummed away, hunting idiotically for vanished instructions.

Dante Alighieri was already on his way down the hall, down the stairs, through the grand hall, and into the First Citizen's glassed-in garden portico. "*I scellerati! I male-detti—!*"

"*Sivis, sivis Graece modum, Dantille.*" Augustus waggled fingers, waved a hand, and anxious sycophants shied aside as he swung his feet over the side of the couch. "*Noli tant' versari—*"

"Gone!" Dante waved a fistful of papers. "*Gone!*" The steam seemed to go out of him. He drew one breath and another and gasped after a third. "I had it. I *had* it—"

"Indubitably," Niccolo drawled from a chair to the side.

Dante's dark eyes went wide. White showed around his nostrils and along the line of his lips. Then the eyes suffused with tears and the lips parted in a sob after breath. "If I could remember—if I could only remember— but that machine, but this place, but those lunatics, *ma questi—*"

"I know, I know, my dear boy." Augustus put out his hand and patted the poet's hand, which was clenched

65

white-knuckled on his knee opposite him. "You have to be patient, you know. You have to expect these things."

"It is," said Niccolo, extending his feet before him, ankles crossed, "the nature of this place."

Dante bowed his head into his hands. "The damned lights fail, this insane power that comes and goes—" He looked up again, at Augustus's face, at the half-dozen sycophants. At Niccolo and Kleopatra and the visitor-youth who stared wide-eyed at the mad poet. "I was so close. They *know*, don't you think they know? And the lines are gone, *two hundred lines*—"

"You'll remember them again. I'm sure you will."

"If it made any difference," said Niccolo.

"Damn you!" The poet leaped up and for a moment violence trembled in his hands, his whole body. Then his countenance collapsed, the tears fell, and Dante Alighieri turned and ran from the room.

"Do you know," Niccolo said to no one in particular, "I did once admire the man."

"Shut up, Niccolo," Augustus said.

Niccolo Machiavelli stretched his feet the further and made a little wave of his hand. *"Dimittemi."*

"Sorry won't mend it. Dammit, Niccolo, do you have to bait him?"

"The man's dangerous. I tell you, *Auguste*, you ought to have him out of the house. Visit him on Louis. *Two* madmen ought to get on well together. They can commiserate. Bestow him on Moctezuma. They can plot strategies together."

"Be still, I say!"

A second flourish of the hand. "You always had a fondness for the arts. It served you well. This man will not."

"Niccolo—"

A third lift of the hand, this time in surrender. *"Signore."*

"Out!" That was for the sycophants, the collection that hovered and darted like gnats throughout the Villa. Petty functionaries and bureaucrats in life, they haunted the place and came and went in perpetual facelessness, trying for points. One scurried up with papers, a pen.

"If the Imperator would—"

"Out!"

The sycophant fled. The newly arrived youth, who had come wandering into the downstairs hall with some sort of petition, gathered himself to his feet and tried for the door.

"*You*," Augustus said, and transfixed the fugitive in midstep. "*What's your name?*"

"B-B-B-Brutus, if it please you, sir."

"*Di immortales*. Which?"

"W-w-w-which?"

"Lucius, Decimus, or the Assassin?"

"A-a-a-assass-in?"

"S-s-s-sounds like the First Lucius," Niccolo said.

"Shut up, dammit, Niccolo. *Which are you, boy? Uterque?*"

"M-Marcus. Marcus Junius Brutus."

"Ye gods." Kleopatra got off her couch, on the other side. Niccolo sat stiff and with his hand quite surreptitiously on the dagger at the back of his belt. And the Akkadian got up with his hand on his sword.

"What's wrong?" young Brutus asked, all wide-eyed. "What's the matter?"

"You just got here, did you?"

"I—don't know." Wide eyes blinked. "I—just g-g-got this notice—" Brutus reached into his robe and Sargon's sword grated in its sheath. Brutus stopped cold, a terrified look on his face. "Did I do something?"

"Never mind the paper," Augustus said. "I've seen them. Official directive. An assignment of zone. Where have you been all this time, boy? Downstairs?"

"I—don't know. I—I think I'm d-d-d-dead—"

"How?"

"I don't know!"

"The Administration has a sense of humor."

"*Quid dicis?*"

"Never mind." The house shook. The lights blinked again. Augustus raised his eyes ceilingward as the lights swayed. A wild sob drifted down the corridors. *Damn!* —from far up the hall.

"Viet Cong," Niccolo explained. Young Brutus looked pathetically confused. "The park. *Viet Cong*. They make

overshots. Plays merry hob with the power lines—You
don't know about that either."

A slow shake of the head. A steady gaze of quiet, helpless
eyes.

"Sometimes," Niccolo said, "you really know it's Hell."

"The man who lost something," Brutus said over lunch
in the garden court. "What did he lose?"

Niccolo blinked, looked at the boy across the wire and
glass table—Kleopatra had joined them, demure and dainty
in a 1930s cloche and black veil. And Hatshepsut. It was
an unlikely association, the Greek with the Egyptian, the
Egyptian in a lavender 2090s bodysuit and with a most
distressing armament about her person. But they were all
a little anxious lately. Niccolo kept to his dagger: and a
tiny 25th-century disruptor, when armament seemed
necessary.

"Dantillus," Brutus said.

"Dante. Dante Alighieri. Born long after your time."
Niccolo sipped his wine, waved off a hovering sycophant
who proffered more. The sycophant persisted, sycophantlike.
Niccolo turned a withering look on the fool, who ebbed
away. "Never trust them," he muttered. "Always ask for
the whole bottle."

"Check the cork," said Kleopatra, and Brutus' wide eyes
looked astonished.

"But what did he lose?"

"Oh," said Hatshepsut, "*ka* and *ba*, I think."

"*He psuche*," said Kleopatra. "*Kai to pneuma.*"

"*Animus et anima*," Niccolo said with a twist of his
mouth, and smiled. "His soul. At least that's what he calls
it. —*Dammit*, man!" He rescued his glass from a sycophant
who oozed up to the table so subtly it almost succeeded in
pouring.

"More wine," said Hatshepsut. "The whole bottle."

The sycophant was gone on the breath.

"You see," said Niccolo, "Dante Alighieri was very devout.
He's sure it was a mistake that sent him here." He laughed,
with a second bitter twist of his mouth. "Isn't it always?
That rascal Cesare Borgia made it upstairs—his father was
a pope. And here I sit, because *I* wrote a book."

"You think that's why," said Kleopatra, sipping wine. Her eyes were enormous through the veil. A diamond glittered on her cheek, beside a perfect nose. "I daresay that's what drives poor Dante mad—*thinking*, you understand. He was quite unreasonable from the beginning— began writing out all his works by hand, absolutely certain that he had offended—*ummn*—the Celestial—by some passage of his work. And he went to the computer to speed his reconstruction. Now *that's* become an obsession. Dante and that machine, hour after hour. Checking and checking. Redoing all his work. He gets terribly confused. Then the computer goes down. Poof! One has to feel sorry for him."

"I don't," said Hatshepsut. She leaned elbows on the table. "The man was a fool. *La divina Beatrice*. To put divinity on a lover—*that's* a mistake! I had a lover try to *take* it once; chiseled his way into my monuments—Sssst. Let me tell you, I was a god. So was my friend here— well, god*dess;* times change. Augustus was, of course, but the silly Romans only did it after they were dead. *I* was a real god, beard, atef, crook, and flail, the whole thing; I held my power and I died old. Now I know why I'm here. Politics. Niccolo's here on politics. So's Augustus. And if Dante's here, it's *still* politics. Nothing else."

"Dante's become quite a nervous man," said Niccolo. "He's certain he's wronged someone important." He shrugged. "On the other hand—Perhaps he *doesn't* belong here. I'd truly watch what I told him."

"You think *I* belong here?" Brutus asked in dismay.

"But you have a paper," Niccolo said softly. "It says you do. Just don't trust Dante. The man was brilliant. Never mistake that. But he's not able to accept this. Some never seem to. Not to accept where one is—that's quite mad."

The sycophant arrived with the wine, another with glasses. Niccolo turned and took them, slapped an intrusive hand.

"—As for instance, I survived where others did not. I survive here. I keep company with gods. And a surfeit of sycophantic fools." He waved off a corkscrew and supplied his own from his wallet. "You never know. Poor Cl-Cl-Claudius was deified with a dish of mushrooms. Cesare Borgia had a certain touch." He inserted the prongs and pulled the cork. "Most anything can be deadly. Poison on the glass rim. On one side of a knife both parties share. One has to trust someone sometime." He poured a glass and handed it toward the youth. "As for instance, now."

"He *what*?" Julius Caesar swung down out of his jeep in the driveway, swept off his camouflage helmet, and dusted a hand on his fatigues. "I don't believe it."

"Nevertheless," said Sargon. The Akkadian leaned on the fender while the khaki-clad driver got out and stood staring. "Marcus Junius Brutus."

"There were seven hundred years of Marcus Junius Brutuses."

"The last Augustus said to tell you." Sargon set his jaw and his ringleted beard and hair shadowed his sloe-eyed face in angular extremes. "He's seventeen."

Julius looked at his driver. Decius Mus gnawed at his lip, took the rifles out, and slung them over his shoulder as if he had heard nothing at all. "Dammit, Mouse—"

"He doesn't remember," Sargon said. "I told you: he's seventeen."

"Oh, *hell*."

"Yeah," Sargon said.

Octavianus Augustus paced to the window and gazed outward where the Hall of Injustice towered up into Hell's forever burning clouds. Looked back at Julius, who sat in a spindly chair, booted feet crossed. Mud was on the boots, flecks of mud spattered on Julius's patrician face. Julius always brought a bit of reality with him; and when he was under the roof Augustus felt like Octavianus again; felt like plain Octavius, jug-eared adolescent scholar.

Get out of Rome, Julius had advised his widowed niece Atia once upon a time, a dangerous time of civil unrest; and sent her whole family to obscurity in Greece. But there had been letters from Julius. There had been the long understanding: careful tutelage of her son Octavius, the pretenses, the cultivation of this and that faction—not least of them the army. To meet with Julius under these circumstances, in the quiet of his private apartments—it brought back the old days; brought back secrecy; and hiding; and as always when uncle Julius talked business, Augustus Pater Patriae, First Citizen, felt his ears a bit too large, his shoulders a bit thin, felt his own intellect no match for the raw scheming charisma that was Julius.

Augustus was a god, posthumously. Julius sneered at gods and worshiped luck. His own. Julius deliberately created his own legends. Even in Hell. And Augustus felt helplessly antiquated, in his light robes, his Romanesque villa, before this man who took to modernity like a fish to water—

Julius spurned the *most* modern weapons. Not to be thought ambitious. Of course.

"It's us they're aiming at," Augustus said finally. "This little gift comes from high Authority. The refinement, the subtlety of it: that argues for—" Augustus' eyes shifted toward the skyscraper that towered at the end of Decentral Park. And meant His Infernal Highness. The Exec.

"Well, whoever set this little joke up has certainly bided his time," Julius said. "If it was planned this way from the start, that lets Hadrian out as originator—Brutus was in storage a damn long while before *he* got here. Has to be someone who predated us."

"I've wondered—" Augustus' voice sank away. He came back and sat down, hands clasped between his knees, in a chair opposite his great-uncle. A boy again. "How high up—and how far back—do the dissidents go?"

"Making the boy a cats-paw for that lot?" Julius rubbed the back of his head where a little baldness was; it was a defensive habit, a nervous habit, quietly pursued. "Damn, I'd like to know how long he's held in reserve and where he's been."

"No way to find that out without getting into Records."

"And deal with the fiends. No. That's vulnerability. Open ourselves up to his royal asininity—"

Hadrian, Julius meant. Supreme Commander. Lately kidnapped by the dissidents. So much for High Command efficacy. Augustus flinched at the epithet. "He's in favor—"

"Asses are always in fashion. They make other asses feel so safe."

"*Absit mi!* For the gods' own sake, Gaius—"

"Isn't it the way of empires? You set one up, then you

have to let the damn bureaucrats have it. Only thing that
saved Rome, all those secretaries, with all those papers—no
one after us ever did run the government. Couldn't find
the damn right papers without the secretaries. The thing
got too big to attack. Even from the inside. It just tottered
on over the corpse of every ass who thought he could shift
it left or right. Same thing going on down at the Pentagram
right now. The dissidents work for the government. They
don't know it; but they do. Whole thing runs like a
machine." Julius ticked his hand back and forth. "Pendulum.
It gets the great fools and the efficient with alternate
strokes. Now here's Hadrian gone missing—you think the
government's really going to miss Hadrian? Not before
snowfall. You think it cares, except for the encouragement
it affords fools? His *secretaries* know where all the damn
papers are. The Exec'll put some other ass in if they lose
him. If they get him back they'll let him serve a while
before they advise him to retire—he's lost prestige, hasn't
he? But appoint me in his place? Not a chance in Hell.
They'll pick some damn book-following fool like Rameses."

"You think all of this is interconnected."

"You miss my point. *Chaos* is the hierarchy's medium.
They don't plan a damn thing. Half the chaos comes from
the merest chance some insider with a capital S has a
coherent plan. The rest of it comes of every damn nut
outside the system who thinks he's just figured it out. The
waves of the bureaucracy will roll over it all eventually.
But you have to think of that chance: that very briefly,
someone in a Position wants to neutralize us. Beware the
bureaucrats. Beware the secretaries."

"*Prodi*. You escaped them."

"Oh, no, no, no, *Augustulle*. What do you think, the
geniuses masterminded my demise? It was the bureaucrats.
The fools. And who survived it all? *You* killed the
conspirators and inherited all the secretaries. And where
are those same secretaries?" Julius waved a hand toward
the wall, the window, the Skyscraper. "Still at it. All those
damn little offices. You wonder why I stay out in the field?
The army's the only bureaucracy you can sit on. I *really*
don't want to find his imperial asininity. I'd *like* the damn
dissidents to send Hadrian's head in. That'd take him out

of circulation a while. I'm terribly afraid they won't. But someone in those offices is either afraid I'll take out the dissidents—or thinks I might use this operation to gather troops for myself—"

"Of course you're not doing that."

"Frankly I'm not. I always preferred Gaul. It was much safer than Rome. *Wasn't* it?"

"You never were a politician."

"Never."

"Niccolo says kill him."

"Pah. Kill him! What would that stop? I tell you: what they've done in sending this boy is damned effective. I'd rather face a regiment."

"Than kill him? *Pro di,* when the State's at risk, one life—*any* life—"

"Now that's Niccolo talking. No. I'll tell you another thing. I have a soft spot." Julius picked up his helmet. Looked at it and fingered a dent ruefully as if it held an answer. "Maybe it's my head, what do you think?"

"I think he's a problem you want to ignore." Augustus got to his own feet with a profound sigh. "I'll tell you where the soft spot is. It's age that gets to you. It's battering down the fools time after time and finding they're endless. It's getting tired of treachery. There's a point past which Niccolo's advice has no meaning. There's this terrible lassitude—"

Julius looked up at him, a stare from deep in those black eyes, and Augustus/Octavius flinched. "Do you think they know that—the secretaries?"

"Like rats know blood when they draw it. They're playing a joke."

"Does it occur to you that they're playing it on him as well—on Brutus? Maybe he's offended someone."

"Dante."

"Offended *Dante?*"

"No. *Offended someone.* That's how they manage us, you know. There's always that nagging worry. Who it could offend. Who might know. How far the ripples might go. Dante's obsessed with it. It's a disease. It's the chief malady in Hell. I have it. You have it. We're all vulnerable. *Prodi, win* the damned war!"

Julius smiled that quirkish smile of his. "I do. By continuing to fight it."

"Damn, I'd as soon argue with Mouse!"

"No one argues with Mouse. He doesn't *want* anything. He knows this is Hell. You and I keep forgetting it, that's our trouble. They make it too comfortable for us long-dead. And then they do something—"

"Like this."

"They find something you want. It doesn't take a great mind to do that. A fool can do it. What they can't see is where it leads. And how it leads back to them. Mouse teaches me patience, *Augustulle*. A man who *chose* this place of his own volition has nothing they can hold him by. I have no intention of winning my war. Or of killing this boy. Now I know about him what I should have known all those years ago."

"That he's your son?"

"That, I knew. No. *Now* I know how to hold him."

"Like Antonius. Like Antonius, brooding over there with Tiberius and his damned—"

Julius quirked an eyebrow. "*You* were my trouble with Antonius, *Augustulle*. You still are. Antonius refuses to come where you are. And my only Roman son knew I couldn't acknowledge him. For my reputation's sake. For that bitch Rome. I'll tell you another secret. I never expected to live as long as I did. It's the women; the Julian women—gods, if we could persuade my aunt in here. Old aunt Julia pushed and shoved Marius; did the same to me; and trained my sister, who taught your mother, who trained you. Brutus didn't have a Julia, that was what. Just the little society-minded fool I got him on. I turned him away. And lo, in fate's obscure humor, he turns out to be the only *Roman* son I ever sired. I always thought I had time. You, off in Greece—you were insurance."

"You'd have killed me if you and Calpurnia—"

"*Prodi*, no. What was Alexander's will? To *the strongest*? I knew which that was. You don't hold a grudge, do you? *Don't* create me another Antonius, nephew. Brutus, I can handle."

Augustus opened his mouth, trying to find something to

say to that. But Julius turned and left, closing the door gently behind him.

The floor shook to a distant explosion. The lights dimmed and brightened again.

Julius never paused in his course down the hall. The troops had the Cong baffled. The Cong made periodic tries on the villa. It was perpetual stalemate.

It was a raison d'être. And a power base.

He snapped his fingers and a half a dozen sycophants heard the sound and converged beside him as he walked along. No sycophant ever resisted such a summons.

"I want," he said, "the young visitor: in the library."

He walked on. There were orders to pass. Some of them were for Mouse.

"He's out of his mind," said Sargon.

"His son," Kleopatra said, drifting on her back. The pool was Olympic-sized, blue-tiled. Kleopatra righted herself and trod water while Sargon sat on the rim and dangled his feet in. "Son, son, son. Dammit." She swam off, toward the other end, neat quick strokes, and Niccolo, standing chest deep, wiped his hair back and gazed after her.

"Ummnn," Niccolo said. While Kleopatra seized the baroque steel ladder and climbed out, black and white striped 1980s swimsuit and a very little of it. "Doesn't *look* like a mother, does she?"

"Caesarion."

"Very touchy. *Very* touchy." Niccolo waited till the diminutive figure had walked away toward the dressing rooms, lips pursed. Then: "Half a dozen children and estranged from all of them."

"This damned boy is setting the house on its ear."

"He'll do more than that. It's a master stroke. Marcus Junius Brutus. Julius' natural son. Augustus had more than one reason to kill him, didn't he? Brutus couldn't have *claimed* his paternity and built on Julius' foundations without acknowledging himself a parricide. But Augustus could take no chances. Brutus murders Julius; Augustus takes out Brutus—Kleopatra's brats all side with their dear papa Antonius, completely his. Even Julius' other son, the noble Caesarion. Dear, *ambitious* Caesarion: Augustus killed both of Julius' natural sons, you know. So in Hell Julius sides with his heir Augustus; Kleopatra sides with Julius, completely ignoring Augustus's little peccadillo in murdering one of her children—Isn't love marvelous? While Marcus Antonius sulks in Tiberius' merry little retinue, drinking himself stuporous. *There's* the man who wanted most to be Julius' heir. There's the man who handed Julius his soul to keep; and Julius just used it and tossed it. Do you know the worst irony? Antonius still loves him. He loves Kleopatra. And those kids. And his sister and *her* little crew of murderers and lunatics. Antonius loves everyone but Augustus, who destroyed him. And lo! Brutus—who always was the greatest threat Antonius understood. This just might bring the poor fellow back."

"Neutralize Caesar."

"Someone in the Exec's service planned this one. Someone *Roman.* Someone who understands enough to know where the threads of this run."

"Tiberius?"

"Tiberius was never subtle. Try Tigellinus. Try Livia. Try Hadrian himself."

"Before he was kidnapped?"

"*If* he was kidnapped. What if *he* ran the dissidents?"

"You dream!"

"I put nothing beyond possibility. I'm surprised by nothing."

"*Brutus* certainly surprised you."

"Only in his youth. He would arrive someday. That he hadn't only meant that he would. It was irresistible to someone."

"Maybe he just served out his time in the Pit, eh?"

Niccolo leaned his arms back on the rim of the pool, his eyes half-lidded. "The Pit is a myth. I doubt its literal existence."

"Then where do they go? Where *are* the ones we miss?"

"In torment, of course. Wondering when *we're* going to show up. And when it palls, when at long last it palls and we all stop worrying—" Niccolo made a small move of a scarred hand. "*Eccolo.* Here they are."

Sargon's hands tensed on the pool rim. He slid into the water and glared.

"There are people we *all* worry about finding," Niccolo said. "Look what they've done to Brutus. *Innocence. Ignorance.* Whips and chains are a laugh, Majesty. It's our *mistakes* that get us. The Pit is here. We're in it."

"You have a filthy imagination!"

"Intelligence is my curse. I am a Cassandra. That is *my* hell, Majesty. No one listens *all* the time. Always at the worst moment they fail to heed my advice." Niccolo rolled his eyes about the luxurious ceiling, the goldwork, the sybaritic splendor. "I will not even solicit you. I *know*, you see, that if I gain you, you will fail *me*, Majesty, Lion of Akkad. That is the worm that gnaws me."

"Insolence ill becomes you. *You* are the worm that gnaws this house. Sometimes I suspect *you*—"

Niccolo's dark brows lifted. "*Me*. You flatter my capabilities. I have no power."

"Remember you're in Hell, little Niccolo. Remember that everything you do is bound to fail. *That* is the worm that gnaws you. Power will always elude you."

"I adopt Julius' philosophy. Cooperate in everything. And *do* what I choose. Which is little. Fools are their own punishment and they are ours."

"Fools are in *charge* down here!"

"That's why they suffer least. Are you content, Lion? Does nothing gnaw at *you*? No. Of course not. You're like poor Saint Mouse. The one virtuous man in Hell. The one incorruptible soul. He has no hope. But you do. Why else do you live in this house? You were no client king. You ruled the known world."

"Flatterer. I also adopt Julius' philosophy. And you will not stir me, little vulture. No more than you stir *him*." Sargon leaned into the water and swam lazily on his back. "I am immune." His voice echoed off the high ceiling and off the water. "Better a foreign roof than Assurbanipal's court. If you want intrigue, little vulture, try your hand there. My own ten wives are *all* there. Not to mention the heirs. Why do you think I'm *here*? Not mentioning all the other kings, and all the other queens and concubines. Don't teach *me* intrigue, little vulture. Take notes."

He reached the ladder. He climbed up to the side,

water streaming from dark curling hair and beard and chest. And Niccolo smiled lazily, not from the eyes.

"I am writing a new book," Niccolo said. "Dante inspires me. I am writing it on the administration of Hell."

"Who will read it, little vulture?"

"Oh. There will be interest. In many quarters."

Sargon scratched his belly and wiped his hand there. "Damn, little vulture. They'll have you in thumbscrews if you go poking around Administration."

"For instance, do you know that Julius exchanges letters with Antonius?"

Sargon stopped all motion.

"Mouse takes them." Niccolo turned and heaved himself up onto the rim of the pool, turned on his hands and sat, one knee up and hands locked about it. "I wonder what he's going to write today. He will write. Mark me that he will." He smiled, not with the eyes. "He'll have to tell Antonius that Brutus has come, you know. Antonius would never forgive him if he didn't. And never's such a damned long time down here."

"Damn your impertinence to the Pit. I had a wife like you. I strangled her. With my own hands."

Niccolo spread wide his arms. "I could never equal your strength, Lion. I should never hope to try."

Sargon glared a moment. Then he seized up a towel and wiped his hair and beard with it. Hung it about his neck with both hands, and there was a glint in his almond eyes. "Come along, little vulture. I have uses for you. How many others do? Hatshepsut? Augustus?—Hadrian?"

"How should I betray confidence? Lion, do you attempt to corrupt me?"

"Impossible."

The lights flickered. A screen went dark, and Dante leaped from his chair. "Ha!" he cried, "*Ha!* I got you, you thrice-damned sneak!" With a note of hysteria crackling in his voice and a maniacal stare, man at cyclopic machine. "Thought you got me! I had it saved! *Saved,* do you hear me?" He jerked the recorded disk from the drive and waved it in front of the monitor. "*Right here!*"

"Do you really think they hear you?"

He dropped the disk and spun about, hair stringing into his eyes. He wiped it back, blinked at something that did not, for a change, glow monitor-green, and straightened a spine grown cramped with myopic peering at minuscule rippling letters. That something which did not glow was a man in 20th-century battle dress. Was the owner of a pair of combat boots that flaked mud onto his Persian carpet. Of a large black gun at his hip, a brass cartridge belt, brass on his shirt, a black head of hair, and a face that belonged on coinage.

"Caesar."

"Marvelous machines." The Imperator-deified walked over to the computer which had come up with READY, and picked up the disk.

"Don't—d-don't." Dante Alighieri perspired visibly. Knotted his large, fine hands.

"Oh?" Julius tapped a few keys. DRIVE? the monitor asked. "Wondrous," Julius said. "Do you know, I need one of these." He looked the disk over, one side and the other. Slipped it into the drive. Called up MENU.

"Please—"

"I did quite a bit of writing myself, you know. I still keep notes and memoirs. Old habits. You're sweating, man. You really oughtn't to work so hard."

"Please." Dante flipped the drive drawer, ejected the disk into his hands. "Please. I'd hate to lose it."

"The great epic? Or your little list of numbers?"

"I—" Dante's mouth opened and shut.

"*Never* trust the sycophants. I'll *give* you a number, scribbler. I want you to run with it. I understand you're quite talented."

"*Io non mai—*"

"Of course you do." Julius reached out and gathered a handful of the poet's shirt. "*Prodi,* you do it all the time, *mastigia*. With our equipment, on our lines, with our reputation. Let's play a little game. You like numbers? Let me give you the one for the War Department."

"I—I—I—"

"It even works."

Brutus paced the library, paced and paced the marble

patterns, up and down in front of the tall cases of books and scrolls. He waited. That was what the message had told him to do. He paced and he worried, recalling innuendo, Niccolo's small barbs, and the brittle wrath in Kleopatra's eyes. He had amused the Egyptian, Hatshepsut. There had been mockery in the way she looked at him. There had been invitation.

And he was very far from wanting *that* bed or another bottle of wine with Niccolo Machiavelli or another of those looks from Octavianus Augustus né Octavius, plebeian— who regarded him as if he had coils and scales and still dealt with him in meticulous courtesy—*wise,* he thought of Octavianus; *wise man*—with instinctive judgment. And he would not give a copper for his life or his safety with the others without whatever restraint Gaius Octavianus Augustus provided.

Did he *order me to wait here?* Brutus wondered in confusion. *He knows me. I don't remember him. With the adoption suffix on his name. I didn't catch the new clan. And gods, what clan has Augustus for a cognomen? No, it's got to be a title. Imperator, they called him. A war hero. And a god, prodi! And goddesses! And Dantillus and Niccolo—Are they serious?*

They're laughing at me, that's what. They hate me. I threaten them. Why?

What am I to wait on here?

He found the wine uneasy at his stomach, and his skin uneasy in the chill air, in this awful half familiarity with things-as-they-were. He did not like to look out the window, where a building towered precariously skyward, vanishing into red, roiling cloud. The sight made him nauseated. It would fall. It would sway in the winds. What skill could make such a thing?

Is it like this, to be dead? What happened to the world, that books are mostly codices and lights come on and off by touching and how do I know these things and why do these people I never met in my life all know me?

Is this what it is, to be dead? Are these shades and shadows?

Is this man Niccolo one of us?

Is he a god like Hatshepsut?

Am I?

What did I die of? Why can't I remember?

The door opened. A man in clean, crisp khaki walked in, a handsome man of thirty with dark hair and lazy amusement in his eyes.

"Is it you?" Brutus asked—for he doubted everything around him. "*O gods, is it you?*"

"*Et, tu,*" Julius said, and closed the door behind him. "My son."

Brutus drew a gulp of air. Stared, helplessly.

"We've had this interview once before," Julius said. "Or have we? Massilia?" Julius walked toward him, stopped with head cocked to one side and hands in his belt. "You'd surely remember."

"I remember."

"Well, gods, sit down. It's been too long."

Brutus retreated to the reading table and propped himself against the edge with both hands, trembling. "My mother— told me—"

"So you said in Massilia."

"But—when did I die? You *know*, don't you? Everyone knows something I don't—*Prodi*, can't someone be honest with me?"

Julius gave him that long, heavy-lidded stare of his. The mouth quirked up at the side the way it would and the lock that fell across his brow the way it would. This was the Caius Julius Caesar who had gone over the wall in Asia; made scandal of the king of Bithynia; set the Senate on its ear.

Are all those things gone, above?

"So," Julius said. "*Honest* with you. You stand here less than twenty. And you don't remember anything."

"*Me di—*"

"That might be a benefit."

"Why? What happened? Where did I—?"

"—die? That's a potent question. What if I asked you not to ask yet?"

"I—"

"Yes," Julius said. "*Hell* of a question to hold in check, isn't it? Hell is doubt, boy, and self-doubt is the worst. Doubt of my motives—well, you must have made some sort of mistake up there, mustn't you? Or here. You can die in Hell too, you die down here and you can come back right away or a *long* time later. When do you think you came?"

Brutus stood away from the table edge, waved a helpless hand at sunlight no longer there. "I was riding along a road, there by Baiae, just a little country track, it was just—an hour or two—Then—I woke up—*di me iuvent!* —on a table—this—this unspeakable old man—"

"The Undertaker. Yes. I do well imagine."

"Did I fall? Did my horse throw me?"

"You weren't to ask, remember. For a while."

"It was something awful! It was something—"

"Can't let go of it, can you? Especially self-doubt. I tell you that's the worst for you. Be confident—look me in the eyes, there. See? Better already. Straighten the back. Fear, fear's the killer. Kills you a thousand times. Somebody put that in my mouth. *Nice* writer. There now—" Julius came close and adjusted a wrinkle in Brutus's tunic. "You just take what comes. You and I—well, there're worse places. Assuredly."

"Is my mother here?"

"I really don't think she wants to see me. I don't hear from her. Never have. One thing you learn down here, boy, is not to rake up old coals. People you think you might want to see—well, time doesn't exactly pass down here. Oh, there are hours in the day—eventually. Sometimes you know it's years. Sometimes you don't. Whatever time it's been, you're not the boy who was riding down that road outside Baiae, now, are you? Death is a profoundly lonely experience. It changes everyone. But—You don't have that, do you?"

"I *don't*! I haven't, I can't remember—"

"Without that perspective. Gods. Poor boy, you can't well understand, can you? You just—"

"—blinked. I blinked and I was *here*, on that table, with that nasty old man, that—*creature*. I—"

"Can you trust me?"

Brutus took in a breath, his mouth still open. His eyes flickered with the cold slap of that question.

"Can you trust me?" Julius asked again. "Here you are.

You never liked me much. I've told you that the dead change. You don't know what direction I've changed. You came to me at Massilia and I never did figure out exactly what you expected of me. We talked. You remember that. You asked were you truly my son and I said—"

"—only my mother knew. *Pro di immortales*, was that a thing to say to me?"

"But *true*, boy. Only she does know. I had to tell the truth with you, the absolute truth: it was all I could give you. Self-knowledge. I had to make you know your situation. And what certain actions could cost. Protect your mother; protect your father's name—the name you carry; protect myself—yes; from making the feud with the Junii worse than it was. Politically I didn't need it. Maybe it was misguided mercy that I was as easy on you as I was. It was a hard trip for a boy to make. It alienated your father's family, humiliated your mother; and if it weren't for your mother's relatives and that little military appointment you got after that interview, the scandal would have broken wide open. It was a damned stupid thing you did, coming to me. Too public. Too obviously confrontation. And you're still the boy who made that trip, aren't you? I see it in your eyes. All hurt, all seventeen, all vulnerable and full of righteousness and doubt. And you needing so badly to trust me. Have you an answer yet?"

"Damn you!"

"You said that then, too. Well, here we are, both of us. Damned and dead. Can you trust me? Can you trust life and death made me wiser, better? I know you. You're a boy looking for his father. And you've found him. You've got all this baggage you've brought to lay at his feet and ask him to do something magical to make you not a bastard and *not* whispered about in your family and not at odds with your relatives, and not, not, not every damn thing that was wrong with your existence when you rode to Massilia. A lot of problems for a seventeen-year-old. You think I could have solved them with a stroke."

"You could have done something."

"Well, you're a *few* months older, at least. In Massilia that winter you wanted everything. Let me give you the perspective of my dying, since you lack your own: everything and anything I did with you that day was doomed to fail. You were the only one in that room who had the power to do anything. Do you know—you still are?"

"Dammit, don't play games with me!"

"Not a game. You're seventeen. It's the summer after. You haven't figured it out yet. I failed to handle your existence. Your mother failed. Your father of record failed. They found a compromise that let you live ignorant until he died and you were old enough to pick up the gossip. Then it started, right? Must've been hell, you and the Junius family gods. Manhood rites. *That* must have been full of little hypocrisies. February rites: praying to Junius ancestors, not that they heard it. Hell on earth. All your seventeen years. And I regret that, boy. But what could I do that late? Make it a public scandal instead of a private one?"

"Was I a suicide?"

"There you are, back to that question. So you considered suicide after talking to me. Maybe you considered killing yourself all that long ride home. Am I right?"

"Yes." A small voice. Brutus rolled his eyes aside, at the wall, at anything. "I *didn't* kill myself. Not on that road, that summer. I'm sure of that, at least. I was happy—I loved a girl—"

"Good for you. So you did find an answer of sorts. I told you, it had to be your own answer. Your existence was centerless as long as you looked to me to justify you; as long as you looked to your mother or to Junius. You were your own answer, the only possible answer. Do you understand me now?"

"I was the only one who cared."

"Not the only one who cared, son. The only one who could *do* anything. You could have killed yourself. Or me. Which would have been even worse for you. Or you could go back to Rome, go out to Baiae and be seventeen and in love. How was she?"

"*Dammit,* do you have to put your lecherous hand on everything?"

Julius made a shrug, hands in the back of his belt. "It probably made a difference in your life—one way or the other. *Prodi,* you were so vulnerable."

"*Was* she. *Was* she. Is! Is! *Dammit*—"

"You're dead. I assure you, you're dead and so is she. Whoever she was. And remember what I said about the dead changing. You're late. I've been waiting for you— thousands of years. Now do you see what you're into?"

"*Di me iuvent.*"

"You're a lost soul, son. One of the long wanderers, maybe. This is Hell. Not Elysium. Not Tartarus. Just— Hell. And it rarely makes any sense. Do you trust me yet?"

Brutus stared at him in horror. "How can I?"

"That's always the question. Here you are. Here you'll remain. I offer you what I couldn't in life. But the problem of your existence is your problem. You want me to embrace you like a father? I can. I can't say I'll feel what you want me to feel. I know you won't. Remember that you're a long time ago for me. And you're a long way from Massilia."

"*Gods!*" Brutus sobbed. And Julius obligingly opened his arms, invitation posed. "*Gods!*" Brutus fled there, hurled himself against the khaki shirt, put his arms about his father, wept till tears soaked the khaki and his belly was sore. And Julius held him gently, stroked his hair, patted his back till the spasms ebbed down to exhaustion.

"There," Julius said, rocking him on his feet, back and forth. "There, boy—does it help?"

"No," Brutus said finally, from against his chest. "I'm scared, I'm *scared*?"

"You're shivering. It was awful, I know, the Undertaker and all."

"It's not that."

"Me? Am I what you're afraid of? A lot of us are to be afraid of. Marcus Antonius, for instance. But he's not in this house. I warn you about him simply in case. You want a commission, dear lad? I can manage that. I'll show you the best side of this place. Gaius doesn't bite. Octavianus. Augustus. My niece Atia's boy—I adopted him. You see? I *needed* a son. It came down to my niece's son, finally. Caius Julius Caesar Octavianus Augustus—nephew of mine's got so damn many names and titles I can't keep up with them myself. And Mouse. You'll like Mouse. He lived a long time before us. Vowed himself to hell to save the country—charged Rome's enemies singlehanded—"

"Decius Mus!" Brutus reared a tear-streaked face and looked Julius in the eyes. "*That* Mouse!"

"Damn good driver. Not much scares him. I told you you can get killed down here. It still hurts. I really appreciate a man with good nerves. Got a lot of good men. Mettius Curtius. Scaevola."

"Marius?"

"Poor uncle Marius got blown to local glory. Haven't found him since. Little fracas with Hannibal—gods, two hundred years ago as the world counts it. Mines. You know mines? Of course not. A little like *lilae*. Worse. Hell, they invented a lot of ways to kill a man up there." He slapped Brutus's shoulder. "You want to dry that face? You want to stay here by yourself and rest a while, or do you want to take a tour around with me? Mouse has got the jeep, but he'll be back. You know cars? Did you walk here?"

"I—I—" Brutus made a helpless gesture at the view out the library window. "I thought this was another part of the building where I woke up. But I don't know. I walked down a hall—"

"Well, things like that happen here. Don't try to figure them. You've figured out the lights, the plumbing's fancier, but ours *worked*. You can ride wherever you like, horses we've got—but you'll want to learn to drive. Augustus isn't much on modernity, but he makes up for it on quality. He has an excellent staff, never mind the sycophants—"

Something roared overhead. Low. Brutus flinched and ran to the window. Julius stayed where he was. "They *fly* here too. I don't advise taking that up. Awfully chancy." There was a boom from the other side of the house, a series of pops. "Fool's overflown the Park. The Cong take real exception to that."

"I'm going mad!"

"No, no, no, it's just change. Novelty. I tell you, it's attitude. Doubt's your enemy. Disbelief is another. Believe in airplanes. Believe in yourself. Believe in visiting the moon and you extend yourself. I believe it happened. There's a limit to what I believe—I just like to have a *little* touch with the ground, you know; like feeling the mud under my feet, like the smell of gasoline—"

"What's gasoline?"

"It runs jeeps. Come along, come along, boy. *Gods,* there's so much to catch you up on—"

"What in the name of reason is he up to?" Kleopatra cried. A sycophant bobbled her nail polish and she shoved the creature down the chaise longue with her foot, sent a bright trail flying over the salon tiles in the sycophant's wake. Ten more took that one's place, mopping polish, seeking after the gesticulating hand, in a susurration of dismay and self-abasement, while the stricken sister wailed and snuffled hardly audibly. *"O fool, fool—!"*

"They'll never improve," said Hatshepsut. She lay belly-down on a marble slab while a masseur worked slowly on her back.

"I don't mean her! It! I mean *him!* O, damn! I don't believe it. He can't. He *hasn't* acknowledged that boy."

"It hardly makes any difference, does it? *Everyone* knows. Ummmn. Do that again. You're better than my architect."

"Dammit, he can't, he can't, I won't have it!" Kleopatra fisted a freshly lacquered hand and pounded the cushion. "He—" Her eyes fixed beyond, incredulously. Hatshepsut rose up on her elbows, looking toward the window, where a jeep pulled into the drive, and her mouth flew open as wide as Kleopatra's, whose lacquer-besmirched hand was instantly enveloped by frenetic sycophants.

"Ohmygods."

"Who?" Augustus cried. *"Who?"* I'll have his—"

"Not publicly," Niccolo drawled, and carefully drew back the curtain, peering down onto the drive as Mouse got out one side and a stocky, curly-headed man in tennis shorts bailed out the other. "Look at that. Even Mouse looks perplexed."

"The hell he does." Augustus came and took a look of his own out past the curtain. The handsome, lop-eared face showed a hectic flush. "What in the name of reason is he thinking of?"

"Antonius?"

"My uncle, dammit!"

"Ah." Niccolo smiled, a fleeting cat smile, long-lashed eyes lowered in contemplation of the scene on the driveway. "On that man I take notes, I never presume to guess him."

"*Antonius?*"

"Your uncle."

"That little bastard downstairs got him once. That *ass* out there tried to get *me*—He's got Kleopatra's brats over at that pervert Tiberius'—*Prodi!* He's got *Caesarion* in his camp!"

"Whom you murdered."

"A lie."

"*Auguste,* all statecraft is a lie and lies are statecraft, but split no hairs with me. This earless ass in your driveway is a schism in your house and a damned uneasy pack animal. I don't think he'll bear patiently at all. And I wonder what he'll do to young Brutus."

"Wine," said Sargon from the far side of the room. "It worked with my ass of a predecessor. Of course—I could just shoot him."

Niccolo turned and lifted a brow. "Like Sulla?"

"Not on my doorstep." Augustus turned from the curtain and snapped his fingers. A horde of sycophants appeared, saucer-eyed. "Get me a Scotch. Where's Caesar?"

Some sped on the first order. A few lingered, feral grins lighting their eyes. These had more imagination. Not much more. "Dante," the whisper came back. "Brutus," came another.

"Mouse went to Antony," said a third, not too bright.

"Out!"

It wailed and departed.

"Be civil," Niccolo said, "my prince. Learn from your uncle. Aren't we still guessing what *he's* up to? Welcome your enemy. Forgive him. If the divine Julius wants a minefield walked, why, he sends for Antonius." Niccolo tweaked the curtain further aside and stared down his elegant nose at the drive. "Ah, there, now, one question answered. There comes Julius and young Brutus. Now, there—they meet. How touching. Father with son on his arm. Antonius' gut must be full of glass. He *counts* on

Caesarion. He's been trying to seduce Caesar and Kleopatra out of here for *so* long, and he so hopes Caesarion will prove the irresistible attraction—Look. An embrace, a reconciliation, Julius with Antonius."

"Watch for knives."

Niccolo grinned. "None yet. Antonius is too devoted, Julius too convolute, the boy too innocent. And look—now the divine Julius draws Antonius aside, now he speaks to him while Mouse holds young Brutus diverted with the jeep and the gadgetry and the guns—O fie! Fie, Saint Mouse, where is your virtue? Adoration, positive adoration shines in young Brutus' face—boy meets the hero of his youth. Meanwhile the divine Julius is whispering apace to mere mortal ass—Antonius glowers, he glares, he swallows his wrath—oh, where are sycophants when they might be useful?"

Something whistled, distantly. Boomed. Power dimmed. "*Maledetto!*" wailed from down the hall.

"Got him again," Sargon said.

"I can't!" Kleopatra said, and fidgeted as a sycophant buttoned her silk shell blouse. Another fastened her pearls, a third adjusted the pleats of her couturier skirt. "I *can't* face him."

"Yes, you will." Hatshepsut shut her eyes and, leaning forward, submitted a bland, smooth face to the ministrations of clouds of sycophants armed with kohl pots and brushes. The sable eyes lengthened, took on mauve and lavender tint about the lids that accorded well with the mylette glitter-suit. Fuchsia beads hung in her elaborate Egyptian coiffure. Some of them winked on and off. So did the diode on the star-pin she wore. And the ring on her hand. And the circlet crown, which swept a trail of winking lights coyly over one strong cheekbone and back beneath the wig, and into her ear where it whispered with static and occasional voices in soldierly Latin. "Ssss. Aren't they friendly? Talk about the weather, talk about the house, talk about the boy—all banal as hell."

Kleopatra rolled her eyes. "Oh, *gods*. How can I put up with this?"

"They're coming this way."

Kleopatra's red lips made a small and determined moue. Her tiny fists clenched. Hatshepsut took an easy posture, arms folded, as a half-dozen sycophants suddenly deserted them to dither this way and that around the door.

It opened. Sycophants on the other side beat them to it while the sycophants inside were undecided. A trio of men who knew better stood behind a boy who knew not a thing.

"How nice," Kleopatra said with ice tinkling on every word. "A whole clutch of bastards."

"Klea!" Julius said.

"Do come in. I was just leaving."

"Maybe—" Brutus said, stammered, his young face blanched. "Maybe we ought—"

"Not likely," Julius said. "I want you upstairs, Klea. Both of you."

"The hell."

"Klea." The man in tennis shorts looked soul-in-eyes at her, advanced holding out his hands. "I've come to make peace. You, me. Augustus. Brutus."

She looked past him to Julius, whose face carefully said nothing.

"And to what do we owe this?"

"She's difficult," Julius said. "She's always difficult." He put his hand on Brutus's shoulder. "Klea, this is a boy. This is a nice boy. *Don't* be difficult."

"I—" Brutus said. And shut up.

Kleopatra cast a look in Hatshepsut's direction. Hatshepsut lowered elaborate eyelids, lifted them again in a sidelong glance, and Kleopatra walked deliberately past Julius with a shrug of silken shoulders. There was a sudden and total absence of sycophants. "Well, well, well. Tell me, *mi care Iuli*—just what *did* bring you back from the field?"

Julius's brows lifted. Kleopatra walked on, sharp echo of stiletto heels on tile, sway of petite hips and pleated skirt. "Come now," she said, snagged Brutus by the elbow, hugged it to her and drew him a little apart, conspiratorially. "These are my husbands. My second and third. How do you like the villa?"

"I—" Brutus cast a desperate look over his shoulder to Julius and Antonius and Decius.

"He doesn't have the perspective," Julius said. "He remembers a road outside Baiae. He was on vacation. Two blinks later he's here. *Think* about it, Klea."

Kleopatra froze a moment. Took her hands carefully from Brutus' arm.

Brutus looked from one to the next to the next. Last and pleadingly, at Decius Mus.

"Come here, boy," the hero said. Held out his hand. Brutus retreated there, to the firm grip of Mouse's hands on his shoulders.

"Let's talk reason," Julius said. "Upstairs. The plain fact is, Klea, we're under attack."

"Brilliant," Niccolo said, ear inclined to the library doors as he leaned there with his shoulders. He rolled his head back to face Sargon, who stood with arms folded, sandaled feet square, and a keen curiosity on his dark-bearded face. "Brilliant. Julius has Brutus in there as a hostage. Augustus, Kleopatra, Antonius—all sitting there on best behavior, knowing full well that any one of them could blurt out something that might jog Brutus the innocent right over the edge—And Hatshepsut sits silent as the sphinx—the cooling influence: he has her there, an outsider-witness to keep this loving family from too much frankness; while the silent, the redoubtable Mouse is a damper on everyone. *No* one bares his weaknesses to that iceberg."

"It's not only his own life Julius's gambling in there," Sargon muttered. "Someone'll have to kill the boy if he's not careful. And *is* Mouse incorruptible? Beware a man of extremes, little vulture. Mouse is a passionate man. Ask his enemies."

Niccolo looked back and raised a brow, turned his ear to the door again. "More of family matters. The politeness in that room is thick enough to stop a man's breath. Antonius vows selflessness, with tears in his voice he swears he's changed profoundly; Augustus swears he wishes to sweep all complications away—as he has come to love, he says, Kleopatra as his sister—as he will regard Antonius as his friend and this engaging young stranger as his younger brother—oh, and Augustus means it, Lion, he always means such things. And will mean them to the day some offense inflames him—then, *then,* he strikes without a qualm. There is no liar, Lion, like a sincere and reasoning man."

"A plague on his reason. What's the old fox got in his mouth?"

"Julius won't be hurried. That's a certainty. He's ranked his pieces, made his move—You ought to have taken this invitation to conference, Lion."

"I? I'll be waiting when the sun comes up on these oaths and protestations. They'll come to one who wasn't witness to their oaths, when they want to break them."

Niccolo made a grimace of a smile. "Ah, well, to *you,* Lion, they come for moral advice; but to *me* they come only when they've set their course. And come they will, to us both—to me when they wish to be rid of this young leopard. To you when they wish to justify it. Even in Hell we must have our morality."

Sargon chuckled softly. "What's the boy doing?"

"Silence, of course, silence—a *tabula rasa,* blank and oh, so frightened. Julius plies him with such a wealth of trust as would daze any prodigal son—and the leopard cub yet is leopard enough to look for blood on the old leopard's whiskers. But being cub, being cub quite lost and desperate, he nuzzles up to any warmth—if *Hatshepsut* clasped him to her bosom he would call her mother and weep for joy."

"He'd be far safer."

Niccolo laughed, merest breath. "Oh, with either of *us* he'd be safer, Lion, at least his life would be. —Ah! Now, now, we get to business! Attack, says Julius: he names enemies—"

Sargon stepped closer, applied his own ear to the door, royal dignity cast aside.

". . . an executive-level operation," Julius was saying. "We've got the fool Commander in dissident hands; and what put him there was a ragtag nothing having a chance dropped into their laps—administrative blundering or a leak in the Pentagram; or you can draw other conclusions. *Hadrian,* son. Publius Aelius Hadrianus, so damned modernized he's forgotten his own name. Supreme Commander of Hell's Legions. Remember you're thousands of years late. Hadrian ruled Rome—*ruled,* exactly so. He was—never mind what he was. There's a group of rebels— just think of the civil war and you've got it. The rebels grabbed Hadrian while he was gadding about on another of his damn tours; the headquarters is in its usual mess; you walked into a situation, boy. The Administration's embarrassed; the dissidents have scored a big one. And you can count on an embarrassed Administration to make some moves to distract *anyone* they don't trust. That's one level of thinking. There are others. There's one level that says we may have personal enemies that want to take advantage of the chaos and the Administration's lack of attention. You want to ask a question, son?"

"I—"

"It's a confusing place. Seventeen and you don't know any real facts about how your own country ran, you didn't understand why Rome tore its own guts out—"

"I know about Marius. *And* Sulla."

"Well, think of it like that, then. Gods help you, we're thousands of years old; you're seventeen. You wonder what you're doing in this room? You have to learn. You're going to learn." The sound of footsteps crossing stone. "There's something in the wind. *Antoni*, tell them what you told me."

"Rumors," Antonius' voice said. "That's all I can call it. Talk. The dissidents—they're laying plans for some kind of strike—Klea—Klea, forgive me—Caesarion—"

"What? What about Caesarion?"

"He's left, Klea, he's—gone. He's joined them."

"Oh, my GODS! Joined the dissidents?"

"I didn't want to tell you, I wanted to tell you—down there—I—"

"Do something!" The sharp impact of stiletto heels on the stone. "Zeus! You're his father! DO SOMETHING!"

"That," said Julius's low voice, "is why I think we're in trouble. From both sides of this affair. Caesarion moves to the dissidents. And—"

Upstairs a door opened and closed. Footsteps pelted down the hall upstairs and down the steps—Niccolo heard it coming, turned in utmost vexation and Sargon hardly a moment slower, as a disheveled black-clad figure came bounding down toward them and the door, papers in fist,

trailed by a chattering horde of sycophants. "*L'ho fatto!
L'ho fatto! Scusi, prego, prego, scusi—*" as he came barreling
up to the doors. "Here, is he here?"

"*Yes-yes-yes,*" hissed the sycophants, fawning and whisking right on through the closed door so brusquely Niccolo
sucked in his gut in reflex. Sargon retreated in dismay as
Dante shoved the doors open and charged on, papers in
hand. Sargon's mouth stayed open, his feet planted. But
Niccolo Machiavelli strolled on through the doors as
smoothly as if he had been following Dante Alighieri from
as far as upstairs, right into the library and the conference.

Dante never stopped. He walked right up to Julius and
waved a paper in Julius' vision. "There, there—it's *here*—"

It evidently had import. Niccolo's brows both lifted as
Julius took the paper in his own hand and read it carefully,
as Julius listened to the poet chatter computerese at him
and jab with a pencil here and here and here at the
selfsame paper. And the people in the room had risen
from their chairs, Sargon had trailed through the door,
everything had come to a thorough stop.

"Out!" Julius snapped suddenly; but that was for the
sycophants, who went skittering and wailing and tumbling
over one another in panic flight from the room. No one
else budged, except Dante Alighieri, who ventured another
poke with the indicating pencil at the paper that trembled
in Julius' fist. A quick whispered: "There, *signore,* there,
I'm quite sure—"

Julius flicked pencil and hand away with a lift of his
hand. "We've found who sent you here," he said, looking
straight at Brutus. "How's your current events, son? Six
eighty-five from the founding of the City. Your year. Who's
the man to fear—in all the world: who's worst?"

Hesitation. Brutus stared at Julius like a bird before the
serpent.

You, that look said. It was painfully evident. Then:

"In Asia. Mithridates."

"The butcher of Asia," Julius said. "*Mithridates* is one of
our problems—he's the one who plotted this little surprise,
holding you out of time. And if he's sprung it—" Julius
gave a sweeping glance to all of them. "If he's spent this
valuable coin, it's for no small stakes." Julius shook the

paper, as if it were legible. "Rameses has moved up to acting commander."

"Ummmn," said Sargon.

"Ummn, indeed," Julius said. "We've got imminent—"

Something whistled over the roof, whumped in a great shattering of glass that rocked the floor and sent shards of the great library window flying in a dreadful glitter of inward-bound fragments in the same instant that everyone dived for cover; everyone except the poet—Niccolo grabbed him on his way down, landed on him, and lay in the shower of glass nose to nose with Dante Alighieri, in utmost shock at the reflex that had betrayed him to heroism.

"*Prodi*," Augustus murmured from under a table. Another strike whumped down. "Efficiency. What's Hell coming to?"

"*Pol! Iactum habent isti canifornicatores ter quaterque matrifoedantes Cong!*" Julius scrambled up in the glass shards, hardly quicker than Mouse and Sargon and Antonius, with Brutus and Hatshepsut a close third. Augustus elbowed a glass-hazarded way out from under his table and Kleopatra staggered up on tottering heels, smudges all over her haute couture. Niccolo delayed, mesmerized by his own stupidity and the utter shock in Dante's eyes. "*Agite!*" Julius was shouting. "Up and out! *Move!*" And Sargon's hand landed on Niccolo's collar and hauled him up by one hand, shaking him.

"Out!" Sargon yelled, "Julius is right, they've got the range—*move*, man!"

Niccolo spun loose and ran when the rest started to run. From somewhere Hatshepsut had gotten a deadly little pistol, Julius was waving them out of the imperiled room, which swirled with smoke and wind-borne dust—

Julius passed him then, headed down the hall through which sycophants rushed and screamed in terror. He overtook Antonius, grabbed Antonius' arm and shouted at him: "*Get over that hill, get that brood of yours moving—* Take the Ferrari!! Klea, have you got the keys?"

Kleopatra stopped against the wall, rummaged her black handbag. Came up with keys. Antonius snatched them and ran, as the house quaked to another explosion and Augustus stopped and looked in anguish at a crack sifting dust from the hall ceiling. Mouse tore by him and hit the stairs down-bound, while Sargon and Hatshepsut hit the same set going up.

Niccolo opted for the latter, grabbed the banister, and ran the steps two at a time.

Weapons, that was what the others were after; their private arsenals.

He had another concern that sent him flying up that stairway like a bat out of hell—

He reached his own apartment, thrust the key in the lock as the floor shook to another shell somewhere in the rose garden. He ran inside, fumbled after more keys, unlocked one desk drawer and drew out the disruptor, unlocked another and snatched up a notebook which he thrust into his shirt.

Then he ran, as another impact shook the villa, somewhere in the vicinity of the swimming pool. Down the hall, Sargon and Hatshepsut were headed for the stairs, Hatshepsut with a laser rifle, Sargon with an M-1 in his hand and a 1990s flex-armor vest about his kilt.

Niccolo overtook them on the second turn, as plaster sifted from the ceiling and the chandelier swayed to another hit.

The Ferrari shot out of the garage in a squeal of tires on gravel; slewed as the man in the tennis shorts spun the wheel and hit the gas. Dirt rained down, and bits of sod.

"He's clear!" Kleopatra cried, and got her head down behind the driveway wall again as dirt and clods and rosebush fragments pelted their position. "You damn dogs!" Her face was smudged and white when she lifted it, and she had a .32 automatic braced in her hand as she peered over the rim of the driveway's bricks. "Let me try," Brutus was saying, while Mouse backed the jeep around and Augustus and Julius swung the rear-mounted launcher into action.

"Don't fire!" Julius yelled at Kleopatra. "Get down, you'll draw attention."

She ducked. "Shells," she told a gibbering sycophant which turned up next to her. "In my bedroom in the top of the closet, in the shoebox—go, fool!"

It gibbered, and whether that was where it was going was anyone's guess. It yelped as it reached the stairs and Sargon and Hatshepsut and Niccolo Machiavelli came tearing out. It scuttled.

"All of you," Julius yelled, "get the hell out of the driveway! Sargon, take left flank round back! Klea, Brutus, get to cover! Mouse, get back inside, take that second-story center window, and save it till we've got targets. And get the hell back down here if they get you spotted!" He dropped a shell into the launcher and it whoosed off in an arching streak toward Decentral Park, over a rhododendron hedge, a stand of oaks, kicking up a cloud by the time Julius swung the mount over a degree and Augustus popped another one in, laying stitches down a line.

Kleopatra ran low, barefooted over the grass, and scuttled in behind ornamental rock and an aged stand of pine. Brutus hit the ground by her side, eyes wide, about the time a shell landed in the front of the drive and blasted gravel and shrapnel that tore through the thicket, ricocheted off the ornamental boulders, and shredded bark off the pine. A barrage of shells left the jeep-launcher.

"*Pro di, pro di,*" Brutus mumbled in a state of shock. His face was ashen. "*Di—o Iuppiter fulminator maxime potens—*"

"Catapults," Kleopatra said. "Keep *down,* boy!"

Another shell hit. The jeep-launcher returned fire in a steady stream as fast as Julius and Augustus could drop rounds in. Kleopatra risked a look up, just as a cloud of fire erupted in the smoke beyond the park oaks.

"Got the bastards!" she yelled, and remembered to her embarrassment who was beside her, as somewhere a motor began to grind toward them and an incredible long snout poked through the rhododendrons across the street, with crunching and cracking of branches: a Sherman tank, lurching and crashing its way up to street level.

Brutus gave a moan and froze like a rabbit as black-clad Cong followed that juggernaut, attackers pouring out of that gap in the rhododendrons, around either side of the tank. Kleopatra took aim, both hands braced on the rocks, and sent rounds into the oncoming horde. Bullets spanged back, and she ducked and Brutus yelped and ducked as the tank ground across the pavement toward the lawn.

The ground exploded massively as the treads crunched the curb and hit the grass.

"Mine," Kleopatra gasped, huddling with her arms over the shuddering teenager. "Ours."

Brutus just gulped and tried to keep his lunch down.

Another tank broke through.

Hatshepsut steadied the laser on the rim of the flower bed and took cool aim at the tank as Sargon blasted away at the black-pajamaed horde that tried to storm their position. Steady fire came from Mouse's position up in the second-floor window.

Niccolo took aim of his own, no good on heavy iron atoms, his little pistol, but effective enough against water-containing flesh. Cong dropped and writhed.

Then a Fokker roared over, and a screaming whine ended in a whump and a deluge of rosebushes and rhododendron.

"Damn!" Sargon yelled, and Hatshepsut rolled over and got a shot off after the plane as it headed for a turn. "Range," she complained. "Damn scatter—Where's the Legion, dammit? Where's Scaevola? Asleep?"

"I imagine," Niccolo said, picking off one and the next targets, "the Cong have *them* pinned. Air support. This is a—"

A shell hit the front porch.

"Mouse!" Brutus cried. *"Down!"* Kleopatra snapped, and fired off a series of shots, paused and had to reload. Not hide—or wisp of the sycophant with the shells. The box she had picked up in the garage was near empty now.

Cong poured through the bushes, and the plane came around for another pass as Julius and Augustus sent missile after missile on as short a trajectory as they could. "We've got to pull it back," Julius yelled and scrambled over the seat, got the jeep into motion backward and then in a gravel-spitting turn around and over the lawn, headed behind Kleopatra's position and the cover of the pines and rocks.

About this time an incoming round hit the retaining wall of the driveway and sprayed the front ranks of the Cong breakthrough at that point with brick, geraniums, and shrapnel.

"*Fall back!*" Kleopatra yelled, elbowing Brutus into motion ahead of her. "*Get to the jeep—we're getting out of here!*"

The boy moved, got to his feet, and ran for his life. Kleopatra sprinted after him, low as she could while Augustus got the launcher swiveled round again and sent a ranging shot over their heads into the park.

A returning shell hit the pines—hit the gravel nearby, and Kleopatra went skidding, blinked in astonishment at pain in her back and at the wild-eyed boy who had staggered to one knee, blood starting from half a dozen wounds as he scrambled up and ran back for her.

"Dammit!" she yelled. She had died the focus of heroic fools. She had no more appetite for futilities. She thrust herself up to her knees, grabbed her gun and got that far before the boy got to her, snatched her into his arms and swung into a lumbering run with shots kicking up the pine needles and the fragments everywhere around him.

"*Age! Agite!!*" Julius yelled at them, while Augustus lobbed another shell overhead. Julius flung himself into the driver's seat, put the jeep's flank between them and the Cong. Augustus abandoned the launcher to haul Kleopatra up and over the side into the floor of the jeep. "Get in!" Julius yelled at Brutus, while shots spanged off the body-work and the launcher. Augustus came up with a grenade and threw it as Brutus clawed his bloody way into the passenger seat. Then the jeep cut tracks out of the lawn as Julius hit the gas and turned, shots whining past their ears. Brutus took a wild look back over the seat rim at a wave of Cong running past the pines.

Then the sky went up in a sheet of flame and the whole of Hell lurched. Julius swerved the jeep wildly out of control and stabilized it again as the air shock rolled over them and bits of trees and rhododendron and worse stuff began to rain down.

"Ran into their own fire!" Augustus was screaming. "*They blew up!*"

In truth there was a billowing cloud where the pines had been, and that group of Cong was a scattered few

survivors staggering about in the smoke. Julius swerved
and blasted the horn, taking the jeep across behind the
house, jouncing and bumping across flower beds and the
remnants of the rose garden, dodging shell holes. And
Sargon and Niccolo and Hatshepsut came straggling
disheveled and dusty from the portico of the east wing,
firing back as they ran.

Another huge impact rocked the park beyond the house,
blew out a last corner of glass from the second story and
toppled a cascade of roof tiles.

Then a gathering babble howled beyond the house, as
the Cong regrouped their forces.

A second bedraggled pair came staggering out the back
door, through the patio. Mouse and Dante Alighieri—
holding each other up.

"He got into Pentagram communications," Mouse gasped
as they and Sargon's company reached the side of the
jeep. "He fed in attack instructions on the Cong's coordinates
and the Pentagram zeroed in a couple of *their* rounds right
into them. There may be more rounds incoming—"

"Get in!" Julius said. They were already climbing; Sargon
boosted Niccolo and Hatshepsut up to hang on over the
fenders, scrambled up himself and turned the M-1 behind.
The overloaded jeep bounced and wove its way around the
craters in the lawn, headed away at speed as Cong poured
in a black wave around either side of the house and
Sargon, Niccolo, and Hatshepsut sprayed fire across their
ranks.

That was when Antonius and Agrippa showed up over
the hill in front of them and Mettius Curtius and the First
Cav. came rumbling over the rise of the west, with Scaevola
and the Tenth Legion hard behind.

The harried Cong veered north, toward open parkland
and the urban outskirts.

About this time, Attila's division arrived over that hill,
on the bizarrest instructions from the Pentagram he had
ever gotten.

"Prosit," said Augustus, lifting his glass. It was a bizarre
setting, even for Hell, the red-and-white-striped canopy in
the shell-pocked rose garden, with the salvaged furniture—

but there was not a window left in the villa and sycophants were in frenzied activity inside, sweeping and patching. *"Prosit heroibus nostris omnibus!"*

"Quite," said Kleopatra, lifting her glass with her left hand. She was in a rose satin dressing-gown, all in flounces, her right arm in a tasteful beige silk sling. "To our heroes!" Inside the villa a plank fell. Saws buzzed. Glass tinkled.

And Kleopatra included Marcus Junius Brutus in that sweep of her glass, so that Brutus hesitated with his own drink in hand, his young face aflame and his eyes filled with a new worship.

Dante Alighieri stood up and stammered out a *"Grazie."* Mouse, accustomed to honors, simply gave a bland nod of his head. And Sargon stood up and raised fragile wine glass in herculean fist.

"To us!" Sargon said with royal modesty, and Hatshepsut added, lifting hers: "To all us heroes!"

"Prosit," said Julius, and drank that one too. And laughed.

But Niccolo Machiavelli walked away from that gathering with a troubled heart, in the mortifying recollection of Dante Alighieri's ace nose to nose with him on the library floor.

He had betrayed himself, the most consummately rational man in Hell, as a fool among the shrewd and the calculating—all of whom had advantage to gain from their actions; but he had had none, had absolutely no ulterior motive in that leap which had preserved Dante Alighieri (and gotten him painful slivers of glass in several sensitive portions of his anatomy). He glanced back, at the poet and the boy-assassin basking in the warmth of praise from the powerful; and flinched and walked away in the ruin of all his self-estimation.

THE BOTTOM OF THE GULF

Barry Pain

Three hundred and sixty-two years before Christ a chasm opened in the Roman Forum, and the soothsayers declared that it would never close until the most precious treasure of Rome had been thrown into it. It is said that a youth named Mettus (or Mettius) Curtius appeared on horseback in full armor, and before a very fair audience, exclaiming that Rome had no dearer possession than arms and courage, leaped down into the gulf, which thereupon closed over him. This incident, like most of the legendary history of Rome, has been subjected to severe criticism. Those who too hastily disbelieve in it will reconsider their opinion on reading the account, not previously published, of what took place at the bottom of the gulf.

Curtius and the horse fell in the order in which they had started, with the horse underneath. After a few minutes' rapid passage the horse stopped falling somewhat suddenly, broke most of itself, and died. Curtius, who, though a little shaken, was uninjured, sat up on his dead horse and looked round to see if he could discover the nearest way back. As he looked upward he saw the top edges of the cavern close together, and the daylight shut out. But a curious greenish light still lingered in the cavern in which he found himself, and from one of its recesses came a voice which startled Mettius considerably. It said interrogatively:

"Did you hurt yourself?"

"Not much," replied Curtius. "I didn't know there was anybody down here. You quite startled me. Do come out and let me see you."

"No, thanks," said the voice.

"Did you really believe that you would die when you jumped down the gulf?"

"Certainly I did."

The voice laughed, a mean little snigger.

"So you will, too. You'll die of suffocation, slowly, when the air in this cavern is exhausted."

"Then we'd better get to work at once," said Curtius. "I have an excellent sword here and a couple of daggers. I put them on for the occasion. I didn't fall so far as I expected, and if we both of us work hard we shall be able to cut our way out."

"Thanks," said the voice, "but I'm not going to do any work. I'm not of the same kind as yourself. I don't need the air of the outer world. In fact, I don't think much of the outer world, even its best specimens. That's why I live down here. You've got to die. Sorry, but there's no help for it. I've set my trap, and I caught you, and if you're the best specimen they can provide on top, my low opinion of them is confirmed."

"What do you mean by the 'trap'?" asked Curtius.

"Well, it was I who caused the chasm to open, knowing the kind of tomfool thing your soothsayers would remark about it. I sat here wondering what I should get. Shouldn't have been surprised at a brace of vestal virgins. They would have exclaimed, 'Purity and devotion,' instead of 'Courage and arms,' amid loud applause, of course. Or it might have been an elderly matron, with a good old tag that Rome held nothing more precious than the tender love of her mothers. It might have been a soothsayer, it might have been anything. As it is, it's you, and I think very little of you. Arms? Of what use do you think all those tin-pot arrangements which you have hung about you are likely to be? Courage? Why, man alive! you've got no courage at all."

"I have," said Curtius stolidly; "I fully expected to die, and I was willing to die."

"Just for one moment," said the voice, "when you had

got all that mob of howling fools around applauding you. Applause is an intoxicant, and you got drunk on it. Now you are sober again, and you don't want to die at all. The man who can die alone, slowly and terribly, is courageous. But you've got no more courage in you than a piece of chewed string. You're as white as chalk."

"That's the effect of the green light," interposed Curtius.

"Rubbish!" replied the voice, "green light doesn't make a man shake all over, does it?"

"That's just the shock from the fall," said Curtius. "But I can't stop here arguing with you; I'm off to explore the cavern. There must be a way out somewhere."

"There isn't," said the voice; you can explore."

"I can't die like a rat in a trap," said Curtius, whimpering.

And off he went on his exploration. He looked in at the recess from which the voice had proceeded and found nothing. The cave was enormous. For many hours he tramped on and on, and never through one tiny chink in the roof did he see the light of day. Exhausted and ravenous, at last he flung himself down on the floor of the cave, and almost immediately the voice, which had been silent all this time, began again. First of all came that faint, mean little snigger; then it said:

"Hungry?"

"Worn out with hunger," sobbed Curtius; "I'm thirsty, too. My mouth is so parched that I can hardly speak, and there doesn't seem to be one drop of moisture in this damned cavern."

"There isn't," said the voice, "nor one crumb of food either, with the exception of your horse, and I don't think you will be able to find that again. You can try back if you like. Now I come to think of it, you won't die of suffocation, but of starvation. Cuts my entertainment rather shorter than I had hoped, but I must put up with that."

"I can't die like this," sobbed Curtius.

"Courage and arms," replied the voice, "are the things which Rome holds most precious. Go on, my boy; you'll last some time yet."

Then Curtius drew his sword, and went to look for the proprietor of the voice in order to slay him. But he didn't find him. He resumed his explorations.

In a few hours he was too weak to walk any further. He fell into a kind of doze, and when he woke again his arms had been taken from him.

"Where is my sword?" he exclaimed.

"I've got it," replied the voice, this time from the roof of the cavern; "what do you want it for?"

"Want to kill myself," said Curtius.

"If I give you your sword, will you own that you were merely a drunken theatrical impostor?"

"Yes."

"And that you are a coward, and are dying the death of a coward?"

"Yes."

The sword clattered down from the roof on to the floor of the cavern at the feet of the hero.

He picked it up and set his teeth.

AN ELIXIR FOR THE EMPEROR

John Brunner

The roar of the crowd was very good to his ears, just as the warm Italian sunshine was good on his body after three years of durance in the chill of Eastern Gaul. Few things made the general Publius Cinnus Metellus smile, but now, for moments only, his hard face relaxed as he made his way to the seat of honor overlooking the circus. There was winding of buccinae by trumpeters of his own legions, but the sound was almost lost in the shout of welcome.

This was what the populace liked from their generals: a profitable campaign, a splendid triumph and a good day of games to finish with.

Slowly the cries faded into the ordinary hum of conversation as Metellus took his place and glanced around at his companions, acknowledging them with curt nods.

"It'll be good to see some decent games again, Marcus," he grunted to the plump elderly man next to him. "If you'd had to sit through the third-rate makeshifts one suffers in Gaul . . . You did as I asked you, by the way?"

"Of course," lisped Marcus Placidus. "Though why you were worried, I don't know. You brought enough livestock back with you to keep the arena awash for a week—some of those Germanic wolves, in particular . . . No, you're paying well. You'll get the best games Rome has seen in years."

"I hope so. I certainly hope so." Metellus let his eyes

rove across the gaudy crowd. "But I'm not going to risk being cheated by some rascally lanista who wants to cooper his bets! And . . . and things have changed here since I've been away. I feel out of touch."

He made the confession in a voice so low it reached no one but Marcus Placidus, and immediately looked as though he regretted uttering it at all. Marcus pursed his fleshy lips.

"Yes, there have been changes," he concurred.

After a brief pause, Metellus shifted on his chair. He said, "Well, now I'm here, where's the ringmaster? He ought to be on hand to open the show."

"We're waiting for the Emperor, of course," Marcus said with real or feigned surprise. "It would be an insult to begin without him."

"I didn't think he was coming!" Metellus exclaimed. His gaze fastened on the gorgeous purple-hung imperial box. "I thought the insult was going to pass in the opposite direction. After all, he's snubbed me before, hasn't he? You were there, Marcus! He said I bled my provinces white! A fine emperor, that wants no tribute for Rome! He doesn't even seem to realize that you have to keep your foot on the neck of those barbarians. If you don't, you wake up one morning with your throat slit. I've seen."

He started forward on his chair, staring about him for the missing ringmaster. "Nothing would please me better than to show the world what I think of his milk-and-water notions. I'm the editor of these games, and I say when they open!"

Marcus laid a restraining hand on the general's arm. He said apologetically, "The people wouldn't stand for it, you know."

"I know nothing of the sort! Since when would a Roman crowd prefer to sit broiling in the sun like chickens on a spit, rather than start the games?"

"Since you've been away, perhaps," Marcus murmured, and hauled his bulky body out of his chair. "Here he is now, anyway."

Scowling, Metellus also stood up. Shields changed as the ranks of the guard completed the perfectly drilled movements of the salute, and the yell went up from the crowd. *The* yell—not just from the bottom of the lungs, but from the bottom of the heart. It went on. It lasted longer than the applause which had greeted Metellus, and seemed still to be gaining volume when the Emperor took his place.

As the roar echoed and reechoed, the general clenched his fists. When, two years before, a courier had brought the news of Cinatus's accession, together with the warrant for the renewal of his proconsulship, Metellus had shrugged his shoulders. It was a wonder, of course, that they had ever allowed the old man to assume the imperial toga in succession to his childless nephew—whose short and bloody reign was memorable to Metellus for one thing: his chance to pick the plum of Eastern Gaul.

But with rival factions sprouting all over the Empire, it was probable the old man had been chosen because he wouldn't offend too many influential people. He certainly had not been expected to last so long. Or to handle his impossible task so well . . .

"Aren't they ever going to stop screaming?" Metellus snarled. "Who's editing these games, anyway?"

"You don't understand how they feel," was Marcus's only reply.

At that moment Cinatus, having made himself comfortable, caught Metellus's eye and shook his head in the Greek affirmative that was one of the few affectations. As though by magic the giant ringmaster popped into view in the arena.

"*At last,*" grunted Metellus, and signalled for the games to be opened.

After the ritual procession, the ringmaster took his stand before the imperial box. All talking died away as the crowd waited eagerly to learn which of the many fabulous acts they'd just had a foretaste of would constitute the first spectacle.

"What did you decide to start with?" Marcus inquired behind his hand. "You were in two minds when I spoke to you yesterday."

"A perfect item, I think," Metellus answered. "It should put the crowd in a good humor straight away."

"A battle!" screamed the ringmaster. "Of the sunbaked

110 *An Elixir for the Emperor*

South—against the frigid North! Six wild Germanic wolves from the forests of Eastern Gaul, brought hither by special command of the general—"

The next words were lost in a shout of excitement. Marcus gave a nod. "Ah, the wolves!" he commented. "I said they looked promising. But against what? Each other?"

"Not quite," Metellus said. "You'll see."

Once more the ringmaster bellowed. "And opposing them . . . !" He turned with a flourish, and all eyes followed the movement as a gate was thrown back to admit into the arena—head bowed to avoid a final blow from his jailer—an elderly dark-skinned man clad only in a ragged kilt and worn sandals after the Egyptian pattern, whose back was laced with the marks of the scourge. In one hand he clasped a sword, which he seemed not to know what to do with.

A gale of laughter went up from the crowd, in which Metellus joined rather rustily. "Excellent," he muttered to Marcus. "I told my procurator to find someone—some criminal—who would look really ridiculous. And there he is. Afterward, you see, there's a giant bull—"

"I warn you," said Marcus in a very flat voice, "the Emperor is not laughing."

The general swung around. Indeed, Cinatus's face was set in a stern frown. He whispered to one of his attendants, who called to the ringmaster over the front of the box.

"Caesar desires to know with what crime this old man is charged!"

At a gesture, the ringmaster's assistants caught hold of the dark man and dragged him across the sand to answer for himself. He seemed to have recovered his wits, for as he straightened and looked up he gave a passable salute with his sword.

"My name is Apodorius of Nubia, O Caesar! And the crime of which I am accused is one I freely confess. I hold that neither you nor any other man who has assumed the purple thereupon became a god."

A low *o-o-oh!* went around the circus. Metellus sat back, satisfied. Surely Cinatus would not take that lightly. But a hint of a smile played on the Emperor's lips. He spoke against his aide, who relayed the question: "Why say you so?"

"Gods are not made by the will of men, and not all the words in the world can create divinity!"

"By the same token, then," came the good-humored answer, "not all the talk in the world can unmake a god. Ringmaster, release this man, for it pleases Caesar to be merciful."

Aghast, Metellus turned to Marcus. "Can I believe my ears? Does he intend to ruin my games, as well as insulting me about the way I ran my province? Surely the people will not stand for this!"

"They are standing for it," said Marcus calmly. "Can you hear any objections?"

Indeed there were very few, quickly drowned out by a roar of cheers.

"But how is this possible?" Metellus demanded.

"You don't understand," said Marcus again. "They love their Emperor."

Though the rest of the show proceeded without interruption, Metellus hardly paid any attention. He sat with a scowl carved deep on his features, disturbed only when he growled—at frequent intervals—that it was a plot to make his accomplishments look small, that Cinatus was jealous of his popularity with the plebs. Marcus endured his complaints patiently, but it was a relief when the last item on the program ended and the sated crowd surged like a flood toward the exits. Rising with a curt word of farewell, and an even curter salute to Cinatus, Metellus ordered his retinue to clear a way to the street and stormed from the circus.

Following more slowly, looking thoughtful, Marcus Placidus listened to the comments of the departing audience. As he passed one young couple—an elegant and handsome youth accompanied by a pretty girl whom he had noticed in a front-row seat on the shadow side, naked as was the custom among the more expensive courtesans—he eavesdropped with the skill of long practice.

"Good games," the youth said.

"Was it not gracious of Caesar to pardon that old man?" the girl countered.

"It was so. We have seen many wear the purple who would rather have ordered that the wolves' teeth be specially sharpened because the meat on his old bones must be tough!"

"Would that such an emperor could be with us forever!"

Marcus stopped dead in his tracks for the space of a heartbeat, and then continued forward. After a while he did something quite out of keeping with his senatorial dignity: he began to hum a popular song which was going the rounds of the Roman brothels.

He was humming it again when his litter was set down before the house of Metellus late that evening, but under the astonished gaze of his torchbearer—who doubtless knew where the song was current—he composed himself and followed the path to the door.

Over the splashing of the little fountain in the atrium he heard an enraged yell in Metellus's parade-ground voice. "If that's someone to see me, tell him to come along with the rest of the *clientes* in the morning!"

"It is the senator Marcus Placidus, General," said the respectful nomenclator, and Metellus gave a grunt which the slave interpreted as permission to show the caller in.

The general was reclining on a couch with a jug of Falernian wine at his side. A pretty Greek slave was massaging his neck.

"It had better be important, Marcus," he said shortly. "I'm not in the best of tempers, you know. And you know why!"

"It is."

"All right. Make yourself comfortable. Pour the senator some of this filthy Falernian!" he added to the Greek girl, and she hastened to obey.

Marcus spilt a drop in ritual libation and swigged a healthy draught of the wine. Then he set the cup aside and produced something from the folds of his toga. On the open palm of his plump pink hand he showed it to Metellus. It was a rose.

The general came to an abrupt decision. "Get out," he

told his slaves, and as they vanished soundlessly he added, "Well?"

"How would you like to be Emperor, Metellus?"

"I know you too well, or I should think you'd been chewing ivy, like a Bacchante!" the general said caustically. "Or have you changed along with everything else in Rome?"

"I assure you I'm perfectly serious. You were probably going to point out that Cinatus is firmly ensconced—which is true. It's also true that the court, and all Rome, are less turbulent than they've been in my lifetime. But Cinatus has made enemies apart from yourself. You know about my grounds for disliking him, to begin with."

"Something to do with a debt, wasn't it?" Metellus said, and gave a harsh laugh.

"A trifling matter," Marcus told him. "A question of a few tens of thousands. But it was the principle of the thing. He gave judgment against me, and I had to resort to most undignified methods to recover what I was owed. If I hadn't needed it so badly—"

"You're being strangely candid."

"I wish you to see how I would benefit from a change of Caesar. Others like me have been—shall we say, embarrassed by decisions on the part of Cinatus? A petty slight against someone in my position can rankle and ultimately fester. I suspect that those other whose cooperation I intend to enlist will agree chiefly because they imagine that once *we* have tumbled this immovable Caesar, it will be a matter of weeks before *they* topple his successor and install their own favorite. But I think they would find you hard to shift. Besides, you are popular with the plebs already. What more natural choice than our most successful general to assume the purple?"

"And how do you propose bringing this minor miracle to pass?"

Marcus told him.

At the end Metellus had a faraway look in his eyes. "Suppose, though, that Cinatus finds out from whom the suggestion originated? Will he not smell a rat?"

"Trust me for that, Metellus. I can arrange matters so subtly that the actual proposition will come from someone he relies on implicitly—who will himself believe he's making the suggestion in good faith."

"Ye-es," said Metellus doubtfully. He rose and began to pace the floor, head down, hands clasped behind his back. "But will Cinatus act on the proposal when it's made? Won't his accursed skepticism cause him to laugh the idea to scorn? Oh, Marcus, it will never succeed!"

"You're a man used to direct action," the senator said. "You're ill accustomed to the twists and turns of a court intrigue. I, however"—he gave a modest cough—"have some not inconsiderable skill in the latter field. I've already thought of the risk you mention. I'll forestall it by having Cinatus consent in order to be rid of those who keep plaguing him with concern about his health."

"We'll consult the auspices," Metellus said suddenly. "If they're favorable, I'm with you."

Marcus smiled like a contented cat. He had not expected so swift a victory.

First, he planted a rumor that the Emperor was a sick man. Since Cinatus was elderly, not to say old, people were ready to believe it. So often did he hear the whispered report from others, he soon almost credited it himself. Every time he saw Cinatus he studied him for signs of infirmity. However, the Emperor remained annoyingly hale.

So he planted his second seed. This was a single nebulous concept, whose pattern of growth he had chosen with extreme care. And, as the idea was relayed to more and yet more courtiers, it took exactly the form he had hoped for.

When it came finally to the ears of Cinatus himself it did so—as Metellus had been promised—from a close friend who honestly believed he was making a valuable suggestion.

"If it were only possible for Caesar to remain with us for another twenty years, we might see Rome even greater than she had been in the past."

"Faugh!" said Cinatus. "I'm fifty-four years old, and if I last another five under the strain of your pestering I'll have done well. Besides, who told you I wanted to put up with twenty more years of this job?" And, to drive home his point, he finished, "Anyhow, there's no way of making an old man young, so the notion is ridiculous."

"Is it?" his friend persisted. "These are stories of men who have chanced on potions to confer long life and good health. In Asia they tell of a king who discovered such a drug—an herb—but a serpent stole it from him before he could use it. And the Jews claim that their ancestors lived to an age comparable with that of the heroes—seven hundred years!"

"I'm not a Jew, and I'm rather glad," said Cinatus feelingly, for at that time those intransigent inhabitants of Palestine were once more in spirited revolt against their Roman rulers. "Are you suggesting I should become one?" he added with a glare. "If so, you can precede me. I'm told the process is rather painful!"

"Not at all, not at all," soothed the trusted friend, and then and there recounted the wholly fictitious news Marcus had so dexterously invented.

Cinatus did not yield at once. But after a month's importuning by more and more of his oldest friends, he gave in—as predicted—for the sake of peace and quiet.

"What did I tell you?" Marcus said smugly when he next called on Metellus. "Listen, I have the text of the proclamation here—it's to be made public tomorrow."

"How did you get hold of it?" the general demanded, and Marcus raised a reproving eyebrow.

"Do I inquire the secrets of your strategy? I think I may keep my own methods under the rose, then! But hear this. After the usual trifles about the graciousness of Caesar and how everyone wants him to reign a thousand years, it goes on:

" 'If any man bring to Rome medicine which after trial proves to bestow long life and good health he shall be richly rewarded, but if any man bring a medicine which is useless he shall be banished from the city and if any man bring a medicine which is harmful he shall be punished and if any man bring a poison his life shall be forfeit.' "

Apologetically refolding the wax tablets he had been reading from, he added, "Three penalties for one hope of reward, as you notice. I'm sorry, but that was the only way we could get Cinatus to seal the proclamation."

"Hmm!" Metellus rubbed his chin. "Do men bet against such odds in this strange Cinatified Rome of ours? I mean, will there be any candidates at all?"

"Beyond a doubt. They may not love Cinatus as much as they say they do, but they'll come—to puff some cult or other, or for the hope of gain, or for notoriety . . . And anyway I've arranged a steady supply of quacks to keep the interest of the plebs whipped up."

Metellus gave a reluctant smile. "Yes, I've noticed the city is full of sorcerers and favor-seeking acolytes of the mystery cults. Some of them even have the gall to come howling at *my* door. Well, let's assume a man turns up and produces some noxious drench: what then?"

"Why, then we try their potions on some slaves, do we not? For instance, you're aware that Cinatus has a trusted body-slave, a Greek called Polyphemus for his one eye?"

"I've seen him," Metellus granted.

"In your name I've offered him his manumission if he helps us. He's made good use of his position at court, and has a small private fortune. But Cinatus won't release him—says he depends on him too much. It's the worst mistake he's committed.

"Now, this Polyphemus thinks he can outwit me. Of course I have no intention of letting him go free with such a secret, and he suspects this, but he wants his liberty so much he's willing to gamble on the chance of blackmailing me afterward." Marcus sat back with a pleased expression.

"What secret are you talking about?"

"Why—! See: when *our* sorcerer, *our* doctor, comes to offer his potion to the Emperor, it will be something no more harmful than water."

"Not so harmless, that," grunted Metellus, thinking of the stinking stagnant liquid he had often encountered in the field. "But go on."

"Well, it's a detail we can settle. Make it a tasteless powder to be administered in wine, if you prefer." Marcus dismissed the point with an airy wave. "But I've arranged for Polyphemus, over the next few weeks, to feign occasional illness, severe enough to make Cinatus worry about losing him. When the medicine has been tested on some slaves and proved at worst innocuous, he's then going to volunteer to be the last experimental subject and will promptly make a miraculous recovery.

"It will then be the task of this same one-eyed Greek to give the potion to Cinatus. He'd trust no one else to administer it. And what he gives the Emperor will be—ah—stronger than water."

"I see. You're devious, Marcus, but clever, I concede! So we shall have to find culprits: the pretend doctor, and while we're about it, why not the one-eyed slave? Yes, neat and tidy like a good plan of battle!" In an access of uncharacteristic enthusiasm Metellus almost clapped his hands, but cancelled the impulse on realizing it would bring slaves into the room. Then his mood changed.

"We'd better move swiftly, though! For if I mistake not, people are beginning to forget the tribute my campaigns brought to Rome."

"We shall be swift enough," smiled Marcus, and stowed in the bosom of his toga the tablets on which was inscribed the proclamation even now being carried to the four corners of the world.

Long, long, before the sages of Egypt and the Druid mystics of Europe heard the news and began their preparations, the word came to Apodorius the Nubian as he shivered over a wood fire in a stinking little inn beside the Tiber. He was awaiting a ship that would bear him back to Africa.

Already he had travelled very far. He had sat at the feet of philosophers in Athens retailing the wisdom of their ancestors like parrots; he had bowed in the temples of Alexandria and the sacred groves of Asia; he had been initiated into mystery cults from Persia to the Pillars of Hercules; he had acquired very much knowledge. In fact, as he disputed anew with priests and adepts in every place he visited, he had begun to suspect that few men anywhere had studied so widely and absorbed so much.

And the suspicion had given him a certain courage.

The fact that a whim of Caesar had saved him an agonized death in the arena counted little with him. He was not as attached to his mortal frame as he had been when he was a youth. He cared more that he had sensed in the elderly Cinatus a quality unique among the many rulers he had seen: hardheaded common sense.

Apodorius, though Romans had almost cost him his life, was not blind to the benefits Roman mastery had brought to the world. He had been in many countries enjoying more peace and greater prosperity than ever under governments of their own. But should Caesar be weak, his deputies corrupt, the Empire could—did—bring misery.

The world needed the Empire. The Empire needed a good Caesar. Apodorius made up his mind.

Publius Cinnus Metellus *Augustus*—Caesar himself, latest of the wearers of the imperial purple—yawned. If he had been able to find a way around the right of all citizens to appeal in person to the Emperor, he would have done so. He hated dealing with petty squabbles, disputes over money, pretended claims against judges he had himself appointed . . . Unfortunately it was unavoidable. People who had enough funds to bribe their way past the various subordinates with whom he had surrounded himself, however, were also rich enough to be influential, and he had to continue going through the motions at least where they were concerned.

Marcus Placidus felt differently, of course. He enjoyed watching people scheme and weave devious plans, for the eventual pleasure of outwitting them. Metellus prevented his face from lapsing into a frown—just in time—as the senator himself entered the audience hall.

Too clever by half, the Emperor thought. *Something might have to be done about him. . . .*

"Well?" he demanded. "I understood today's audience was at an end."

"I think," Marcus murmured, "you may be interested in one more of those who have been waiting at the door. Look, O Caesar!"

The doors opened again. Through them stepped a dark-skinned figure, very thin, old, ragged, yet bearing himself with a certain dignity. To his chest he clutched something reddish-brown—a pottery jar sealed with a lump of wax.

He bowed vaguely in Metellus's direction; it was obvious that his sight was failing and an usher had to push him toward the throne.

Metellus's first impulse was to demand who had let this flea-ridden bag of bones into the hall. Then he checked. If Marcus had expressed interest in him, there must be a reason. He puzzled for a long moment, and at last said, "I see nothing significant about this scarecrow!"

"No? Think back, O Caesar," Marcus urged. "Think what that jar he clutches may contain. Do you not recall a day of games following your triumph when——?"

"That Nubian? The one Cinatus pardoned—may the empty-headed fool drown in Styx! Why, of course!" Metellus snapped his fingers. "Ap . . . something. Apodorius!"

The Nubian, apparently more by guesswork than sight, for it was plain to Metellus now that his eyes were filmed with cataracts, halted facing him.

"Caesar remembers me?" he said with faint astonishment.

"Indeed we do," Metellus confirmed grimly. Watching, Marcus allowed a sly smile to creep across his face.

As though vaguely troubled by the sound of the Emperor's voice, Apodorius hesitated, lovingly stroking the earthenware pot he cradled in his skinny arms. Seeming to draw confidence from it, he spoke up.

"I come in answer to a proclamation of Caesar more than a year ago, which said that if a man brought medicine to Rome for the health of Caesar he would be rewarded. I want no reward. You gave me my life, and in return"——he thrust his jar forward convulsively—"I bring you *everlasting* life!"

There was a long slow silence, which soughed through the hall like an ice-cold wind.

It was broken by an undignified gurgle of laughter from Marcus. Metellus shut him up with a murderous glare and leaned forward.

"Why have you delayed so long, Apodorius?" he asked silkily.

"I beg Caesar's indulgence! It was often hard to come by the ingredients, so I had to search far and wide."

"And why, seeing you have this medicine, are you yourself old and sick, and nearly blind?"

"The ingredients were costly," said the old man apologetically. "I had little money. I could buy no more than would make one dose . . ." He tapped the pot. "And that dose is for Caesar, not for me."

Metellus slapped the arm of his throne. "Know, O stupid conjurer, that your kind is not welcome in Rome!"

"But—but there are no others of my kind, Caesar. None but I could have brewed this elixir!"

"If your eyes were unveiled," Metellus said, rising to his feet so that he towered over the Nubian, "you would realize that I am not Cinatus, who spared your worthless life in the arena, but Metellus, who ordered you into it! And sorcerers of your breed are unwelcome because one like you came to Rome offering an elixir which proved to be poison and from whose effects Cinatus—Augustus—died."

At each of the last three words Apodorius winced, as if under successive blows. Slowly, slowly, he lowered his cherished jar. He stood very still, a broken man.

"Guards!" barked Metellus. Two brawny soldiers closed on the Nubian. "Take that jar from him."

A fist moved swiftly and seized it.

"Break the seal and pour this charlatan's muck down his own throat!"

The order galvanized the old man. He stiffened, and babbled the beginnings of a plea. A broad palm shut his mouth for him.

"We notice you are less eager to drink your elixir than to have Caesar drink it," Marcus said dryly. "Go ahead, soldier!"

Forcing Apodorius's mouth open, the man spilt rather than poured a clear grayish liquid from the jar between the Nubian's bare gums. A quick jab in the stomach made him swallow convulsively, and again, and until the jar was empty.

"Let him go," Metellus directed, and Apodorius slumped to the floor in a faint.

"As I thought," Marcus murmured. "Oh, the subtlety of these philosophers!"

Metellus ignored him. He was too pleased with his own acumen to listen to self-praise from the stout senator. "Now take that bundle of skin and bones and dump it in the Tiber," he instructed the guards. "And let me hear no more of sorcerers."

"*Just* as I thought," Marcus said more loudly, and Metellus rounded on him.

"And what do you mean by that?" he demanded.

"Reflect, O Caesar! It is truly possible that a man abiding anywhere in the Empire should have failed to hear of your succession, or that having failed he should not have learned the facts on reaching Rome? No, doubtless this fellow thought that by pretending he was so blind he imagined he was offering his potion to Cinatus he could make you as gullible as his old benefactor and induce you to take his poison."

"Then why should he not have come sooner?" frowned Metellus.

The question troubled him for a few moments; moreover Marcus had no immediate answer. Then he dismissed it from his mind and called for wine, wishing he had conceived a more spectacular fate than mere drowning for this skillful would-be regicide.

Consciousness returned after what seemed like the passage of aeons to Apodorius. He was lying on a rough and hard support, a wooden bench, and was so astonished to find he had not been thrown in the river already that he sat up by pure reflex before he had taken in his surroundings. For the first time in many months he did not feel his usual twinge of rheumatism.

His eyes, too, were clearer. Though the light was bad, he could see he was in a stone-walled cell; its ceiling oozed green damp. A grille of metal bars cut him off from another, identical cell, where a man with one eye sat counting the fingers of his left hand.

Seeing the Nubian rise, however, he let the hand fall to his side and cautiously approached the bars. When he spoke, it was with a strong Greek accent.

"You're the last of the conjurers, aren't you? You're going to Father Tiber tonight, aren't you? Oh, yes! You've come back, and I knew you would, because I'm still here and I'm trapped the same as you."

He talked with a kind of explosive bitterness in which

insanity rang dully like a counterfeit coin on a moneychanger's table.

"Marcus Placidus did for us both very nicely," the one-eyed man went on. "I thought I was cleverer than he was, but I was wrong, and he proved it to me. He proved it slowly, for a long, lo-ong, LO-O-ONG TIME!"

From a conversational level his voice rose to a screech. As though challenging Apodorius to doubt his words he thrust the stump of his right arm through the grille. It had no fingers left. The thumb was a mere blob of flesh and the skin from palm to elbow was seared with the marks of the torturer's iron.

"Who are you?" Apodorius said slowly.

"Polyphemus," said the Greek, and giggled. "Only I'm luckier than the real Polyphemus. Marcus didn't put my eye out with a hot stick, oh no! Marcus isn't as clever as Odysseus, but I'm not as clever as Marcus."

Abruptly he altered his tone again, and now cocked his head so that his one-sided gaze could study his new companion's face. "You came too late to poison Caesar, you know," he said. "I did it a long time ago. Marcus told me he'd manumit me for it, but he lied—he was clever! He proved it," he added inconsequentially, and thrust his left hand also through the grille so that he could count its fingers again, this time by touching them in turn to the blob marking the site of his other thumb.

Apodorius felt facts mesh together in his mind. Hoping against hope for a few minutes' clarity from the Greek's disordered brain, he spoke as things presented themselves to him.

"It was a plot by Marcus Placidus to poison Cinatus. You pretended to be a doctor and—no, that can't be right. You said you knew I'd be back . . . Ah. You were imprisoned here with the man who posed as a doctor and brought poison instead of medicine, who'd been put up to it by Marcus, and hence presumably by Metellus. You must have been one of Cinatus's slaves, promised your freedom if you substituted poison for the elixir."

"You know all that," Polyphemus said petulantly. "Why go on about it? You gave me the poison before you went to

Caesar with water. Water! Even water can kill you, if you drink as much of it as there is in the Tiber!"

Footsteps sounded in an echoing corridor. Polyphemus moved away from the grille and listened intently. "I think they're coming to take you away," he said, unholy joy in his voice. "But you'll be back. Sooner or later you'll be back. You keep coming and going, but . . . I'm the proof, you know. The senator told me so. If ever he can't cope with Metellus, he said, he'll use me to prove it was a plot of Metellus's to poison Caesar. I hope he doesn't have to use me as proof, because they torture slaves before they make them talk, and I've been tortured. Did you know?"

He finished with a pathetic attempt at confidence, "But Marcus will be able to handle Metellus! Marcus is clever! Marcus is clever! Marcus is—"

"Shut your mouth, you!"

Apodorius turned, not too quickly, to see that the speaker was an officer of the guard who had halted beyond the grating set into the door of his cell. Bolts jarred back as the soldiers accompanying him heaved on their handles. The officer stepped inside.

"Awake, are you?" he grunted. "Hah! Can't have been very powerful poison, then. Still, no matter—it will please Caesar when I tell him you were conscious enough to enjoy the taste of the river." He gestured to the soldiers, and they moved purposefully forward. It would have been senseless to offer resistance; Apodorius let them do as they liked.

When his arms had been lashed behind his back and his legs so hobbled he could barely stumble along, he was jabbed into the corridor at the point of the officer's sword. The sound of Polyphemus counting—up to five, and then again up to five—died slowly in the distance.

"If it weren't ridiculous," the officer muttered, "I'd swear you were actually the better for that muck you swallowed. Not that it's going to make any difference now."

He swung open a door and they emerged on a stone ledge, under which the river ran chuckling. It was very dark, and the night breeze had a chill to it.

"*Vale*, brewer of elixirs," the officer said, and drove the point of his sword deep into Apodorius's left buttock. Yelling, he plunged into the water—and vanished.

The soldiers waited long enough to be sure he would not surface, and dispersed with no further thought of the matter. It was all in their day's work.

But deep in the swift-flowing Tiber, Apodorius was hoarding his breath, conscious mainly of how glad he was they hadn't sewn him in a sack before they threw him in.

"At this hour?" said Marcus Placidus irritably. "Who?"

"He is a Nubian, senator," the slave explained, unaware of the effect he was about to have on Marcus's state of mind. "He is very wet and muddy, and if he had not sworn by all the gods that it was a matter of life and death I should have kicked him into the street. But he says I must tell you that his name is Apodorius."

"Wine," Marcus said faintly. "Help me to a couch. And quick—*get that man in here!*"

"I have come, Senator," said the unmistakable voice of Apodorius from the curtained doorway. Marcus's eyes bulbed in his fat face. He gasped and swayed, and the slave anxiously aided him to the nearest couch.

"I regret the state in which I call on you," the Nubian went on. "But Tiber is at the best of times an unclean river, and I had some trouble breaking free of my bonds."

"Come—come here," whispered Marcus. "Let me—No! You, slave! Touch this man and see if he is substantial!"

Astonished, the man obeyed. "He is warm flesh," he reported. "But slippery with mud, as you observe."

"No ghost . . . Praise be, praise be! What do you want with me?" Marcus wheezed.

"I have a grim kind of business with Caesar," Apodorius answered dryly. "But why should I approach him when it is known to all Rome and the Empire that the words are his and the thoughts are yours?"

Marcus could not help preening himself a little, and recovered some of his ordinary composure. "Slave!" he rapped. "Cleanse this man—he's my guest! Wipe him, give him a fair new toga, bring wine for him, and be quick!"

And he watched as his orders were put into effect, unashamedly goggling.

"I find it hard to accept that you're here," he said at last. "Still, I must do so or never again believe my senses. And such a trick as you must have employed to escape is one worth knowing. Speak!"

Refreshed, neatly clad, Apodorius gave a smile.

"Why, Senator, my elixir which you took for a lie was potent enough! Ask the guards who dropped me in the Tiber whether they did not see me sink with arms and legs bound!"

"I . . ." Marcus hesitated. "Granting that's true, why have you come to me?"

"To offer a bargain. A fair one, I think. You are in a position to give me what I most desire: revenge upon Metellus for what he did to me. Likewise I am able to give you what you want—what I already have against my will. I doubt you'll care much which Caesar wears the purple when you wield the power."

Marcus leaned forward with greed brilliant in his eyes.

"Destroy Metellus," Apodorius said, "and I will give you my elixir."

Marcus pulled at his lower lip. After a moment's reflection he said cannily, "Your elixir! How do I know it's not a sham? How do I know you weren't pretending to be old and blind, and sloughed the appearance of age as easily as you slipped your bonds in the river?"

Apodorius winced and rubbed a chafed ankle. "Do not term that 'easy,' Senator," he complained. "But I have proof for you. Setting aside the point that no hale man with any alternative open would have gone willingly to be torn apart by wolves—you remember?—I have taken so great a dose of my medicine that I am growing younger almost by the hour. See!" He opened his mouth and indicated his visibly toothless gums. "I feel an ache which may even portend . . ."

Marcus rubbed his finger along the shrivelled flesh and gaped in awe. Surely no conjurer's deception could make sharp new teeth grow in an ancient's jaw!

Even so, it was not until three days later when the first tooth was cut, gleaming and indisputable, that he sealed the bargain Apodorius had proposed. Then he was committed. In truth, what was it to him if Metellus went down to join the shades? An immortal man could become the power behind not one Caesar, but all Caesars!

Apodorius watched him grow drunk on the heady liquor of his dream.

He asked for what he wanted, and Marcus supplied it with no demur at the cost, which—as had already been said—was immense. The senator's desire for secrecy suited him; in a quiet room at the back of the house he worked with the strange mixture of substances bought for him, and weeks slipped by.

After two months, however, Marcus was at the limit of his patience, and Apodorius judged it unwise to make him wait any longer.

Accordingly he waited on him when he returned from the Senate, and to his fevered demand for news of progress gave a simple headshake of affirmation.

"Yes, I have prepared the elixir again. It goes quicker when one can buy from a bottomless purse instead of having to beg and even steal . . . What have you done to keep your side of the bargain?"

Marcus rolled his eyes to heaven and clasped his hands. He whispered, "I have arranged that next time Caesar goes to the circus a pillar below his box will be loosened. An elephant will be goaded into terror and caused to break the pillar down. If Metellus is not trampled to death, the care of such doctors as I have recommended to him can be counted on to help him join the shades."

"Good," said Apodorius. "Then come with me."

Marcus entered the room where the Nubian had been working, and stopped dead. Everything had been taken from it—all the pans, jars, braziers—all but a single small table on which rested a crock containing a grayish fluid. His eyes lit up as he recognized the color of the liquid that had been forced down Apodorius's throat.

He stretched out his hand toward it, and then checked himself. "No!" he croaked. "You first! Sip it before I do—and do no more than sip it, mind!"

"Have no fear," said Apodorius quietly. "I have made

enough this time for more than a single dose." He picked up the crock and set it to his lips.

Marcus's eyes, alert for any hint of deception, followed his movements as he drank three slow mouthfuls of the stuff. Then he replaced the crock and rested his hand on the table to steady himself.

"You may feel a little giddy at first," he husked. "Remember, when I was forced to drink before Caesar I fell in a swoon. But you are not so old and weak as I was then."

His breathing grew easier and he straightened. Convinced there was no trickery, and impatient beyond endurance, the senator seized the crock and drained it in frantic gulps.

When he set it down, it was with a crash that shattered it and sent the shards flying across the floor. A burning began in his stomach. Dark veils crept across his vision as he sought to fix his eyes on the Nubian's face.

Through a rushing torrent of pain he heard Apodorius's voice, very cool, very detached.

"You are a dead man, Senator."

"What?" he whimpered. "What?"

"I have drunk the elixir—the real elixir. You have not. In that crock was the strongest poison I have ever found. I drank it, and I live. But you die."

Marcus Placidus clutched his belly as though he would squeeze the poison from it like water from a sponge. But blueness was already showing on his lips and around his fingernails. In a moment he could stand no longer, and crumpled to the floor. His eyes rolled; his chest barrelled out in a final despairing gasp of air. And he was dead.

"But that will make no difference to Metellus," Apodorius said to the corpse. "Not yet. Even if his doctors save him after the accident at the circus. I am sure, Senator, you were sufficiently skilled in flattery to let him imagine your decisions were his own. By himself—well, he is no Cinatus!"

And, his thoughts ran on, *his fall will probably bring the Empire down* . . . Another wave of murdered Caesars, and then barbarian invasions from the outskirts of the Empire—oh, the ultimate collapse of so mighty an edifice would take centuries, but it was now inevitable.

And afterward?

"We shall see," murmured Apodorius. And then corrected himself with wry amusement. "Or rather: I shall see!"

He dipped his finger in a drop of poison which remained in a fragment of the broken crock, and thought of the care he had taken to make its color exactly the same as that of the real elixir. He still felt queasy from the three mouthfuls he had swallowed. Enough of that poison would perhaps pierce his invulnerability.

Rising, he spoke to the air.

"Does it make you smile, Cinatus Augustus, there in the land of shades? You gave me my life, and I've avenged you. But Metellus outdid your gift! He gave me everlasting life, and because of that I have destroyed him. Do you understand, Cinatus? I think you do. I think if I had come to you, you would have turned me away.

"Perhaps, then, I would have been offended. But now I know why I brewed my elixir for an emperor, and not for me."

He stared down at the poison in the broken crock, and did not see it. He was contemplating the endless centuries ahead, and feeling himself grow cold.

"Next time I brew," he said, "which will I choose? This? Or a renewal of the other?"

The fat dead body of the senator did not answer him. Its mouth, though, was already curved in the sardonic corpse's leer known as the Hippocratic smile.

SOME VERY ODD HAPPENINGS AT KIBBLESHAM MANOR HOUSE

Michael Harrison

I was standing at the bar of the new Marine Hotel, looking through the plate glass picture windows at the promenade and the sea, when I saw a little old man, shriveled of face and tottery of legs, come into view. His eyes were sunk in the enormous hollows of his skeletal face, and this death's-head was framed in wispy grey hair— for he wore a long beard. Yet, for all the shocking difference in his appearance, I could not hesitate a moment in recognizing Andy, the very Compleat Sportsman of pre-war years, and my intimate friend for a decade or so before the coming of Hitler had disrupted so many of our lives. I had gone into the Army; Andy into the Navy, that "Senior Service" in which his dashing style as one of Britain's most spectacular yachtsmen soon earned him speedy and impressive promotion. And now, as I stared at him through the plate glass window of the Marine Hotel's bar, I saw a shriveled-up old man who, once his startled gaze had met mine through the glass, was evidently intent on avoiding me.

I felt, I confess, that I was taking rather an unfair advantage of my old friend when I realized that only his inability to quicken his step prevented his making a determined effort to disappear before I had time to leave the bar and catch him up in the street.

But I did catch him up in the street, and when I said, "Andy! how wonderful seeing you again!"—like that—and

129

put out my hand, he returned the clasp, for all that his grin was a bit rueful; as much, I couldn't help thinking, because he hadn't been able to escape me, as because he knew how his appearance had shocked me.

As Englishmen of our way of upbringing do, we began tentatively to probe the situation from behind our traditional defenses of banal remarks: "What a marvelous day it is, isn't it?" "You living down here now, Andy?" "Let's have a drink . . . unless you prefer some other place?" "No . . . I quite like the Marine. I go there, every now and then." And so on.

But, at any rate, I got him to turn back, and to join me at a table in a corner of the big bar, out of the direct heat of the sun. When the waiter had brought our drinks, Andy anticipated all my questions by saying.

"You know that my parents died, did you? Yes, you'd have seen that. And Verena's dead, too. . . ."

"No," I said, pretending to see something on the table, so that I should not have to meet his eyes. "No, I didn't know that. She . . . she never got any better?"

"No," said Andy. "There's that dreadful old phrase about 'a merciful relief.' Well, in this case—in Verena's case—it was true enough. You could well call it a merciful relief. You could, indeed." And, quite shockingly, he began to laugh. I looked up, and he saw what I was thinking. "No . . . you don't understand. When I said it was a merciful relief, I wasn't referring to Verena, poor darling. I was referring to us—to what was left of the Johnstones. Poor old Father. Mother. Me. And now there's nothing left of the Johnstones but me. And, as you see, there's precious little left of me."

"When did they die?" I asked, to show that I could take this sort of matey outspokenness, that I hadn't developed weak nerves in the years since the war. "Your people, I mean. . . ."

"Father died just after the war, as you know. They *said* it was cancer. Mother died about a year later. They didn't have time to think anything up. She just died. But, as you knew that already, you meant, when you said, 'When did your people die?'—'When did Verena die?' She died when they pulled Kibblesham down. I'd got her into a very

special home . . . I may tell you about it, later. I may not.
I don't know." He passed a shaking hand across his skeletal
face, and shivered, as though with ague. "And then I sold
Kibblesham."

"I'm sorry about Verena," I said. "I would like to have
seen her again."

Andy stared at me, and then—again, and even more
frighteningly this time—he began to laugh.

"My God, Tim, you don't know your luck! Thank
everything you pray to that you can't even *imagine* what it
was you missed!"

Old friends—especially old friends of the same sex—
should be able to ask questions, to ask the other to explain
exactly what is meant by a half-understood remark. But I
couldn't. I hadn't the courage. I didn't know what it was
that I feared to know. But I was certain that, in this, as in
so many other things of past days, Andy was right. Better
that I should not even begin to guess what it was which
had taken Verena upstairs to her bedroom—suddenly and
(for all the outer world knew) inexplicably—never to leave
it, save to go to what Andy had called 'a very special
home.'

I remembered then the curious atmosphere surrounding
the fact of Verena's illness. Juliet had gone down to
Kibblesham—it was still the countryside thirty miles from
London, then—to meet me; we were to join Andy and
Verena, and to go to one of those Hunt Club hops without
which, so they used to say, Christmas, my dear fellow,
wouldn't be complete.

But when I got down to Kibblesham by the six P.M.
train from Paddington, I found that we were to go to the
dance one short. Verena was in her room, had been confined
to her room for several days past, and wouldn't, on any
account, let either of us up to wish her a Happy Christmas
and say how sorry we were that she would have to miss
the dance. Verena, a tall, horsy blonde, would almost
certainly have been the one to borrow the hunter from the
stable, and ride him through the dance.

"Sends you both her salaams," said Andy, briefly, "but
she'd just as soon you saw her when she's a bit better."
'Just as soon,' in our idiom, meant, 'positively forbids you

to.' We didn't see Verena that night. We never saw Verena again.

I said, to bring the conversation back to normality, "Who bought Kibblesham in the end?"

"A local order of nuns. They wanted the site for a new school."

"Oh, so some bright boy didn't get the chance of developing—as *you* should have done!"

"Well, the nuns did. They put up flats and shops, and have let them all. They built their school where the Five-acre Meadow used to be. They've shown a good deal of business sense. Mother, as you may remember, always used to support her convent. So, when they approached me, I let them have it."

"You must have lost a good bit on the deal."

"If you mean by that, that I could have got more in another market, I suppose so. But . . . but there were reasons why I wanted to get rid of Kibblesham . . . no, not because the family had died; there were other things, things you don't know about . . . and I let them have it. Funnily, the better offer came from the Rector. His Bishop, apparently, wanted to build a school, too—London won't be long before it gobbles up Kibblesham, and all these far-seeing characters buy for the eventual property rise."

"Why didn't you let the Rector have it?"

"I was going to. I was baptized and confirmed in his church, and much as I admire the nuns, I'm not as R.C. In fact," said Andy, absently, frowning down at the rings that he was making on the tabletop with the bottom of his glass, "I had nearly said yes, when suddenly the significance of his church's name struck me."

"St. Theobalds . . . ? Why, what's the significance of *that*?"

"It's not Theo-balds," said Andy, impatiently. "The local pronunciation is 'Tibbles'—St. *Tibbles*."

"Well . . . ?"

"Well," he said, sullenly and shiftily, " 'Tibbles' is the same as 'Kibbles'—and 'Kibblesham' means 'the Village of Kibble.' Or 'of Tibble.' It's the same thing. You don't know what 'Kibble' means, you say?" he asked, anxiously.

"Nor of 'Tibble,' if it comes to that," I said, facetiously.

"It's nothing to laugh at," said Andy. "Waiter! bring us another drink."

"Do you remember what Kibblesham looked like before all that rebuilding changed the look of everything?"

"Andy, I've never been back. So far as I am concerned, it's the same."

"Oh well. Then you remember how everything was. The Manor House, the Parish Church, the row of shops, the tied cottages . . . that sort of thing. You remember, across the road from the Manor House, there was a big field—it was under barley, the last time I saw it—with a windbreak of enormous elms in the top left-hand corner? Yes, I know you do. And do you remember my telling you that the ploughman—it was farmer Richard's land—used to plough up colored *tesserae* . . . bits of a Roman tessellated pavement, and that I suggested that you and I should excavate for the Roman villa which *must* lie under Richard's land, under the road which cuts between . . . *cut* between . . . his land and ours, and, supposedly, under the Manor House itself?"

"I remember. I've seen the Ordnance Survey Map of Roman Britain, since then. It's all Roman-settled country 'round Kibblesham. It's quite likely that there *was* a Roman villa under the Manor House. It's even possible that the Manor House is the direct descendant of the villa itself."

"Kibblesham is Roman," said Andy. "But it wasn't a villa . . . it was a temple. That's why I'm glad that it was the nuns who bought it . . . to pull it down. If anyone can make the break between Kibblesham's past and Kibblesham's present, they can. I wish to God . . . but what's the good? Kibblesham's gone; the others have gone, and I won't be long. It's what I'm . . . it's what I *might* be going to be . . . which scares the daylights out of me. Do you really want to know what happened to Verena . . . ?" The waiter brought the drinks. I paid, and when the man had gone, Andy said, "Look, we'll finish this up, and you can come to my place. I've got furnished rooms at the back of this place, and there's something I'd like to show you. If *I* know, there's no reason why you shouldn't." He picked up his glass and drained it in one swallow—just like the Andy

of the old days. I felt my heart lift at this evidence, slender
as it was, that all of my old friend had not vanished in
these strange changes which had overtaken him. "Know
what a *gallus* is?"

"Isn't it an old-fashioned word for what the Americans
call 'suspenders,' and we call 'braces'?"

"It's a certain kind of priest," said Andy. " 'Gallus.'
Come on, let's go back to my place. I'm sorry I tried to
avoid you. I should have known you wouldn't take the
brush-off. Anyway, you're old enough a friend to hear
what happened to us all at Kibblesham Manor House."

"I know you remember everything of Kibblesham. We
didn't, as you know, keep up a big establishment, but I
want to emphasize that there were some fourteen or fifteen
people coming or going about the house—I mean, besides
ourselves and our guests—and never once did we have a
single complaint that the house was haunted."

"*Was* it haunted?"

"Yes," said Andy. "Very haunted. Haunted in the worst
possible way."

I was on exceedingly dangerous ground—my common
sense told me that. But my curiosity, at that moment, was
stronger. I simply couldn't resist asking, "What's the worst
possible way in which the dead can haunt a house?"

"When they're still alive," said Andy.

Outside an ice cream van chimed its way along the
quiet street. All the inhabitants of Worthing, on this sunny
day, were by the sea. Except for the noise of the ice cream
man's chimes, dying away to a distant, elfin tinkling, a
Sunday silence had fallen on the seaside town.

But inside the room, there was not only quiet, there
was chill as well. I said, "We never got around to digging
for that Roman villa."

"But Verena did," said Andy.

"Did she really!"

"And she found something. She thought they were a
pair of Roman nutcrackers, and in a way," Andy said, with
a wry, tortured grin, "that might have been one way of
describing them. She cleaned them up with metal polish,

and she got quite a polish on them, but in spite of that, Mother wouldn't ever touch them because 'you don't know where such things have been,' and Father because, though he'd faced practically every savage tribe in the world one way and another, he firmly believed that anything dug out of the earth which wasn't a vegetable was alive with what he called 'tentanus germs.' You couldn't have got the Governor to touch that object for a stack of five-pound notes."

"And you . . . ?"

"I never touched them because Verena got a bit miffed that my people weren't more impressed with what she'd found, and in a huff she took them up to her room and put them in an old tea caddy in which she kept needles and cotton and that sort of thing. I was away at the time. Had I been at home, why yes, I almost certainly would have handled them. Why not? But I didn't. Verena put them away, and not until . . . until later . . . did I see them and realize what they were."

"What were they . . . ?"

"I'll tell you in a minute. What do you know of Cybele, the Great Mother?"

"Not much. Exotic religion, imported into Rome when— was it Hannibal?—threatened, and the oracle advised the Senate to have a word with the Idaean Mother. Doesn't Livy tell the story? The priests—here! Yes, I *do* remember! —the Galloi: Gauls, because no Roman was permitted to demean himself by becoming a priest of so outlandish a religion . . . screaming through the streets of Rome, gashing themselves, and dressed in women's clothing, and . . ."

And then I remember why the ritual of Cybele, the Great Mother, used 'nutcrackers,' and what it was that they crushed.

"She put them into her workbox," said Andy, staring vacantly through the window, "and that night she heard the piping. You hear all sorts of noises in what they call 'the quiet of the countryside,' and all sound damned odd at night, and not a few sound damned frightening as well. But Vee was a levelheaded girl, and she didn't pay too much attention to the piping, except that it kept her awake wondering what on earth it could be. She only thought she heard voices, chanting, that night—she wasn't sure, but what startled her was the dream which followed when she fell asleep at last.

"She was dancing down a street that she knew, in her dream, wasn't in Rome, but in London. The architecture was vaguely classical, but it had a homely sort of look, as though everything had been done on a fairly tight budget. It was definitely provincial, but quite grand, nevertheless. The streets were lined with dense crowds, and she was dancing with a lot of other men, all dressed as women. Only Vee wasn't dressed as a woman; she was still dressed as a man . . ."

"Why the change? Men dressed as women; women dressed as men . . ."

"Oh," said Andy, as though I'd missed a simple point. "Vee was dressed as a man because she *was* a man. Still a *man*, I mean. She was gashing her arms like the others and screaming out, 'Io! Io! Magne Mater! Mater Omnium! Mater Omnium Deorum!'—and in some odd fashion, she seemed to be something special in the procession. People looked at her differently, and some made signs as she came near. She felt she was someone—something—special, but what that was, she didn't know. So she went on slashing herself, and flinging the blood over herself and over the people standing by. She remembered that she had been at some special ceremony and was bound for another. The procession came to London Bridge and went into a temple alongside the northern entrance to the bridge. The rest was a bit shadowy, but she remembered being led down some steps to a boat, rowed by sailors, but with a single sail. There was a procession of boats up the river, until they all came to a place that she thinks must have been about where Maidenhead is now. Then there were more celebrations, and another walk, and then they were all taken in creaking bullock-carts to Kibblesham—the Settlement of Cybele. And there," said Andy, "her initiation should have ended."

"*Should* have ended . . . ?"

"Well, poor Vee couldn't quite remember that bit . . . it was all in a dream, you understand . . . and some details were sharp and clear, and others were dim and a bit shadowy. But she got the sense that if she did something that she had to do—some tremendous obligation, a test, a ritual—something terrific would happen to her. And then, she told me, she had an overwhelming sense of having failed someone—failed that someone, and failed herself. You know how fond she used to be of Tennyson? Well, she said she felt as Sir Bedivere must have felt when he found that he had failed in his duty. Like that."

"What had she failed to do . . . ?"

"The next night," said Andy, as though I hadn't spoken, "she heard the piping again. But this time, she heard clearly the voices—the chanting that she had thought she'd heard on the previous night. The words were the same as those that she'd heard in her dream. They were calling on the Great Mother . . . and they sounded near. Very near, indeed. It was at that point," said Andy, staring down at his great freckled hands, "that she began to change.

"Every night," he continued, "she dreamt of the *Galloi*— the priests of Cybele. Every time she expected to become one of them—and every damned night she failed to do something or other, which prevented her actually joining them. She remembered a lot—in her dream, of course—of what had happened to her earlier. She had seen other people undergo the *taurobolium*—where they used to stand under a grating, whilst a bull was killed above: a baptism of blood. She saw the crushers being used, and learned, she said, how to weave the screams into the melody that she was jangling out with her *sistrum*. But though, in her dream, she was a man, no one used the crushers on her—nor would they, she told me, until she had passed the Final Test. She couldn't tell me then what it was . . . and I'd no idea. Have you?"

"No. What did you mean, Andy, when you said just now that she began to change. I heard a funny story . . . could it possibly have come from the servants. I heard that Venera had changed her sex!"

Andy shook his head.

"If it had been only that!"

"Then what did change?"

"She herself."

"I don't quite understand you. She was Verena . . . the Verena whom we both knew and liked. What did she become?"

"She became what the Chosen Ones became . . . she became the Great Mother Herself. . . ."

I stared at my old friend in horror. He had talked of the 'very special home' to which Verena had gone to die—but for what 'very special home' did this lunacy to which I was now listening qualify *him*.

He stared at me, and reached down into the 'poacher's pocket' of his tweed hacking jacket.

"Know what these are?" he said, casually. He reached over, and before I knew what I had done, I had unthinkably accepted a pair of rust-stained forceps, the arms of which were set with tiny heads, amongst which I recognized those of some Roman gods. "They're the forceps used for the ritual castration—when the novice, having passed his tests, made the final renunciation of his manhood to the Great Mother. Henceforward, having lost his manhood, having sacrificed the severed parts to Cybele, he would no longer be a man. He would dress as a woman; speak as a woman. On the Day of the Great Mother, he would come out into Rome, and all the other cities of the Empire where the Great Mother was worshipped, and down the streets he'd run and dance, gashing himself, scourging himself. . . ."

"Why?" I wondered. "Why on earth did they do it?"

"Eh?" said Andy, as though I had asked a question whose answer was obvious. "Why, *for the rewards*, of course."

I gulped. How much of all this wild stuff that Andy was talking had a basis in fact? Did *any* of it have a basis in fact?

Andy was mumbling now—and I had to strain my ears to catch the words.

"Great rewards, though," he muttered, "don't come to one except for having done great acts. Only a few could ever find the strength to go through with it . . . with the trials, I mean . . . and the tests . . . and the final renunciation. But," Andy continued, staring through the window with unseeing eyes, "castration and all that were nothing, really, compared with the greater renunciations . . . ."

"The greater renunciations . . . ?"

"Why, yes," he turned towards me, faintly astonished that I should have cared to reveal my ignorance. "Castration, transvestism, squeaky voice, self-wounding and so on . . . these are merely *physical* renunciations. The Great Mother, in return for the rewards that She alone could give, demanded renunciations far more important than these. Dehumanization called for a complete break with all one's past, with all one's *mores*, with all social traditions and obligations. Particularly it called for the complete severance of family ties."

"Well, yes," I said, desperately striving to introduce even the semblance of normality into our conversation, "but don't all religions call for the break with one's family?"

"The Great Mother wanted something more than that the Chosen Ones should say good-bye to their family ties. She wanted something a great deal more positive. A great deal more final. Something which would *prove* the neophyte's sincerity. Something so *horrible*—so against nature—that the very act of doing it would not only prove the neophyte's sincerity, but would cut him off forever from humankind. Only then could he enter into the Goddess—become one with her. Become Her, indeed."

"Something so horrible . . . ." I whispered. "What could be so horrible that one would dehumanize oneself in the very act of doing it? What sin against the Holy Ghost could it be which would prevent one's ever becoming human again?"

"There's a moral in that story of Arthur's taking the sword out of the stone. The sword was for him—for him only. Yet, the moment that he had got the sword, he was the King. The forceps . . . the forceps have the same sort of power. . . ."

"What do you mean?" I asked, my blood running cold in panic fear of I knew not what.

"They are the instrument of the priest, but they are, in

a fashion I don't quite understand, the controller of the priest. *No one can handle them and ever be the same again.*"

I stared down in horror at the rusty object in my hands, and cast it violently from me.

"It doesn't matter now," said Andy, in a tired voice. "What you and I want doesn't matter. We are the slayers and the slain. We are the priests and the victims. We are the sacrifice and the Goddess herself. I don't know . . . but when I heard Father scream like that . . . scream, scream, *scream* . . . I knew that he was the very special sacrifice, and that, in using the forceps on Father, Verena was proving that she could perform the act which would cut her off from all humanity.

"I don't know whether Father ever realized what had happened. He wasn't a young man, but he was physically very strong. He said nothing . . . after that terrible scream. Mother was in her own room, and Father—God knows how he did it—said that he'd had a terrible nightmare when Mother came in to see what the noise was all about.

"He saw Dr. Lawrence—and you know that country doctors aren't like the modern city boys: the country doctors *still* don't talk. They fixed up a crack plastic surgeon, and repaired the damage to Father. Then, a few months later, behind a door on which the locks had been changed, Father committed suicide, without fuss, without scandal."

"How on earth did he do that?"

"He was a diabetic . . . I don't suppose you knew that? Well, he was. So all that he had to do was to 'forget' to take his insulin, fall into the diabetic coma, and die. He left it to me to see that Verena was dealt with suitably . . . poor old Governor! What an end! To be castrated by one's own daughter . . . no wonder he was glad to die!"

I was swamped in the horror of the tale, whether or not it were true. If true, it passed the bounds of decent terror; if untrue, it marked the depths to which Andy's madness had plunged. But suppose that it *were* true . . . ?

Still striving to get this insanity back on to a rational basis, if such a thing sound not too absurd, I managed to choke out: "But Verena wasn't a man. She was a woman. I thought the *Galloi* were all men . . . ?"

"Not all," said Andy. "There were exceptions. Verena was Chosen. It didn't matter what she had been at the beginning, and in the end her original sex mattered not a bit. After she'd ceased to be human, she became what the Great Mother changed her to. That's what killed Mother. I forgot to keep Verena's door locked and Mother walked in. I'd told her that Verena wanted no one to see her but me, but . . . well, you know what Mother was. She walked in, saw what was lying in Verena's bed, and collapsed. Dr. Lawrence shot her full of sedatives, and—fortunately for poor Mother—she died. That's when I decided to get Verena off to a very special home. Dr. Lawrence arranged that, too. Verena hasn't long. She might as well be where people are paid a great deal of money to have nerves of steel . . . it isn't any everyday nurse who can face the sight of the Great Mother and stay even half sane. I know," he added, "because I've seen Her. . . .

"You are trying to ask me where I stand in all this," said Andy, with a wan smile. "I'm not a Chosen One. I'm just a simple priest . . . a *Gallos*."

And then, for all the horror that I had known, came the most terrible experience of all.

"I must get out of these clothes," Andy said. "*She* isn't served best in this kind of clothing." And, opening a drawer, he began to take out filmy, lace-trimmed garments of silk . . .

That was six weeks ago. I got out of Andy's rooms somehow, and stumbled down the stairs into the blessed dust and sunlight of the Worthing back street.

The horror persisted, but, like all other human emotions, even horror dims a bit with time. After a fortnight or so, I found that I could think, without shuddering on all that Andy had told me. I began to feel a strong impulse to revisit Kibblesham and see how total had been the changes wrought by the nuns who had bought the property.

There were changes indeed! Not merely in the land on which Kibblesham Manor House had once stood, but in the village—now the town—of Kibblesham itself. Kibblesham had become as faceless, as characterless, as any other London suburb.

Where Kibblesham Manor House had stood, with its meadows and paddocks and stabling and ponds and kitchen gardens and rose-walks, now rose an eight-story block of flats above a four-story strip of shops with flats above.

The new convent, of mixed glass and shining concrete, stood isolated in the midst of its asphalted playgrounds, and the noise of children's voices came loud and clear across the open space. Then the children filed into their classrooms, and I heard one nun call to another, "Oh, Sister Francis Xavier, will you be taking the French class this afternoon?"—and the younger nun answered, "Yes, Mother."

Mother . . . but in what a different context was the word used here! Bright, clean, airy buildings, even though designed without imagination, were better raised where an ancient evil had once had possession—and the nuns' innocence would keep that evil forever at bay. The multiple-stores were filled with shoppers, all making their small and ordinary purchases. Andy's horrors . . . and the touch of the rusted forceps . . . seemed curiously remote. I felt the terror of the night slipping from me, as though I had been suddenly released from the bondage of a nightmare not of this world.

The silence of a suburban lunchtime descended on the new Kibblesham. The shops closed, the children went into their midday "dinner." Even the dogs retired for either a meal or a sleep.

I got into the car, and was about to start up, when I heard it.

I sat, frozen, trying to tell myself that what I had heard was nothing—the wind in a television antenna (except that there was no wind on that still day), that an errand boy was whistling (save that there was no errand boy), that it was the song of a bird (save that, now, there were no more trees, and no more birds to sing at Kibblesham). I waited, remembering what Andy had said about those who even touched the forceps of the Great Mother.

I did not have to wait long. This place was consecrated to a force from which a little modern rebuilding could hardly drive it—both Andy and I had been foolish to believe that the Ancient Mysteries may be expelled from their Ancient Places.

I did not start the car. I sat in the noonday silence of Kibblesham and waited.

The piping had begun. . . .

TIME GRABBER

Gordon R. Dickson

Feb. 16, 2631—Dear Diary: Do I dare do it? It's so frustrating to have to be dependent upon the whims of a physicist like Croton Myers. I'm sure the man is a sadist—to say nothing of being a pompous ass with his scientific double-talk, and selfish to boot. Otherwise, why won't he let me use the time-grapple? All that folderol about disrupting the fabric of time.

He actually patted me on the shoulder today when I swallowed my righteous indignation to the extent of pleading once more with him. "Don't take it so hard, Bugsy," he said—imagine—"Bugsy"—to me, Philton J. Bugsomer, B.A., M.A., L.L.D., Ph.D., "in about twenty years it'll be out of the experimental stage. Then we'll see if something can't be done for you."

It's intolerable. As if a little handful of people would be missed out of the whole Roman Empire. Well, if I can't do it with his permission, I will do it without. See if I don't. My reputation as a scholar of sociomatics is at stake.

Feb. 18, 65: MEMO TO CAPTAIN OF THE POLICE: The emperor has expressed a wish for a battle between a handful of gladiators and an equal number of Christians. Have gladiators but am fresh out of Christians. Can you help me out?

(signed) Lictus,
CAPTAIN OF THE ARENA

Feb. 19, 65: MEMO TO CAPTAIN OF THE ARENA: I think I might be able to lay my hands on a few Christians for you—possibly. And then again I might not. By the way, that's a nice little villa you have out in the Falernian Hills.

(Signed) Papirius,
CAPTAIN OF POLICE

Feb. 19, 65: Papirius:
All right, you robber. The villa's yours. But hurry! We've only got a few days left.

L.

Feb. 21, 65: Dear L:
Thanks for the villa. The papers just arrived. By an odd coincidence I had overlooked the fact that we already had sixteen fine, healthy Christians on hand, here. I am sending them on to you.

Love and kisses,
P.

Feb. 22, 2631: Dear Diary: Congratulate me! I knew my chance would come. Late last night I sneaked into the physics building. That fool of a Myers hadn't even had the sense to lock the door of his laboratory. I opened it and went in, pulled down the shade, turned on the light, and was able to work in complete security. Luckily, I had already played on his credulity to the extent of representing myself as overawed by the mechanical mind, and so induced him to give me a rough idea of how he operated the time-grapple (this over the lunch table in the Faculty Club) so, with a little experimenting, and—I will admit it—some luck, I was able to carry off my plans without a hitch.

I bagged sixteen young males from the period of Nero's reign—along somewhere in the last years. By great good luck they happened to be Christians taken prisoner and destined for the Roman Games. Consequently, the guards had them all huddled together in a tiny cell. That's why the time-grapple was able to pick up so many at one grab. They came along quite docilely, and I have quartered them in the basement of my house where they seem to be quite comfortable and I can study them at my leisure.

Wait until the Sociomatics department here at the University sees the paper I'll write on this!

Feb. 23, 65: MEMO TO CAPTAIN OF POLICE: Where are my Christians? Don't you think you can gyp me out of my villa and then not deliver.

> (signed) Lictus,
> CAPTAIN OF ARENA

Feb. 23, 65: MEMO TO CAPTAIN OF THE ARENA: You got your Christians. I saw them delivered myself. Third cell on the right, beneath the stands.

> (signed) Papirius,
> CAPTAIN OF POLICE

Feb. 24, 65: MEMO TO CAPTAIN OF POLICE: I tell you they're not there.

> (signed) Lictus,
> CAPTAIN OF THE ARENA

Feb. 24, 65: MEMO TO CAPTAIN OF ARENA: And I tell you they are.

> (signed) Papirius,
> CAPTAIN OF POLICE

P.S. Are you calling me a liar?

Feb. 25, 65: MEMO TO CAPTAIN OF POLICE: I tell you THEY'RE NOT THERE. Come on over and look for yourself if you don't believe me.

> (signed) Lictus,
> CAPTAIN OF THE ARENA

Feb. 25, 65: Listen, Lictus:

I don't know what kind of a game you think you're playing, but I haven't time to bother with it right now. Whether you know it or not, the Games load a lot of extra work on the police. I'm up to my ears in details connected with them, and I won't put up with having you on my neck, too. I've got the receipt signed by your jailer, on delivery. Any more noise from your direction and I'll turn it, together with your recent memos, over to the Emperor himself and you can straighten it out with him.

Papirius

Feb. 25, 2631: Dear Diary: What shall I do? How like that sneaky, underhanded physicist to be studying historical force lines in the Roman era, without mentioning it to me. Myers came into lunch today fairly frothing with what can only be described as childish excitement and alarm. It seems he had discovered a hole in the time fabric in the year 65, although he hasn't so far been able to place its exact time and location (this is, of course, my sixteen Christians) and he tried to frighten us all with lurid talk about a possible time collapse or distortion that might well end the human race—if the hole was not found and plugged. This is, of course, the most utter nonsense. Time collapse, indeed! But I can take no chances on his discovering what actually happened, and so I realized right away that I had to plug the hole.

The idea of putting back my Romans is, of course, unthinkable. They are beginning to respond in a most interesting manner to some spatial relationship tests I have been giving them. Therefore I clearly sounded out Myers to find the necessary factors to plug the hole. I gather that any sixteen men would do, provided they conformed to the historically important characteristics of the Roman group. This sounded simple when he first said it, but since then the problem has been growing in my mind. For the important characteristics are clearly that they all be Christians who are willing to die for their faith. I might easily find such a group in Roman times but in order to hide the gap my replacements will make I will have to take them from some other era—one Myers is not studying. I have only a day or two at most. Oh, dear diary, what shall I do?

PHYSICIST GIVEN KNOCKOUT
DROPS

(University News)
(Feb. 27, 2631). When Croton Myers, outstanding physicist
and professor of Physical Sciences at the university here
showed a marked tendency to snore during his after-lunch
classes, his students became alarmed and carried him
over to the University Hospital. There, doctors discovered
that the good professor had somehow been doped. There
were no ill effects, however, and Dr. Myers was awake
and on his feet some eighteen hours later. Authorities
are investigating.

Feb. 29, 2631: Dear Diary: SUCCESS! Everything has
been taken care of. I am so relieved.

Feb. 28, 1649 (From the Journal of John Stowe)—Today,
by the will of the Lord, we are safely on our way from
Appleby, fifteen men under the valiant leadership of
Sergeant Flail-of-the-Lord Smith, having by our very
presence in Appleby served to strike fear into the hearts of
the papist plotters there, so that they dispersed—all of the
troop in good health and spirits save only for one small
trouble, of which I will relate.

It hath come to pass, that, being on our way from
Appleby to Carlisle, there to join the forces of Captain
Houghton, if God shall suffer such to come to pass, we
have found ourselves at nightfall in a desolate section of
the country, wasted by the late harrying and pillaging. We
decided to pitch camp where we found ourselves rather
than adventure farther in the dark.

Therefore, we made ourselves comfortable with such
simple fare as contents a servant of the Lord, and our
provisions supplied, and having sung a goodly hymn and
given ourselves over to an hour or so of prayer for the
pleasing of our souls, some among us fell to talking of the
nature of the surrounding waste, recalling that from heathen
times it hath had the name of being a place of most evil
and supernatural resort. But our good Sergeant Flail-of-
the-Lord, speaking up cheerily, rebuked those who talked
so, saying "Are we not all servants of the Lord, and strong

in his wrath? Therefore, gird ye up your courage and take heart."

But there were still some among us—and I do confess some sort of the same weakness in myself—who found the blackness and desolation press still heavily upon our souls, reminding us of manifold sins and wickedness whereby we had placed ourselves in danger of the Pit and the ever-present attacks of the Enemy. And our good Sergeant, seeing this, and perceiving we needed the sweet comfort and assuagement of the Word of the Lord, he bade us sit close by him, and opening his Book which was the Word of the Lord, read to us from II Kings Chapter 9, concerning the overthrow and just fate of Jezebel, whereat we were all greatly cheered and entreated him that he read more to us.

But it happened at this time that a small trouble was thrust upon us, inasmuch as it appeared to all of us that the wide and empty fields of night which surrounded us were whisked away and the appearance of a cell, stone on three sides, and a thick iron grating on the fourth, surrounded us. Whereat we were at first somewhat surprised. However, our good Sergeant, looking up from his Book, bade us mind it not, for that it was no more than a manifestation of whatever unholy spirits plagued the spot and which they had called up in jealous defiance of the sweet virtue of the Lord's word, as he had been reading it.

On hearing this, all were reassured, and, the hour being late, lay down to rest, inasmuch as we are to march at the first break of dawn. So, now, as I write these words, by God's mercy, nearly all are disposed to slumber, saving that the enchantment of the cell doth make somewhat for cramped quarters and I do confess that I, myself, am somewhat ill-at-ease, being accustomed to the good pressure of my stout sword against my side as I go to sleep. This, however, may not be helped, for, since it is the custom of our troop to lay aside all sharp tools on coming into the presence of the Lord our weapons are hidden from us by the enchantment and it would be a mark of lack of faith to pretend to search for them.

And, so, thanks be to the Lord, I will close this entry in my journal and dispose myself for a night of rest.

March 1, 65: MEMO TO CAPTAIN OF POLICE: I notice you finally got cold feet and got those Christians over here after all. But I warn you. I'm not yet altogether satisfied. They look like pretty odd-appearing Christians to me. More like barbarians. And if you've rung in something like that on me, I warn you, the Emperor will hear of it. My gladiators are too valuable to risk with a group of Goths or Vandals.

(signed) Lictus,
CAPTAIN OF THE ARENA

March 1, 65: MEMO TO CAPTAIN OF ARENA: Papirius has unfortunately been called out of the city on police business, and it is uncertain when he will be able to get back. I am sure, however, that if the Captain said that these men were Christians, they are Christians. However, if you're doubtful, there's nothing easier than to test the matter. Give any of them a pinch of incense and see if they'll sacrifice to the gods to gain their freedom. If they won't, they're Christians. You know how these things work.

(Signed) Tivernius
Acting CAPTAIN OF POLICE

(From the Journal of John Stowe) March 2, 1649: Lo! Satan is upon us and his devils do surround us. Trusting in the Lord, however, we have no fear of them.

Early this morning we awoke to find the enchantment still strong about us. Whereupon we took counsel together concerning our conduct in this strait. After several hours of discussion, it was decided that we could not necessarily be considered remiss in our military duties for not pushing on to Carlisle when bound and held by devils. This settled, it remained only to decide on our course of conduct toward these imps of Satan, and Sergeant Flail-of-the-Lord hath determined this by ordering that all present be industrious in prayer and considering of the good works of the Lord.

So it fell out that about the third or fourth hour after sunrise when we were engaged in singing that hymn of sweet comfort—

Lo! We shall crush His enemies,
And drown them in their blood,

—that a fat, balding devil of middle age, somewhat wrapped and entwined in a sheet of bed linen approached the outer grating of our cell and did speak with us.

At first we were slow in understanding; but as it did happen that by good chance I had had some teaching in my youth in papist ways, it was not long before I realized that this devil was speaking a particularly barbarous and unnatural form of Latin; and, on my conveying this information to Sergeant Flail-of-the-Lord, it was decided that I should speak with the devil for all of us.

I began by abjuring him to turn from the ways of the devil and cast himself upon the mercy of the Lord. But, so imperfect were the creature's wits and so inadequate his grasp of the tongue in which we conversed that he failed to grasp my meaning. Whereupon, I demanded of him by what right he held us and he did name several devils with Romish names and, producing several objects of strange manufacture, seemed to call on us for some kind of action.

At this point, Sergeant Flail-of-the-Lord interrupted to order me that I draw the devil out in conversation and learn whatsoever I could, that the knowledge might be a means to breaking the enchantment. Therefore, I did show interest and beseeched the devil to further explain himself.

Whereupon he did so. And it was apparent immediately that our wise Sergeant, praise the Lord, had correctly judged the state in which we were held. For after a great deal of words which I had some trouble interpreting, it became apparent that this spawn of the Devil, this creature of Satan was endeavoring by means of foul enticements and false promises of release from our enchantment, to cozen us into bowing down to graven images.

No sooner had I understood this, than I was filled with the wrath of the Lord, and, feeling His hand upon me, spoke words of fire to the lost being before me. I observed that he quailed, although odd as it seems, some of our troop claim to have noticed a slight trace of satisfaction upon his hellish visage. Whereupon he closed the interview with a question.

"Are you all Christians?" he demanded of me.

I answered, "Yes," and, rubbing his hands together with an expression of glee he hurried off.

I related all this to my comrades and the Sergeant. The Sergeant then advised us that we continue as he had before, saying that no doubt we were not alone at the mercy of the Devil, but that we were being somewhat tested by the Lord, and as long as our faith in Him remained steadfast, no harm could surely come from this.

So hath the day past, very decently in praying and godly conversation. From scraps of conversation I have overheard from neighboring cells it becometh apparent that tomorrow we are to be thrown into the 'Arena,' which I take to be a devilish word for the pit. So be it. We abide the issue, all of us, with firm faith and quiet hearts. Amen.

March 2, 2631: Dear Diary: What a vexatious group! What on earth shall I do? These Romans seem to be pining away and losing interest in my tests, taking them lackadaisically, if at all. I'm sure I don't know what's wrong. I've given them the most attractive apparatus I can find, different colored little balls and pegs and objects, and brightly-lit shadow cards to study. I've piped all sorts of cheerful music into the basement and given them authentic Roman diets of the period and all they wanted to eat. They just don't seem to have any interest. I can't imagine what's wrong.

(From the notebook of Croton Myers) March 2, 2631:

11:02 P.M.—Dial settings. A-26.24, B-5.1, C-2 73779 Calibration check, Vernier check. (Run 73)

Found it. Year 65, our calendar, Feb. 22, 10:15 P.M. (Approx). Sixteen individuals. Time scar to present date and year. Hole plugged on or about Feb. 27. Structure therefore safe middle late Roman era, disregarding minor time-thread damage which runs out anyway. However—took general check on hunch, and hunch confirmed. There's another hole even closer to our time. I can tell by the strains on the major time-threads. No time to trace it down now. We've got about five hours worth of elasticity in the present time-fabric before there'll be (a) a time collapse, or (b) an attempt by the fabric to rearrange itself to relieve the strain. Even the rearrangement could do for us. This second hole's too close to our own period.

I'm no Sherlock, but to me it adds up to only one answer—Bugsomer. I'm going over and see if I can force the information out of him.

The damn fool!

March 3, 65: TO THE CAPTAIN OF THE ARENA: Order your gladiators to stretch out this battle with the Christians. I don't want a sheep-slaughter. I want some sport. Some running around and excitement. See to it.

NERO, Imp.

March 3, 65: TO THE EMPEROR: Hail Caesar! I will do whatever I can when the time comes. But you know how uncooperative these Christians are. They won't even pick up their swords and armor. They want to be martyrs. However, I promise that the Emperor will not be disappointed.

(signed) Lictus
CAPTAIN OF THE ARENA

Dear Diary: I have no idea what the date is, so I just won't put any down. If the world goes topsy-turvy, it's not *my* fault. I'm all in a flutter. I hardly know where to begin writing.

I guess it all began when that pigheaded Myers came breaking into my house in the middle of the night. Breaking in, literally! My front door was locked, naturally, so he just kicked in a window and walked through it. I was down in the basement with my poor Romans, who hadn't been sleeping too well lately. I was trying to get them to take some barbiturates, but they seemed afraid to do so for some reason. They preferred to turn and toss on their cushions all night.

Well, at any rate I heard a noise. And then the next thing I heard was his bull voice calling, "Bugsy! Bugsy!"

Before I could head him off he was at the top of the steps and clumping down. My poor Romans just stared at him.

"So here you are," he said triumphantly.

"Is that odd?" I replied. "After all, it's my house. And, while we're on the matter, I'd like to know how you got in, and by what right—"

"Oh, shut up," he said and pointed at my Romans. "Are these the sixteen you stole first?"

"I don't know what you're talking about," I answered coldly. "These are some foreign students from one of my classes. We're holding a seminar in Roman customs."

He just snorted, and ignoring me entirely, turned to the nearest Roman and started jabbering at him in barbarous high-school Latin. I even had trouble following him, but my Roman didn't. His face lit up and before I could say a word he was telling Myers all about what had happened to them, and the tests I'd been giving them. And right then and there, I learned something about Roman ingratitude. Can you believe it? Those sixteen young fellows weren't the least bit thankful for being saved from death in the Arena. All that concerned them was the fact that they were homesick. Homesick! For lions and gladiators!

I interrupted and asked my Roman whether he hadn't been well treated. And he turned on me and said—almost in those very words—that he had—he'd been too well treated. He'd been a hardworking artisan and Christian all his life and it didn't come natural to him to loll around on cushions and play with children's toys. He ended up by saying that if I gave him another test he'd ram it down my throat.

Well, after something like that, I was only too glad to get rid of them. I told Myers so and we started up the stairs. Just at that moment there was the most curious shiver—decidedly unpleasant—and we all suddenly found ourselves back at the foot of the stairs again. Myers turned white as a sheet.

He gasped. "Good God, I didn't think it would start this quickly!"—And I don't mind telling *you*, dear Diary, that for a second even I felt a touch of fear.

We hurried, all eighteen of us, across the darkened campus and up to his laboratory. Twice more those curious shivers threw us back a step or two in time, and we had to do things over.

"It's cracking faster," said Myers, and herded my Romans into an area marked off by chalk lines on the floor. Myers took me by the arm.

"Listen," he said, "and listen good, because I don't have time to say it twice. I've got the sixteen Romans waiting in a trigger area. There's a trip mechanism that will throw them back to their own time the minute there's an opening for them to fit into. I'm going to stay here and operate the machine. I want you to ride the time-grapple back to the Arena and see that the others—you said they were Roundheads?—and nobody but they get into the time-grapple for transference back to their own time."

"Me?" I said. "Into the time-grapple. I certainly will not—" Before I could finish he seized me by the shoulders and pushed me into the time-grapple area.

The moment I stumbled across the line the laboratory faded around me. I felt a moment of nausea, and then I was swinging, unsupported and apparently invisible above the royal box in the arena. When I leaned down I was right on a level with Nero himself. I took one horrified look at him, gasped and turned away.

I looked down in the arena, and saw immediately why Myers had sent me back. The time-grapple would, of course, have to get the Roundheads all on one grab and it would be impossible until they were all close together. I knew that, back in the laboratory, Myers could see me apparently standing on the floor in front of him and his devilish machine. He could also, of course, see Nero and part of the Royal box. I would have to direct him to the Roundheads when the time came.

I looked out in the arena, and groaned. The door to the cells was just opening and the Roundheads were filing out onto the field. The gladiators were already out; the Roundheads were too far dispersed for the time-grapple to grab them.

"Get together, get together!" I cried—but of course they couldn't hear me as long as I was in the time-grapple field.

Just then Nero spoke up next to my ear, and I *could*

hear him, because of the auditory equipment built into the field.

"My dear," he was saying petulantly to a thickly powdered, fat-faced woman beside him. "Look at those Christians! And Lictus promised me that I shouldn't be disappointed. Look how sober and dull they are. They usually come on with their faces lit up, almost exalted."

"Perhaps," said the woman, "this group doesn't feel so much like being martyred. Maybe they'll run around a bit more."

I could stand no more of this, and signaled Myers to move the field down toward the Roundheads. The idiots were still too far apart to be picked up and were talking together in the odd, seventeenth-century English.

"What think you, Sergeant," said one fresh-faced youngster, "are we to be put to trial by those armored demons, yonder?"

"It may be, John," replied the individual addressed as Sergeant.

The young man sighed. "I feel the hand of the Lord strong upon me," he said. "None the less, had I but my claymore—"

"Fie, John Stowe," reproved the Sergeant. "Let not your mind dwell upon earthly matters. Look rather upon yon armed demons, with a mind to marking their true natures. See yon demon with the chased shield, which is surely Pride. And the other beside him, whom, by his lean and envious face I clearly read as Covetousness."

And the Sergeant went on giving names to the various gladiators, so that the other Roundheads became interested and drifted over. I was beginning to have hopes of snatching them up immediately when the Sergeant wound up his little discussion.

"And besides, John Stowe," he said, "if the Lord wisheth us to have weapons, He surely will provide them."

At this moment, an attendant of the Arena leaned over the stone parapet that encircled the field and dropped a bundle of swords and armor.

"What did I tell you?" said the Sergeant.

So they dispersed in the process of putting on the armor, and the chance was lost.

"What's holding things up?" boomed the voice of Myers in my ear.

"The battle," I snapped. "They're supposed to fight those gladiators."

"What!" yelled Myers. "Stop them. Don't let them do it. They've all got to get back alive."

"What can I do?" I asked bitterly. "It's up to the Roundheads."

And, indeed it was. There is no way of knowing how many lives were depending upon those Roundheads at that moment.

At any rate, there was a toot on a horn, or some kind of signal like that, and off they went.

"Do you take Pride, Stowe," said the Sergeant. "And so each of the rest of you pick out a cardinal sin. I, myself, will take Covetousness." He lifted his Roman short sword over his head and shouted like a wild man.

"Now, LET GOD ARISE!" he shouted, and the Roundheads charged toward the enemy.

"I'm moving you back to Nero," said Myers' voice in my ear. "Maybe we can put pressure on him somehow."

I was swooped back to the royal box. But by the time I got there the situation was such that neither of us could think of anything to do. Nero was bouncing around like a fat toad, squeaking at the top of his lungs.

"Why—what—what—" he was squealing. "What are they doing? You Christians, stop chasing my gladiators, do you hear me? Stop it! Stop it!"

Somebody blew that silly horn again, and the gladiators stopped, but the Roundheads went right on.

"Guard thyself, Pride!" the stentorian voice of John Stowe floated up to us in the royal box. Beside Stowe there was a clang and a thud as the Sergeant decapitated Covetousness.

Gladiators were getting cut to pieces right and left. But not for long. Nero was ordering his own guard out of the stands, down into the Arena.

"I've got an idea," I called to Myers. "Drop me on the field."

"It better be good," he grunted. "Or you'll go the same way they're going!"

He dropped me. I came into sight of those Romans suddenly, and the shock of my appearance temporarily halted the Praetorian Guard. They looked from me to Nero and back again.

"To me!" I yelled, running over the field, waving my arms. "To me, Roundheads!"

Well, they looked up at the sound of my English voice and, to make a long story short, gathered around in short enough space for Myers to pick them up. The field faded around us. . . .

March 3, 65: TO THE CAPTAIN OF THE ARENA: I thought I ordered you to produce Christians for slaughter! What devilish magic have you loosed upon Rome under the guise of Christians? I order you to capture those sixteen hell-spawned devils who murdered our gladiators. At once!

NERO, Imp.

March 3, 65: TO THE EMPEROR: My Caesar! I know not how the sixteen Christians escaped from the arena— replacing themselves with sixteen others. I have contacted Papirius, Captain of Police, and he informs me it must be a plot on the part of the Christians for an uprising throughout the City. I believe the missing sixteen are in hiding. My Guard will be ordered out at once to apprehend them

(signed) Lictus,
CAPTAIN OF THE ARENA

March 3, 65: TO CAPTAIN OF POLICE: I have at hand information from Lictus, Captain of the Arena, concerning the plot of the Christians to overthrow Roman rule with today's events in the Arena as a signal for insurrection. Drastic action must be taken. Burn out every festhole in Rome where the Christians are massed. At once!

NERO, IMP.

*March*3, 65: TO THE EMPEROR: Hail, Caesar! Your command has been obeyed. Even now the Christians burn in their catacombs!

(signed) Papirius,
CAPTAIN OF POLICE

March 3, 65: TO THE CAPTAIN OF POLICE: Are you mad, you fool? By whose authority have you put the torch to Rome? The flames are spreading throughout the city—underground—and already are at the Arena dungeons! Send help to quench the fires!

Lictus,
CAPTAIN OF THE ARENA

March 3, 65: TO THE CAPTAIN OF THE ARENA: Don't call me a fool, you idiot! How was I to know the fire would spread through the catacombs! I can't send you any men. I'm appealing to the Emperor for help myself. The fires are getting beyond control!

Papirius,
CAPTAIN OF POLICE

March 3, 65: TO THE EMPEROR: Mighty Caesar! The Christians have turned the fires against us and our city is in danger of being consumed. What shall we do?

(signed) Papirius,
CAPTAIN OF POLICE

March 3, 65: TO THE CAPTAIN OF POLICE: You imbecile! I order you to burn out the Christians and you set fire to the entire city! Already my palace is on fire! Consider yourself under arrest! Report to me after you have the flames under control. Or perhaps you'd prefer throwing yourself into the closest inferno and cheat me of the pleasure of roasting you alive later!

NERO, Imp.

March 3, 65: TO THE EMPEROR: The city is engulfed, my Caesar! I shall die fighting the flames. But what of you, my Emperor? I shall pray to the Gods that you be spared my fate.

(signed) Papirius,
CAPTAIN OF POLICE

March 3, 65: TO THE EX-CAPTAIN OF POLICE: The Gods be damned—I'm getting the hell out of Rome!

NERO, Imp.

April 1, 2631: Dear Diary: Myers has seen to it for my transfer. Oh, he's clever and all that to keep the fact hidden that I used the time-grapple. But I can't see what all the fuss is about. We corrected the time stress before anything critical could happen. The way he carries on you'd think we did something (I, that is) that would go down in history. A ridiculous thought, but then Myers is a physicist and you know what suspicious natures they have. . . . I often wonder though how the games did turn out that afternoon. . . .

SURVEY OF THE THIRD PLANET

Keith Roberts

Superradio to Hy Caslon, somewhere in Sector twelve three-five oh-seven:

Hy, Best Pal and Dealer,

For once I've beaten you! I've warped three vessels into observation orbits 'round the third planet of System Ninety, which I think fulfills Galactic Regs: the pickings are mine! Instrument checks indicate a type seven oxy-nitrogen atmosphere, good humidity, mean equatorial temp very reasonable, etc., etc., and as you know the chlorophyll absorption bands showed up from way out in the heavens, so I think this could be a nice little world. Inhabited almost certainly, hominids for a bet, I'd say from the setup Class IV or V Primitives. Very nice indeed, too bad I'm not in the mood for sharing. Though any time you want to, just look in on me; you'll find me cooling my feet in one of those blue oceans I can see right from where I sit. Only one thing wrong in my little old life right now, I don't like the primary; I never could stand the emission from these dingy yellow brutes. But as ever, I'm prepared to suffer for the sake of Trade. Wire my coordinates in to our people will you, there's a dear good chap, and tell them I'm going down. I'll keep you posted on developments.

Raf Trigg, dealer.

On board ship, somewhere at sea.

Dear Uncle Mark,

Excuse the air of secrecy but you know what military regs. are like; one can't be too careful, especially when there's a bit of a flap on! As a matter of fact, I couldn't be much more explicit as to my whereabouts if I tried. I'm taking passage back in a troopship, and so far the only thing I've found out for sure is that I hate troopships. Not that I didn't know that before! We hug the coast, stop here, drop men off there; I was bored the first day out and the succeeding five or six haven't made things any better. No space, gear piled all over the decks, characters being sick from time to time on your feet, food bad and next to nonexistent; but you didn't want to hear a catalogue of complaints I'm quite sure and anyway it's pretty good to be coming home at all, particularly under the circumstances.

You asked me to give you an off-the-cuff report on the so-called Mystery War. I'll do my best, though that probably won't satisfy your thirst for knowledge; I know you of old! I can't deny I was pretty intimately involved, though that doesn't mean I'm in a position to be too definite about anything.

You know the God-forsaken hole I was drafted to a couple of years back so there's no point going into details. Enough to say that I rapidly got as fed up as the rest of the blokes on camp, and being ADC to the Old Man didn't exactly help my state of mind. Things weren't too bad while I was settling in but I soon got into the sort of deadly routine I expect you know only too well. Mornings I'd take a stroll 'round camp, sign the duty rosters, inspect the guardhouse; supervise punishment parade if there was one. Most of the time our people were too bone-idle to get into much in the way of scrapes. Then I'd have a look at the Old Man's flower beds and whistle up a fatigue party to water them if the damn plants looked too dry. And that was virtually that for the day. Lunch in the mess, siesta till about four, an hour for bathing and changing and down to one of the local hovels for a few stoups of mead. Then to bed, with the whole ghastly cycle starting again in a few hours' time.

There were odd excitements of course; we had a desertion once and there was a solitary court-martial. Rather low type got involved with one of the local popsies, the details are horribly sordid and anyway I've forgotten half of them. And all the time the rain, the fog, the drizzle; doesn't that blasted country ever get any sun?

But I've already wandered well off the point. Sticking to facts, the first intimation of trouble came just about two months ago. It was late at night. I'd been nursing a toothache for a couple of hours and I could see I wasn't going to get much in the way of sleep. I gave it up as a bad job, dressed, and had a walk 'round camp. It was lousy weather as usual, cold and with a spitting rain; things were dead quiet and looked like staying that way. As it happened, they didn't. I was standing in the guardroom yarning with the duty officer when Hell's delight broke out just beyond the perimeter; yells, howls, shrieks fit to wake the dead. At the outset there wasn't much doubt in my mind as to what was going on. As you know, the temper of the locals could hardly be called jovial at the best of times and there aren't many of them that can resist taking a sly poke at the occupying forces when they think they see half a chance. For what it's worth, my own opinion is that the rain sends them all more or less permanently crackers. . . .

I stepped out fairly smartly expecting we were in for some sort of night attack. They didn't happen all that often and when they did they never amounted to much; one or two of our people might get slightly knocked about but we usually managed to bowl over half a dozen locals before they gave it best. In fact, we more or less looked forward to the odd dustup; it all helped break the monotony.

For once though, I was wrong. I'd hardly taken a dozen steps before I was bowled over by a rush of natives, all rolling their eyes and waving their arms and yelling blue murder. Torches were showing here and there; by their light I saw a mass of humanity struggling with the guards at the main gate. Our chaps were being shoved back from the perimeter already, and if the din was anything to go by, there were plenty more wogs still out on the heath. I ordered a general turnout. That was fatal of course; within minutes the Old Man was yelling for his boots and the war had started with a vengeance.

By the time we'd secured the perimeter and got things more or less under control a couple of dozen of the invaders had been rounded up and shoved in the guardhouse. You could have heard them a mile away all yelling and jabbering in that infernal language of theirs. The Old Man didn't waste any time arguing; he simply marched in, ploughed his way to the orderly table, bellowed like a bull and brought his hand down flat on the wood with a smack that nearly lifted the roof off the place. That means shut up in anybody's dialect. The locals shut up, abruptly, and we started trying to get some sense out of them.

That wasn't easy. The only chap we had who was really fluent in the lingo was away on some damn fool course or other, and I'd never bothered to learn more than the few words I needed to haggle in the local markets. The Old Man of course had a system with foreigners; it consisted of yelling at the top of his voice, waving his arms and sticking a few extra 'oes' on the ends of words. Sometimes it worked better than others; this was one of the times it didn't work at all. I think the wogs were all too badly scared to start with.

It was obvious they weren't a war party. The men weren't armed, a good proportion of them were only half clothed and they had women and children with them. Some of the faces looked familiar; it seemed they came from a biggish village some four or five miles from camp. I saw one chap I'd had odd dealings with. He'd struck me before as being a little brighter than average; I managed to get the Old Man to quieten down long enough to try to talk to him. He told me some sort of story, mostly by sign language; the others backed him up, wailing and howling by turns. I gathered finally there'd been an attack on the village. Who'd done the attacking and how many of them there had been I couldn't find out. I don't think the people knew themselves. They'd scattered in all directions apparently, though a good proportion of them seemed to have run our way. That struck me as typical; they'd call us everything they could lay their tongues to until there was a bit of bother, then they'd come scuttling for protection. I asked the chap exactly how the attack had been mounted, how the enemy had been armed. I didn't get very far with that either. He started yelling and quivering all over again; he seemed to be talking about some sort of light but when

I repeated the word to him in his own dialect he shook his head and jabbered worse than ever, using the sounds for "fire" and "burning." Had there been a light or a fire or both? "Both," he said, "yes, both. Light. Fire. The same." So that left me with a phrase. A fiery light. The light that burned. I shook my head; I'd never heard of such a thing.

To support their argument one of the refugees produced a little pouch or sack, shook its contents out on the table. The Old Man's eyes dilated; somebody screamed and there was a general surging backward movement. On the table lay a human hand, severed at the wrist. Yet not severed in any normal fashion. There was no blood; the end of the stump was blackened, as though it had been cauterized with a hot iron. Whatever had lopped it off had seared the veins in the same instant, sealing them shut. I felt an odd sensation in the pit of my stomach. This strange thing had been done by the 'light that burned.'

We stood to until dawn, watching the orange reflection on the skyline where the village still burned. Just before first light the rain became heavier, extinguishing the flames. We organized a scouting detail; the men tramped off into the downpour stolidly enough but it was fairly obvious they didn't care for the job overmuch. I didn't blame them; I'd seen something myself of the guerrilla tactics the locals used. Pretty effective even against a well-armed column. At that time of course, we still thought we were dealing with a normal enemy, some raiding party or other down from the hills.

Our people came back some time later with nothing to report except that for some distance 'round the village the grass was unaccountably charred and stones and rocks had been split as if by great heat. The natives started to wail again. This had been done by the 'light that burned.'

But this time of course our C/O was in a rage that I can only describe as ecstatic. To begin with, he'd lost a good part of a night's sleep, and the base was littered with refugees complete with their goods and chattels. Quite a few natives had managed to make their way to us and they were camping anywhere and everywhere inside the perimeter; there were kids and dogs underfoot and things were generally chaotic. The Old Man issued an ultimatum;

get these people out of sight by noon, or watch out. It was all very well for him to talk, the bastards wouldn't go. We tried to convince them there was nothing to be scared of; the raiders, whoever they'd been, had moved on and it wasn't likely they would return as the village held nothing of much value. In the end we compromised, they said they'd go back if we would send a party along as a safe-conduct. I agreed to that and detailed a couple of dozen men. I went with them myself to see if I could find anything out.

It was all much as the scouts had described. The village was rather scorched but in the main it hadn't suffered much damage. There had certainly been no looting. One or two fires had restarted themselves; we dealt with them easily enough, and hung 'round for a couple of hours watching the people trying to sort things out. Then as nothing much seemed to be happening, I re-formed the men and headed back toward camp. A mile down the road we met an old boy hobbling along on rheumaticky legs and swearing blue fire. He claimed his home had been attacked, his wife and numerous daughters carried off. The aggressors had been armed with peculiar weapons; wherever they were pointed, things had burst into flame. Wood and earth, metal, human bodies, sizzled and vanished.

The pattern sounded horribly familiar. My first impulse was to follow the old chap's urging and try to deal with the thing immediately but I had no authority to act on my own like that; I reminded myself our camp was undermanned, we were a holding garrison, not an army. The temptation was pretty strong but in the end I decided to go by the book, report back and leave the decision to the C/O. It was just as well I did; when I got back I found the camp under emergency alert. The invaders had been in sight from the perimeter; they had observed us for a time, well out of reach of anything we could lob at them, then they had retired. Nobody quite knew what was supposed to happen next.

I made my report. The Old Man was pacing up and down in front of a map of the area. Half a dozen more sightings had come in while I had been away; it looked as though we were fairly well surrounded.

The C/O was in an unusually thoughtful mood. It seemed two main facts had emerged: (1) that the attackers, though few in number, were highly mobile and (2) that they were armed with some weapon that made conventional resistance hazardous. I was shown a piece of metal that had been split by one of the rays; the cut faces had boiled and run as though they had been in a furnace. The Old Man had sent messages to Sector H/Q but so far nothing had been heard. Under normal circumstances the procedure would have been fairly clear; take half a dozen sections of men, beat the surrounding terrain, flush out the nuisance and destroy it on the spot. But the reports and the evidence of the heat-weapons had made even the general cautious. This was something outside all our experience.

I shall never forget the night that followed, or its sequel. We could see the enemy lights moving out on the heath; they were glaring and blue, like no lights I had ever seen. Toward dawn I was snatching a few minutes' rest when the Old Man sent for me. I remember him standing, face lined with tiredness, watching the will-o'-the-wisps glowing out there across the grass. "Well, Paul," he said, "there's something here I don't understand. But I know this. If we don't hit them they'll hit us. . . ."

The plan was simple. We split our infantry into two groups; one was to move out just before dawn and engage the enemy on a close front, the other, by far the larger, would attempt an encircling action. They would start off from camp a couple of hours before so as to be in position when the first party went in. The theory was fine but the results were disastrous.

The invaders had established their camp in a slight hollow overlooked on three sides by rising ground. At first sight they seemed to be in rather a bad position. Even at night the place was easy to find; there was a constant flaring of light from it and 'round about the enemy had rigged up a series of towers. Hanging from them were objects that reminded me of gigantic ploughshares. What their purpose might be I couldn't guess.

I was in charge of the outflanking operation; the Old Man directed the primary attack. We got into position about half an hour before dawn; our people went in at first light and a fairly satisfactory flap started down below. The enemy scuttled about in all directions; I saw many of them shinning up the struts of the towers. The time seemed to be right; I gave my chaps the signal and we started downhill in open order, moving briskly with weapons at the ready. Then it happened. Abruptly, the things that looked like ploughshares broke free of their columns and sailed up into the air. They were nearly soundless; the only noise from them was a faint piping mixed with an odd muttering and grumbling. For a few moments they swirled about aimlessly, spinning like leaves; then they swooped at us, and the rest was confusion.

I dropped flat; one of the things passed low over my head, there was a rushing, a sensation of great heat. I heard screaming; a man blundered past me with his clothes on fire, another fell to his knees staring blankly at the stump of an arm. I saw a line of smoke whip across the grass, then another. It missed me by a yard, passed on and hit a knot of our people. More cries, and a smell of scorching cloth and flesh. Flames were already licking up across the hillside and my men were starting to break and run like rabbits.

It was a massacre, and I could do nothing but watch it. The infantry of the first wave were totally wiped out; I saw my C/O cut down with them. The ploughshares swerved and ducked, glinting in the dawn light; and everywhere they moved the ground beneath them caught fire with a hissing and boiling. As the smoke thickened, I saw beams of light lancing through it. I realized then too late what I was looking at. This was the 'light that burned.'

Resistance was impossible. I was half blinded by smoke; 'round me were nothing but corpses and dying men. I can't remember what my feelings were at the time; I was possibly too stunned for coherent thought. I know I yelled at our people, trying to get the survivors under some sort of control; I stood up and waved, urging them back over the crest of the hill.

The retreat ended a mile or more away. The flying contraptions followed us for a while, piping and swooping; then they whirled back from where they had come and we were left to lick our wounds and count our dead.

I had less than two sections left, and some half dozen walking wounded. Several of them had lost fingers, one man a part of his leg. The rest of the chaps were too paralyzed by fright to speak; it was terrifying to see how quickly a disciplined unit had been reduced to a rabble. I did what little I could for the injured, then I got the survivors into some sort of marching order and headed back to camp.

We moved carefully, taking advantage of what cover we could find, and of course we were slowed by the injured men, so it was midday before we came in sight of the place. I had another shock. The first thing I saw, planted menacingly in the middle of the parade ground, was one of the enemy towers. Half a dozen ploughshares hung from it, their sharp noses pointed outward aggressively. There was no movement 'round about, but there was a litter of bodies. It was hopeless to go on; the invaders had taken our base.

I don't think I've ever felt more inadequate or more alone. I wasn't over the shock of the Old Man's death; I'd cursed him often enough in the past but he was a fine soldier and the whole affair had hit me very hard. And there I was with a handful of men, half of them unfit for combat, cut off from my arms and supplies and facing something I'd never experienced before. I sat on the grass and stared at the distant tower and wondered what in Hell I was going to do.

While I was still trying to make my mind up a couple of the machines rose and began quartering the ground between us and the camp, burning any clumps of bushes that might afford cover. We, the hunters, were being hunted in our turn. We withdrew from the menace; out of sight of the heat-things I formed the men up again and we started a forced march. It was obvious that in our present condition, lacking transport and weapons, we were in no shape to put up a fight even against a normal enemy; my intention was to reach Sector H/Q and hand over what was left of my command.

We walked till evening with only a couple of breaks. By that time I judged we'd put a safe distance between us and the strangers, but I was wrong. As night fell I saw the horizon glowing in a dozen places, ahead and behind. The enemy had extended their operation, encircling us.

A couple of hours after dark we suffered another attack. One of the ploughshares passed almost directly over us. We heard the piping and grumbling in the sky and scattered but we weren't quick enough; the thing wheeled back and the ray from it claimed another victim, the chap with the damaged leg. I came close to dying myself; the fire passed within inches of me as I lay huddled, scorching my arm from elbow to wrist. Then the machine vanished in the dark.

By the small hours it had become obvious we were not going to reach H/Q. The whole sky ahead was bright with flame reflections. I turned away; both the men and I had had enough, my only desire now was to reach the coast.

It seemed the whole countryside was on the move. Several times we passed columns of refugees, some of them hauling their household possessions with them. I commandeered a cart from one group; I could see my injured men weren't going to get much farther without help. The peasants tagged along behind us, calling down a variety of curses on our heads and generally adding to the confusion.

A little before dawn we reached an isolated farmhouse. It was a fairly large place, and some attempt had been made to put it into a state of defense; windows had been barricaded, and a couple of heavy wagons turned on their sides to form a breastwork in front of the door. All useless of course; one might as well have tried to stop thunderbolts with a sunshade as shield oneself with wood against the 'light that burned.'

We were challenged when we came in sight of the place; I went forward alone and managed to persuade the people inside not to start letting fly at us. I got my men under cover in the outbuildings and saw to it they had water, of which we all stood badly in need. I learned the owner of the spread was away on a business trip; what little had been done had been at the instigation of his wife and twenty-year-old daughter.

The mother was too panicky to talk sense. I had a word with the daughter. She was a pretty thing with big eyes and long dark-brown hair; she was badly scared herself but at least, thank God, she spoke my language. Not only spoke it; the very sight of my uniform brought a flood of accusation. We were the occupying forces, she said. We oppressed the country, kept the people poor; but as soon as trouble started we were the first to run. And there was a lot more in the same vein.

I was filthy and stinking of sweat, I'd been on my feet continuously for twenty-four hours and the burn was throbbing mercilessly. I shut her up; from what I could see her family hadn't done badly out of the occupation and I told her so. I described something of what I'd seen on the heath, and the destruction of our troops. Then I pulled away the remnants of my sleeve and held up my glistening arm, "Take your folk out," I said, "and fight them with pitchforks if you wish. For we can do no more."

She changed her tune at that, and brought dressings and ointment. I was still furious; I refused to let her touch me until her people had seen to my men. Before they were through word was brought that the enemy were in sight. I ran outside. Three of the flying devices were visible a mile or so away; they bobbed and dipped, and as they moved the ground beneath them volleyed smoke.

There was no time for argument, the girl at least appreciated that. On her orders the farm animals were turned loose and people started to scuttle about grabbing up what valuables they could take with them. We carried the old lady out squawking and clucking, her hands full of trinkets. We were barely half a mile away when one of the ploughshares appeared over the roof of the farm. It hung purring, tile and brick exploded from beneath it and flames licked up brightly. The girl stood watching the place burn. "I was born there," she said to me. "I never lived anywhere else. It was everything we owned." Then she turned away and started to walk again. That was all; there were no tears.

The column headed for the sea, my men marching in front and to the rear. The farm folk shambled along, bunched 'round the wagon that carried the injured. If anything, the second day was a worse nightmare than the first. Our wounded were in a bad way, we had little water and less food. Night found us some dozen miles from the coast, at the foot of a low range of hills. Before us the sky burned red again and the enemy were close behind. I took a couple of men and went forward to see what the situation was. Our road climbed into the hills; a couple of miles on we came in sight of a line of towers. They stretched right and left as far as we could see over the crests of the downs. Each one was topped by the gaunt shape of a ploughshare.

Immediately ahead and almost beside the road was an enemy camp, the biggest I'd seen so far. We worked our way close up to it and I counted some score of invaders. They were strolling and talking, or sitting 'round what I would have taken for braziers had not the light from them been an odd pale blue. The men were small for the most part and looked normal except for their dress; some of them were carrying queer-looking devices that I took to be weapons, but the majority seemed to be unarmed.

I suppose the sight and the knowledge that we were not completely cut off should have made me afraid. Under normal circumstances it probably would have done but I'd been retreating for two days and I was sick of the whole business. I got very angry; it seemed to me better to end the affair positively one way or another than to crawl about on our bellies any longer being hunted like animals. I went back to our camp and got my men 'round me; and a sorry-looking crowd of ruffians they were!

I didn't waste time getting to the point. I told them briefly what was ahead and that we were trapped. "Now look here," I said. "You all know me; I'm not going to give you a load of bull about the glory of the Empire, I'm just going to tell you the way I see things. We can't go back, and God knows how far those towers reach. I don't fancy trying to outflank them; we can't move fast, and if we're not clear by first light the little people behind will pick us off rather easily. So it looks as if we've got to go through. Now what I propose is this. We'll close up the transport and the injured as near as we dare; then the rest of us, all those that can walk, will nip in and start beating the bastards up. Obviously if they get those damned flying devices of theirs airborne we'll have had it; but I don't think they can do that *as long as we keep them away from the towers.* I expect some of us will get knocked over, but while the shindy is going on the rest will have a chance of slipping through. And just beyond is the sea; there'll be boats of some sort, we can get out of this for good. Now what do you say?"

I could have ordered them of course, but I don't think in that case they would have gone. As it was they talked things over among themselves, then agreed to a man to play it the way I wanted. All in all, they were a damn fine crowd of blokes.

I don't remember much about the actual attack except that I was scared as Hell. We achieved total surprise; the enemy hadn't even bothered to post sentries, I can only assume they thought they'd got us well beaten. There weren't very many of us but when we went in we were making enough noise for an army. Things started to fly almost at once; I took a swing at one of the strangers, odd-looking little chap with a face like an elderly ape, and he ducked and brought up the tube he was holding. The weapon in my hand seemed to catch fire; molten splashes flew from it and I dropped it cursing. I seemed momentarily to see red; I got hold of him 'round the waist, heaved him up and tossed him at one of the braziers. The thing went out with a roar and I headed for the nearest of the towers, picked off a couple of wogs who were shinning up the struts. I saw a ploughshare diving, then there was a flash that hurt my eyes and a series of concussions that knocked me flat. I got up in darkness; fighting was still going on all around me, there were crashes and shrieks. I heard the noise as the wagons started through the pass; then—and this is going to be the most difficult part to believe—the entire sky began to glow with a milky sheen that got brighter and brighter.

I covered my eyes. I was nearly deafened by the racket; a roaring, a sighing, I can't describe it. I didn't see what happened next with any clarity but I had an impression of a . . . shape, something huge, monstrous, settling down onto the camp. All the underside of it seethed with light; some force came from it that blew men sideways, rolling them across the ground. I tried to stand against it but it was like fighting a hurricane. There was an endless time of bellowing and brilliance; I'd given myself up for dead; it seemed the sun had settled on my back and I was witnessing the end of the world. Then I became aware that the din was lessening. I got up blindly; when I could see again there was nothing overhead but a tiny disc that wobbled and diminished, sailed up and up till it seemed to vanish among the very stars.

And there was a cool breeze, blowing against my face.

Well, sir, that's about all there was to it. When we'd sorted ourselves out we found miraculously that none of us had been damaged. It took us longer to realize the fantastic thing that had happened. The camp was deserted; the strangers had gone and their towers and ploughshares and the braziers that had glowed. Nothing remained but shards of twisted metal, tents of some strange fabric that flapped slowly in the night wind. The whole mass of men and equipment had been evacuated in seconds by that . . . sky engine. I don't know another phrase that describes so well what I saw.

Or thought I saw. I've wondered since whether we were all the victims of some hallucination. I'd be prepared to believe I dreamed the whole thing except that there's a scar on my arm that I don't suppose I shall ever lose; and of course there's Martha, the girl I took from the farmhouse. But I don't have the space to talk about her here!

I've read through this letter most carefully and I don't think there's a thing I can add except that I'm looking forward to seeing you in the very near future. Until I do, please give my fondest love to my family, to Mother and Father and to my sister Julia; the last time I saw her I could pull her plaits, but kids grow so fast these days I expect by now she's one of the town beauties, with her own string of suitors!

I'm sending along to you one of the oddments I picked up on the campsite the morning after the attack. As you'll see it's a weird contraption, a sort of twisted tube of some unknown metal with all manner of bits and pieces attached to the broader end. Whether or not it's a weapon I can't say but please handle it carefully, Uncle; I do want to meet you again in this world!

Oh, and while I think of it; the chap who hands you this

letter is my batman. He's an excellent type but he does have a frightful thirst and his pay is sadly in arrears. If you could stake him for beer money I'd be much obliged; I'll square up with you when I see you. I should say he's earned all he can drink; I've got a feeling maybe we all have!

Your Affectionate Nephew,
Paul

Superradio to Hy Caslon, Sector twelve three-oh five-eight:
Dearest Pal,

By the Seven Holders of the Key of Truth, but I'm glad to be talking to you again! We're clear of that accursed planet now, heading for rendezvous nine, repeat *nine*, oh-five-eight. Your Escorters are in station, God bless 'em, all fields are working and the ship is in order; but Hy, the *ground gear!* The wreckage, and the *expense!* And even now I'm wondering how it all happened. . . .

I can tell you one thing though; nothing, repeat *nothing*, would get me near that Hell-hole again; never in a lifetime's Dealing have I come across a cultural *mess* like that! As I said, the natives *were* hominids and they *were* low-level, barely Class Fours. We landed with no trouble at all and started standard Occupation procedure, set up the laser-planes, collected a few study specimens; everything was going fine and according to the book until *that night!* There I was sitting peacefully, not a care in the cosmos; initial geosurveys were complete, the Analyzers were giving us the paws-up, everything was set for a fine fat haul and *crash* . . . into our midst erupts a crowd of smelly, dirty, brainless *barbarians*, and for a few minutes I was sure I'd never see a blue sun again!

In a way of course it's lucky I *did* panic and it's a good thing the Synchronous Orbiter detected me and roboed in as fast as she did; but of course her decision packs had flipped the switch before I was even aboard and my entire groundgear set was atomized; Hy, I lost the *lot!*

I'm putting in a report to the Grand Dealer himself; I'm recommending the planet be closed to Trade from here on in, because what those creatures would be like after a few generations of cultural diffusion is more than I can imagine.

Hy, just *think* of it; Class Fours with a military organization tough enough and flexible enough to retaliate like that! We'd already beaten them once and they *counterattacked* . . . and that with no weapons, no technology, *nothing but their hands* . . . All I can say is, give them a few years to soak up our brand of know-how and they'd be out here *with* us and we should be through, Dear Brother, *through.* Savages, with a military organization . . . it's outside the Principles of Trade!

I'm quite *convinced* the Master will second my ban but until he does there's a fine rich planet that's yours for the taking. Only if you go down you're a *maniac,* a positive *maniac!* Maybe I shouldn't be tipping you off like this; with ninety thrallworlds you must already be the richest Dealer in Galaxy and my mirth-pits would expand to see you lose a *magnum* but I wouldn't do it, not even to you! As it is, GalacTax are already hanging 'round my venerable neck for a cool billion credits, I've got to replace a complete laserset and how the Trigg empire is going to stand up to an intensive program of thulium-mining I just *don't know!*

Goodbye for now, see you (figuratively speaking) in the Warp,

> *Yours in Misery,*
> *Trigg.*

P.S. Have just heard of a *sweet* little world in System Ninety-Seven; have laser barrels and chambers but no spare host-lattices, can you help me out, *please* . . .

Dear Paul,

Many thanks for your letter, which arrived this morning against all expectations. Am sending this to you in the hope that it will reach you at your port of disembarkation. I'll say now your story fascinates me; I'm looking forward to many hours of discussion! As to the *object* your man brought, it's being studied by the best available brains but so far no conclusions whatever have been reached. For my own part, I have strange certainty that nothing more *will* be learned in our lifetimes at least; this whole affair is too far from normal experience for our comprehension. Did those creatures come from the *stars? Could* they have done? The speculations are endless . . .

You'll be glad to hear that your parents and sister are well and that great preparations are being made for your arrival. I think when you finally get home you'll find you're quite a famous man! I would write more, but time prevents me. So until I see you in the flesh I remain

Your Loving Uncle,

L. Marcus Trebonius,

Senator.

a.d.V Kal. Dec.

P.S. Julia says you might very well be a hero, but did you remember to buy her the red cloth in Gaul. . . . ?

DON'T BE A GOOSE

Robert Arthur

Professor Alexander Peabody, with his sister Martha's final emphatic words still ringing in his ears, opened his eyes and blinked at the strange landscape about him. For a moment he felt dizzy, and his head buzzed, with Martha's blunt admonition, "Don't be a goose, Alexander!" seeming to echo through the buzzing.

But some unpleasant symptoms were to be expected. After all, his personality had just hurtled a gap of hundreds of years and taken up temporary abode in a strange body. Such a violent shifting about of the essential ego could not be accomplished without a certain amount of stress and strain.

Gradually the buzzing ceased, the dizziness passed away, and Alexander Peabody, his eyes glistening with excitement, began to examine the details of his surroundings.

He seemed to be sitting on the grassy bank of a small pond, about which grew rushes of unusual height, since they reached well above his head. Beyond them stood a line of curious trees. They were twisted and gnarled, and bore glossy green leaves, but their height astonished him. If they had not been so tall, he would have called them olive trees. But olive trees eighty feet high—No, they must be some new species.

Professor Peabody started to rise from his sitting position, but quickly sat down again. His legs felt odd. All the muscles of his body seemed strange and uncoordinated. And the movement had brought back the dizziness.

That, no doubt, was due to the fact his personality was not yet adjusted to the new body it had taken. Professor Peabody decided to wait for a few moments, until he became a little better integrated, before starting out to explore his surroundings.

There was, after all, no tremendous hurry. It had taken him twenty years of preparation, since he had found that rare magical spell in a very old book, to reach this moment, and if it had not been for Martha's sarcasm, he might not even yet have summoned up the courage to take the plunge.

But for Martha to laugh and tell him not to be a goose when he had told her that he was tired of teaching physics in an obscure college, and that he had determined to experience at least once in his life danger, adventure, excitement, and perhaps romance—that had been galling in the extreme.

Martha's incredulity had come out in those scornful words when he had added that the great, secret yearning of his existence was to affect the course of history in some manner, however slightly.

"Don't be a goose, Alexander!" she had exclaimed. "History isn't made by men like you!"

And she had gone out, slamming the door to his study, before he could even explain his plans.

There is no doubt, Professor Peabody thought—tentatively twisting his head and finding that the dizziness was almost gone—that she was partially right. He was small and unimpressive, with a baldish head, horn-rimmed spectacles, a long, thin neck, and a somewhat receding chin.

But he had never intended to try to affect the course of history in the age in which he lived. His plan, if Martha had only waited to hear it, was to return to an earlier era, when his knowledge, intelligence, and general abilities would loom far larger than they did in the twentieth century.

He could do it. Once, at least. And if Martha had only listened, he could have given her the gist of the magical spell which, after twenty years of work, he had mastered: he could force his personality back through the time-pressure of vanished centuries into some corporeal body that had lived long ago.

But Martha had not waited to hear.

"After all, Martha," Alexander Peabody had said with quiet dignity, "I seem to remember that another Alexander made history once."

But he had said it to a closed door. Perhaps it was just as well. If Martha had stayed, there was no telling what she might have retorted.

The proof, after all, was that, smarting under the sting of her words, he had gone ahead with his plans and—here he was!

Professor Peabody opened his eyes wide, blinking. In the momentary confusion of those first few minutes, he had quite forgotten to wonder *where* he was, in what land he found himself. And for that matter, in what century, what year. He chuckled to himself at the realization. Certainly, before he could plan any moves, he must know those two things.

And a third, equally important. The identity of the body in which his ego now—

Alexander Peabody, glancing down at himself automatically, ceased thinking with horrid abruptness. And his brain reeled in a wild dizziness a dozen times worse than it had before.

He was—he was covered with white feathers!

Professor Peabody shuddered and closed his eyes, keeping them shut lest the dizziness that rocked him unnerve him completely. In heaven's name, what—what—

Then he was startled by a lilting, feminine voice.

"Hello, handsome," it said. "What're you doing 'way off here all by your lonesome? How about coming for a swim? I know a place where we can get some dandy mud worms."

Alexander Peabody's eyes remained shut. He did not want to be impolite, but the unknown female would have to wait for an answer until he felt less giddy. Besides, in his present distress he certainly didn't want to go swimming, and mud worms were the last things he could have desired.

Some corner of Alexander Peabody's reeling brain found itself wondering, however, what language the girl was speaking. He had prepared himself for his great adventure by learning Old English, Old French, Latin, and Sanskrit, and he knew that the curiously harsh, hissing tongue that she spoke was none of these.

"Okay, stuck-up!" the girl spoke again. "Don't answer. Sit there and moult, for all I care!"

Professor Peabody heard a splashing in the pond, and opened his eyes. But there was no girl to be seen. There was no one and nothing, save a large white swan swimming away across the little lake, her tail seeming to express disdain.

No, not a swan, though she looked big enough to be one. A—a goose. And—and—it could only have been she who had told him to "sit there and moult."

"Great heavens!" Professor Peabody groaned aloud, his voice harsh and strange in his ears. "Then I *am* a-a—"

He could not say it. But he did not have to. The goose had been talking to him because *he* was a goose, too!

Something of wild despair rang in Alexander Peabody's brain. He had set out to find adventure, to know romance, to affect history; and he had wound up as a barnyard fowl!

His sister Martha was to blame, of course. With those last scornful words, she had set up some psychic channel which must have led him, when he completed the old spell, into this feathered body.

He would have wept, if a goose had been capable of tears; would have sobbed aloud, if a goose could cry.

Then, bit by bit, he got a grip on himself. He was not an uncourageous man—goose, rather. Handicapped he was, but perhaps all was not lost. In any event, it behooved him to learn what he could of this time and country in which he found himself.

With that decision, he rose and started for the water. He settled comfortably down upon the surface of the pond, and found natural instincts enabling him to swim with ease.

Floating thus on the surface, he arched his neck and found that he could examine his appearance by staring at the inverted reflection of himself.

He was, undeniably, a goose. But he gained a crumb of comfort from the fact he was a large goose, a handsome one, with a long, flexible neck; a large, well-shaped head; bright eyes, with a curious dark ring about them, as if he wore spectacles; and a sturdy, well-muscled body.

Experimentally he flapped his wings. Though he did not

rise from the water, the effort made him move with good speed across the pond. Swiftly enough, in fact, to overtake the goose that had spoken to him.

Alexander Peabody found himself hurrying after her as she swam toward a small stream. He even found himself admiring her, in a way. She was young, streamlined, a pure dazzling white, with a coquettish flirt to her tail. And she had called him handsome.

It was a new experience to Alexander Peabody to be called handsome, and even coming from a goose it was pleasant. It might be entertaining to converse with her. . . .

Professor Peabody coughed—or tried to—abruptly. Obviously a strong residue of personality remained in the feathered body he now inhabited. His thoughts seemed to be part human and part goose. He must not let himself become confused. It was absurd to think of himself, Alexander Peabody, B.S., M.S., and Ph.D., admiring a barnyard fowl. However, she might be a source of much-needed information.

A moment later he drew alongside her and slowed.

"Er," he began. "That is—ah—good afternoon."

It was remarkably difficult to think what to say to a goose, and his initial effort drew no response. Professor Peabody tried again.

"I—that is, I hope I wasn't rude just now," he said.

His companion tossed her head, and he caught her peering at him from the corners of small, bright eyes. Still she said nothing.

"The truth is," Peabody continued, "I was a bit dizzy, and I had my eyes closed till the dizziness went away."

"Oh, that's all right," Miss Goose said now, evidently considering his apology humble enough. "I know how it is. You can call me Edna."

"Ah—Edna," Professor Peabody repeated. "A pretty name. But I was wondering, Miss—er, Edna, if you could tell me the date."

"Date?" Edna looked at him in puzzlement.

"I mean, what year is it?"

"Year? What is a year?"

"Uh—that is, it doesn't matter," Professor Peabody answered. Naturally, a goose could be expected to know nothing of time. "But perhaps you can tell me where we are, though?"

"Where?" Edna glanced at him sidewise. "Why, here, of course."

"Yes, quite so," Professor Peabody agreed, a little desperate. "But where is 'here'? I mean, what is the name of the place?"

"Name?" Edna said. "It hasn't any name. It's just here. There are only two places—here and there. And we're here."

"Thank you." Peabody sighed, as nearly a sigh as he could manage. "To be sure. May I also inquire where this stream upon which we are now swimming takes us?"

"How you do talk!" Edna exclaimed, pleased. "I never heard language like you use before. Why, it takes us to the river. Where the people are."

"Ah!" Peabody brightened. "The river. And people. You don't know their names, do you?"

Edna shook her head, her lissome neck undulating pleasantly. "Do people have names?"

"Yes," Alexander Peabody told her as a bend in the stream brought into view a town.

It was not a very imposing town, being merely a largish aggregation of stone and wood houses on the edge of the river into which the stream flowed. But beyond it, on the crest of a hill, was a more imposing structure, almost a fortress, with stout stone walls.

Within the confines of this stronghold, Professor Peabody glimpsed the tops of buildings, and he caught sight of human beings on the walls, scanning the horizon in the manner of sentinels.

"What is that?" he asked eagerly, and Edna looked toward the town.

"That's just home," she said. "It's sort of dull. Nothing ever happens there. I just came out for a swim, and because I was hungry for some mud worms. Would you like some? I know a dandy place to get them."

"No, thank you," Alexander Peabody replied hastily. "I—uh, I'd like very much to see where you live."

"Would you?" Edna seemed pleased. "Then come along. What is your name anyway, good-looking?"

"Call me Alex," Professor Peabody suggested.

"Alex. I like that name," Edna told him. "It's a good name for a big, strong fellow like you. All right, Alex. We swim down to that dead tree, then we go up the path, and there's a hole in the wall . . ."

Forty minutes later, Professor Peabody squeezed through a crevice in the stone wall of the fortress and found himself inside. The route Edna had led him had taken them near no human beings. But now there were plenty of people in sight. There were numerous buildings of stone within the walls, and a large one in the center was really very imposing, with lofty pillars and broad marble steps.

The streets were muddy, and filled with refuse, but no one seemed to mind. Individuals strode along about their business, skirting the worst puddles and giving no heed to the garbage.

A short distance away was what seemed to be a market. Nothing was for sale, however, save a few carcasses of small animals. These were being bought by housewives in loose white gowns amidst much bargaining.

All the men in sight were armed, either with swords, or pikes, or both. All wore tunics of white cotton or homespun, and most had leather jerkins or at least leather straps outside these, from which shields were suspended. Professor Peabody realized that he should be able to tell from the dress of the inhabitants where he was. But he couldn't. He was, after all, a scientist, and not a historian. Though something struck a familiar note in his mind, he could not place it.

However, he must somehow make contact with them, and let them know that the body of the fowl he now wore concealed a human soul and mentality.

He was turning his next move over in his mind when he observed a large white fowl approaching him and Edna. It was another goose, a male goose, in fact, and it waddled toward them with an arrogance that Alexander Peabody found distasteful.

"Why, it's Carl!" Edna exclaimed, with a little hiss of interest. "Dear me, Alex, I should warn you: Carl is very fond of me."

"He is, is he?" Professor Peabody responded, finding, to

his own amazement, that there was a distinctly ominous tone in his voice.

"Hello, Edna," the oncoming Carl hissed. "Where'd you pick up that mangy-looking bird with you?"

"He's a gentleman friend of mine," Edna answered, with a toss of her head. "We've just been having a little walk together."

"You have, have you?" Carl fixed a beady eye on Alexander Peabody. "Well, tell him to take another walk, before I kick his feathers off."

"Huh!" Edna answered, provocatively. "I guess he can take care of himself. Can't you, Alex?"

"Eh?" Alexander Peabody felt a certain alarm. Carl's intentions were obviously hostile. And despite the curious urge within him to reciprocate that hostility, Professor Peabody was after all a man of peace, who had never engaged in a conflict in his life. "Why—why—"

Carl gave him no chance to make up his mind. Hissing and clacking, Carl charged.

Carl was large, and obviously of a bellicose nature. His first rush knocked the professor off his feet. While he lay on his side, beating his wings and giving out cries of distress, Carl plucked large handfuls of feathers from his anatomy. Then with his powerful beak he nipped Peabody in numerous places, all of which hurt.

Ruffled and flustered, Peabody scrambled to his feet and attempted to strike back. But he was unaccustomed to combat, and Carl bore down on him in so fearsome a manner that the professor's courage gave way. He turned and fled.

As he squawked down the street, feathers flying, wings beating, Carl took a few last nips. Then he ceased, to return to Edna.

"There he goes," Peabody heard his rival hissing behind him. "You won't see that bird again, bright eyes."

The professor turned a corner, and skidded to a wobbly stop as he almost ran into the legs of a man hurrying toward a flight of marble steps. At first he'd thought it was a woman, because of the white draperies fluttering about the sandaled feet.

But the harsh voice that spoke was distinctly masculine,

and what it said was, "Be gone from my path, bird, before I kick you loose from your giblets! On my word, if you weren't sacred to Minerva, I'd wring your neck and pop you into the cooking pot, or my name's not Marcus Manlius!"

A glow of excitement overspread Professor Peabody even as he fluttered to one side. The language was Latin. And he must be—yes, the hill and river made it positive. He was in Rome.

Exultation flamed in Peabody's breast. Rome! At an early date, obviously, for the place was not much more than a provincial village. But Rome, where most of the world's history was made for a thousand years!

He must communicate with the inhabitants quickly, learn the date, discover into just what stage of Rome's history he had been precipitated. Then, having all the facts, he could put his brain and intelligence to work; and handicapped though he was by the body of a goose, he might yet triumph over his misfortune.

He scuttled up the muddy steps and got ahead of the ascending man. The fellow strode with the air of a commander.

Professor Peabody summoned his best Latin.

"*Hic, haec, hoc!*" he shrilled at the glowering Marcus Manlius, to get his attention. "*Gallia est omnis divisa in partes tres!* Listen, please! I am a friend. It's all a mistake that I look like a goose. I must talk to you!"

To Professor Peabody, waiting expectantly, the purest of Latin seemed to have tripped off his tongue. But the togaed one only glowered.

"Cease, fowl, your hissing and clacking!" he roared at Professor Peabody. "By the gods, you make my ears ring! If it weren't for the blessed Minerva's protection, I'd break you into seventy-seven bits. Now, out of my way!"

Dismayed, Professor Peabody tried to scuttle aside. He was too slow. A foot caught just beneath the tail feathers. He sailed through the air and down the steps.

Gasping for breath, Professor Peabody spread his wings, flapping furiously. But unacquainted as he was with the art of flight, something went wrong. He went into a side slip, then into a stall, and in getting out of that, into a tailspin.

A moment later he made a landing on the bottom step that jarred all remaining breath from his body.

On the steps above, harsh laughter sounded. Then Marcus Manlius was gone.

Slowly Professor Peabody recovered his breath, his wits, and his courage. He had failed to make the man understand. Probably his accent had been wrong. Or more likely, his vocal cords were not adapted to clear reproduction of human speech.

Yet somehow he must communicate with the Romans, or twenty years of labor and a lifetime of ambition were gone for nothing.

It was a problem requiring the utmost concentration. He decided to stroll about the town while he pondered it. Besides, he did not feel like sitting down. Not just now.

Slowly and with dignity, Professor Peabody proceeded down the muddy lane that served for a street. From the corner of his eye he saw Edna and Carl strolling in the other direction. For a moment a flush of humiliation flooded Peabody. Then, putting trivial personal matters from his mind, he concentrated on how to communicate with the Romans.

Presently his eyes brightened. Seated on a doorstep ahead of him, to get the last light of the afternoon, was an individual marking on parchment with a quill pen, which he dipped now and again into a pot of ink beside him.

Hope rose in Professor Peabody. This was a scribe, an educated man. He approached cautiously. The intent scribe, a scrawny fellow with a bald spot in the middle of his pate, took no notice of him. Peabody went closer.

If, he thought, he could take the quill pen in his mouth—his beak, rather—and write a message with it—No, that was impractical. But still—

He cleared his throat. He'd try speech again first. He did, uttering a few preliminary sentences, but the scribe only glanced up in annoyance.

"Shoo!" he said. "Get hence, bird. No, pause a moment!"

Alexander Peabody, having started back, stopped. The scribe's expression was more friendly. Taking heart at this sign of interest, Peabody bent his neck, inserted his beak into the smooth mud beside the doorstep, and began to make awkward capital letters.

"H-I-C," he wrote, sprawlingly but plainly. "H-A-E-C . . . H-O-C."

Triumphantly he stood back. There! That would demonstrate he was intelligent. Get the scribe's attention. Then he would write a real sentence. Then—

He looked up. The scribe made a swift grab at him. A large hand seized his wing. Pain shot through Professor Peabody. He leaped forward, straight between the fellow's legs. His wings flapping, he shot into the clear, and behind him the scribe tottered, grabbed at air, and sat down with a resounding smack in the mud—fair on the words Alexander Peabody had written!

Peabody groaned. The furious writer was struggling to his feet with a handful of feathers and a stone. He hurled the stone. Peabody dodged around a corner.

Confound the fellow! He had only wanted some feathers to make new goose quill pens. Using him, Professor Alexander Peabody, B.S., M.S., Ph.D., as a source of writing materials!

Then Peabody's neck sagged, his tail feathers drooped. Evening was coming on, and a cold, raw wind was whisking through the streets of Rome. He'd failed to communicate with anyone, and gloomily he could see that no matter what he tried, he'd fail again. Who would pay any attention to a goose?

He sighed, and then a determination crystallized. He'd go back, and see Edna again. Maybe she was just a goose, but she was company, someone to talk to, and he was lonely.

As for Carl, if he could find him now, he'd thrash him to within an inch of his life!

He turned about, and went in search of Edna and Carl.

A curious thing was happening to Alexander Peabody, and he was only half aware of it. The residue of goosish personality in the body his ego was inhabiting seemed to be coloring his thoughts and actions. He was gradually losing interest in human affairs, even in the mission which had brought him here.

Conversely, the more he thought of Edna, the more he

desired her company. The more he thought of the uncouth
Carl, the more he desired a chance to engage him in
combat again, to beak-whip him until his pinfeathers came
loose.

In a highly bellicose state of mind, Professor Alexander
Peabody waddled down the muddy streets of Rome, ruffling
his feathers.

But he could not find Carl and Edna, and night had
come on. He began to be hungry. He found a crust
dropped beside a doorway, and his beak broke it up into
crumbs. He swallowed them, washing them down with
water from a puddle, and felt refreshed.

Now, however, in the darkness he was quite lost. The
town had gone to bed shortly after nightfall. Occasionally a
cloaked figure, sword at his side, shield slung over his back,
passed. These seemed to be sentries, for Professor Peabody
saw them take up places at the walls.

But as the night wore on, and the raw wind grew
keener, he saw the sentries leaving their exposed positions
and seeking protected niches where they might keep warm.
Peabody, however, was not interested in them. A wan
moon was rising, and down the street he could now see the
temple outside which he had parted from Carl and Edna.

He hastened toward it.

And there they were, crouched cozily side by side in a
corner, behind a fluted column, sleeping with their wings
touching.

Indignation and jealousy made Professor Peabody emit
a hiss of rage that brought the two sleepers to startled
wakefulness. Then Edna blinked coyly.

"Why, it's Alex!" she said.

"Listen, you bag of feathers," Carl clacked, "beat it, or
I'll pull you wing from wing."

"You and who else!" Peabody retorted, remembering in
time a favorite answer of youth to such challenges. "You
pusillanimous fowl, I'll beat you down into goose grease!"

"Oh, Alex!" Edna sighed. "What lovely language you
use! And how handsome you are when you're angry!"

"Take a last look at him then, bright eyes," Carl told
her. "Because when I finish with him, he won't have
enough feathers left to cover a sparrow."

And he rushed to the attack.

Professor Peabody gave way at first, mainly because he wanted the combat to take place on a different field of honor—the flat surface beyond the temple. The marble of Minerva's temple was slippery, and he wanted firm footing for this chivalric joust in which he was engaged.

So he scurried backwards and down the far steps, into the vacant lot where the rising moon gave a clear if subdued light. Carl pursued, hissing in triumph, and the sound of battle brought scores of sleepy geese running after them from the corners of the temple.

In the middle of the open space, Professor Peabody took his stand. He stopped running and began to attack.

The change in tactics took Carl by surprise, and Professor Peabody got in half a dozen sound, smacking beak-blows to the head. Then Carl screamed in redoubled rage and closed with him.

The other geese gathered about to watch, hissing in shrill excitement. Above all the voices, though, Edna's could be heard most clearly, and her "Oh, Alex, don't let him hurt you!" was sweet music to Professor Peabody's ears.

Professor Peabody, however, for all his valor, was unversed in the best fighting strategy of the fowl world. He was slowly getting the worst of the terrific wing-to-wing, beak-to-beak tussle when an interruption occurred. A torch flared near by, and a voice which he recognized roared in terrible rage.

"By the sacred bones of my ancestors, I'll slice the gizzard from the goose with the black marking around its eyes, Minerva or no Minerva! Today on the Forum steps it made my ears ache with its hissing, and tonight it must engage in battle and make the air hideous noise, waking honest Romans from their needful sleep. I'll toast its liver and grill its gizzard and stew its bones and—"

Another voice cut the first short.

"Marcus Manlius! They come. The enemy come stealing up the hillside path!"

Then indeed did the night become sonorous with the sound of battle. Men rushed forth into the street, buckling on shields and short swords. Torches flared bright. From the city wall came shrill barbaric war cries, the gasp and scream of wounded men.

But Alexander Peabody heeded it not. He had his own fight to attend to. Carl was still strong and fresh, and pressing him back. So Peabody, in desperation, altered his tactics.

His new fighting method was a combination of all he could recall of the best features of chivalric jousting of knights with lances, and modern pursuit plane dogfighting. Extending his neck like a spear, he rushed into Carl. His hard beak bored through Carl's defenses and bowled him over. Following up his advantage, Professor Peabody took to the air.

With a great flapping of wings, he gained an altitude of three feet, and from there dive-bombed Carl. Carl, struggling up, received all of Peabody's weight on the side of his head and went down again, stunned. Alexander Peabody, withdrawing a yard or so, rushed in once more with the leveled spear technique.

Carl gave ground. Professor Peabody pursued. Carl turned and ran for safety, and Peabody delivered one last triumphant blow. Then Carl's agonized squawks were receding down the street into the night, and Edna was snuggling up to Alexander Peabody as he leaned against the temple steps, panting for breath.

"Alex," Edna said, "you were *wonderful.*" And she rubbed her long, lissome white neck against him.

A strange thrill warmed Professor Peabody's blood. He had conquered an enemy in combat, and he had won the admiration of a fair lady.

"It wasn't anything really, Edna," he said modestly. "That Carl, he's just an overrated bully."

"It *was* something," Edna breathed. "You're a hero, Alex. Anyway, you're *my* hero."

"It was for you I did it," Alexander Peabody said boldly. "And I'll always fight for you—if you'll let me."

"Oh, Alex!" Edna sighed, and pressed close against him.

They were alone, the other geese having gone back to sleep. And in his absorption, Professor Peabody was quite deaf to the diminishing sound of fighting at the city's walls. It was not until some time later when the light of torches came toward them, making him blink, that he remembered the Romans at all.

Then, as he looked up, a burly figure clad in animal skins leaped from the midst of a band of Roman soldiers and, snatching a sword from one, rushed at Professor Peabody.

"We'd have had you, cursed Romans," a bull voice roared in bad Latin, "had it not been for this goose hatched of Satan! I saw him myself, as we were about to charge over the wall, fighting with another to awaken you. And he shall die for it!"

Edna screamed in fright as the huge soldier came at them, sword swinging. But Alexander Peabody felt no fear. He launched himself forward, beak extended, hissing ferociously. He leaped, and struck for the eyes as the glittering blade descended.

One ferocious jab he got in, while behind him Edna's anguished voice cried, *"Alex! Alex!"* Then the edge of the sword met his neck, and Professor Alexander Peabody knew only darkness.

The blackness may have lasted for a minute or an hour. Peabody could not tell. But as it lifted slowly, he heard Edna crying still, "Alex! Alex!" and shaking him by the wing with her beak to arouse him. Professor Peabody opened his eyes, blinking.

"It's all right, Edna," he gasped. "I'm all right. I—"

Then he stopped, for it was his sister Martha he was staring at.

She stepped back, letting go his shoulder, and Alexander Peabody saw that he was in his Morris chair, in his study, and that it was night outside.

"Alexander!" Martha exclaimed. "What has happened? I came in and—and you seemed to be asleep in your chair. But though I shook you for the longest time I couldn't seem to wake you up."

She stopped and stared at him.

"Who is Edna? What has happened to you? You—you look different."

Alexander Peabody did not answer her immediately. He rose from the chair, marched to his bookcase, drew down a volume of the encyclopedia. And there he found the name he sought. For a moment he stared at the page.

MARCUS MANLIUS CAPITOLINUS. A patrician. Roman consul in 392 B.C. According to tradition, when in 390 B.C. the besieging Gauls were attempting to scale the walls of the Capitol, he was roused by the cackling of the sacred geese, rushed to the spot, and threw down the foremost assailants. The attack on Rome was defeated.

Slowly Peabody closed the volume and looked up, to meet Martha's gaze.

"I *am* changed," he proclaimed. "I have known adventure. I have routed an enemy in single-handed combat. And I have affected the course of history.

"I am responsible for the fact that the Gauls did not capture Rome in 390 B.C. If Rome had fallen then, the Roman Empire might never have been. If the Roman Empire had not existed, the history of the world would have been vastly different. So I have affected history more than any modern dictator can ever hope to do. I, Alexander Peabody. And I'm satisfied."

Martha goggled at him. Then gradually she relaxed and shook her head.

"You've had a dream, I see," she commented. "But don't try to tell me you believe that your dream actually happened. Please don't be a goose."

Alexander Peabody gazed at his sister, not with resentment, but with a bright, faraway look in his eye, as if he were thinking back to some special moment in his life.

"Certainly not, Martha," he replied with dignity. "In any case, you know, I would be a gander."

DOMITIA.

Mrs. Richard S. Greenough

I was born in a far-distant land, beside the Tiber, upon one of the seven hills of Rome. My father was the head of the great house of the Savelli; my mother was Geltrude of Milan. I was their eldest child. Five years after I was born, a little sister came into the world; and after six more of waiting and of prayers, an heir was born, to my parents' great relief, and to the joy of the whole house, and, indeed, I may say of all Rome; for it would have been felt as a misfortune to the city had so ancient a house become extinct.

The Pope sent his chamberlain to congratulate my father, and to bear a precious jewel with his benediction to my mother; and my father feasted the poor of the city for six successive days.

From that time, the happiness of the palazzo was without a cloud. I look back upon the ensuing years as does a prisoner upon the remembrance of green hills, and smiling gardens, and blue, open skies.

I was always a grave and thoughtful child, and my spirits had hitherto been secretly depressed by the reflection that it was my duty to have been a boy; but now I became reconciled to my sex, and when I sat beside my mother, and watched her as she played with my little laughing brother, I felt as much happiness as a child's heart can contain.

My sister was very unlike myself. She was a fair and

frolicsome child, the favorite of all who saw us, as indeed it was but right that she should be, for she was far more gay and mirthful than I had ever been. But our mother never showed any partiality between us. She seemed to love me as well as she did my sister; and, even when the heir was born, it diminished in nothing her tenderness and care.

We saw but little of our father. He was always busied in weighty matters, or engaged in the civil feuds which desolated the city. He was a man of proud and distant bearing, and we feared more than we loved him. Our affection was lavished on our mother. As I look back upon her, I thank God for the inestimable blessing of having been tended and nurtured by one so like to an angel.

We lived in Rome during the winter, but, during the summer, at our castle above the Alban Lake. It was always a season of rejoicing to my sister and myself when we saw the long line of covered carts which bore our household gear, escorted by their mounted guard, issue from the massive gate of our palace in Rome, and wind its way across the Campagna, towards our summer stronghold; for, when we were at Rome, our parents lived in great state and ceremony. There were constant entertainments to be given or to be attended, and we saw our mother but at rare intervals. We were left much to the care of our nurse Flavia. She had been my father's foster mother, and held dearer than aught else the renown and glory of our house. She used, in the long winter evenings, while we sat 'round the lamp, to tell us stories of the ancient deeds of our forefathers, and of the beauty and grace of our ancestresses. Sometimes she would mingle with these histories, legends wild and fearful of the former masters of the city, until we scarcely dared to draw our breath, and would be undressed and laid in our beds, silent and shivering with dread. Those were happy evenings, when our mother would send for us to come to her tiring-room, and would talk to us while her women braided her long hair, and adorned it with jewels and strings of pearls, and while they attired her in her magnificent robes; but she had little time for us, and often she would whisper, as she kissed me good-night,—

"Courage, Leonora mia! the summer will soon come."

And she was as happy as were my sister and myself, when she could leave all the pomp of the city, and retire with us to the hills of Gandolfo, where we were together all the day long, and no vexatious festival called her from us at night.

She would sit at her embroidery-frame in the great window that overlooked the Campagna; and Cecilia and I would sit on our little cushions at her feet, and she would teach us many things, all made sweet to us by her gentle smile and loving voice. Then, when the heat of the day was past, she would wander along the slopes of the hills around, leading us by the hand, or sit on some mossy stone while we wove coronals of flowers to deck her fair white brow. I have never seen anyone so beautiful as was my mother.

Around the outer wall of the castle, between the terrace and the moat, were small grated windows which communicated with the dungeons below. It was one of the great pleasures of my sister and myself, to save the daintiest portion of our daily fare, then to creep with it to the terrace, and throw it stealthily down to the prisoners, running away as fast as we could for fear that the guards would see us.

We fancied that they never guessed our errand; but doubtless they had orders from our mother not to interfere with us.

One day we had saved some apricots, and had stolen softly with them to the grating of the dungeon of an old man, who was our especial favorite. As we peeped down, he saw us; and, joining his hands, in the dim twilight below, he implored us by all that we loved best to hasten away, and tell our father that he had found that which was worth his ransom a thousand times over.

We dared not attempt to approach our father, who then chanced to be on one of his rare visits to the castle; but we ran to our mother, and told her all. She went immediately to our father, and, as we learned afterwards from our nurse Flavia, requested leave to send her leech to the old prisoner. Our father, supposing him stricken with illness, consented; and she forthwith despatched the leech—a wise and prudent man, in whom she had great confidence—to the prisoner.

As he followed the keeper of the dungeons down the damp and narrow stone steps, they heard fearful shrieks issuing from the old man's cell. They made all the haste they could; but, ere the keeper could undo the heavy fastenings of the door, the sounds had ceased. When they entered, the old prisoner was lying on his back; his glazing eyes were staring wide in horror; his features were frightfully distorted. They sought to raise him. He was dead.

The dungeon was thoroughly searched, but nothing was found there. This event greatly distressed and terrified my sister and myself, and it was long before we had the courage to pass that side of the terrace; and when the night was closing in, and the wind waved the trees in the castle-garden, we often used to fancy that we heard the death moans of the old prisoner, and would whisper ghastly guesses to each other of the cause of his mysterious end.

But years passed on; and little by little we forgot, as children do, to speak or to think of the old prisoner; little dreaming how fearfully he was to be recalled to our memories, and with what shudderings of terror and anguish we were to receive the key to that buried mystery.

But I must not tarry. It was the summer time. Early one morning my mother and myself, mounted on our Spanish jennets, and attended by our escort, left the castle for a canter around the lake, and through the cool and leafy galleries which led over the hills towards the villages beyond. We were talking and laughing gayly, as we circled the hollow cup in whose depths lie the placid waters of the lake, when suddenly, from amidst the ruins of the Emperor's villa, which my great grandfather had destroyed in order to build the fortress, rose a kestrel. It soared high into the air above her heads; then, dropping like a stone, it alighted on the head of my mother's horse, and pecked furiously at its eyes.

The blinded animal, maddened by pain and fright, plunged wildly to and fro, unwitting whither it went; then, just as my mother was freeing her foot from the stirrup, in order to leap from its back, it sprang towards the precipitous bank, tottered, and rolled down the steep declivity, bearing her with it.

I cannot dwell on this great anguish. Few words must suffice me now.

She was borne to the castle, and laid upon her bed. She still breathed faintly; but we knew that her hour had come. Mercifully, her consciousness did not return. She was spared the last farewell.

We knelt, weeping and praying, about the bed, until the leech, who had his hand upon her pulse, laid it down reverently by her side. Then our sobs and tears broke forth unrestrained; and the priest advanced to bless her lifeless clay. But, as he stood before her, her eyelids were suddenly lifted, revealing a look so fierce, so haughty, that he started back in terror. We sprang to our feet, and crowded around her. With an impatient motion of her hand she waved us away, and, slowly rising, stood upon her feet.

She cast her eyes gloomily around her, then walked to her inner room, entered, and closed the door.

My sister and myself stood gazing in consternation upon each other. Could this indeed be our gentle, gracious mother? Had she been snatched from the jaws of death to be given back to us thus changed?

The priest was the first to speak. He approached us, and, in an uncertain and troubled tone, begged us to come, with all the household, to the chapel, there to give thanks for our mother's preservation. White and anxious, we obeyed.

The chapel was but dimly lighted by its narrow windows, cut high in the walls. Before the altar burned four great waxen tapers. The air was so damp—for the chapel was partly underground—that each candle seemed surrounded by a small, yellow cloud.

The priest began to recite the consecrated words of thanksgiving, but his face was pale, and his voice trembled as it left his lips; and the responses of the assembled household, kneeling before him, rose on the chilly air like groans.

When the service of thanksgiving was over, I took my sister's hand, and went with her to the door of our mother's

apartments. We knocked softly. She did not answer. We
tried the lock; it was fastened from within. We listened.
We heard a faint, tapping sound. It ceased, then recom-
menced. It seemed to come from different parts of the
chamber in turn. There was something in the sound that
frightened us still more. The servants gradually assembled
at a little distance from us. They, too, heard the low
sound. They whispered to each other below their breath.

At last the hour of the midday meal sounded; and the
maestro di casa, with his wand, came to announce to my
mother, as was his office, that she was served.

As he ended, the sound ceased; then, after a little
pause, the door was thrown open, and our mother appeared
on the threshold. She seemed to tower above our heads,
so haughty was her bearing. Her eyes, once so soft, had
now a cold and cruel stare; her lips, whose wont it was to
be so smiling, were now compressed and stern. She moved
on with a stately step, passing my sister and myself without
a glance. We followed her, as she swept slowly down the
corridor, and timidly took our accustomed places beside
her at the table. She frowned.

"Draw back, ye little apes," she said. And, the tears
streaming down our cheeks, we rose, and took our seats at
the foot of the table.

Our mother looked with a mixture of curiosity and disgust
upon the viands on the table. There was only one dish that
she tasted. It was composed of lampreys stewed with
honey and spices; and the manner of its preparation was a
secret handed down among the servants of the *credenza*.

She demanded Falernian wine to drink; nor did she
once touch to her lips the water which formed her habitual
beverage.

When the meal was ended—Cecilia and myself had
eaten nothing—our mother rose, and returned to her own
apartments.

My sister and myself had no longer courage to follow
her. We went to the room which we shared together, and
there abandoned ourselves to all the agony of our grief.

When we grew calmer, and I was able to reflect, I came
to the conclusion that this sudden and unaccountable change
in our mother must be the result of the shock she had

received; and, after bathing my eyes, and composing my demeanor, I ordered the leech to be summoned.

He had lived in the castle ever since I was a child, and I had a great affection for him. But, when he appeared, with his kind and compassionate look, I knew now how to frame the questions I wished to ask. My sister sat weeping by my side, and her affliction gradually melted away all my self-command; and I began to weep also, not having been able to say a word.

"My gracious young lady," he said at length, seeing me incapable of explaining why I had summoned him, and knowing but too well the cause, "let not your mind be disturbed by the contemplation of a phenomenon which, in its nature, is but temporary. The vital spirits of the Princess have received so great a shock as to be for the moment displaced; and those which belong to the spleen and the liver have gone to the brain. But this disturbance is accidental; and the balance will soon be restored by the healing power of Nature. Meantime, I earnestly pray you, that your affection for the Princess, your mother, may not incline you to lay too much stress upon any casual differences in her deportment; for it is not to her daughter that I need say, that God never before assembled such a multitude of excellent and lovely graces in a human form as he has deigned to show to the world in the person of that most exalted lady, your mother."

Having said this, and perceiving me to be somewhat comforted by his words, the leech withdrew.

But, alas! neither the morrow nor the next day, nor all the days that followed, saw the hoped-for change in our mother. We seemed to be living in a dream; our former life had disappeared, and, with it, all our pleasures and happiness were gone. No more did we sit at her feet, and learn wisdom from her gentle lips; no more did we wander by her side over the green hills, no more weave gay flowers into garlands to deck her head. We were forbidden to approach her presence; and, did she ever chance to meet us wandering disconsolately through the silent corridors, she would scowl at us, and bid us to our chamber. On our little brother only did she ever smile; but, strange to say, the child, who had hitherto adored her, now shrieked whenever he was brought before her, giving every sign of the utmost terror and dislike.

She never confessed nor went to mass. She was imperious and exacting towards everybody; so difficult to please, that her women trembled whenever their duties summoned them to attend her. But the greater part of the time she spent shut up alone in her apartments; and then again was constantly heard the same low tapping.

So weeks passed on, each day seeming more dreadful than the last. My little sister pined and faded; her gayety was all gone. She would sit silent, hour after hour, looking on the ground, the tears stealing down her cheeks, until I would take her in my arms, and we would weep together.

Our father was away, warring with the Pope against Venice; the old priest had no comfort to give us; the leech, when we questioned him, only shook his head, and bade us pray and try to hope. We prayed, earnestly and constantly; but we had lost the power to hope.

I have said that my mother never confessed nor heard the mass; but something even more dreadful I discovered at this time.

In one of the great halls of the castle, among the ancient statues ranged along the walls, was a small bronze figure of Mercury, greatly prized by our father because of its delicate workmanship, and the precious jewels which formed its eyes. One day this disappeared, nor could any one tell what had become of it. It was in its accustomed place at night, and in the morning it was gone. There was great grief and distress through the castle at its loss; for all the servants and retainers feared that they might be suspected of having stolen it.

Among the changed habits of our mother was this—she would allow no one to enter her oratory. She would often shut herself up there, and sing strange songs that we had never heard before. The priest was one day passing, and he stayed to listen; but all at once he crossed himself, stopped his ears, and hastened away. He forbade any one in the castle, for the future, to pass through that gallery; nor would he ever tell what it was that he had heard.

One day Flavia came to me with her finger upon her lips, and whispered to me to follow her. She led me to a room in which the linen was kept. It was built in a projecting angle of the courtyard, and on one side was a high, lozenge-shaped window. She bade me mount upon a table under this window, and look out. I did as she told me, and saw that the window commanded across the courtyard a view of the interior of my mother's oratory. But all within was changed. The great ebony crucifix lay on the ground; the picture of St. Catherine of Sienna, on which I had gazed with reverence ever since my infancy, had been torn down; the bowl of holy water had disappeared; and the books of devotion were cast in a heap on one side. In the center of the room, upon an antique altar of carved ivory, which had formerly served my mother as a stand for flowers, stood the little bronze statue of Mercury; and before it was a basket containing a piece of honeycomb, and a vase filled with what looked like milk. My mother sat in front of the statue. I saw her lips moving, but I could hear nothing; the distance was too great.

As I gazed upon this unexpected sight, the room grew indistinct, and everything seemed wavering about me. Then I felt old Flavia's arms clasp me; and the next thing I knew I was lying on the floor, and she was rubbing my hands.

When I recovered, I remained for a while as if stunned. I could scarcely bring myself to believe that the pious hands, which had so often clasped my own, and held them up in supplication to the holy Virgin and the blessed Jesus, had prepared that pagan offering, and performed those sacrilegious rites; that those pure lips, whose daily wont it had been to chant sweet hymns of gratitude and praise, could be perverted to the deadly sin of breathing forth adoration to a heathen god of bronze. The horrible thought that my mother had forfeited her salvation, that her soul was forever lost, filled me with unutterable grief and terror.

When I could speak, I bade Flavia, who was rapidly telling her beads, say what cause she could imagine for all that was so dreadful and so strange. And she, looking fearfully around, said that not only she herself, but all the household, were persuaded that her mistress had been bewitched by the kestrel; and that old Rinaldino was watching night and day, hidden among the bushes by the lake, hoping to bring it down with his crowbow. For, that if it were killed and cooked, and my mother should eat but the tiniest morsel of its flesh, the enchantment would be broken, and she would become as she was before.

But, although Flavia's faith in the bewitchment was firm, I was not persuaded; nor did old Rinaldino ever bring home the kestrel, so that the experiment could never be tried.

I made Flavia promise that she would tell no one of the unholy rites in my mother's oratory; and she kept her word. It remained a secret, known but to us two alone.

The strange tappings, which so constantly sounded from my mother's apartments, at length ceased, to our great relief; for, incessant though they had been, none of the household could ever become accustomed to the sounds, and they continually alarmed every one. But, after a few days of quiet, our mother ordered another suite of rooms on the same side of the house to be prepared for her, and she took possession of them when they were ready. No sooner was she established in her new apartments, than the strange, tapping sound began again, greatly disturbing all in the castle. Once the priest came in his consecrated robes, and brought holy water, and sprinkled it on the door, and said the awful form of exorcism; but the faint, unremitting tappings went on all the while, and continued after he had ceased; and he went away shaking his head.

So time went on. One night I could not sleep. My sister and myself had always of late retired at sundown. It was less painful to be in our own room together, than to be wandering in the great unlighted halls below, or standing at the door of our mother's apartment, never opened to us now. Cecilia was quietly sleeping by my side; but I was lying plunged in mournful thought, when I heard some-one enter the room beside us—old Flavia's. The door leading into our chamber was ajar, and I heard all that passed.

"What! are you already abed, Flavia mia?" said the voice of Caterina, one of my mother's tiring-women. "Much peace may you find there! Know ye not that nowadays the whole household is afraid to sleep? Half of us watch, while the other half take their rest. Who knows what may happen, any night, ere morning? And the days are bad enough, the saints know. What think you! Yesterday, as I was braiding the Princess's hair, I did not arrange it to suit her, and she caught up the long golden bodkin which lay on the table before her, and plunged it a full inch into my breast, and she menaced Camilla with being thrown into the lake to feed the fishes because she fastened on a bow awry."

"Heaven defend us!" exclaimed Flavia. "Surely we have need to pray that old Rinaldino may speedily bring down the kestrel, to end this accursed spell."

"Of course we do," replied Caterina. "We pray morning, noon, and night. It is no time to neglect the saints when people are in danger of their lives."

"But tell me, what was it about the merchant yesterday?" inquired Flavia. "I was here with my gracious young ladies, and saw and heard nothing."

"It was strange enough!" answered the tiring-woman. "The Princess saw him from her window, as he entered the courtyard, and ordered that he should bring his goods to her. She tossed them over scornfully, though he had the most exquisite head-tires, and silks, and velvets for bodices, and laces and embroideries, that were ever seen; nor would she allow the poor man to say a word in praise of his wares. At his first sentence, she fastened such a look upon him that he stammered and drew back, and stood mute, until she asked him what it was that he had in a drawer that he had not opened. He said that it was something he had bought from a peasant—an antique lyre. She commanded him to show it instantly; and he produced a discolored piece of ivory, curiously carved with eagles' heads and foliage work, with all the strings gone. The Princess immediately bought it, and ordered him to carry away all the rest of his merchandise; and she forthwith despatched a messenger to Rome, for a goldsmith, and commanded that he should bring gold wire; and he has been at work all today."

As she spoke, a strain of music floated up through the open window, so strange in its intonations that I had never listened to the like; and I heard from below my mother's

voice, singing in cadence; but I could not catch the words.
It was a low, irregular chant, at times swelling into a
fierce, vindictive wail. My flesh crept as I lay hearkening
to it.

"Holy Virgin! whoever heard such sounds as those?"
exclaimed Caterina, in affright. "How shall I ever dare to
go through the corridors to my own room! Thank Heaven
that it is not my night to disrobe the Princess. I would
rather walk barefoot over red-hot ploughshares. But I
must go. The longer I tarry the more afraid I shall be."

And I heard her timid footfall die along the echoing
length of the gallery.

The strange measure ceased after a while, but still I
could not sleep. Midnight tolled from the great watch-
tower, and still I had not closed my eyes, when I fancied I
heard a muffled tread passing along the corridor. I sat up
in bed, and distinctly saw a gleam of light shoot along the
ground, shining from beneath my door. I rose hurriedly,
threw a robe over my shoulders, and, when I could no
longer hear the footsteps nor see the light, I noiselessly
unclosed the door and passed out into the gallery.

I followed softly the direction the footsteps had taken; at
length I saw a faint beam before me. Still more cautiously
I pursued my way. I tracked it to the chapel. I paused and
looked in as I gained the door. The chapel was empty. The
moonbeams streamed down from the narrow and lofty
windows, and showed a black opening before the altar,
where a stone had been raised and laid aside. I advanced
and looked down. At my feet, I saw a rapidly descending
passage. The faint light of the moonbeams showed but its
opening, then it lost itself in utter darkness.

I drew back an instant, then, with a prayer to the
blessed Madonna to protect me, I entered the subterranean
way. I was obliged to grope my steps, holding by the side
wall, for I could see nothing. I walked in this manner a
long while, always going deeper and deeper into the earth,
as I perceived by the rapidly descending slope. At length I
saw from below a faint, grayish light. I pressed on, and
finally arrived at the extremity of the passage.

Hidden myself, I looked without. Before me lay the
calm, still waters of the lake. Between rose the crumbling

foundations of Domitian's villa, with scattered blocks of stone heaped upon one another, half-covered by rank weeds and clambering vines. But my eye rested only an instant on these. There was that before my sight which riveted it.

Upon a broken column, the moonlight shining full upon her, sat my mother. On the ground before her crouched a withered, witchlike form.

"Speak, counsel me!" said my mother, in the harsh, commanding tones now habitual to her. "Ye were crafty once; at my behest be crafty yet again."

"Yes, once," answered the croaking voice of the hag; "but how can I now propitiate him who inspires with craft? His temples are ruins, his altars are cast down."

"Not all," replied my mother. "Milk and honey still send up their pleasant odors to his nostrils. Mercury, O favorable god, listen and hear!"

And she clasped her hands, and looked upward to the silent sky.

I pressed tightly on my heart to still its throbbings, and bent my ear again.

"Ye have searched in the private chambers so far with no reward," said the old woman; "yet ye are certain that it lies towards the north?"

"Most certain," replied my mother. "He would not dare deceive me."

"And ye have by night sounded the walls and floor of the halls below, and still have found nothing?"

"Ye know it," answered my mother, in her imperious voice.

The hag sunk her head upon her knees, and pondered awhile in silence. Then she rose, gathered up some pebbles, which she carefully examined, rejecting many, and replacing them with others. This done, she climbed upon a heap of stones that rose out of the lake, and, repeating a low chant, threw them in, one by one. The last fell from her hand. There was silence; then, mournfully rising from the opposite bank of the lake, came the cry of an owl. The creature hooted three times, then twice, and again once.

The hag chuckled, and, rubbing her hands together, returned to my mother, who still sat on the ruined column.

"Ye heard," she said. "Did you understand?"

"I heard," replied my mother; "but am I a loathsome witch, to understand?"

"Nay, great as ye are, ye have need of old Catta," rejoined the old woman, laughing hideously.

"Cease prating, and expound to me," said my mother, scowling.

"Look in the dungeons, O august one!" answered her companion. "Minerva herself assures you that you shall find it there."

My mother rose.

"I'll reckon with you, sorceress, should you have told me false."

"Nay, mighty one," whined the hag, "have I not many a time merited and received reward from those hands? Have ye forgotten who it was that, when Domitian——"

"Hush!" interrupted my mother, stamping her foot and clenching her hand; "ye make me wish for that same dagger now."

The hag cowered down among the stones, and my mother turned away towards the entrance of the subterranean passage.

As I saw her coming towards me, I felt every limb turn into ice; then the blood made a rush in my veins, and I fled up the passage. I gained the chapel; I flew through the corridors; reached my own room, locked the door, and barred it with the articles of furniture nearest at hand; then sank upon the ground with a hope that I was dreaming. But again the stealthy footsteps and the glimmering lamp glided past, and then I knew that all was true.

I lay, I know not how long, before I rose and crept shivering to my bed. I folded the sleeping child in my arms as if to shield her. She nestled close to me, and kissed me in her slumber. After this I remember nothing save one long, frightful night, during which I seemed to be ever falling from the brink of some precipice, or hunted by beasts of prey, or buried in the subterranean passage, or drowning in the waters of the lake.

At last my consciousness returned: but I found myself too weak to speak or to move. I could see through my half-closed lids that I was in my own room, but that my sister was no longer beside me. Old Flavia sat sleeping in a chair at the foot of the bed; a night-lamp was burning in the corner. Eleven o'clock struck—midnight—still Flavia slept on.

As I lay, I heard again the stealthy footsteps, and again I saw the gleam of light pass beneath my door.

I felt a wave of feverish strength run through me. I rose, and, creeping from the room, I followed as before. Again I passed through the dark passages to the chapel; the gaping stone stood open; down the subterranean way I pursued my mother. I looked out again upon the gleaming waters of the waveless lake. I saw her again sitting among the ruins, and before her stood the hag. Through the stillness the sound of their voices came again, clear and distinct to my ear.

"And still it remains hidden?" my mother was saying.

"Sealed in a hollow stone, beneath the highest step leading to the vestibule," repeated the old woman. "It would puzzle the architect himself to say where that is now."

And she glanced around on the ruins with a low laugh.

"Peace with your jests!" said my mother, sternly. "Your business is to listen to one who allows small comment."

The hag shrank back.

"I have searched every cranny of the fortress save one," she continued, "and that I shall examine tonight. And now follow me. We will explore it together."

I turned as she rose, and sped up the passage till I reached the chapel. There I hid myself behind the altar and waited.

Presently I heard the footsteps of my mother and the old woman. As they ascended into the chapel, I heard the hag sniff the air.

"Do I not scent human breath?" she said.

And my mother answered, "Not a soul in the castle but sleeps. The sentinels on the outer wall alone wake at this hour."

They left the chapel, and I followed them through many windings not known to me before; for I had never been allowed to go into this part of the castle. At length they passed through a heavy door, and down a flight of stone steps. When I had reached the foot of the steps, looking out from the shadow of an angle, I saw her apply a master-key to the door of a cell. They passed within. I stole to the door and looked.

My mother drew a small bronze dagger from her girdle, and tapped in succession upon each stone. Each returned the same dull sound. Around the walls, over the floor she moved, tapping gently upon every separate block. The hag stood watching her.

The lamp upon the floor shed its faint light upon my mother's stately, white-robed figure, and dimly showed the wrinkled hideousness of the old woman.

Suddenly my mother smote upon a stone beneath the grated window. I heard a sound different from all that had preceded it—a faint tramping, a low wailing, as of a distant multitude hurrying to and fro, in fear and dread, below the ground.

She flung down the dagger and stood erect, her eyes blazing like those of a tiger when it sees its coveted prey. The old woman sprang forward with the lamp, and bent over the stone. She scratched away the mould that covered it.

"Here is the sign in very truth, O august one!" she said. "Now let us raise it."

And she sought with her bony fingers to draw it from its cavity. She paused, after striving in vain, and muttered low curses.

My mother bent over it, and examined it for a moment.

"See you not the Christian sign, made by the slaves who placed it here?" she exclaimed.

The hag drew back in terror. "We can never raise it," she said. "O mighty one! leave this place. I feel already the torments. Come, let us go." She caught hold of the folds of my mother's dress.

"Peace, fool!" said my mother, frowning upon her companion. "Shall Domitia tremble because of your grovelling fears? Speak, say what will avail to raise the stone?"

"The hand of a Christian only," stammered the hag, looking fearfully at the block.

"I have not far to seek," said my mother. "That fair-haired child will suit my purpose well."

And she moved towards the door.

I tarried no longer in the shadow without. I advanced, and stood before them.

The old hag turned her bleared and evil eyes upon me. My mother towered up as if about to crush me into the earth.

"O thou that bearest the semblance of my mother!" I said, "behold I offer to your need the hand of a Christian maiden to raise the stone. That fulfilled, I adjure you, by the living God, vanish, and disquiet my father's house no more."

My mother shivered as I spoke, and the old hag cowered and moaned.

I moved onward to the stone. I signed three times over it the holy cross, then raised it from its bed. When I lifted it, again I heard the faint trampling, the low wailing, as of a distant multitude, rushing to and fro in fear and dread, below the ground.

As I gave it into my mother's hands, I saw that her form had begun to fade and grow indistinct, and that of the old woman also. As I stood, they became fainter and fainter. At length I could see the lines of the stone wall through their transparent figures. So, slowly and without a word they vanished, bearing with them the close-sealed stone with its hidden secret.

When their last trace had vanished, I knelt on the dungeon floor and prayed. And as I prayed I heard, as it were within my soul, a voice, saying, "My child, you have given me rest. My mortal body now will be undisturbed. The gates of paradise are opening to my soul."

I felt an air-pressed kiss upon my forehead. Then there was silence and stillness all around.

As the stars began to fade, I regained my chamber. Flavia still slept. I lay down upon my bed, and waited till the day had fully dawned; then I wakened her, and ordered her to dress me and lead me to my mother's apartments. With many wondering and apprehensive words she obeyed.

The door was locked. I commanded it to be forced. The whole household was gathered around.

When the door at length yielded, we entered. Within,

upon her bed, lay my mother, as we had placed her, when we brought her up, dying, from the borders of the lake. A gentle, radiant smile was on her face, a look as of a reflection from eternal peace.

With stifled cries and ejaculations the more timid shrank back, while the bolder, softly drawing near, stood and gazed and wept.

The priest advanced and blessed the lovely, lifeless clay; and, as he spoke, the morning sun rose, and its rays streamed through the open window and rested on her face, sweet and gracious as that of one of God's holy angels.

All day, with my little sister and brother, I knelt beside our mother; and, when the night came, we buried her in the chapel; and over the tomb our father raised a monument to her who rests in God.

SURVIVAL TECHNIQUE

Poul Anderson and
Kenneth Gray

THE EMPIRE STATE UNIVERSITY
New York 30, N.Y.
College of Science and Engineering
Department of Physics

May 20, 1967

Mr. James K. Maury
c/o Adventurer's Club
430 Hudson Street
New York 14, N.Y.

Dear Mr. Maury:

Your name has been given to me by Mr. Roger McIntyre, and I am therefore writing to ask whether you would be interested in joining a most unusual expedition sponsored by this department and the history section of the Arts College under a research grant from UNESCO.

You are doubtless aware from both newspaper and professional accounts that the Homolka reformulation of general relativity theory has been triumphantly confirmed by Goldberg's experiments in spatiotemporal projection, and that the device loosely known as a "time machine" is not only possible but is actually being completed in our laboratories. Pilot models have already sent human volunteers into distant regions of the earth and recent sections of the past, and brought them back unharmed. For the final test, a three-man expedition to Augustan Rome, 1 A.D., is being planned, and on the basis of Mr. McIntyre's recommendation we should very much like to include you.

Without going into the theory of the projector, I shall briefly discuss the practical aspect. Our three explorers will be sent from the laboratory of this year to first-century Rome. They will, of course, have been previously instructed in the Latin language and customs, and will be given appropriate garb and sufficient, proper money for a three-week stay. During that time they will not reveal their identity, except in the improbable event of extreme emergency—not that the past can be "upset," but it would complicate their mission, which will be simply to mingle with the people and take notes on those small questions of detail (mores, attitudes, etc.) which are not discussed in surviving contemporary chronicles. At the end of the period, they will return to the exact spot of their materialization, and the projector field will again be generated to return them to this point of space-time.

Actually, they will return three weeks later than they left, because of the balance effect. In simple terms, the laws of conservation require that when a given mass is displaced into the past, the same mass must be brought up to the present; in fact, it must be both physically and chemically similar, within narrow limits of tolerance. In short, when we send our three men to ancient Rome, the field will automatically select three Romans of roughly equal size from the vicinity and carry them to our laboratory. By questioning these Romans during their stay with us, our historians expect to gain much other valuable information. At the end of the arbitrary three-week period, they will be returned as our men come back to the present.

Needless to say, our personnel must be carefully chosen. Though furnished with automatic pistols, and any other inconspicuous equipment that may be indicated, they should use them only as a last resort. Quite apart from humanitarian considerations, such use would vitiate the scientific purpose of the expedition, since it would make them conspicuous figures, regarded with awe and therefore cut off from the daily life which they have been sent to observe. We need men not only of courage, resource, and training, but of tact and quick wits.

Already we have co-opted Mr. McIntyre, as you know a skilled anthropologist, and Dr. Simon Harbold, who is a noted Classical historian. In addition we need a man who is an athlete with experience of alien cultures. Your record as soldier and explorer makes you eminently qualified.

Accordingly, I am happy to offer it to you. If you are interested, I will supply any further details you wish, and salary can be discussed. I trust to hear from you at your earliest convenience.

> Very sincerely yours,
> J. Worthington Barr
> Chairman of the Department

J. WORTHINGTON BARR = DEPT. OF PHYSICS EMPIRE STATE UNIVERSITY = NEW YORK NY = YOU BET =

MAURY =

*Official transcript from tape
recording
July 14, 1967*

DR. BARR: At this great moment, gentlemen, at this great moment in the advance of mankind from savagery to undreamed-of heights, I think it wisest not only to film this great event as it happens, as it occurs, but to keep a running commentary. Although representatives of the press are among us, the sacred obligation of science is to have a record as given by trained observers. Underline that: *trained observers*. . . . Ah . . . Present are myself, J. Worthington Barr, Chairman of the Department of Physics; President Johnson of this great university; Dean Clausewitz of the College of Arts; Dr. Langdon, professor of Latin; and, of course, the various technicians and scientists, as well as representatives of—Ah! Mr. Maury! Here come Mr. Maury,

Mr. McIntyre, and Dr. Harbold, our three intrepid emissaries to ancient Rome. Come over here, please, gentlemen. The projector is quite ready to go. Have you any statements you wish to make?

MAURY: Yes. How the devil do I keep this toga on straight?

DR. BARR: Hah-hah, you will have your little joke.

MCINTYRE: One thing worries me. I feel adept enough at Latin—I ought to, after that course they put us through! —but how, uh, I mean are we *sure* our costumes are authentic?

HARBOLD: I thought you knew, Roger. They probably aren't. We can't be sure of all these little details. That's what this expedition is for, to find out such things.

MCINTYRE: OK, OK. But if we're not supposed to admit we're time travelers—

MAURY: Just a precaution, Mac. They wouldn't believe us, that's all, and we don't want to be locked in the nut house when the time comes for us to go back.

HARBOLD: Don't worry too much about the clothes. Our accent is doubtless wrong too. But we're not going to claim to be Romans. We'll be foreigners, Germans with a smattering of education, like Arminius you know. Rome was full of outlanders.

MAURY: And if we should run into real trouble—well, I've been in trouble before now. One time in the Sinkiang Desert—

MCINTYRE: You have the guns. I'll leave the shooting to you.

MAURY: There shouldn't have to be any. Actually, with all our technical knowledge, we could support ourselves very nicely. Introduce pinball games and steam engines and whatnot. Or Harbold here could set up as a prophet—he'll know what's going to happen next.

DEAN CLAUSEWITZ: That will not be necessary. You have ample funds.

MAURY: I know, I know. We'll just investigate the customs . . . and I understand those Roman customs were very interesting!

DR. BARR: Ahem! Naturally, the reputation of this institution —decorum—

MAURY: Don't be afraid, doc. It won't *all* get in the official report.

DR. BARR: I believe the press representatives would like to see you. You have ten minutes till, ah, zero hour.

MAURY: Sure. And don't worry about us. We've got two thousand years of progress behind us. If you must worry about something, worry about Rome! . . .

DR. BARR: There they, ah, go. Good-by, gentlemen! Good luck!

DEAN CLAUSEWITZ: Stand by, here come the Romans!

PRESIDENT JOHNSON: Good heavens . . . there, under the lens . . . three of them! Are the guards ready?

DR. LANGDON: Yes. But I don't expect these people will get violent. Look at them huddling—the poor creatures must be half mad with fright. They're going to have to be protected from the psychic shock of transportation into a culture as far ahead of theirs as ours is.

DR. BARR: Why—why, one of them is a young woman!

PRESIDENT JOHNSON: Er, not unattractive, is she? But so, um, poverty-stricken.

DR. BARR: They all are. Look at those dirty tunics—in rags! And the two men haven't shaved for a week, I'll be bound. Look at the big one—what a brute!

DEAN CLAUSEWITZ: It was to be expected on the basis of probability, you know. More paupers than aristocrats in any century. And, of course, to make them less conspicuous, our men were sent into what we believe was a slum area.

DR. BARR: True. The machine, ah, selected the three nearest humans to balance . . . They're standing up! That man there, the small one, he's walking off the platform toward us!

DR. LANGDON: I'd better go reassure them.

DR. BARR: A great moment. Where's that microphone? A great moment in the onward march of science.

DEAN CLAUSEWITZ: I wonder how our men are making out . . . or did make out . . . really, time travel ought to have a separate verb form.

DR. BARR: No reason to worry about them, Dean Clausewitz. Not only are they men of courage and resource, but they, ah, know the score . . . know what to expect . . . a great advantage. Believe me, I anticipated all the contingencies. I am not lacking in imagination.

DEAN CLAUSEWITZ: What's the matter with old Langdon? He's jabbering at them and they're jabbering back and nobody seems to understand.

DR. BARR: Could these be, ah, non-Romans too? Visiting foreigners that were by unlucky chance selected—

DEAN CLAUSEWITZ: Surely not. They look right, you know, just about like modern Italians. . . . Hmmm, they appear to be recovering their self-possession. Look, the young woman's smiling. I'll bet if you washed her face and gave her some makeup she'd be quite stunning.

DR. LANGDON: Gentlemen!

DR. BARR: What is it? What's the matter?

DR. LANGDON: They don't understand me, and I don't understand them. Just a word here and there is all.

DEAN CLAUSEWITZ: What on earth?

DR. LANGDON: Oh, it's simple enough. Classical Latin apparently was not pronounced as we have assumed. Our scholars only guessed at it, after all—and to make matters worse, these are slum dwellers. They're talking some equivalent of cockney.

DEAN CLAUSEWITZ: Good Lord! But this ruins the whole experiment! In three weeks we can't find out—

PRESIDENT JOHNSON: And what about our poor time travelers?

DR. BARR: Oh, they will get by, I am sure. But we here seem to be in a quandary.

MR. MORELLI: Excuse me. I think I get that lingo.

DR. BARR: Oh, Mr. Morelli. This is Mr. Morelli of our physics department. Don't tell me *you* understand them?

MR. MORELLI: After a fashion. You see, I speak Italian, and know a little Church Latin to boot. I kind of get the "feel" of it. They want to know what's happened to them.

DR. LANGDON: Excellent! Between us, we ought to—yes, of course, I might have guessed. Italian derives from a Latin corrupted by ignorant folk in the Dark Ages. The Classical pronunciaton among the lower classes must have been basically similar. Come on, Morelli, let's see what we can do.

DR. BARR: Good. Remove the, ah, subjects to the prepared quarters as soon as possible. Oh, just a moment, here is the photographer from *Life*. Would you like me to pose with the Romans?—This is a great day for science, a great day!

* * *

Memorandum dated July 21, 1967

FROM: *Dr. Charles Langdon, Dept. of Classical Languages*
TO: *Dr. K. V. Clausewitz, Dean of the College of Arts*
SUBJECT: *Daily report on spatio-temporal research experiment*

We are making rapid progress now that I have the "hang" of their twisted argot. All three are cooperative and express themselves well pleased with the treatment they have received, with an exception noted below.

The man Publius describes himself as an unemployed sailor. He has a large stock of anecdotes about his past adventures; frankly, I doubt his strict veracity, but true or not, his stories furnish a priceless compendium of the details of everyday life. At last the riddle of the trireme has been solved! His words are, of course, being recorded, and a transcript is being prepared. I suggest, however, that access to this transcript be given only to a few properly authorized scholars, since his language and reminiscences may be described as racy. In fact, I do not believe even the original could go through the mails, let alone a translation.

So far Julius has remained evasive about his own life. I gather that he lived by his wits. In brief though colloquial terms, he was a confidence man or racketeer.

The young woman Quintilia has proven extremely cooperative, indeed to a somewhat embarrassing extent. As a *fille de joie*, she seems to feel called upon to pay for her lodging in the only coin she has. To safeguard the good name of this institution, though without making any insinuations of misconduct to date, I suggest that young Dr. Martens be transferred from this project.

The burden of discussion today dealt with their complaints. Their awe of us has worn off with surprising rapidity. Whether they really understand the idea of spatio-temporal transference is debatable, but at least an accomplished fact no longer impresses them. They unanimously demand to be let out of their quarters and offered entertainment. I have given them magazines, but the illustrations only seem to whet their appetites. I suggest that, if possible, some films be shown them, simple slapstick comedy within the grasp of their minds. Furthermore, in view of Quintilia's profession, I think it would be wisest to lock them into their separate rooms at night.

Tomorrow it is planned that we will take anthropometric measurements.

THE EMPIRE STATE
UNIVERSITY
New York 30, N.Y.
Office of the President

July 22, 1967

Dr. J. Worthington Barr
Department of Physics

Sir:

Since you are in charge of the time project, I must hold you answerable for the catastrophe which has occurred. Kindly let me have the precise circumstances, the names of all concerned, and the steps contemplated to deal with the situation.

Yours truly,

James M. Johnson
President

THE EMPIRE STATE UNIVERSITY
New York 30, N.Y.
College of Science and Engineering
Department of Physics

July 23, 1967

Dr. James M. Johnson
Office of the President

Dear Sir:

This letter will confirm our conversation of yesterday and serve as my official explanation of the difficulty. I must, however, decline to bear personal responsibility for the incident, nor is my department actually to blame. May I point out that the project was undertaken jointly with the History Dept.?

Briefly, then, as closely as the facts can be ascertained, yesterday at 1:30 P.M. the Roman subjects were called into the common room of their assigned quarters for the scheduled anthropometric studies. Present were Dr. Langdon as interpreter and Drs. Cabot and Simmons of the Department of Anthropology. It was noted that the woman Quintilia had put on modern dress, kindly lent to her by Dr. Langdon's wife. She had requested such garments three days previously after seeing some pictures in *Mademoiselle*.

I can only conclude, and my colleagues join with me in this, that the Romans had prepared their scheme in advance and waited until the original precautions of the campus police were relaxed. The report of what happened suffers from a deplorable paucity of precise detail, but the observers agree that Publius volunteered to be measured first. He and Julius removed their clothes. Dr. Langdon requested Quintilia to leave the room meanwhile, but she refused quite profanely. It must be remembered that the Classical world had a different attitude toward nudity from that of our Western Christian Civilization.

Publius sat down in a chair and Drs. Cabot and Simmons bent over him with calipers and notebook. Being a large and powerful man, Publius reached up and, I gather, knocked their heads together. Meanwhile Julius used some variety of judo on Dr. Langdon. Before any of our unhappy colleagues had fully recovered consciousness, they were stripped, bound, and gagged with Dr. Langdon's garments. Publius and Julius donned the clothes of, respectively, Drs. Cabot and Simmons, and all three subjects thereon left the room.

There are no witnesses to their further actions. They must simply have mingled with the crowd, as this was a period between summer classes, and walked off the campus. Their motives are uncertain, but Dr. Oliver of the Department of Psychology is making an intensive study and has advanced the preliminary hypothesis, subject to correction, that it was a matter of boredom, curiosity and greed. After all, three slum dwellers might not relish the prospect of being returned to their unfavorable environment. However, on the basis of Gestalt theory, Dr. Hayward disputes this suggestion. Both will submit reports as soon as practicable.

The occurrence is unfortunate, but there is no ground for alarm. I should particularly wish to reassure you in your concern for Maury, McIntyre and Harbold. True, we cannot recover them from the past without projecting three other humans back; but if necessary, the corpses of our three subjects will suffice.

However, such a tragic denouement is hardly probable. I have been in conference with Inspector Brannigan of the Metropolitan Police Force, and he assures me that strangers from another era, totally ignorant of our language and customs, cannot long remain undetected. Indeed, it seems most likely that the fear of such unfamiliar objects as skyscrapers and automobiles will force them to return to us voluntarily. Meanwhile, a police dragnet is out, but chiefly for the protection of the Romans themselves, who in their helplessness could possibly meet with some accident.

I await the return, voluntary or enforced, of our subjects at any moment. It is clear from the above, as your own well-known sense of fairness will readily admit, that neither I nor my department can be held in any way responsible; but naturally we offer our fullest cooperation.

Very truly yours,
J. Worthington Barr
Chairman of the Department

FEDERAL BUREAU OF INVESTIGATION
Department of Justice
Washington, D.C.

July 30, 1967

Dr. James M. Johnson
Office of the President
Empire State University
New York 30, N.Y.

Dear Sir:

I am in receipt of your telegram of the 30th inst. regarding the disappearance of three Romans of the Augustan Era and the failure of the local police to apprehend them.

Since these people are not American citizens and have not been granted visas, their case would normally fall under the jurisdiction of the Department of Immigration and Naturalization. But since special permission was obtained for your experiment, this bureau is prepared to enter the case. We should, in fact, have been notified immediately, and your delay in doing so will itself have to be investigated.

In the meantime, our New York office will take over the search.

Yours truly,
K. Edward Windhover

*Memorandum dated
December 18, 1967*

FROM: *Dr. Alfred Morelli, Dept. of Physics*
TO: *Dr. J. Worthington Barr, Chairman*
SUBJECT: *Development of sweepfield attachment for spatio-temporal projector*

This is to let you know that the pilot model of the sweep-field attachment has been tested and proven so satisfactory that a full-scale device can now be constructed. I estimate that we can have it ready in about six weeks, provided we can get the funds. Setting it for the physical characteristics of Maury, McIntyre and Harbold, we can then scan the entire central Mediterranean area of 1 A.D. (or, by then, 2 A.D.) and pick them up wherever they are—or their bodies if they have died.

I'm not so worried about this, though. With their modern background and equipment—well, they can't change the past, but maybe it'll turn out that Augustus Caesar had three powerful ministers who really ran the Empire and didn't get into the history books!

The main stumbling block, aside from the cost, will be getting three humans to exchange for our boys. Since

those blasted Romans haven't turned up yet . . . poor
devils, they're probably in the East River by now. I'd
guess they got scared, tried to come back to us, and never
made it for some reason. Well, if we don't find them, we'll
just have to go ahead and use three unclaimed bodies from
the morgue. Can you arrange that with the cops? I'm
attaching an IBM tabulation of the required physical
measurements.

JOURNAL OF THE AMERICAN
MEDICAL ASSOCIATION
April 7, 1968
Studies of Physical and Psychic
Lesions Incident to
the Hazards of Time Travel
by C. Galen, M.D., Ph.D.,
School of
Medicine, Empire State
University
and E.S. Oliver, Ph.D.,
Department of
Psychology, Empire State
University

By now the misadventures of the University expedition
to Augustan Rome are common knowledge, but it was felt
that a scientific study of James K. Maury, Roger McIntyre
and Simon Harbold would prove of interest and possibly of
value to physicians who may in the future have to treat
patients with a similar experience. The following data are
published with the permission of the men in question and
of the University authorities.

Briefly to recapitulate, they materialized in a slum area
at midnight, as planned. The streets of that time being
unlighted, and few people abroad, they were not noticed.
Elated by their success, they studied the location carefully
so they could return to it at the appointed time, and then
set out to find lodging for the remainder of the night.

Their account is rather confused. Presumably, as they
went past a dark alley, they were set on by robbers, who
were common in that part of town. About four men attacked

them, and Harbold suffered a knife wound in the upper left biceps. Maury drew his revolver and disposed of one bandit. The noise attracted the attention of an official patrol, which arrived on the scene and began to club all present into submission. Naturally, Maury did not fire on them, but all he gained by his forbearance was a mild concussion. Being terrorized, McIntyre fled and managed to elude pursuit.

Confined in separate cells, though with numerous fellow prisoners, Maury and Harbold spent a miserable time, much annoyed by vermin. It was two days before the former was brought before a magistrate. In the meantime Harbold apparently contracted a variety of plague from louse bites; furthermore, his wound was badly infected. His immunizations appear to have been ineffective, which suggests that there has been a radical mutational change in a number of viruses during the past two millennia and further suggests the necessity of extensive bacteriological studies before any such expeditions are again undertaken.

Maury had been stripped of all his gear by the police, and was not allowed to have it back to prove his claims of great powers. He was, in fact, considered to be suffering from delusions—insofar as anyone understood his version of Latin—and was in all events an unregistered alien, presumed to be of some Germanic tribe. Though this was before the battle of Teutoburger Wald, there was considerable tension and Germans were suspect. The upshot was that Maury was enslaved and sold to the master of a galley in the Egyptian trade. He spent the rest of his seven-month stay in the past pulling an oar under most unsanitary conditions.

However, the case had aroused the interest of the quaestor, who had Harbold brought to him. Though semi-delirious from fever, Harbold asked for his medical kit, and after the usual linguistic difficulty this was given to him. Under improved conditions of detention, and with the help of penicillin injections, he recovered very slowly. Much impressed, the quaestor finally asked him to demonstrate the other twentieth-century equipment captured from the expedition, and this he did. Naturally, he expected to be treated as an important figure, and the psychic shock

must have been considerable when he was accused of
witchcraft and all the apparatus was destroyed. It seems
that magic was illegal under Roman law; and being a
people utterly devoid of scientific curiosity and positively
hostile to technological innovation—which could upset their
slave-labor economy—they had no further interest in him.
Harbold was condemned to be thrown to the lions as soon
as he got well enough to provide good sport. The temporal
sweepfield was developed just in time to save him.

Meanwhile McIntyre, fleeing, survived the night but
the next day had his money stolen by some cutpurse. He
tried to sell his gear, but no one was interested enough to
give him more than scrap metal prices, and he learned later
that he had been cheated even on that transaction. In a few
days, McIntyre found himself a penniless foreigner, unable
to get work since he lacked the manual skills of the era and
certainly unable to convince anyone of the facts. Wisely, he
did not even attempt to do this, but eked out a precarious
existence as a beggar. He was near starvation when rescued.

The full account may, of course, be found elsewhere.
Turning to the medical and psychiatric examinations . . .

FEDERAL BUREAU OF
INVESTIGATION
Department of Justice
Washington, D.C.

May 21, 1968

Dr. James M. Johnson
Office of the President
Empire State University
New York 30, N.Y.

Dear Sir:

I am in receipt of your communication of the 15th inst.
regarding the case of the three missing Romans. Rest
assured, this bureau will not give up the case. This bureau
never gives up a case. You will be notified when the
subjects have been found and arrested.

Yours truly,
K. Edward Windhover

Headquarters of the National
Committee of
THE ALL-AMERICAN PARTY
Roosenhower Building
Chicago 19, Illinois

August 9, 1993

Mr. Julio Arminelli
Anglosaxon Arms Hotel
New York 8, N.Y.

Dear Julius,

This is going to be kind of a hard note to write,
considering how long we have been friends and all, and
believe me I still think of you as my old pal and as soon as
I can I will see you again and I won't forget your wife and
kids neither. But for the time being we had better stop
seeing each other. People are starting to talk, and I can't
afford that. You know how it is.

Me Hercule, it seems like a long time ago we came to
the good old USA! And it is, you know, 26 years about. By
now we would probably have been down in Pluto's boarding
house from some or other filthy disease if that time machine
had not yanked us up to now. These doctors they got
nowadays are Georgios verus, huh, old pal?

Remember how scared we was at first? Even after we
had busted out, we was scared, all the cars and stuff. I
remember Quintilia was about ready to break and run for
it, till I told her these things did not hurt other people so
why should they hurt us? Only it was you figured out the
traffic light system, you always was a sharp boy, Julius.
Otherwise we would likely have been arrested then and
there. I guess it was us all together who found a low class
part of town. We have got a nose for that.

Plain luck, I admit, that there was this big Italian section
where we could make ourselves understood and get us a
flophouse where they do not ask questions. Not that we
have ever been in much danger, even since we got famous.
The only people who got a close look at us before we
busted out was these science boys at the U., and they are

schnooks who could not identify their own grandmother in a lineup.

Remember how Quintilia got to work? Some doll, and her job don't change none in two thousand years! I am glad, though, you made me stop after I mugged that one guy in Central Park. It was a two-hundred buck haul, but you are right, crime don't pay.

And then that fortune-telling racket you started. Did that ever pull them in! After we had bailed you out the first time and got wise to the law and called it an Orphic religion, we had them, boy, we had them. These religions nowadays don't know a damn thing about showmanship. But don't forget, I was the one who cleaned out that big crap game and got us our capital. I am still good at it. When you learned to throw them scientific on the deck of a lousy little galley in a mistral wind, you never forget how, even if the shape is different nowadays.

I don't think you was right in your last letter, where you said it was luck Quintilia roped that Park Avenue swell and got him to set her up in a swank apartment and all. That doll knows her stuff, I tell you. If we had stayed in Rome, she might have ended up with Caesar. Better this way, though. Wives don't poison mistresses any more. Not very often. Of course, it was nice having connections through her boyfriend so we could get forged papers. This century is almost as bad as Rome when it comes to wanting official papers in triplicate. Imagine me, old Popeye Publius the sailor, with a birth certificate in Boston!

How do you like my English, by the way? I am trying it on you this time. I never did learn to write English so well, though you know I got a Brooklyn accent nobody could tell was put on. I remember the Italians where we hid out at first was surprised how fast we all learned the lingo. But hell, when they spoke a hundred languages in the Roman Empire, you had to be good at them or go under, isn't that so? You write just like a college professor, take it from me.

In fact, our busting loose was only the second-best thing that ever happened to us. The best was being born in the Roman slums, or the Ostia waterfront in my case. Sounds funny? Well, just think of it as the good old School of Hard

Knocks. We learned how to handle people back then, because if we did not know how, we would end up heaving an oar or feeding the lions, which we did not want to do, and people do not change much. Not big-city working stiffs, anyway.

But I am writing too much about the old days. It is just to show that I still think a lot of you and I am not forgetting you even if we can't meet again for a while. You see, I am on the National Committee now and I can damn near handpick the next candidates for governor of you-know-what three states—and elect them, by Jupiter's right eye! Only till our boys are in the saddle, with me behind them pulling all the strings, it just would not do for Big John Brutto, the People's Pal, to be so close to Julio Arminelli who everybody knows owns all the rackets in New York even if they can't pin it on him. Once the elections is over, I will look you up for sure, because there is plenty you can do for us and I do not think you will mind getting on the gravy train.

Well, so now I got to close. I had a letter from Quintilia the other day. She has built a new house in Beverly Hills and having ditched Husband Number Six, or is it Seven, she is going to make another movie. Maybe she is over forty years of age now, but mammis Veneris, that gal can still pull them in!

Your Old Friend,
Publius (Big John)

RANKS OF BRONZE

David Drake

The rising sun is a dagger point casting long shadows toward Vibulenus and his cohort from the native breastworks. The legion had formed ranks an hour before; the enemy is not yet stirring. A playful breeze with a bitter edge skitters out of the south, and the tribune swings his shield to his right side against it.

"When do we advance, sir?" his first centurion asks. Gnaeus Clodius Calvus, promoted to his present position after a boulder had pulped his predecessor during the assault on a granite fortress far away. Vibulenus only vaguely recalls his first days with the cohort, a boy of eighteen in titular command of four hundred and eighty men whose names he had despaired of learning. Well, he knows them now. Of course, there are only two hundred and ninety-odd left to remember.

Calvus's bearded, silent patience snaps Vibulenus back to the present. "When the cavalry comes up, they told me. Some kinglet or other is supposed to bring up a couple of thousand men to close our flanks. Otherwise, we're hanging. . . ."

The tribune's voice trails off. He stares across the flat expanse of gravel toward the other camp, remembering another battle plain of long ago.

"Damn Parthians," Calvus mutters, his thought the same. Vibulenus nods. "Damn Crassus, you mean. He put us

233

there, and that put us *here*. The stupid bastard. But he got his, too."

The legionaries squat in their ranks, talking and chewing bits of bread or dried fruit. They display no bravado, very little concern. They have been here too often before. Sunlight turns their shield-facings green: not the crumbly fungus of verdigris but the shimmering sea-color of the harbor of Brundisium on a foggy morning.

Oh, Mother Vesta, Vibulenus breathes to himself. He is five-foot-two, about average for the legion. His hair is black where it curls under the rim of his helmet and he has no trace of a beard. Only his eyes make him appear more than a teenager; they would suit a tired man of fifty.

A trumpet from the command group in the rear sings three quick bars. "Fall in!" the tribune orders, but his centurions are already barking their own commands. These too are lost in the clash of hobnails on gravel. The Tenth Cohort could form ranks in its sleep.

Halfway down the front, a legionary's cloak hooks on a notch in his shield rim. He tugs at it, curses in Oscan as Calvus snarls down the line at him. Vibulenus makes a mental note to check with the centurion after the battle. That fellow should have been issued a replacement shield before disembarking. He glances at his own. How many shields has he carried? Not that it matters. Armor is replaceable. He is wearing his fourth cuirass, now, though none of them have fit like the one his father had bought him the day Crassus granted him a tribune's slot. Vesta . . .

A galloper from the command group skids his beast to a halt with a needlessly brutal jerk on its reins. Vibulenus recognizes him—Pompilius Falco. A little swine when he joined the legion, an accomplished swine now. Not bad with animals, though. "We'll be advancing without the cavalry," he shouts, leaning over in his saddle. "Get your line dressed."

"Osiris's bloody dick we will!" the tribune snaps. "Where's our support?"

"Have to support yourself, I guess," shrugs Falco. He wheels his mount. Vibulenus steps forward and catches the reins.

"Falco," he says with no attempt to lower his voice, "you tell our deified commander to get somebody on our left flank if he expects the Tenth to advance. There's too many natives—they'll hit us from three sides at once."

"You afraid to die?" the galloper sneers. He tugs at the reins.

Vibulenus holds them. A gust of wind whips at his cloak. "Afraid to get my skull split?" he asks. "I don't know. Are you, Falco?" Falco glances at where the tribune's right hand rests. He says nothing. "Tell him we'll fight for him," Vibulenus goes on. "We won't let him throw us away. We've gone that route once." He looses the reins and watches the galloper scatter gravel on his way back.

The replacement gear is solid enough, shields that do not split when dropped and helmets forged without thin spots. But there is no craftsmanship in them. They are heavy, lifeless. Vibulenus still carries a bone-hilted sword from Toledo that required frequent sharpening but was tempered and balanced—poised to slash a life out, as it has a hundred times already. His hand continues to caress the palm-smoothed bone, and it calms him somewhat.

"Thanks, sir."

The thin-featured tribune glances back at his men. Several of the nearer ranks give him a spontaneous salute. Calvus is the one who spoke. He is blank-faced now, a statue of mahogany and strap-bronze. His stocky form radiates pride in his leader. Leader—no one in the group around the standards can lead a line soldier, though they may give commands that will be obeyed. Vibulenus grins and slaps Calvus's burly shoulder. "Maybe this is the last one and we'll be going home," he says.

Movement throws a haze over the enemy camp. At this distance it is impossible to distinguish forms, but metal flashes in the virid sunlight. The shadow of bodies spreads slowly to right and left of the breastworks as the natives order themselves. There are thousands of them, many thousands.

"Hey-*yip!*" Twenty riders of the general's bodyguard pass behind the cohort at an earthshaking trot. They rein

up on the left flank, shrouding the exposed depth of the
infantry. Pennons hang from the lances socketed behind
their right thighs, gay yellows and greens to keep the
lance heads from being driven too deep to be jerked out.
The riders' faces are sullen under their mesh face guards.
Vibulenus knows how angry they must be at being shifted
under pressure—under his pressure—and he grins again.
The bodyguards are insulted at being required to fight
instead of remaining nobly aloof from the battle. The
experience may do them some good.

At least it may get a few of the snotty bastards killed.

"Not exactly a regiment of cavalry," Calvus grumbles.

"He gave us half of what was available," Vibulenus
replies with a shrug. "They'll do to keep the natives off our
back. Likely nobody'll come near, they look so mean."

The centurion taps his thigh with his knobby swagger
stick. "Mean? We'll give 'em mean."

All the horns in the command group sound together, a
cacophonous bray. The jokes and scufflings freeze, and
only the south wind whispers. Vibulenus takes a last look
down his ranks—each of them fifty men abreast and no
more sway to it than a tight-stretched cord would leave.
Five feet from shield boss to shield boss, room to swing a
sword. Five feet from nose guard to the nose guards of the
next rank, men ready to step forward individually to replace
the fallen or by ranks to lock shields with the front line in
an impenetrable wall of bronze. The legion is a restive
dragon, and its teeth glitter in its spears; one vertical
behind each legionary's shield, one slanted from each right
hand to stab or throw.

The horns blare again, the eagle standard slants forward,
and Vibulenus's throat joins three thousand others in a
death-rich bellow as the legion steps off on its left foot.
The centurions are counting cadence and the ranks blast it
back to them in the crash-jingle of boots and gear.

Striding quickly between the legionaries, Vibulenus
checks the dress of his cohort. He should have a horse,
but there are no horses in the legion now. The command
group rides rough equivalents which are . . . very rough.
Vibulenus is not sure he could accept one if his parsimonious
employers offered it.

His men are a smooth bronze chain that advances in lock step. Very nice. The nine cohorts to the right are in equally good order, but Hercules! there are so few of them compared to the horde swarming from the native camp. Somebody has gotten overconfident. The enemy raises its own cheer, scattered and thin at first. But it goes on and on, building, ordering itself to a blood-pulse rhythm that moans across the intervening distance, the gap the legion is closing at two steps a second. Hercules! there is a crush of them.

The natives are close enough to be individuals now: lanky, long-armed in relation to a height that averages greater than that of the legionaires. Ill-equipped, though. Their heads are covered either by leather helmets or beehives of their own hair. Their shields appear to be hide and wicker affairs. What could live on this gravel waste and provide that much leather? But of course Vibulenus has been told none of the background, not even the immediate geography. There is some place around that raises swarms of warriors, that much is certain.

And they have iron. The black glitter of their spearheads tightens the tribune's wounded chest as he remembers.

"Smile, boys," one of the centurions calls cheerfully, "here's company." With his words a javelin hums down at a steep angle to spark on the ground. From a spear-thrower, must have been. The distance is too long for any arm Vibulenus has seen, and he has seen his share.

"Ware!" he calls as another score of missiles arc from the native ranks. Legionairies judge them, raise their shields or ignore the plunging weapons as they choose. One strikes in front of Vibulenus and shatters into a dozen iron splinters and a knobby shaft that looks like rattan. One or two of the men have spears clinging to their shield faces. Their clatter syncopates the thud of boot heels. No one is down.

Vibulenus runs two paces ahead of his cohort, his sword raised at an angle. It makes him an obvious target: a dozen javelins spit toward him. The skin over his ribs crawls, the lumpy breadth of scar tissue scratching like a rope over the bones. But he can be seen by every man in his cohort, and somebody has to give the signal. . . .

"Now!" he shouts vainly in the mingling cries. His arm
and sword cut down abruptly. Three hundred throats give
a collective grunt as the cohort heaves its own massive
spears with the full weight of its rush behind them. Another
light javelin glances from the shoulder of Vibulenus's cuirass,
staggering him. Calvus's broad right palm catches the
tribune, holds him upright for the instant he needs to get
his balance.

The front of the native line explodes as the Roman
spears crash into it.

Fifty feet ahead there are orange warriors shrieking as
they stumble over the bodies of comrades whose armor
has shredded under the impact of the heavy spears. "At
'em!" a front-rank file-closer cries, ignoring his remaining
spear as he drags out his short sword. The trumpets are
calling something but it no longer matters what: tactics go
hang, the Tenth is cutting its way into another native
army.

In a brief spate of fury, Vibulenus holds his forward
position between a pair of legionaires. A native, orange-
skinned with bright carmine eyes, tries to drag himself out
of the tribune's path. A Roman spear has gouged through
his shield and arm, locking all three together. Vibulenus's
sword takes the warrior alongside the jaw. The blood is
paler than a man's.

The backward shock of meeting has bunched the natives.
The press of undisciplined reserves from behind adds to
their confusion. Vibulenus jumps a still-writhing body and
throws himself into the wall of shields and terrified orange
faces. An iron-headed spear thrusts at him, misses as
another warrior jostles the wielder. Vibulenus slashes
downward at his assailant. The warrior throws his shield
up to catch the sword, then collapses when a second-rank
legionary darts his spear through the orange abdomen.

Breathing hard with his sword still dripping in his hand,
Vibulenus lets the pressing ranks flow around him. Slaughter
is not a tribune's work, but increasingly Vibulenus finds
that he needs the swift violence of the battle line to
release the fury building within him. The cohort is advancing
with the jerky sureness of an ox-drawn plow in dry soil.

A windrow of native bodies lies among the line of first contact, now well within the Roman formation. Vibulenus wipes his blade on a fallen warrior, leaving two sluggish runnels filling on the flesh. He sheaths the sword. Three bodies are sprawled together to form a hillock. Without hesitation the Tribune steps onto it to survey the battle.

The legion is a broad awl punching through a belt of orange leather. The cavalry on the left stand free in a scatter of bodies, neither threatened by the natives nor making any active attempt to drive them back. One of the mounts, a hairless brute combining the shape of a wolfhound with the bulk of an ox, is feeding on a corpse his rider has lanced. Vibulenus was correct in expecting the natives to give them a wide berth; thousands of flanking warriors tremble in indecision rather than sweep forward to surround the legion. It would take more discipline that this orange rabble has shown to attack the toadlike riders on their terrible beasts.

Behind the lines, a hundred paces distant from the legionaires whose armor stands in hammering contrast to the naked autochthones, is the commander and his remaining score of guards. He alone of the three thousand who have landed from the starship knows why the battle is being fought, but he seems to stand above it. And if the silly bastard still has half his body guard with him—Mars and all the gods, what must be happening on the right flank?

The inhuman shout of triumph that rises half a mile away gives Vibulenus an immediate answer.

"Prepare to disengage!" he orders the nearest centurion. The swarthy noncom, son of a North African colonist, speaks briefly into the ears of two legionaries before sending them to the ranks forward and back of his. The legion is tight for men, always has been. Tribunes have no runners, but the cohort makes do.

Trumpets blat in terror. The native warriors boil whooping around the Roman right flank. Legionaries in the rear are facing about with ragged suddenness, obeying instinct rather than the orders bawled by their startled officers. The command group suddenly realizes the situation. Three of the bodyguard charge toward the oncoming orange mob. The rest of the guards and staff scatter into the infantry.

The iron-bronze clatter has ceased on the left flank. When the cohort halts its advance, the natives gain enough room to break and flee for their encampment. Even the warriors who have not engaged are cowed by the panic of those who have; by the panic, and the sprawls of bodies left behind them.

"About face!" Vibulenus calls through the indecisive hush, "and pivot on your left flank. There's some more barbs want to fight the Tenth!"

The murderous cheer from his legionaries overlies the noise of the cohort executing his order.

As it swings Vibulenus runs across the new front of his troops, what had been the rear rank. The cavalry, squat-bodied and grim in their full armor, shows sense enough to guide their mounts toward the flank of the Ninth Cohort as Vibulenus rotates his men away from it. Only a random javelin from the native lines appears to hinder them. Their comrades who remained with the commander have been less fortunate.

A storm of javelins has disintegrated the half-hearted charge. Two of the mounts have gone down despite their heavy armor. Behind them, the commander lies flat on the hard soil while his beast screams horribly above him. The shaft of a stray missile projects from its withers. Stabbing up from below, the orange warriors fell the remaining lancer and gut his companions as they try to rise. Half a dozen of the bodyguards canter nervously back from their safe bolthole among the infantry to try to rescue their employer. The wounded mount leaps at one of the lancers. The two beasts tangle with the guard between them. A clawed hind leg flicks his head. Helmet and head rip skyward in a spout of green ichor.

"Charge!" Vibulenus roars. The legionaries who cannot hear him follow his running form. The knot of cavalry and natives is a quarter mile away. The cohorts of the right flank are too heavily engaged to do more than defend themselves against the new thrust. Half the legion has become a bronze worm, bristling front and back with spearpoints against the surging orange flood. Without immediate support, the whole right flank will be squeezed until it collapses into a tangle of blood and scrap metal. The Tenth Cohort is their support, all the support there is.

"Rome!" the fresh veterans leading the charge shout as their shields rise against the new flight of javelins. There are gaps in the back ranks, those just disengaged. Behind the charge, men hold palms clamped over torn calves or lie crumpled around a shaft of alien wood. There will be time enough for them if the recovery teams land—which they will not do in event of a total disaster on the ground.

The warriors snap and howl at the sudden threat. Their own success has fragmented them. What had been a flail slashing into massed bronze kernels is now a thousand leaderless handfuls in sparkling contact with the Roman line. Only the leaders bunched around the command group have held their unity.

One mount is still on its feet and snarling. Four massively-equipped guards try to ring the commander with their maces. The commander, his suit a splash of blue against the gravel, tries to rise. There is a flurry of mace strokes and quickly-riposting spears, ending in a clash of falling armor and an agile orange body with a knife leaping the crumpled guard. Vibulenus's sword, flung overarm, takes the native in the throat. The inertia of its spin cracks the hilt against the warrior's forehead.

The Tenth Cohort is on the startled natives. A moment before the warriors were bounding forward in the flush of victory. Now they face the cohort's meat-axe suddenness— and turn. At swordpoint and shield edge, as inexorable as the rising sun, the Tenth grinds the native retreat into panic while the cohorts of the right flank open order and advance. The ground behind them is slimy with blood.

Vibulenus rests on one knee, panting. He has retrieved his sword. Its stickiness bonds it to his hand. Already the air keens with landing motors. In minutes the recovery teams will be at work on the fallen legionaries, building life back into all but the brain-hacked or spine-severed. Vibulenus rubs his own scarred ribs in aching memory.

A hand falls on the tribune's shoulder. It is gloved in a skin-tight blue material; not armor, at least not armor against weapons. The commander's voice comes from the small plate beneath his clear, round helmet. Speaking in Latin, his accents precisely flawed, he says, "You are splendid, you warriors."

Vibulenus sneers though he does not correct the alien. Warriors are capering heroes, good only for dying when they meet trained troops, when they meet the Tenth Cohort.

"I thought the Federation Council had gone mad," the flat voice continues, "when it ruled that we must not land weapons beyond the native level in exploiting inhabited worlds. All very well to talk of the dangers of introducing barbarians to modern weaponry, but how else could my business crush local armies and not be bled white by transportation costs?"

The commander shakes his head in wonder at the carnage about him. Vibulenus silently wipes his blade. In front of him, Falco gapes toward the green sun. A javelin points from his right eyesocket. "When we purchased you from your Parthian captors it was only an experiment. Some of us even doubted it was worth the cost of the longevity treatments. In a way you are more effective than a Guard Regiment with lasers; outnumbered, you beat them with their own weapons. They can't even claim 'magic' as a salve to their pride. And at a score of other job sites you have done as well. And so cheaply!"

"Since we have been satisfactory," the tribune says, trying to keep the hope out of his face, "will we be returned home now?"

"Oh, goodness, no," the alien laughs, "you're far too valuable for that. But I have a surprise for you, one just as pleasant I'm sure—females."

"You found us real women?" Vibulenus whispers.

"You really won't be able to tell the difference," the Commander says with paternal confidence.

A million suns away on a farm in the Sabine hills, a poet takes the stylus from the fingers of a nude slave girl and writes, very quickly, *And Crassus's wretched soldier takes a barbarian wife from his captors and grows old waging war for them.*

The poet looks at the line with a pleased expression. "It needs polish, of course," he mutters. Then, more directly to the slave, he says, "You know, Leuconoe, there's more than inspiration to poetry, a thousand times more; but this came to me out of the air."

Horace gestures with his stylus toward the glittering night sky. The girl smiles back at him.

KINGS OF THE NIGHT

Robert E. Howard

The Caesar lolled on his ivory throne—
His iron legions came
To break a king in a land unknown,
And a race without a name.

—*The Song of Bran*

1

The dagger flashed downward. A sharp cry broke in a gasp. The form on the rough altar twitched convulsively and lay still. The jagged flint edge sawed at the crimson breast, and thin bony fingers, ghastly dyed, tore out the still twitching heart. Under matted white brows, sharp eyes gleamed with a ferocious intensity.

Besides the slayer, four men stood about the crude pile of stones that formed the altar of the God of Shadows. One was of medium height, lithely built, scantily clad, whose black hair was confined by a narrow iron band in the center of which gleamed a single red jewel. Of the others, two were dark like the first. But where he was lithe, they were stocky and misshapen, with knotted limbs, and tangled hair falling over sloping brows. His face denoted intelligence and implacable will; theirs merely a beastlike ferocity. The fourth man had little in common with the rest. Nearly a head taller, though his hair was black as theirs, his skin was comparatively light and he was gray-eyed. He eyed the proceedings with little favor.

And, in truth, Cormac of Connacht was little at ease. The Druids of his own isle of Erin had strange dark rites of worship, but nothing like this. Dark trees shut in this dark scene, lit by a single torch. Through the branches moaned an eery night wind. Cormac was alone among men of a strange race and he had just seen the heart of a man ripped from his still pulsing body. Now the ancient priest, who looked scarcely human, was glaring at the throbbing thing. Cormac shuddered, glancing at him who wore the jewel. Did Bran Mak Morn, king of the Picts, believe that this white-bearded old butcher could foretell events by scanning a bleeding human heart? The dark eyes of the king were inscrutable. There were strange depths to the man that Cormac could not fathom, nor any other man.

"The portents are good!" exclaimed the priest wildly, speaking more to the two chieftains than to Bran. "Here from the pulsing heart of a captive Roman I read—defeat for the arms of Rome! Triumph for the sons of the heather!"

The two savages murmured beneath their breath, their fierce eyes smoldering.

"Go and prepare your clans for battle," said the king, and they lumbered away with the apelike gait assumed by such stunted giants. Paying no more heed to the priest who was examining the ghastly ruin on the altar, Bran beckoned to Cormac. The Gael followed him with alacrity. Once out of that grim grove, under the starlight, he breathed more freely. They stood on an eminence, looking out over long swelling undulations of gently waving heather. Near at hand a few fires twinkled, their fewness giving scant evidence of the hordes of tribesmen who lay close by. Beyond these were more fires and beyond these still more, which last marked the camp of Cormac's own men, hard-riding, hard-fighting Gaels, who were of that band which was just beginning to get a foothold on the western coast of Caledonia—the nucleus of what was later to become the kingdom of Dalriadia. To the left of these, other fires gleamed.

And far away to the south were more fires—mere pinpoints of light. But even at that distance the Pictish king and his Celtic ally could see that these fires were laid out in regular order.

"The fires of the legions," muttered Bran. "The fires that have lit a path around the world. The men who light those fires have trampled the races under their iron heels. And now—we of the heather have our backs at the wall. What will fall on the morrow?"

"Victory for us, says the priest," answered Cormac.

Bran made an impatient gesture. "Moonlight on the ocean. Wind in the fir tops. Do you think that I put faith in such mummery? Or that I enjoyed the butchery of a captive legionary? I must hearten my people; it was for Gron and Bocah that I let old Gonar read the portents. The warriors will fight better."

"And Gonar?"

Bran laughed. "Gonar is too old to believe—anything. He was high priest of the Shadows a score of years before I was born. He claims direct descent from that Gonar who was a wizard in the days of Brule, the Spear-slayer who was the first of my line. No man knows how old he is—sometimes I think he is the original Gonar himself!"

"At least," said a mocking voice, and Cormac started as a dim shape appeared at his side, "at least I have learned that in order to keep the faith and trust of the people, a wise man must appear to be a fool. I know secrets that would blast even your brain, Bran, should I speak them. But in order that the people may believe in me, I must descend to such things as they think proper magic— and prance and yell and rattle snakeskins, and dabble about in human blood and chicken livers."

Cormac looked at the ancient with new interest. The semi-madness of his appearance had vanished. He was no longer the charlatan, the spell-mumbling shaman. The starlight lent him a dignity which seemed to increase his very height, so that he stood like a white-bearded patriarch.

"Bran, your doubt lies there." The lean arm pointed to the fourth ring of fires.

"Aye," the king nodded gloomily. "Cormac—you know as well as I. Tomorrow's battle hinges upon that circle of fires. With the chariots of the Britons and your own Western horsemen, our success would be certain, but—surely the

devil himself is in the heart of every Northman! You know
how I trapped that band—how they swore to fight for me
against Rome! And now that their chief, Rognar, is dead,
they swear that they will be led only by a king of their own
race! Else they will break their vow and go over to the
Romans. Without them we are doomed, for we cannot
change our former plan."

"Take heart, Bran," said Gonar. "Touch the jewel in
your iron crown. Mayhap it will bring you aid."

Bran laughed bitterly. "Now you talk as the people
think. I am no fool to twist with empty words. What of the
gem? It is a strange one, truth, and has brought me luck
ere now. But I need now, no jewels, but the allegiance of
three hundred fickle Northmen who are the only warriors
among us who may stand the charge of the legions on foot.

"But the jewel, Bran, the jewel!" persisted Gonar.

"Well, the jewel!" cried Bran impatiently. "It is older
than this world. It was old when Atlantis and Lemuria
sank into the sea. It was given to Brule, the Spear-slayer,
first of my line, by the Atlantean Kull, king of Valusia, in
the days when the world was young. But shall that profit
us now?"

"Who knows?" asked the wizard obliquely. "Time and
space exist not. There was no past, and there shall be no
future. NOW is all. All things that ever were, are, or ever
will be, transpire *now*. Man is forever at the center of
what we call time and space. I have gone into yesterday
and tomorrow and both were as real as today—which is
like the dreams of ghosts! But let me sleep and talk with
Gonar. Mayhap he shall aid us."

"What means he?" asked Cormac, with a slight twitching
of his shoulders, as the priest strode away in the shadows.

"He has ever said that the first Gonar comes to him in
his dreams and talks with him," answered Bran. "I have
seen him perform deeds that seemed beyond human ken.
I know not. I am but an unknown king with an iron crown,
trying to lift a race of savages out of the slime into which
they have sunk. Let us look to the camps."

As they walked, Cormac wondered. By what strange
freak of fate had such a man risen among this race of
savages, survivors of a darker, grimmer age? Surely he was

an atavism, an original type of the days when the Picts ruled all Europe, before their primitive empire fell before the bronze swords of the Gauls. Cormac knew how Bran, rising by his own efforts from the negligent position of the son of a Wolf clan chief, had to an extent united the tribes of the heather and now claimed kingship over all Caledon. But his rule was loose and much remained before the Pictish clans would forget their feuds and present a solid front to foreign foes. On the battle of the morrow, the first pitched battle between the Picts under their king and the Romans, hinged the future of the rising Pictish kingdom.

Bran and his ally walked through the Pictish camp where the swart warriors lay sprawled about their small fires, sleeping or gnawing half-cooked food. Cormac was impressed by their silence. A thousand men camped here, yet the only sounds were occasional low guttural intonations. The silence of the Stone Age rested in the souls of these men.

They were all short—most of them crooked of limb. Giant dwarfs; Bran Mak Morn was a tall man among them. Only the older men were bearded and they scantily, but their black hair fell about their eyes so that they peered fiercely from under the tangle. They were barefoot and clad scantily in wolf-skins. Their arms consisted in short barbed swords of iron, heavy black bows, arrows tipped with flint, iron and copper, and stone-headed mallets. Defensive armor they had none, save for a crude shield of hide-covered wood; many had worked bits of metal into their tangled manes as a slight protection against swordcuts. Some few, sons of long lines of chiefs, were smooth-limbed and lithe like Bran, but in the eyes of all gleamed the unquenchable savagery of the primeval.

These men are fully savages, thought Cormac, worse than the Gauls, Britons and Germans. Can the old legends be true—that they reigned in a day when strange cities rose where now the sea rolls? And that they survived the flood that washed those gleaming empires under, sinking again into that savagery from which they once had risen?

Close to the encampment of the tribesmen were the fires of a group of Britons—members of fierce tribes who lived south of the Roman Wall but who dwelt in the hills and forests to the west and defied the power of Rome.

Powerfully built men they were, with blazing blue eyes and shocks of tousled yellow hair, such men as had thronged the Ceanntish beaches when Caesar brought the Eagles into the Isles. These men, like the Picts, wore no armor, and were clad scantily in coarse-worked cloth and deerskin sandals. They bore small round bucklers of hard wood, braced with bronze, to be worn on the left arm, and long heavy bronze swords with blunt points. Some had bows, though the Britons were indifferent archers. Their bows were shorter than the Picts' and effective only at close range. But ranged close by their fires were the weapons that had made the name Briton a word of terror to Pict, Roman and Norse raider alike. Within the circle of firelight stood bronze chariots with long cruel blades curving out from the sides. One of these blades could dismember half a dozen men at once. Tethered close by under the vigilant eyes of their guards grazed the chariot horses—big, rangy steeds, swift and powerful.

"Would that we had more of them!" mused Bran. "With a thousand chariots and my bowmen I could drive the legions into the sea."

"The free British tribes must eventually fall before Rome," said Cormac. "It would seem they would rush to join you in your war."

Bran made a helpless gesture. "The fickleness of the Celt. They cannot forget old feuds. Our ancient men have told us how they would not even unite against Caesar when the Romans first came. They will not make head against a common foe together. These men came to me because of some dispute with their chief, but I cannot depend on them when they are not actually fighting."

Cormac nodded. "I know; Caesar conquered Gaul by playing one tribe against another. My own people shift and change with the waxing and waning of the tides. But of all Celts, the Cymry are the most changeable, the least stable. Not many centuries ago my own Gaelic ancestors wrested Erin from the Cymric Canaans, because though they outnumbered us, they opposed us as separate tribes, rather than as a nation."

"And so these Cymric Britons face Rome," said Bran. "These will aid us on the morrow. Further I cannot say.

But how shall I expect loyalty from alien tribes, who are not sure of my own people? Thousands lurk in the hills, holding aloof. I am king in name only. Let me win tomorrow and they will flock to my standard; if I lose, they will scatter like birds before a cold wind."

A chorus of rough welcome greeted the two leaders as they entered the camp of Cormac's Gaels. Five hundred in number they were, tall rangy men, black-haired and gray-eyed mainly, with the bearing of men who lived by war alone. While there was nothing like close discipline among them, there was an air of more system and practical order than existed in the lines of the Picts and Britons. These men were of the last Celtic race to invade the Isles and their barbaric civilization was of much higher order than that of their Cymric kin. The ancestors of the Gaels had learned the arts of war on the vast plains of Scythia and at the courts of the Pharaohs where they had fought as mercenaries of Egypt, and much of what they learned they brought into Ireland with them. Excelling in metal work, they were armed, not with clumsy bronze swords, but with high-grade weapons of iron.

They were clad in well-woven kilts and leathern sandals. Each wore a light shirt of chain mail and a vizorless helmet, but this was all of their defensive armor. Celts, Gaelic or Brythonic, were prone to judge a man's valor by the amount of armor he wore. The Britons who faced Caesar deemed the Romans cowards because they cased themselves in metal, and many centuries later the Irish clans thought the same of the mail-clad Norman knights of Strongbow.

Cormac's warriors were horsemen. They neither knew nor esteemed the use of the bow. They bore the inevitable round, metal-braced buckler, dirks, long straight swords and light single-handed axes. Their tethered horses grazed not far away—big-boned animals, not so ponderous as those raised by the Britons, but swifter.

Bran's eyes lighted as the two strode through the camp. "These men are keen-beaked birds of war! See how they whet their axes and jest of the morrow! Would that the raiders in yon camp were as staunch as your men, Cormac!

Then would I greet the legions with a laugh when they come up from the south tomorrow."

They were entering the circle of the Northmen fires. Three hundred men sat about gambling, whetting their weapons and drinking deep of the heather ale furnished them by their Pictish allies. These gazed upon Bran and Cormac with no great friendliness. It was striking to note the difference between them and the Picts and Celts—the difference in their cold eyes, their strong moody faces, their very bearing. Here was ferocity, and savagery, but not of the wild, upbursting fury of the Celt. Here was fierceness backed by grim determination and stolid stubbornness. The charge of the British clans was terrible, overwhelming. But they had no patience; let them be balked of immediate victory and they were likely to lose heart and scatter or fall to bickering among themselves. There was the patience of the cold blue North in these seafarers—a lasting determination that would keep them steadfast to the bitter end, once their face was set toward a definite goal.

As to personal stature, they were giants; massive yet rangy. That they did not share the ideas of the Celts regarding armor was shown by the fact that they were clad in heavy-scale mail shirts that reached below mid-thigh, heavy horned helmets and hardened hide leggings, reinforced, as were their shoes, with plates of iron. Their shields were huge oval affairs of hard wood, hide and brass. As to weapons, they had long iron-headed spears, heavy iron axes, and daggers. Some had long wide-bladed swords.

Cormac scarcely felt at ease with the cold magnetic eyes of these flaxen-haired men fixed upon him. He and they were hereditary foes, even though they did chance to be fighting on the same side at present—but were they?

A man came forward, a tall gaunt warrior on whose scarred, wolfish face the flickering firelight reflected deep shadows. With his wolfskin mantle flung carelessly about his wide shoulders, and the great horns on his helmet adding to his height, he stood there in the swaying shadows, like some half-human thing, a brooding shape of the dark barbarism that was soon to engulf the world.

"Well, Wulfhere," said the Pictish king, "you have drunk the mead of council and have spoken about the fires—what is your decision?"

The Northman's eyes flashed in the gloom. "Give us a king of our own race to follow if you wish us to fight for you."

Bran flung out his hands. "Ask me to drag down the stars to gem your helmets! Will not your comrades follow you?"

"Not against the legions," answered Wulfhere sullenly. "A king led us on the Viking path—a king must lead us against the Romans. And Rognar is dead."

"I am a king," said Bran. "Will you fight for me if I stand at the tip of your fight wedge?"

"A king of our own race," said Wulfhere doggedly. "We are all picked men of the North. We fight for none but a king, and a king must lead us—against the legions."

Cormac sensed a subtle threat in this repeated phrase.

"Here is a prince of Erin," said Bran. "Will you fight for the Westerner?"

"We fight under no Celt, West or East," growled the Viking, and a low rumble of approval rose from the onlookers. "It is enough to fight by their side."

The hot Gaelic blood rose in Cormac's brain and he pushed past Bran, his hand on his sword. "How mean you that, pirate?"

Before Wulfhere could reply Bran interposed: "Have done! Will you fools throw away the battle before it is fought, by your madness? What of your oath, Wulfhere?"

"We swore it under Rognar; when he died from a Roman arrow we were absolved of it. We will follow only a king—against the legions."

"But your comrades will follow you—against the heather people!" snapped Bran.

"Aye," the Northman's eyes met his brazenly. "Send us a king or we join the Romans tomorrow."

Bran snarled. In his rage he dominated the scene, dwarfing the huge men who towered over him.

"Traitors! Liars! I hold your lives in my hand! Aye, draw your swords if you will—Cormac, keep your blade in its sheath. These wolves will not bite a king! Wulfhere—I spared your lives when I could have taken them.

"You came to raid the countries of the South, sweeping down from the northern sea in your galleys. You ravaged the coasts and the smoke of burning villages hung like a cloud over the shores of Caledon. I trapped you all when you were pillaging and burning—with the blood of my people on your hands. I burned your long ships and ambushed you when you followed. With thrice your number of bowmen who burned for your lives hidden in the heathered hills about you, I spared you when we could have shot you down like trapped wolves. Because I spared you, you swore to come and fight for me."

"And shall we die because the Picts fight Rome?" rumbled a bearded raider.

"Your lives are forfeit to me; you came to ravage the South. I did not promise to send you all back to your homes in the North unharmed and loaded with loot. Your vow was to fight one battle against Rome under my standard. Then I will aid your survivors to build ships and you may go where you will, with a goodly share of the plunder we take from the legions. Rognar had kept his oath. But Rognar died in a skirmish with Roman scouts and now you, Wulfhere the Dissension-breeder, you stir up your comrades to dishonor themselves by that which a Northman hates—the breaking of the sworn word."

"We break no oath," snarled the Viking, and the king sensed the basic Germanic stubbornness, far harder to combat than the fickleness of the fiery Celts. "Give us a king, neither Pict, Gael nor Briton, and we will die for you. If not—then we will fight tomorrow for the greatest of all kings—the emperor of Rome!"

For a moment Cormac thought that the Pictish king, in his black rage, would draw and strike the Northman dead. The concentrated fury that blazed in Bran's dark eyes caused Wulfhere to recoil and drop a hand to his belt.

"Fool!" said Mak Morn in a low voice that vibrated with passion. "I could sweep you from the earth before the Romans are near enough to hear your death howls. Choose—fight for me on the morrow—or die tonight under a black cloud of arrows, a red storm of swords, a dark wave of chariots!"

At the mention of the chariots, the only arm of war that had ever broken the Norse shield-wall, Wulfhere changed expression, but he held his ground.

"War be it," he said doggedly. "Or a king to lead us!"

The Northmen responded with a short deep roar and a clash of swords on shields. Bran, eyes blazing, was about to speak again when a white shape glided silently into the ring of firelight.

"Soft words, soft words," said old Gonar tranquilly. "King, say no more. Wulfhere, you and your fellows will fight for us if you have a king to lead you?"

"We have sworn."

"Then be at ease," quoth the wizard; "for ere battle joins on the morrow I will send you such a king as no man on earth has followed for a hundred thousand years! A king neither Pict, Gael nor Briton, but one to whom the emperor of Rome is as but a village headman!"

While they stood undecided, Gonar took the arms of Cormac and Bran. "Come. And you, Northmen, remember your vow, and my promise which I have never broken. Sleep now, nor think to steal away in the darkness to the Roman camp, for if you escaped our shafts you would not escape either my curse or the suspicions of the legionaries."

So the three walked away and Cormac, looking back, saw Wulfhere standing by the fire, fingering his golden beard, with a look of puzzled anger on his lean evil face.

The three walked silently through the waving heather under the faraway stars while the weird night wind whispered ghostly secrets about them.

"Ages ago," said the wizard suddenly, "in the days when the world was young, great lands rose where now the ocean roars. On these lands thronged mighty nations and kingdoms. Greatest of all these was Valusia—Land of Enchantment. Rome is as a village compared to the splendor of the cities of Valusia. And the greatest king was Kull, who came from the land of Atlantis to wrest the crown of Valusia from a degenerate dynasty. The Picts who dwelt in the isles which now form the mountain peaks of a strange land upon the Western Ocean, were allies of Valusia, and the greatest of all the Pictish war-chiefs was Brule the Spear-slayer, first of the line men call Mak Morn.

"Kull gave to Brule the jewel which you now wear in your iron crown, oh king, after a strange battle in a dim land, and down the long ages it has come to us, ever a sign of the Mak Morn, a symbol of former greatness. When at last the sea rose and swallowed Valusia, Atlantis and Lemuria, only the Picts survived and they were scattered and few. Yet they began again the slow climb upward, and though many of the arts of civilization were lost in the great flood, yet they progressed. The art of metal-working was lost, so they excelled in the working of flint. And they ruled all the new lands flung up by the sea and now called Europe, until down from the north came younger tribes who had scarce risen from the ape when Valusia reigned in her glory, and who, dwelling in the icy lands about the Pole, knew naught of the lost splendor of the Seven Empires and little of the flood that had swept away half a world.

"And still they have come—Aryans, Celts, Germans, swarming down from the great cradle of their race which lies near the Pole. So again was the growth of the Pictish nation checked and the race hurled into savagery. Erased from the earth, on the fringe of the world with our backs to the wall we fight. Here in Caledon is the last stand of a once mighty race. And we change. Our people have mixed with the savages of an elder age which we drove into the North when we came into the Isles, and now, save for their chieftains, such as thou, Bran, a Pict is strange and abhorrent to look upon."

"True, true," said the king impatiently, "but what has that to do—"

"Kull, king of Valusia," said the wizard imperturbably, "was a barbarian in his age as thou art in thine, though he ruled a mighty empire by the weight of his sword. Gonar, friend of Brule, your ancestor, has been dead a hundred thousand years as we reckon time. Yet I talked with him a scant hour ago."

"You talked with his ghost—"

"Or he with mine? Did I go back a hundred thousand

years, or did he come forward? If he came to me out of the past, it is not I who talked with a dead man, but he who talked with a man unborn. Past, present and future are one to a wise man. I talked to Gonar while he was alive; likewise was I alive. In a timeless, spaceless land we met and he told me many things."

The land was growing light with the birth of dawn. The heather waved and bent in long rows before the dawn wind as bowing in worship of the rising sun.

"The jewel in your crown is a magnet that draws down the eons," said Gonar. "The sun is rising—and who comes out of the sunrise?"

Cormac and the king started. The sun was just lifting a red orb above the eastern hills. And full in the glow, etched boldly against the golden rim, a man suddenly appeared. They had not seen him come. Against the golden birth of day he loomed colossal; a gigantic god from the dawn of creation. Now as he strode toward them the waking hosts saw him and sent up a sudden shout of wonder.

"Who—or what is it?" exclaimed Bran.

"Let us go to meet him, Bran," answered the wizard. "He is the king Gonar has sent to save the people of Brule."

2

"I have reached these lands but newly
From an ultimate dim Thule;
From a wild weird climbe that lieth
sublime
Out of Space—out of Time."

—Poe

The army fell silent as Bran, Cormac and Gonar went toward the stranger who approached in long swinging strides. As they neared him the illusion of monstrous size vanished, but they saw he was a man of great stature. At first Cormac thought him to be a Northman but a second glance told him that nowhere before had he seen such a man. He was built much like the Vikings, at once massive and lithe—tigerish. But his features were not as theirs, and his square-cut, lionlike mane of hair was as black as Bran's own. Under heavy brows glittered eyes gray as steel and cold as ice. His bronzed face, strong and inscrutable, was clean-shaven, and the broad forehead betokened a high intelligence, just as the firm jaw and thin lips showed will-power and courage. But more than all, the bearing of him, the unconscious lionlike stateliness, marked him as a natural king, a ruler of men.

Sandals of curious make were on his feet and he wore a pliant coat of strangely meshed mail which came almost to his knees. A broad belt with a great golden buckle encircled his waist, supporting a long straight sword in a heavy leather scabbard. His hair was confined by a wide, heavy golden band about his head.

Such was the man who paused before the silent group. He seemed slightly puzzled, slightly amused. Recognition flickered in his eyes. He spoke in a strange archaic Pictish which Cormac scarcely understood. His voice was deep and resonant.

"Ha, Brule, Gonar did not tell me I would dream of you!"

For the first time in his life Cormac saw the Pictish king completely thrown off his balance. He gaped, speechless. The stranger continued:

"And wearing the gem I gave you, in a circlet on your head! Last night you wore it in a ring on your finger."

"Last night?" gasped Bran.

"Last night or a hundred thousand years ago—all one!" murmured Gonar in evident enjoyment of the situation.

"I am not Brule," said Bran. "Are you mad to thus speak of a man dead a hundred thousand years? He was first of my line."

The stranger laughed unexpectedly. "Well, now I know I am dreaming! This will be a tale to tell Brule when I waken on the morrow! That I went into the future and saw men claiming descent from the Spear-slayer who is, as yet, not even married. No, you are not Brule, I see now, though you have his eyes and his bearing. But he is taller and broader in the shoulders. Yet you have his jewel—oh, well—anything can happen in a dream, so I will not quarrel with you. For a time I thought I had been transported to some other land in my sleep, and was in reality awake in a strange country, for this is the clearest dream I ever dreamed. Who are you?"

"I am Bran Mak Morn, king of the Caledonian Picts. And this ancient is Gonar, a wizard, of the line of Gonar. And this warrior is Cormac na Connacht, a prince of the isle of Erin."

The stranger slowly shook his lion-like head. "These words sound strangely to me, save Gonar—and that one is not Gonar, though he too is old. What land is this?"

"Caledon, or Alba, as the Gaels call it."

"And who are those squat apelike warriors who watch us yonder, all agape?"

"They are Picts who own my rule."

"How strangely distorted folk are in dreams!" muttered the stranger. "And who are those shock-headed men about the chariots?"

"They are Britons—Cymry from south of the Wall."

"What Wall?"

"The Wall built by Rome to keep the people of the heather out of Britain."

"Britain?" the tone was curious. "I never heard of that land—and what is Rome?"

"What!" cried Bran. "You never heard of Rome, the empire that rules the world?"

"No empire rules the world," answered the other haughtily. "The mightiest kingdom on earth is that wherein I reign."

"And who are you?"

"Kull of Atlantis, king of Valusia!"

Cormac felt a coldness trickle down his spine. The cold gray eyes were unswerving—but this was incredible— monstrous—unnatural.

"Valusia!" cried Bran. "Why, man, the sea waves have rolled above the spires of Valusia for untold centuries!"

Kull laughed outright. "What a mad nightmare this is!

When Gonar put on me the spell of deep sleep last night—or this night!—in the secret room of the inner palace, he told me I would dream strange things, but this is more fantastic than I reckoned. And the strangest thing is, I know I am dreaming!"

Gonar interposed as Bran would have spoken. "Question not the acts of the gods," muttered the wizard. "You are king because in the past you have seen and seized opportunities. The gods of the first Gonar have sent you this man. Let me deal with him."

Bran nodded, and while the silent army gaped in speechless wonder, just within earshot, Gonar spoke: "Oh great king, you dream, but is not all life a dream? How reckon you but that your former life is but a dream from which you have just awakened? Now we dream-folk have our wars and our peace, and just now a great host comes up from the south to destroy the people of Brule. Will you aid us?"

Kull grinned with pure zest. "Aye! I have fought battles in dreams ere now, have slain and been slain and was amazed when I woke from my visions. And at times, as now, dreaming I have known I dreamed. See, I pinch myself and feel it, but I know I dream for I have felt the pain of fierce wounds, in dreams. Yes, people of my dream, I will fight for you against the other dreamfolk. Where are they?"

"And that you enjoy the dream more," said the wizard subtly, "forget that it is a dream and pretend that by the magic of the first Gonar, and the quality of the jewel you gave Brule, that now gleams on the crown of the Morni, you have in truth been transported forward into another, wilder age where the people of Brule fight for their life against a stronger foe."

For a moment the man who called himself king of Valusia seemed startled; a strange look of doubt, almost of fear, clouded his eyes. Then he laughed.

"Good! Lead on, wizard."

But now Bran took charge. He had recovered himself and was at ease. Whether he thought, like Cormac, that this was all a gigantic hoax arranged by Gonar, he showed no sign.

"King Kull, see you those men yonder who lean on their long-shafted axes as they gaze upon you?"

"The tall men with the golden hair and beards?"

"Aye—our success in the coming battle hinges on them. They swear to go over to the enemy if we give them not a king to lead them—their own having been slain. Will you lead them to battle?"

Kull's eyes glowed with appreciation. "They are men such as my own Red Slayers, my picked regiment. I will lead them."

"Come then."

The small group made their way down the slope, through throngs of warriors who pushed forward eagerly to get a better view of the stranger, then pressed back as he approached. An undercurrent of tense whispering ran through the horde.

The Northmen stood apart in a compact group. Their cold eyes took in Kull and he gave back their stares, taking in every detail of their appearance.

"Wulfhere," said Bran, "we have brought you a king. I hold you to your oath."

"Let him speak to us," said the Viking harshly.

"He cannot speak your tongue," answered Bran, knowing that the Northmen knew nothing of the legends of his race. "He is a great king of the South—"

"He comes out of the past," broke in the wizard calmly. "He was the greatest of all kings, long ago."

"A dead man!" The Vikings moved uneasily and the rest of the horde pressed forward, drinking in every word. But Wulfhere scowled: "Shall a ghost lead living men? You bring us a man you say is dead. We will not follow a corpse."

"Wulfhere," said Bran in still passion, "you are a liar and a traitor. You set us this task, thinking it impossible. You yearn to fight under the Eagles of Rome. We have brought you a king neither Pict, Gael nor Briton and you deny your vow!"

"Let him fight me, then!" howled Wulfhere in uncontrollable wrath, swinging his ax about his head in a glittering arc. "if your dead man overcomes me—then my people will follow you. If I overcome him, you shall let us depart in peace to the camp of the legions!"

"Good!" said the wizard. "Do you agree, wolves of the North?"

A fierce yell and a brandishing of swords was the answer. Bran turned to Kull, who had stood silent, understanding nothing of what was said. But the Atlantean's eyes gleamed. Cormac felt that those cold eyes had looked on too many such scenes not to understand something of what had passed.

"This warrior says you must fight him for the leadership," said Bran, and Kull, eyes glittering with growing battle-joy, nodded: "I guessed as much. Give us space."

"A shield and a helmet!" shouted Bran, but Kull shook his head.

"I need none," he growled. "Back and give us room to swing our steel!"

Men pressed back on each side, forming a solid ring about the two men, who now approached each other warily. Kull had drawn his sword and the great blade shimmered like a live thing in his hand. Wulfhere, scarred by a hundred savage fights, flung aside his wolfskin mantle and came in cautiously, fierce eyes peering over the top of his out-thrust shield, ax half-lifted in his right hand.

Suddenly when the warriors were still many feet apart Kull sprang. His attack brought a gasp from men used to deeds of prowess; for like a leaping tiger he shot through the air and his sword crashed on the quickly lifted shield. Sparks flew and Wulfhere's ax hacked in, but Kull was under its sweep and as it swished viciously above his head he thrust upward and sprang out again, catlike. His motions had been too quick for the eye to follow. The upper edge of Wulfhere's shield showed a deep cut, and there was a long rent in his mail shirt where Kull's sword had barely missed the flesh beneath.

Cormac, trembling with the terrible thrill of the fight, wondered at this sword that could thus slice through scale-mail. And the blow that gashed the shield should have shattered the blade. Yet not a notch showed in the Valusian steel! Surely this blade was forged by another people in another age!

Now the two giants leaped again to the attack and like double strokes of lightning their weapons crashed. Wulfhere's shield fell from his arm in two pieces as the Atlantean's sword sheared clear through it, and Kull staggered as the Northman's ax, driven with all the force of his great body, descended on the golden circlet about his head. That blow should have sheared through the gold like butter to split the skull beneath, but the ax rebounded, showing a great notch in the edge. The next instant the Northman was overwhelmed by a whirlwind of steel—a storm of strokes delivered with such swiftness and power that he was borne back as on the crest of a wave, unable to launch an attack of his own. With all his tried skill he sought to parry the singing steel with his ax. But he could only avert his doom for a few seconds; could only for an instant turn the whistling blade that hewed off bits of his mail, so close fell the blows. One of the horns flew from his helmet; then the axhead itself fell away, and the same blow that severed the handle, bit through the Viking's helmet into the scalp beneath. Wulfhere was dashed to his knees, a trickle of blood starting down his face.

Kull checked his second stroke, and tossing his sword to Cormac, faced the dazed Northman weaponless. The Atlantean's eyes were blazing with ferocious joy and he roared something in a strange tongue. Wulfhere gathered his legs under him and bounded up, snarling like a wolf, a dagger flashing into his hand. The watching horde gave tongue in a yell that ripped the skies as the two bodies clashed. Kull's clutching hand missed the Northman's wrist but the desperately lunging dagger snapped on the Atlantean's mail, and dropping the useless hilt, Wulfhere locked his arms about his foe in a bearlike grip that would have crushed the ribs of a lesser man. Kull grinned tigerishly and returned the grapple, and for a moment the two swayed on their feet. Slowly the black-haired warrior bent his foe backward until it seemed his spine would snap. With a howl that had nothing of the human in it, Wulfhere clawed frantically at Kull's face, trying to tear out his eyes, then turned his head and snapped his fanglike teeth into the Atlantean's arm. A yell went up as a trickle of blood started: "He bleeds! He bleeds! He is no ghost, after all, but a mortal man!"

Angered, Kull shifted his grip, shoving the frothing Wulfhere away from him, and smote him terrifically under the ear with his right hand. The Viking landed on his back a dozen feet away. Then, howling like a wild man, he leaped up with a stone in his hand and flung it. Only Kull's incredible quickness saved his face; as it was, the rough edge of the missile tore his cheek and inflamed him to madness. With a lionlike roar he bounded upon his foe, enveloped him in an irresistible blast of sheer fury, whirled him high above his head as if he were a child and cast him a dozen feet away. Wulfhere pitched on his head and lay still—broken and dead.

Dazed silence reigned for an instant; then from the Gaels went up a thundering roar, and the Britons and Picts took it up, howling like wolves, until the echoes of the shouts and the clangor of sword on shield reached the ears of the marching legionaries, miles to the south.

"Men of the gray North," shouted Bran, "will you hold by your oath *now?*"

The fierce souls of the Northmen were in their eyes as their spokesman answered. Primitive, superstitious, steeped in tribal lore of fighting gods and mythical heroes, they did not doubt that the black-haired fighting man was some supernatural being sent by the fierce gods of battle.

"Aye! Such a man as this we have never seen! Dead man, ghost or devil, we will follow him, whether the trail lead to Rome or Valhalla!"

Kull understood the meaning, if not the words. Taking his sword from Cormac with a word of thanks, he turned to the waiting Northmen and silently held the blade toward them high above his head, in both hands, before he returned it to its scabbard. Without understanding, they appreciated the action. Blood-stained and disheveled, he was an impressive picture of stately, magnificent barbarism.

"Come," said Bran, touching the Atlantean's arm; "a host is marching on us and we have much to do. There is scant time to arrange our forces before they will be upon us. Come to the top of yonder slope."

There the Pict pointed. They were looking down into a

valley which ran north and south, widening from a narrow gorge in the north until it debouched upon a plain to the south. The whole valley was less than a mile in length.

"Up this valley will our foes come," said the Pict, "because they have wagons loaded with supplies and on all sides of this vale the ground is too rough for such travel. Here we plan an ambush."

"I would have thought you would have had your men lying in wait long before now," said Kull. "What of the scouts the enemy is sure to send out?"

"The savages I lead would never have waited in ambush so long," said Bran with a touch of bitterness. "I could not post them until I was sure of the Northmen. Even so I had not dared to post them ere now—even yet they may take panic from the drifting of a cloud or the blowing of a leaf, and scatter like birds before a cold wind. King Kull—the fate of the Pictish nation is at stake. I am called king of the Picts, but my rule as yet is but a hollow mockery. The hills are full of wild clans who refuse to fight for me. Of the thousand bowmen now at my command, more than half are of my own clan.

"Some eighteen hundred Romans are marching against us. It is not a real invasion, but much hinges upon it. It is the beginning of an attempt to extend their boundaries. They plan to build a fortress a day's march to the north of this valley. If they do, they will build other forts, drawing bands of steel about the heart of the free people. If I win this battle and wipe out this army, I will win a double victory. Then the tribes will flock to me and the next invasion will meet a solid wall of resistance. If I lose, the clans will scatter, fleeing into the north until they can no longer flee, fighting as separate clans rather than as one strong nation.

"I have a thousand archers, five hundred horsemen, fifty chariots with their drivers and swordsmen—one hundred fifty men in all—and, thanks to you, three hundred heavily armed Northern pirates. How would you arrange your battle lines?"

"Well," said Kull, "I would have barricaded the north end of the valley—no! That would suggest a trap. But I would block it with a band of desperate men, like those you have given me to lead. Three hundred could hold the gorge for a time against any number. Then, when the enemy was engaged with these men to the narrow part of the valley, I would have my archers shoot down into them until their ranks are broken, from both sides of the vale. Then, having my horsemen concealed behind one ridge and my chariots behind the other, I would charge with both simultaneously and sweep the foe into a red ruin."

Bran's eyes glowed. "Exactly, King of Valusia. Such was my exact plan—"

"But what of the scouts?"

"My warriors are like panthers; they hide under the noses of the Romans. Those who ride into the valley will see only what we wish them to see. Those who ride over the ridge will not come back to report. An arrow is swift and silent.

"You see that the pivot of the whole thing depends on the men that hold the gorge. They must be men who can fight on foot and resist the charges of the heavy legionaries long enough for the trap to close. Outside these Northmen I had no such force of men. My naked warriors with their short swords could never stand such a charge for an instant. Nor is the armor of the Celts made for such work; moreover, they are not foot-fighters, and I need them elsewhere.

"So you see why I had such desperate need of the Northmen. Now will you stand in the gorge with them and hold back the Romans until I can spring the trap? Remember, most of you will die."

Kull smiled. "I have taken chances all my life, though Tu, chief councillor, would say my life belongs to Valusia and I have no right to so risk it—" His voice trailed off and a strange look flitted across his face. "By Valka," said he, laughing uncertainly, "sometimes I forget this is a dream! All seems so real. But it is—of course it is! Well, then, if I die I will but awaken as I have done in times past. Lead on, king of Caledon!"

Cormac, going to his warriors, wondered. Surely it was all a hoax; yet—he heard the arguments of the warriors all about him as they armed themselves and prepared to take their posts. The black-haired king was Neid himself, the Celtic war-god; he was an antediluvian king brought out of the past by Gonar; he was a mythical fighting man out of Valhalla. He was no man at all but a ghost! No, he was mortal, for he had bled. But the gods themselves bled, though they did not die. So the controversies raged. At least, thought Cormac, if it was all a hoax to inspire the warriors with the feeling of supernatural aid, it had succeeded. The belief that Kull was more than a mortal man had fired Celt, Pict and Viking alike into a sort of inspired madness. And Cormac asked himself—what did he himself believe? This man was surely one from some far land—yet in his every look and action there was a vague hint of a greater difference than mere distance of space—a hint of alien Time, of misty abysses and gigantic gulfs of eons lying between the black-haired stranger and the men with whom he walked and talked. Clouds of bewilderment mazed Cormac's brain and he laughed in whimsical self-mockery.

3

"And the two wild peoples of the north
Stood fronting in the gloam,
And heard and knew each in his mind
A third great sound upon the wind,
The living walls that hedge mankind
The walking walls of Rome."

—Chesterton

The sun slanted westward. Silence lay like an invisible mist over the valley. Cormac gathered the reins in his hand and glanced up at the ridges on both sides. The waving heather which grew rank on those steep slopes gave no evidence of the hundreds of savage warriors who lurked there. Here in the narrow gorge which widened gradually southward was the only sign of life. Between the steep walls three hundred Northmen were massed solidly in their wedgeshaped shield-wall, blocking the pass. At the tip, like the point of a spear, stood the man who called himself Kull, king of Valusia. He wore no helmet, only the great, strangely worked headband of hard gold, but he bore on his left arm the great shield borne by the dead Rognar; and in his right hand he held the heavy iron mace wielded by the sea-king. The vikings eyed him in wonder and savage admiration. They could not understand his language, or he theirs. But no further orders were necessary. At Bran's directions they had bunched themselves in the gorge, and their only order was—hold the pass!

Bran Mak Morn stood just in front of Kull. So they faced each other, he whose kingdom was yet unborn, and he whose kingdom had been lost in the mists of Time for unguessed ages. Kings of darkness, thought Cormac, nameless kings of the night, whose realms are gulfs and shadows.

The hand of the Pictish king went out. "King Kull, you are more than king—you are a man. Both of us may fall within the next hour—but if we both live, ask what you will of me."

Kull smiled, returning the firm grip. "You too are a man after my own heart, king of the shadows. Surely you are more than a figment of my sleeping imagination. Mayhap we will meet in waking life some day."

Bran shook his head in puzzlement, swung into the saddle and rode away, climbing the eastern slope and vanishing over the ridge. Cormac hesitated: "'Strange man, are you in truth of flesh and blood, or are you a ghost?'"

"When we dream, we are all flesh and blood—so long as we are dreaming," Kull answered. "This is the strangest nightmare I have ever known—but you, who will soon fade into sheer nothingness as I awaken, seem as real to me *now*, as Brule, or Kananu, or Tu, or Kelkor."

Cormac shook his head as Bran had done, and with a last salute, which Kull returned with barbaric stateliness, he turned and trotted away. At the top of the western ridge he paused. Away to the south a light cloud of dust rose and the head of the marching column was in sight. Already he believed he could feel the earth vibrate slightly to the measured tread of a thousand mailed feet beating in perfect unison. He dismounted, and one of his chieftains, Domnail, took his steed and led it down the slope away from the valley, where trees grew thickly. Only an occasional vague movement among them gave evidence of the five hundred men who stood there, each at his horse's head with a ready hand to check a chance nicker.

Oh, thought Cormac, the gods themselves made this valley for Bran's ambush! The floor of the valley was treeless and the inner slopes were bare save for the waist-high heather. But at the foot of each ridge on the side facing away from the vale, where the soil long washed from the rocky slopes had accumulated, there grew enough trees to hide five hundred horsemen or fifty chariots.

At the northern end of the valley stood Kull and his three hundred Vikings, in open view, flanked on each side by fifty Pictish bowmen. Hidden on the western side of the western ridge were the Gaels. Along the top of the slopes, concealed in the tall heather, lay a hundred Picts with their shafts on string. The rest of the Picts were hidden on the eastern slopes beyond which lay the Britons with their chariots in full readiness. Neither they nor the Gaels to the west could see what went on in the vale, but signals had been arranged.

Now the long column was entering the wide mouth of the valley and their scouts, light-armed men on swift horses, were spreading out between the slopes. They galloped almost within bowshot of the silent host that blocked the pass, then halted. Some whirled and raced back to the main force, while the others deployed and cantered up the slopes, seeking to see what lay beyond. This was the crucial moment. If they got any hint of the ambush, all was lost. Cormac, shrinking down into the heather, marveled at the ability of the Picts to efface themselves from view so completely. He saw a horseman pass within three feet of where he knew a bowman lay, yet the Roman saw nothing.

The scouts topped the ridges, gazed about; then most of them turned and trotted back down the slopes. Cormac wondered at their desultory manner of scouting. He had never fought Romans before, knew nothing of their arrogant

self-confidence, of their incredible shrewdness in some
ways, their incredible stupidity in others. These men were
overconfident; a feeling radiating from their officers. It
had been years since a force of Caledonians had stood
before the legions. And most of these men were but newly
come to Britain; part of a legion which had been quartered
in Egypt. They despised their foes and suspected nothing.

But stay—three riders on the opposite ridge had turned
and vanished on the other side. And now one, sitting his
steed at the crest of the western ridge, not a hundred
yards from where Cormac lay, looked long and narrowly
down into the mass of trees at the foot of the slope.
Cormac saw suspicion grow on his brown, hawklike face.
He half turned as though to call to his comrades, then
instead reined his steed down the slope, leaning forward
in his saddle. Cormac's heart pounded. Each moment he
expected to see the man wheel and gallop back to raise the
alarm. He resisted a mad impulse to leap up and charge
the Roman on foot. Surely the man could feel the tenseness
in the air—the hundreds of fierce eyes upon him. Now he
was halfway down the slope, out of sight of the men in the
valley. And now the twang of an unseen bow broke the
painful stillness. With a strangled gasp the Roman flung
his hands high, and as the steed reared, he pitched headlong, transfixed by a long black arrow that had flashed
from the heather. A stocky dwarf sprang out of nowhere,
seemingly, and seized the bridle, quieting the snorting
horse, and leading it down the slope. At the fall of the
Roman, short crooked men rose like a sudden flight of
birds from the grass and Cormac saw the flash of a knife.
Then with unreal suddenness all had subsided. Slayers
and slain were unseen and only the still waving heather
marked the grim deed.

The Gael looked back into the valley. The three who
had ridden over the eastern ridge had not come back and
Cormac knew they never would. Evidently the other scouts
had borne word that only a small band of warriors were
ready to dispute the passage of the legionaries. Now the
head of the column was almost below him and he thrilled
at the sight of these men who were doomed, swinging

along with their superb arrogance. And the sight of their
splendid armor, their hawklike faces and perfect discipline
awed him as much as it is possible for a Gael to be awed.

Twelve hundred men in heavy armor who marched as
one so that the ground shook to their tread! Most of them
were of middle height, with powerful chests and shoulders
and bronzed faces—hard-bitten veterans of a hundred
campaigns. Cormac noted their javelins, short keen swords
and heavy shields; their gleaming armor and crested
helmets, the eagles on the standards. These were the men
beneath whose tread the world had shaken and empires
crumbled! Not all were Latins; there were Romanized
Britons among them and one century or hundred was
composed of huge yellow-haired men—Gauls and Germans,
who fought for Rome as fiercely as did the native-born,
and hated their wilder kinsmen more savagely.

On each side was a swarm of cavalry, outriders, and the
column was flanked by archers and slingers. A number of
lumbering wagons carried the supplies of the army. Cormac
saw the commander riding in his place—a tall man with a
lean, imperious face, evident even at that distance. Marcus
Sulius—the Gael knew him by repute.

A deep-throated roar rose from the legionaries as they
approached their foes. Evidently they intended to slice
their way through and continue without a pause, for the
column moved implacably on. Whom the gods destroy
they first make mad—Cormac had never heard the phrase
but it came to him that the great Sulius was a fool. Roman
arrogance! Marcus was used to lashing the cringing peoples
of a decadent East; little he guessed of the iron in these
western races.

A group of cavalry detached itself and raced into the
mouth of the gorge, but it was only a gesture. With loud
jeering shouts they wheeled three spears length away and
cast their javelins, which rattled harmlessly on the overlapping
shields of the silent Northmen. But their leader dared too
much; swinging in, he leaned from his saddle and thrust at
Kull's face. The great shield turned the lance and Kull
struck back as a snake strikes; the ponderous mace crushed
helmet and head like an eggshell, and the very steed went

to its knees from the shock of that terrible blow. From the Northmen went up a short fierce roar, and the Picts beside them howled exultantly and loosed their arrows among the retreating horsemen. First blood for the people of the heather! The oncoming Romans shouted vengefully and quickened their pace as the frightened horse raced by, a ghastly travesty of a man, foot caught in the stirrup, trailing beneath the pounding hoofs.

Now the first line of the legionaries, compressed because of the narrowness of the gorge, crashed against the solid wall of shields—crashed and recoiled upon itself. The shield-wall had not shaken an inch. This was the first time the Roman legions had met with that unbreakable formation— that oldest of all Aryan battlelines—the ancestor of the Spartan regiment—the Theban phalanx—the Macedonian formation—the English square.

Shield crashed on shield and the short Roman sword sought for an opening in that iron wall. Viking spears bristling in solid ranks above, thrust and reddened; heavy axes chopped down, shearing through iron, flesh and bone. Cormac saw Kull, looming above the stocky Romans in the forefront of the fray, dealing blows like thunderbolts. A burly centurion rushed in, shield held high, stabbing upward. The iron mace crashed terribly, shivering the sword, rending the shield apart, shattering the helmet, crushing the skull down between the shoulders—in a single blow.

The front line of the Romans bent like a steel bar about the wedge, as the legionaries sought to struggle through the gorge on each side and surround their opposers. But the pass was too narrow; crouching close against the steep walls the Picts drove their black arrows in a hail of death. At this range the heavy shafts tore through shield and corselet, transfixing the armored men. The front line of battle rolled back, red and broken, and the Northmen trod their few dead under foot to close the gaps their fall had made. Stretched the full width of their front lay a thin line of shattered forms—the red spray of the tide which had broken upon them in vain.

Cormac had leaped to his feet, waving his arms. Domnail

and his men broke cover at the signal and came galloping up the slope, lining the ridge. Cormac mounted the horse brought him and glanced impatiently across the narrow vale. No sign of life appeared on the eastern ridge. Where was Bran—and the Britons?

Down in the valley, the legions, angered at the unexpected oppositon of the paltry force in front of them, but not suspicious, were forming in more compact body. The wagons which had halted were lumbering on again and the whole column was once more in motion as if it intended to crash through by sheer weight. With the Gaulish century in the forefront, the legionaries were advancing again in the attack. This time, with the full force of twelve hundred men behind, the charge would batter down the resistance of Kull's warriors like a heavy ram; would stamp them down, sweep over their red ruins. Cormac's men trembled in impatience. Suddenly Marcus Sulius turned and gazed westward, where the line of horsemen was etched against the sky. Even at that distance Cormac saw his face pale. The Roman at last realized the metal of the men he faced, and that he had walked into a trap. Surely in that moment there flashed a chaotic picture through his brain—defeat—disgrace—red ruin!

It was too late to retreat—too late to form into a defensive square with the wagons for barricade. There was but one way possible out, and Marcus, crafty general in spite of his recent blunder, took it. Cormac heard his voice cut like a clarion through the din, and though he did not understand the words, he knew that the Roman was shouting for his men to smite that knot of Northmen like a blast—to hack their way through and out of the trap before it could close!

Now the legionaries, aware of their desperate plight, flung themselves headlong and terribly on their foes. The shield-wall rocked, but it gave not an inch. The wild faces of the Gauls and the hard brown Italian faces glared over locked shields into the blazing eyes of the North. Shields touching, they smote and slew and died in a red storm of slaughter, where crimsoned axes rose and fell and dripping spears broke on notched swords.

Where in God's name was Bran with his chariots? A few

minutes more would spell the doom of every man who held that pass. Already they were falling fast, though they locked their ranks closer and held like iron. Those wild men of the North were dying in their tracks; and looming among their golden heads the black lion-mane of Kull shone like a symbol of slaughter, and his reddened mace showered a ghastly rain as it splashed brains and blood like water.

Something snapped in Cormac's brain.

"These men will die while we wait for Bran's signal!" he shouted. "On! Follow me into Hell, sons of Gael!"

A wild roar answered him, and loosing rein he shot down the slope with five hundred yelling riders plunging headlong after him. And even at that moment a storm of arrows swept the valley from either side like a dark cloud and the terrific clamor of the Picts split the skies. And over the eastern ridge, like a sudden burst of rolling thunder on Judgment Day, rushed the war-chariots. Headlong down the slope they roared, foam flying from the horses' distended nostrils, frantic feet scarcely seeming to touch the ground, making naught of the tall heather. In the foremost chariot, with his dark eyes blazing, crouched Bran Mak Morn, and in all of them the naked Britons were screaming and lashing as if possessed by demons. Behind the flying chariots came the Picts, howling like wolves and loosing their arrows as they ran. The heather belched them forth from all sides in a dark wave.

So much Cormac saw in chaotic glimpses during that wild ride down the slopes. A wave of cavalry swept between him and the main line of the column. Three long leaps ahead of his men, the Gaelic prince met the spears of the Roman riders. The first lance turned on his buckler, and rising in his stirrups he smote downward, cleaving his man from shoulder to breastbone. The next Roman flung a javelin that killed Domnail, but at that instant Cormac's steed crashed into his, breast to breast, and the lighter horse rolled headlong under the shock, flinging his rider beneath the pounding hoofs.

Then the whole blast of the Gaelic charge smote the Roman cavalry, shattering it, crashing and rolling it down

and under. Over its red ruins Cormac's yelling demons
struck the heavy Roman infantry, and the whole line reeled
at the shock. Swords and axes flashed up and down and
the force of their rush carried them deep into the massed
ranks. Here, checked, they swayed and strove. Javelins
thrust, swords flashed upward, bringing down horse and
rider, and greatly outnumbered, leaguered on every side,
the Gaels had perished among their foes, but at that
instant, from the other side the crashing chariots smote
the Roman ranks. In one long line they struck almost
simultaneously, and at the moment of impact the charioteers
wheeled their horses sidelong and raced parallel down the
ranks, shearing men down like the mowing of wheat.
Hundreds died on those curving blades in that moment,
and leaping from the chariots, screaming like blood-mad
wildcats, the British swordsmen flung themselves upon
the spears of the legionaries, hacking madly with their
two-handed swords. Crouching, the Picts drove their arrows
point-blank and then sprang in to slash and thrust. Maddened
with the sight of victory, these wild peoples were like
wounded tigers, feeling no wounds, and dying on their
feet with their last gasp a snarl of fury.

But the battle was not over yet. Dazed, shattered, their
formation broken and nearly half their number down
already, the Romans fought back with desperate fury.
Hemmed in on all sides they slashed and smote singly, or
in small clumps, fought back to back, archers, slingers,
horsemen and heavy legionaries mingled into a chaotic
mass. The confusion was complete, but not the victory.
Those bottled in the gorge still hurled themselves upon
the red axes that barred their way, while the massed and
serried battle thundered behind them. From one side
Cormac's Gaels raged and slashed; from the other, chariots
swept back and forth, retiring and returning like iron
whirlwinds. There was no retreat, for the Picts had flung a
cordon across the way they had come, and having cut the
throats of the camp followers and possessed themselves of
the wagon, they sent their shafts in a storm of death into
the rear of the shattered column. Those long black arrows
pierced armor and bone, nailing men together. Yet the

slaughter was not all on one side. Picts died beneath the lightning thrust of javelin and shortsword, Gaels pinned beneath their falling horses were hewed to pieces, and chariots, cut loose from their horses, were deluged with the blood of the charioteers.

And at the narrow head of the valley still the battle surged and eddied. Great gods—thought Cormac, glancing between lightninglike blows—do these men still hold the gorge? Aye! They held it! A tenth of their original number, dying on their feet, they still held back the frantic charges of the dwindling legionaries.

Over all the field went up the roar and the clash of arms, and birds of prey, swift-flying out of the sunset, circled above. Cormac, striving to reach Marcus Sulius through the press, saw the Roman's horse sink under him, and the rider rise alone in a waste of foes. He saw the Roman sword flash thrice, dealing a death at each blow; then from the thickest of the fray bounded a terrible figure. It was Bran Mak Morn, stained from head to foot. He cast away his broken sword as he ran, drawing a dirk. The Roman struck, but the Pictish king was under the thrust, and gripping the sword-wrist, he drove the dirk again and again through the gleaming armor.

A mighty roar went up as Marcus died, and Cormac, with a shout, rallied the remnants of his force about him and, striking in the spurs, burst through the shattered lines and rode full speed for the other end of the valley.

But as he approached he saw that he was too late. As they had lived, so had they died, those fierce sea-wolves, with their faces to the foe and their broken weapons red in their hands. In a grim and silent band they lay, even in death preserving some of the shield-wall formation. Among them, in front of them and all about them lay high-heaped the bodies of those who had sought to break them, in vain. *They had not given back a foot!* To the last man, they had died in their tracks. Nor were there any left to stride over their torn shapes; those Romans who had escaped the Viking axes had been struck down by the shafts of the Picts and swords of the Gaels from behind.

Yet this part of the battle was not over. High up on the steep western slope Cormac saw the ending of that drama.

A group of Gauls in the armor of Rome pressed upon a single man—a black-haired giant on whose head gleamed a golden crown. There was iron in these men, as well as in the man who had held them to their fate. They were doomed—their comrades were being slaughtered behind them—but before their turn came they would at least have the life of the black-haired chief who had led the golden-haired men of the North.

Pressing upon him from three sides they had forced him slowly back up the steep gorge wall, and the crumpled bodies that stretched along his retreat showed how fiercely every foot of the way had been contested. Here on this steep it was task enough to keep one's footing alone; yet these men at once climbed and fought. Kull's shield and the huge mace were gone, and the great sword in his right hand was dyed crimson. His mail, wrought with a forgotten art, now hung in shreds, and blood streamed from a hundred wounds on limbs, head and body. But his eyes still blazed with the battle-joy and his wearied arm still drove the mighty blade in strokes of death.

But Cormac saw that the end would come before they could reach him. Now at the very crest of the steep, a hedge of points menaced the strange king's life, and even his iron strength was ebbing. Now he split the skull of a huge warrior and the backstroke shore through the neckcords of another; reeling under a very rain of swords he struck again and his victim dropped at his feet, cleft to the breastbone. Then, even as a dozen swords rose above the staggering Atlantean for the death stroke, a strange thing happened. The sun was sinking into the western sea; all the heather swam red like an ocean of blood. Etched in the dying sun, as he had first appeared, Kull stood, and then, like a mist lifting, a mighty vista opened behind the reeling king. Cormac's astounded eyes caught a fleeting gigantic glimpse of other climbes and spheres—as if mirrored in summer clouds he saw, instead of heather hills stretching away to the sea, a dim and mighty land of blue mountains and gleaming quiet lakes—the golden, purple and sapphirean spires and towering walls of a mighty city such as the earth has not known for many a drifting-age.

Then like the fading of a mirage it was gone, but the Gauls on the high slope had dropped their weapons and stared like men dazed—*For the man called Kull had vanished and there was no trace of his going!*

As in a daze Cormac turned his steed and rode back across the trampled field. His horse's hoofs splashed in pools of blood and clanged against the helmets of dead men. Across the valley the shout of victory was thundering. Yet all seemed shadowy and strange. A shape was striding across the torn corpses and Cormac was dully aware that it was Bran. The Gael swung from his horse and fronted the king. Bran was weaponless and gory; blood trickled from gashes on brow, breast and limb; what armor he had worn was clean hacked away and a cut had shorn halfway through his iron crown. But the red jewel still gleamed unblemished like a star of slaughter.

"It is in my mind to slay you," said the Gael heavily and like a man speaking in a daze, "for the blood of brave men is on your head. Had you given the signal to charge sooner, some would have lived."

Bran folded his arms; his eyes were haunted. "Strike if you will; I am sick of slaughter. It is a cold mead, this kinging it. A king must gamble with men's lives and naked swords. The lives of all my people were at stake; I sacrificed the Northmen—yes; and my heart is sore within me, for they were men! But had I given the order when you would have desired, all might have gone awry. The Romans were not yet massed in the narrow mouth of the gorge, and might have had time and space to form their ranks again and beat us off. I waited until the last moment—and the rovers died. A king belongs to his people, and cannot let either his own feelings or the lives of men influence him. Now my people are saved; but my heart is cold in my breast."

Cormac wearily dropped his sword-point to the ground.

"You are a born king of men, Bran," said the Gaelic prince.

Bran's eyes roved the field. A mist of blood hovered over all, where the victorious barbarians were looting the dead, while those Romans who had escaped slaughter by throwing down their swords and now stood under guard, looked on with hot smoldering eyes.

"My kingdom—my people—are saved," said Bran wearily. "They will come from the heather by the thousands and when Rome moves against us again, she will meet a solid nation. But I am weary. What of Kull?"

"My eyes and brain were mazed with battle," answered Cormac. "I thought to see him vanish like a ghost into the sunset. I will seek his body."

"Seek not for him," said Bran. "Out of the sunrise he came—into the sunset he has gone. Out of the mists of the ages he came to us, and back into the mists of the eons has he returned to his own kingdom."

Cormac turned away; night was gathering. Gonar stood like a white specter before him.

"To his own kingdom," echoed the wizard. "Time and Space are naught. Kull has returned to his own kingdom—his own crown—his own age."

"Then he was a ghost?"

"Did you not feel the grip of his solid hand? Did you not hear his voice—see him eat and drink, laugh and slay and bleed?"

Still Cormac stood like one in a trance.

"Then if it be possible for a man to pass from one age into one yet unborn, or come forth from a century dead and forgotten, whichever you will, with his flesh-and-blood body and his arms—then he is as mortal as he was in his own day. Is Kull dead, then?"

"He died a hundred thousand years ago, as men reckon time," answered the wizard, "but in his own age. He died not from the swords of the Gauls of this age. Have we not heard in legends how the king of Valusia traveled into a strange, timeless land of the misty future ages, and there fought in a great battle? Why, so he did! A hundred thousand years ago, or today!

"And a hundred thousand years ago—or a moment agone! —Kull, king of Valusia, roused himself on the silken couch in his secret chamber and laughing, spoke to the first Gonar, saying: 'Ha, wizard, I have in truth dreamed strangely, for I went into a far clime and a far time in my

visions, and fought for the king of a strange shadow-people!'
And the great sorcerer smiled and pointed silently at the
red, notched sword, and the torn mail and the many
wounds that the king carried. And Kull, fully woken from
his 'vision' and feeling the sting and the weakness of these
yet bleeding wounds, fell silent and mazed, and all life and
time and space seemed like a dream of ghosts to him, and
he wondered thereat all the rest of his life. For the wisdom
of the Eternities is denied even unto princes and Kull
could no more understand what Gonar told him than you
can understand my words."

"And then Kull lived despite his many wounds," said
Cormac, "and has returned to the mists of silence and the
centuries. Well—he thought us a dream; we thought him
a ghost. And sure, life is but a web spun of ghosts and
dreams and illusion, and it is in my mind that the kingdom
which has this day been born of swords and slaughter in
this howling valley is a thing no more solid than the foam
of the bright sea."